THE CRITICS RAVE ABOUT
ROMANTIC TIMES
AWARD-WINNER FLORA SPEER!

TIMESTRUCK

"Speer's outstanding talent shouts from each well-written page."

—*Affaire de Coeur*

A TIME TO LOVE AGAIN

"Ms. Speer has penned an interesting tale rich in historical turbulence and resounding with the chivalry of an era long since past."

—*Romantic Times*

A LOVE BEYOND TIME

"I found this book fast-paced and exciting. Every page was a surprise, and readers will be delighted by it."

—*Affaire de Coeur*

LOVE JUST IN TIME

"Flora Speer provides her audience with her usual first-rate read."

—*Affaire de Coeur*

HEART'S MAGIC

"Those who adore the mystical will find themselves held captive by Flora Speer's tale of magic, evil, enchantment and intrigue."

—*Romantic Times*

ROSE RED

"Flora Speer's writing skills flourish with this superb historical romance, an adult fairy tale that will make readers believe in the magic of love."

—*Affaire de Coeur*

LADY LURE

"Ms. Speer crafts a touching romance, full of both sensual fire and tender love. Fans will be more than pleased."

—*Romantic Times*

THE MAGIC OF LOVE

"Are you a sorceress?"

"Yes," Emma said, unable in that instant to utter more than the single word. She saw Dain receive the admission like a blow to the heart. She could only pray the truth hadn't destroyed his new-found tenderness for her.

"Is that why I've wanted you so often and so passionately?"

"No! I told you when I first came here that I was a substitute bride. I begged my father to send me in place of the younger sister he originally intended for you, who was too ill to travel. Dain, what's between you and me is entirely natural. The only magic I've used since coming to Penruan was to help me see my way through the fog, when I was lost."

"Dare I believe you if you swear as much to me?" He took a single step toward her, the first move he'd made in her direction since she had entered the lord's chamber.

"I would never hurt you, or lie to you," she said. "I am pledged to you by a sacred vow. We are man and wife."

A Passionate MAGIC

FLORA SPEER

LOVE SPELL　　　　　　NEW YORK CITY

A LOVE SPELL BOOK®

May 2001

Published by

Dorchester Publishing Co., Inc.
276 Fifth Avenue
New York, NY 10001

Copyright © 2001 by Flora Speer

ISBN 0-505-52439-2

The name "Love Spell" and its logo are trademarks of Dorchester Publishing Co., Inc.

Printed in the United States of America.

Visit us on the web at www.dorchesterpub.com.

For Mary, our family "magician"
who gave me the idea for Emma's mysterious,
magical presents.

A Passionate
MAGIC

Prologue

Lincolnshire, England
A.D. 1129

"Please, Father," Emma begged, "say you will let me be the one to do this."

There were three people gathered in the lord's chamber of Wroxley Castle. Gavin, the baron of Wroxley, sat in his big, comfortably cushioned wooden chair. Mirielle, his second wife, stood behind him, one hand on his shoulder. Gavin's level gaze rested on Emma's face as he noted with some amusement the way in which she was employing her innocent feminine wiles.

Emma had placed herself squarely within the beam of sunlight that shone through the open casement window. A soft mid-May breeze blew into the room, bringing with it the sweet fragrances of flowers and fresh grasses from the meadows outside the castle walls. The sun on the smooth braid of Emma's hair turned it into shimmering black. Her dark brown eyes did not waver when Gavin frowned at her. He was not surprised by Emma's lack of reaction, for he had never given her any reason to fear him. Since their first meeting when Emma was eleven years old and Gavin was newly returned after more than a decade in the Holy Land their relationship had been entirely affectionate. He loved the girl as if she really were his daughter.

"From what Mirielle told me after you returned from the royal court yesterday," Emma said, "King Henry has decreed that you must send one of your daughters to Cornwall to wed Dain of Penruan, and with that marriage bring a peaceful end to the feud between you. But there was no mention of which daughter you are to send."

"The feud should have been resolved by the deaths of the original participants," Gavin said, not hiding his anger. "Dain has revived the quarrel by publicly blaming my father for crimes supposedly committed against his grandfather and his father decades ago. Emma, I have seen Dain in battle. The man is a fierce opponent, relentless and determined. Despite the assurances he offered to both King Henry and me, I do question how well he will treat his Wroxley bride. After hearing his bitter speech to the king, I am sure Dain does not want any bride of my blood. He is a man who would far rather have revenge, but his oath of fealty to Henry has forced him into a reluctant acceptance of the king's decision on the matter of his dispute with me."

"All the more reason for me to go instead of Alys," Emma said, pressing her petition. "Alys is only seven and you know how sick she was this past winter. She still has not fully recovered. The last thing Alys needs is to be sent far from home, to be married off to some fierce, unfriendly stranger.

"Father." Stepping away from the window, Emma went to her knees, clasping her hands together and resting them on Gavin's knee. "You have heard more than once the story of how unhappy I was when my mother sent me away for fostering when I was just seven. Were it not for my dear brother's presence at the same castle, I think I would have died of my misery."

"So was I miserable when I was sent for fostering," Gavin said. "Most children are, at least at first. Dain has promised that his mother will train Alys as her fosterling and teach her what her future duties as lady of Penruan will be after she is old enough for the marriage to be consummated."

"I know such an arrangement is not at all unusual," Emma continued her argument, "but it is my opinion that Alys is far more fragile than I was at her age. She ought to remain here at home for another year or two, and then be sent to people whom you and she know, people who live near enough to Wroxley for you and Mirielle to visit them occasionally and thus see Alys. That way, my little sister will be happier during the next few years, and healthier when the time comes for her to marry. And then you ought to choose a kind and gentle man for her."

"Mirielle?" Gavin turned in his chair to look at his wife. "What are your thoughts on this issue?"

"It saddens me to see any of our children leaving us, but we both do know it will be inevitable as time passes and they grow up," Mirielle responded. "Emma has rightly judged Alys's state of mind, and her physical health."

13

"Whereas I am remarkably sturdy and strong-minded," Emma noted with a low chuckle. "Unlike Alys, who still clings to her mother, I believe the time is right for me to leave Wroxley and begin my own life. After all, I am eighteen now, which you well know is several years beyond the usual age for a girl to marry."

She did not add that she was unlikely to find a husband anywhere near Wroxley. Most noblemen did not want wives as well educated as Emma, and Gavin knew there were rumors of her unusual abilities. Emma must know, as he did, that if she was to marry at all, it would have to be to a man who lived far from Wroxley, who had not heard the gossip about Emma, or about the wicked activities of her late mother. Perhaps the girl was right that she ought to be sent to Cornwall.

On the other hand, Gavin knew of an objection to Emma's going that was well-nigh insurmountable, an objection he could not voice to the eager girl who knelt before him. If Dain, that cold-blooded warrior, ever learned he had been tricked, there was no telling what he would do to Emma.

"Well, Father?" Emma prodded gently.

"I will consider every argument you have advanced," Gavin promised her.

"You do not have long in which to decide. According to what Mirielle has told me, the priest that Dain is sending as his representative to escort the bride to Cornwall will arrive here within a few days, in company with the king's clerics, who will bring the marriage contract and the written peace agreement," Emma said. She rose, smiling a little, as if she was certain she was going to have her way. "I am sure you and Mirielle will want to talk in private, and I have work to do in the stillroom."

When she was gone and the door was shut behind her, Gavin expelled a long breath and Mirielle came from behind his chair to face him. Gavin shook his head, a rueful smile curving his mouth.

"Emma is still young enough to glory in the thought of self-sacrifice," he said. "For my sake, for yours, and for love of her younger brothers and sisters, she will gladly do this."

"She adores you," Mirielle said, "and I know she loves me as a mother. But I do not think sacrifice is all that's in Emma's mind. Like any other girl, she wants a husband and children of her own. I also suspect that deep in her heart there lurks a longing for adventure and a desire to see something of the world beyond Wroxley. She may not recognize it in herself, but I think it's there, all the same."

"I freely confess I have no liking for the notion of sending Alys to Cornwall," Gavin said, "but neither do I want to send Emma into that bloody man's household—or to his bed! Good Lord of Heaven, Mirielle, how can a man demand vengeance or insist on retribution for something that happened decades ago, an old quarrel long forgotten by most of those who heard his angry speech before the king? I wasn't even in England in those days, and the feud originated between my father and Dain's grandfather. The men involved are dead now. At this late date I can neither prove nor disprove Dain's accusations."

"At least he did agree to accept Henry's judgment in the case," Mirielle said. "And so did you agree, both of you, before dozens of witnesses. Thus, we are honor bound to send one of your daughters to marry Dain and never to take up arms against him, nor he against us, so long as he is wed to a daughter of Wroxley."

"Alys is the older of my two daughters," Gavin reminded her. "It's why I decided that she should be the one to go to Cornwall."

"Only you and I know Emma is not your child," Mirielle said.

"We two, and your cousin Brice," Gavin corrected her. "Though Brice did agree to leave it to me to decide whether, or when, to tell Emma that he is her father. But he has been gone from England for so long that I wonder if he is dead."

"I cannot think so," Mirielle said. "If it were so, I do believe I would know it in my heart, or see it in my crystal ball. Still, Brice is another good reason, beyond the sensible ones Emma has offered, why we ought to send her away from Wroxley."

"How is that?" Gavin asked after a moment of silence, during which he allowed himself to be distracted by memories of his faithless first wife. Alda had kept the secret of Emma's true parentage for years, until she could use the information as a weapon against Gavin. After Alda died while misusing her magical abilities, Gavin, Mirielle, and Brice had agreed to protect Emma from knowledge of the true wickedness of her mother. The girl had grown up believing Gavin was her father.

"Brice left Wroxley in hope of redeeming himself after his affair with Alda," Mirielle said. "If he returns to England, he will surely want to see Emma again, and it is always possible that he will want to claim her as his own. Thus, he will likely come to Wroxley first, believing she is here, or that we will know where he can find her. With Emma safe in distant Cornwall, you and I can dissuade Brice from a course of action that would bring grief and pain to our dear girl."

"You want me to send Emma to be Dain's wife in

order to protect her from the homecoming of a father who may never return?" Gavin exclaimed in disbelief.

"That is exactly what I want," Mirielle told him, and met his questioning gaze with only a faint shadow in her eyes.

"What do you know that I do not?" Gavin asked. "I recognize that look. Have you seen something of the future in your marvelous crystal ball?"

"Say, rather, I have a feeling I cannot explain," Mirielle said. "When I think about Emma's future, it seems to me her destiny lies in Cornwall, and she is right to want to go there."

"Dain of Penruan is widely acknowledged to be rapacious, cruel, and utterly without sympathy for his enemies," Gavin said. "When he makes war, what he cannot seize and carry away he destroys by burning. I do not want either Alys or Emma sent to him." Gavin's lips closed firmly on the words, and his expression was hard with the protective instinct that compelled him to keep his womenfolk safe.

"King Henry has left you no choice," Mirielle said. "Gavin, my dear love, do not forget that while you and I were at court, I met Dain. I did not find him as evil, or as heartless, as you think him to be."

"Did you not?" Gavin's brows went up in surprise at his wife's claim and he regarded her for a long, thoughtful moment.

"Emma is strong enough to withstand him," Mirielle said. "Unlike Alys, Emma possesses magical ability inherited from her mother."

"An inheritance properly schooled by you," Gavin said slowly, "which she can hide until Dain is ready to accept her true nature." He nodded, acknowledging Mirielle's point of view. He had always trusted his wife's insights and her skill at judging character.

"Exactly," Mirielle said. "Emma's magic is under her complete control. Her dearest wish is to negotiate a true peace between our family and Dain's, a peace that goes beyond mere grudging adherence to the king's command."

"To do so, she will need to be invincible," Gavin said. "If it's adventure she secretly wants, I expect she will find more than enough to satisfy her. Emma will require all the courage of a lioness and the magic of a great sorceress if she is to be the bride of Dain of Penruan."

Chapter One

"You are not the bride I was expecting," Dain said, punctuating his words with a deep scowl.

"I know I am not," Emma responded. She tried to smile, but in the face of the unconcealed displeasure of the baron of Penruan she found she could not force her lips to curve upward.

She told herself the knot in her chest was caused by physical discomfort, not by fear. Even in mid-July, the great hall of Penruan Castle was cold, and Emma was thoroughly chilled, wet to the skin from riding through a rainstorm, and very hungry. She longed for a warm fire, hot water for washing, and dry clothes. Instead, she was faced with a man who did not trouble himself to hide his irritation at her presence.

Dain of Penruan was unusually tall and gave the impression of sleek leanness despite his broad shoulders and muscular arms. From what she had heard of him, Emma had expected to find a dark and brooding lord. Certainly the man before her was dark-skinned, obviously tanned by long days in the sun. She was surprised by that; she and her companions had encountered so much rain during the last part of their journey from Lincolnshire that she was beginning to doubt if the sun ever shone in Cornwall.

For all the whispers and rumors about Dain's bloodthirsty fierceness, no one, not even Mirielle, had thought to warn her that her new husband was both young and handsome. Emma did wonder about the odd omission. It was unlike Mirielle to be so forgetful.

She gazed in mingled apprehension and admiration at the man to whom she had been married, by proxy, for slightly more than a month. Admiration won. Dain's sheer physical splendor overcame Emma's secret, lingering concerns about her ability to go to her unknown husband's bed with some semblance of willingness.

Dain's hair was the palest silver-gold Emma had ever seen, though his brows and lashes were brown. She assumed his hair was bleached by the same sunlight that had tanned his skin. Below the short, pale hair the man the world knew as a ruthless predator displayed an angel's face. Emma smothered a sigh of pleasure at the sight of him. Dain's face was all smooth, taut planes—high cheekbones, a long, straight nose, and a firm jaw that, unlike the jaws of most other men she knew, was unblemished by any trace of stubble. She thought, irrelevantly, that he must shave every day.

Emma met his eyes and a shiver went through her. Dain's eyes were a peculiar shade of blue-green, a color emphasized by his woolen tunic of exactly the same shade. Such stormy eyes, puzzled and more than a bit annoyed by the sudden arrival of a grown woman in place of the little girl he was awaiting.

"I was told that my wife was seven years old," Dain said. He looked from Emma's rain-dampened face to Father Maynard, the priest Dain had sent to accompany her from Wroxley to her new home.

Father Maynard was every bit as cold and wet as Emma, and she felt sorry for the man who had been unfailingly kind to her during their travels. Out of sympathy Emma offered the explanation that Dain apparently expected from the priest.

"It was my younger sister, Alys, who was first proposed as your wife," Emma said. "Unfortunately, she is in poor health and our parents feared she could not survive the journey to Penruan. I am the eldest of my father's three daughters, and I do assure you, my lord, I am remarkably strong and healthy."

"No one could guess it by looking at you," Dain remarked. There was no hint of welcome or of hospitality in the cold gaze he cast upon her. "You appear to be half-drowned."

"We have ridden through this entire day in heavy rain," Father Maynard informed him. "All of us are wet and cold—and hungry, my lord. We have not eaten since early morning."

In any other castle that Emma knew of, those words would have brought an immediate outpouring of food, drink, and comfort from the host. Not so the lord of Penruan. He pinned Emma under his searching glare for a time before speaking again, and it was not to her he addressed his question.

"Is she truly the granddaughter of Udo of Wroxley?" Dain demanded of the priest.

"I will be happy to tell you so, my lord, if only you will have the courtesy to speak to me directly," Emma said in a loud voice aimed at regaining his attention. "Let there be no question on the matter of my descent. Furthermore, you and I were wed before more than a dozen witnesses in the chapel at Wroxley Castle, with my father's seneschal serving as your proxy. Father Maynard himself blessed our union. It is quite legal. If you break our marriage contract, you defy King Henry's express command."

Dain stared at her as if he could not believe any woman would dare to speak to him so boldly. Emma saw a flash of some emotion in his blue-green gaze. It was gone so quickly that she could not decide whether it was anger or hastily suppressed amusement.

"Not quite legal yet," Dain said, his fine mouth twisting on the words. "All marriages require one final act to make an indissolvable union. I speak, Lady Emma, of the act of consummation. Until I bed you, ours is no true marriage, no matter what the king, or the baron of Wroxley, may claim."

The glint of that unknown, unspeakable emotion shone in his eyes again. He looked so fierce, so like the coldhearted predator he was said to be, that Emma took a step backward, wanting to put a bit more distance between herself and him.

During the ride to Penruan, Father Maynard had undertaken to educate her about Dain's family history. The priest had told her that several of Dain's ancestors were Norsemen, who in the distant past had crossed the sea from conquered Ireland, seeking new lands to wrest for their own. The first Dain had seized Penruan lands by bloody warfare, and his descendants had held tightly to that same land ever since. Meeting the present Dain's cold eyes, Emma could easily believe the tale. But she was determined not to be cowed by him. A voice deep in her heart whispered that while Dain would never appreciate a meek, simpering wife, he would respect a woman of courage, a woman who knew her own worth.

"Are you refusing to accept your bride?" she demanded of him.

"Certainly not," Dain answered her in a dangerously smooth voice. "A refusal would be disobedience to the king's direct command. Unlike your grandfather, I am no dishonest lord."

"You will not have a very fond wife, my lord, if you persist in disparaging her grandsire," Emma warned.

"Whatever made you think I want a wife who will be fond of me?" he asked. "We have wed only because King Henry insisted upon our marriage. You will obey me in all things, you will lie in my bed and accept my embraces when I am in the mood to bestow them upon you, and you will bear my children. I have no other use for you."

"I am trained as a chatelaine," she said. "I have considerable skill in the healing arts. And I do believe it is only fair to tell you at once about my other abilities."

"I am not interested," he interrupted her. "My mother, Lady Richenda, is chatelaine here. You will obey her as you obey me. Perhaps she can find something useful for you to do, to occupy your days. Otherwise, stay out of my way as much as possible."

"My lord," Father Maynard objected, "that is no way to treat a new wife."

"You will please me best by remaining silent,"

Dain told him with a look so fierce and cold that Emma's heart quaked within her when she saw it.

"My lord Dain," Emma declared, righteous anger stirring in her bosom, "as Father Maynard has already told you, every member of our party is cold, wet, hungry, and weary. We deserve better hospitality than this. If you will not offer what is due to us, then I, as new mistress of this castle, will order what we need for our comfort. Let me remind you that you are in violation of the rules of hospitality."

For the second time since meeting her, Dain stared at her as if he could not believe his own ears. When he did not at once respond to her criticism, Emma looked around the hall, seeking a servant to whom she could give orders. She saw the flash of a skirt as a female dashed around a corner into the screened passage, heading toward the kitchen, perhaps in flight from the quarrel that seemed about to break into all-out warfare between lord and lady. Other than that one, vanished woman, there were only a few men-at-arms lounging about the hall, and all of them were rather pointedly ignoring their new mistress. The men-at-arms and their squires who had escorted Emma from Wroxley were either crowded at the entry or still outside in the courtyard, waiting for orders about unloading the packhorses. Hawise, Emma's companion, stood close behind her.

Emma flung the damp folds of her woolen cloak back over either shoulder to free her arms. Planting her fists on her hips, she approached Dain, not stopping until she stood toe-to-toe with him.

"If you continue to deny us proper hospitality," she said to him, "then I and the rest of my party will leave Penruan. We did not come so far to be insulted."

"If you leave," he responded, sneering at her outrage, "you will break the terms of the peace agreement your father and I promised in the king's presence to abide by, and therefore, you will be responsible for the outbreak of hostilities between Wroxley and Penruan."

"It will take months for you to march an army to Wroxley," she said. "By then, I can ride to court and tell the king how badly you have treated me and my company. What do you think King Henry will say to that?"

"What makes you think I don't already have an army based in Lincolnshire?" he asked.

"That is impossible!"

"Really? Are you foolish enough to imagine I don't have friends?" His blue-green eyes danced with fiendish amusement. "I could name several men who are jealous of the power of the baron of Wroxley and of his close friendship with King Henry. Such men would delight in any opportunity to do harm to Gavin on his own lands."

"Inciting others to attack Wroxley is as much a violation of your agreement with my father as is the way you are treating me," Emma exclaimed.

"How would you know? Have you read the agreement?" he asked in tones of such contempt that she all but screamed her response at him.

"Of course I read it! I read every cursed word! And every word of our marriage contract, too. Never think, my lord, that I came to Penruan ignorant of what is expected of me."

"You can read?" For the first time since she had entered the great hall Dain looked at her with an interest that went beyond contempt and disparagement.

"I learned to read at an early age," she said, grasping at the chance to elicit some respect from him. "I can also write and count. There are a great many things I know how to do."

"There is only one thing you need to do here at Penruan. You are to bear me a son. We will attempt to conceive one tonight."

Emma considered his words as calculated to intimidate her. She wasn't going to allow it; she was going to fight back.

"You will not bed me when I am cold, wet, and hungry!" she shouted at him. "Nor while my attendants are uncared-for."

"I grow weary of your repeated complaints," he said.

"If you will only have the courtesy to respond to them, the complaints will cease," she told him.

"Perhaps I do not care about your condition," he said, regarding her disdainfully.

"Perhaps you should care, my lord, if you want a healthy son from me!"

"If not from you," he replied, "then from some other woman. It matters not at all to me."

"I think it does," she said, suddenly calm. His indifference to her was feigned; she was certain of it. "For a reason I do not yet comprehend, you wanted a granddaughter of Udo of Wroxley for your wife. You wanted it so much, in fact, that you were willing to wait years until my sister Alys was grown to womanhood before getting a child on her. You will not have to wait so long with me. That fact ought to please you, not discomfit you. Unless you are afraid of me, my lord?"

She thought he was going to hit her. She had chosen her words deliberately, knowing no man liked to be called a coward and certain he would be angered. She watched his reaction with some surprise and dawning respect for his powers of self-control. She did not doubt his anger. It blazed in his beautiful eyes and hardened his finely boned face. On first seeing him, she had found it difficult to reconcile his handsome appearance with his fearful reputation. She did not find it difficult now.

He did not strike her. Slowly he unclenched the fists he held close to his sides. Emma watched in amazement as his face smoothed from an expression of fury to one of bland disinterest. When he spoke his voice was soft, yet she heard the underlying danger in it.

"You have no idea how mistaken you are about what I want." Abruptly, he changed the subject. "How many female attendants have you brought with you?"

"Just one, my lord, according to the terms of the agreement between you and my father. I have also an escort of twenty men-at-arms and squires, all of whom will return to Wroxley after a day or two of rest." She did not add that the returning captain of the men-at-arms would bear the letter she intended to write to Gavin, describing her reception at Penruan. She thought Dain would understand as much without her telling him.

"There is room for your men in the barracks," Dain said. "I will have someone show you and your maidservant to the lord's chamber."

"I will want a bath," she said, pressing her advantage. "Also food and drink for myself and those who came with me. I assume the midday meal is over." She looked around the great hall, noting the empty tables.

"Order what you want," he told her. "I will join you later, after you have rested." There was a world of unmistakable meaning in that last sentence.

"Do you wish me to appear at the evening meal?" she asked, willing to be concilliatory now that she had won simple hospitality for herself and her companions. "If so, I will have Hawise unpack my best gown."

"There will be time enough tomorrow for me to present you to my people."

She could not help but wonder if he would acknowledge her as his wife at all, if she did not please him when night came.

"I should like to meet your mother," Emma said.

"Lady Richenda is away from home, visiting her sister in a convent," Dain informed her. "She will return in a week or two." With that, he turned his back on her and walked away.

"There goes the rudest man I have ever seen or heard," gasped Hawise, who had been Emma's personal maid for so long that she sometimes forgot her place in favor of defending her beloved mistress. "Nor can his mother be well mannered, if she absented herself from Penruan during the very weeks when she must have known you would arrive. If my lord Gavin were here—"

"But he is not here," Emma interrupted her loyal companion. "Let us make the best of our situation. It seems to me we have no other choice, for we are very far from home."

"It's a good thing it's you who came to Penruan and not Lady Alys," Hawise said. "If little Alys were here, she'd have been weeping half an hour ago. But you will stand up to him, my lady. You will see to it that he treats us as we ought to be treated. And if he continues to be rude, you will use your magic on him."

"Hush," Emma cautioned, laying a finger on Hawise's lips. "We agreed not to say anything about

28

my magical abilities until after I have decided the time is right for me to speak to my lord Dain on the subject."

She found herself wondering if it was going to be possible for her to talk to Dain in a rational way on any subject. When he learned she could work magic, what would his reaction be? The chill that went up her spine at the thought had nothing to do with the lack of a fire in the great hall or with the absence of a charcoal brazier when she and Hawise finally reached the lord's chamber.

Chapter Two

"How cold it is," Hawise said, looking around the lord's chamber. "How bare and gloomy."

Emma did not say so aloud, but she agreed with Hawise. They had been conducted to a bedchamber well suited to a lord who lived near the end of the world on a cliff at the edge of the sea. It was a room very different from the lord's chamber at Wroxley. Here, there were no tapestries to warm and brighten the unplastered gray stone walls. There was no rug on the floor, no chair made comfortable with thick, bright cushions.

True, the room was large and well proportioned, and perhaps it was a more cheerful place when the sun was shining. On this day of rain and wind the shutters were securely latched over the unglazed double window that was set into a niche in the thick wall. With the shutters closed the room was a place of deep shadows made even more gloomy by the lack of comforts. Stone benches were built into each side of the window niche, where ladies might sit together to ply their needles in the light, but there were no cushions to ease the chill of the stone. Only two pieces of furniture graced the room. The head of a large bed with plain, dark brown hangings was pushed against the inner wall, and an oblong wooden clothes chest rested at the foot of the bed.

"My lady, you will freeze in here," Hawise protested, looking around at the chilly emptiness.

"Lord Dain did tell me to order what I wanted," Emma said, and proceeded to list for Hawise everything she would require. While Hawise carried her orders to the castle servants, Emma made a quick search of the other two rooms on the same level of the tower keep. The first room, which opened directly onto the staircase, held a supply of arrows and assorted other arms, all arranged close to the arrow slits, so they would be readily at hand in case of attack.

The second, smaller room also opened onto the tower steps, and in addition it had a door connecting it to the lord's chamber. Since it was empty, and since the window that looked out over the edge of the cliff was slightly larger than an arrow slit, Emma decided the room would serve well as a place for Hawise to sleep and as a storeroom for the belongings brought from Wroxley until they could all be unpacked.

When Hawise returned to the lord's chamber Emma set her to work changing the bed linens. Soon the scent of the lavender in which the sheets had been packed at Wroxley filled the room. Two of the servants whom Hawise had commandeered arrived, one carrying a brazier, the other with a scuttle full of charcoal. Immediately afterward a boy about twelve years old by the look of him, who was evidently a page, rushed in bearing a candlestick as tall as he was and an armful of fat candles that looked as if they had come from the chapel.

"Father Maynard sent them," the boy said, confirming Emma's guess.

"I'm Blake, my lady," the boy continued, "and I am very glad to have a nice lady at Penruan. Father Maynard says you are nice. Not that Lady Richenda isn't nice," he added hastily. "She is a very good woman, and extremely devout, but she isn't much fun."

"Please take my thanks for the candles to Father Maynard," Emma told the boy. She knew better than to comment on his opinion of Lady Richenda.

An hour later Emma was feeling greatly refreshed, having eaten a meal of cold meat, bread, and cheese, washed down by fresh cider. She had also enjoyed the hot bath she so much wanted. Preferring her companion to be as clean as she was, Emma offered the still-warm bathwater to Hawise to use, so she could also wash away the grime and chill of travel. The emptied tub was being carried out and Hawise, shiny faced with cleanliness and grateful to her thoughtful mistress, had retreated to her own small room to find fresh clothes for herself, when Dain stalked into the lord's chamber.

He stopped short, a startled expression spreading across his face as he looked from the freshly made bed with Emma's bright green quilt from Wroxley spread atop the snowy sheets to the candle burning beside the bed, to the wide, round brazier onto which Emma was sprinkling aromatic herbs. He took a breath, preparing to speak, then stopped with a frown and a slight cough.

"What are you doing?" Dain asked, wrinkling his nose at the fragrance.

"Juniper and rosemary will freshen the air," Emma answered. She stayed where she was, with the brazier standing like a sentinel between her and her husband. She told herself the trembling that suddenly threatened to overcome her was foolish. There was nothing for her to fear. Dain was a man like any other man, and she had the king's will and her father's stalwart strength to protect her. Women had for centuries gone to the beds of men they did not know, brought there by the contracts made by parents or guardians or rulers. It was the way marriages were arranged between nobles.

At least she was not part of the spoils of some dreadful battle. She discounted Dain's remarks about having friends who would attack Wroxley on his order. So long as she carried out her part of the agreement, she believed no harm would be visited upon Wroxley, and all of her beloved family would be safe.

She reminded herself that she came willingly to this marriage, to a husband who was handsome, apparently healthy, and reasonably clean. She would grant him her innocence in order to seal the peace between him and Gavin, and she would do everything she could to give him pleasure. Mirielle had made certain that Emma was well informed about what would happen in the marriage bed, and for her stepmother's wise advice Emma was grateful.

Still, her actual experience with men was limited to a few hasty, stolen kisses during Christmas or May Day celebrations. She did not know how it would feel to be completely possessed by a man. Emma sensed that Dain, known as a formidable opponent in battle, was most likely a passionate lover once he was aroused. Possibly he was a violent lover. Suddenly, she recalled Hawise's whispered gossip in the previous year about the harm done to a serving maid by one of the men-at-arms at Wroxley, and how Gavin, upon learning the story, had imprisoned the man and later sent him away to a distant island monastery where there were no women for him to attack. Surely Dain would not treat his wife so brutally. Would he?

Emma took a long breath to calm her thoughts and her trembling limbs. She scattered the last of the herbs over the hot coals, then let her hands fall to her sides and stood there, in the circle of heat from the brazier, and waited.

Dain approached her, skirting the brazier, and Emma turned a little to face him. Her hair was loose and still a bit damp from washing it. Dain's long fingers stroked the smooth tresses from brow to ear to shoulder, a sensitive, almost gentle touch that gave rise to tender hope on Emma's part. Perhaps he would not be rough with her. Perhaps, when they were together in his bed, Dain would lay aside the hatred he bore toward her father and treat her with kindness.

His hand came to rest on her shoulder, and the brilliant eyes that had been searching every aspect of her face next fell to her throat. Suddenly, Emma was painfully aware of being clad only in a loose linen shift, covered by the woolen shawl she had snatched up and wrapped about her shoulders for modesty's sake while the servants carried out the buckets of bathwater and the tub. The shift was ankle-length and the long, straight sleeves reached to her wrists, yet Emma felt as if she were wearing nothing at all. The garment had a wide neckline, and one of Dain's fingers slipped beneath the edge of the fabric. His fingertip caressed her collarbone. He tugged at the linen, pulling it across her shoulder, and then he bent his head and put his mouth on her bare skin.

Emma went perfectly still, transfixed by the sensation of warm, soft lips on her shoulder and of a hot, moist tongue licking at her skin.

Dain kept his mouth where it was, but his hands were busy, pulling the shawl out of her numbed grasp, dropping it on the floor.

Still Emma could not move. Dain slowly trailed his lips along her shoulder to a spot just below her ear. Again his mouth and his tongue worked their singular magic, and Emma discovered that her earlobe and the area around it were both wonderfully receptive to Dain's calculated touch.

For what he was doing was carefully calculated. It could not be otherwise; Dain did not love her, he did not know her, and after his rude reception of his bride she believed he did not even like her, yet they must lie down together and consummate this marriage between strangers, and try to conceive a child whose existence would be the surety of lasting peace between their families.

Emma believed her only hope for a reasonably contented life at Penruan lay in pleasing her husband. And so she rested her hands on his arms to steady herself, and when Dain's mouth seared across her cheek she offered up her lips and let her hands slide up the sleeves of his tunic, noticing with her fingertips, if not with her preoccupied mind, the hard muscles of his upper arms and shoulders.

Then, when his arms suddenly clasped her about the waist and pulled her close against him, and one of his hands splayed down over her buttocks to push her closer still, and his lips seized hers in a kiss that rocked her to her very soul, she knew he was not going to be a gentle lover. Dain was going to plunder her body and take everything she had to offer.

She wanted him to take her. She wanted to belong to him completely, utterly, and she knew in her heart it was what she had wanted from the first moment she had seen him. In the single, shattering instant when his mouth claimed hers, Emma recognized in Dain her predestined mate.

The magical recognition left her defenseless against him, for while she was eager to give him both her body and the love she had stored in her heart for her eighteen years of life, along with all her hopes and dreams for their future together, Dain wanted only her body. And revenge.

She was lost in his kiss, in the wild, heated sensation of his hands on her back, on her shoulders, and on her breasts. His kiss deepened. Dain's mouth forced her lips open and his tongue plunged into her, tangling with her tongue as if in a mysterious, passionate dance. Emma gasped.

With his lips still on hers, Dain loosened his grip on her a little. Emma was aware of his hand stroking down her thigh, of her shift being drawn upward, and his hand warm on the soft skin of her upper leg. His fingers skimmed across her thigh and into her warm, moist, most private place—and stayed there, even when she moaned and tried to pull her mouth away from his. He ignored her protest, instead thrusting a finger farther still, touching—touching—

An exquisite, piercing sweetness enveloped Emma, and she found herself pushing back against the pressure of his hand. Finally, Dain lifted his head, releasing her mouth from his.

With one arm still supporting her, for she was by now quite incapable of standing by herself, he used his other hand to wreck havoc upon all her senses until she was at the brink of a marvelous discovery. Longing to share her wonder with him, Emma opened her eyes.

Dain was watching her, and there was cold triumph in his beautiful, blue-green gaze. Watching her! Disinterested, coolly judging her reaction to his lovemaking that was not lovemaking at all. His hand stayed where it was, between her thighs, and to her horror Emma realized she wanted him to continue what he was doing to her. Worse, she wanted him to carry her to the bed, for she knew she was unable to walk even those few steps, and in his bed she wanted him to complete what he had started.

Dain smiled at her—a superior, knowing smile— and let his finger sink a little deeper into her. Seeing his smile, Emma rebelled at last.

"No!" She pushed hard against his chest, shoving him away from her at the same time that she lurched backward.

She almost fell into the brazier. Its edge burned her arm, and the pain of the injury returned her to her proper senses.

She was shaking so violently that she knew she could not stand for more than a moment or two without some source of support. The bed—no, that was the last place she wanted to be. The only other furniture was Dain's clothes chest. She could sit on it, but it was large—large enough for him to push her down on it and—

She fled to the window niche, to lean against the

cold stone while she cradled her burned forearm in her other hand. When Dain approached she caught the shutter latch and unfastened it, pulling the shutter wide open. Cool air blew in, damp and salty from the sea. Emma took several restoring breaths.

"Don't be a fool." Dain reached across her to slam the shutter closed and fasten it again. "It is hundreds of feet to the rocks below, and the waves catch anything that falls and hurl it into the deep sea. Nothing that drops from this tower is ever found again."

"I wasn't going to jump," she said, feeling remarkably calm.

"I did wonder." He turned to face her, and in the glow of the single candle his eyes were shadowed. Emma could not guess what he was thinking. She was certain of only one thing.

"You don't care about me at all," she whispered.

"Why did you think I would?" he asked with perfect reasonableness. "I was merely doing what I— and you, too, my lady—am obligated to do. I regret any offense I caused, but surely you are aware that certain actions must be taken by us in order to consummate our marriage. I was attempting to make the event as pleasant as possible for you."

"The event?" She swallowed hard, knowing he was in the right and that she was a fool, indeed, to expect true affection from him.

"Shall we try it again?" Dain held out his hand to her. "On the bed this time. It will be simpler that way, and more quickly done." Incredibly, he was smiling at her, clearly expecting her to place her hand in his.

"Now?" She wanted to hit him. She wanted to scream and yell and throw something at him. Her burned arm hurt and she was perilously close to tears, and this uncaring brute who was her predestined love wanted to toss her onto the bed and put his—

"We could wait until later," he said, still smiling, "but it is my opinion that it will be better to have the act over and done with at once."

"Oh?" she said.

"The first time is always difficult for a virgin. I'm sure you have been told about that. Afterward, it will be easier."

"You miserable cur," she muttered, not caring whether he heard her or not. He did hear her. So indifferent was he to her feelings that the insult did not mar his coolness. His smile never faltered.

"You have no choice, my lady. My advice to you is to give in gracefully and do your duty."

"You don't know or like me," she said.

"No more than you know or like me. My opinion of you does not matter, nor yours of me. We are bound together, you and I, and I will have what is rightfully mine."

"If I refuse, will you force me?" She wasn't afraid, only more angry than she had ever been in her life.

"There will be no need for force," he said, his eyes sparkling with an emotion she could only guess at. "After our one, brief embrace, I am convinced that you are a woman of rare passion. I have only to remove that shamefully sheer piece of linen you are wearing and then begin to caress you, and before long you will accept me eagerly, despite your virgin state."

"No, I won't," she protested.

"I need only sit on the bed," he said, suiting the action to his words, "and tell you what I intend to do to you, and you will come to me, lured by the possibility of even greater ecstacy than I have already shown you. What you felt when I touched you a few moments ago is only the barest taste of the passion you will experience in my arms.

"Now, do not scowl at me so fiercely," he said, looking amused. "You know that what I say is true, and so, my lady, you will lie down where I tell you to lie down, and open yourself to me when I order it, and when I am ready, I will make you mine."

"Stop it!" The horrible truth was that his caressing tone was reheating the earlier fires he had kindled within her. Emma longed to join him on the bed. She ached to experience his hands on her again, to feel once more the exquisite torture of his fingers stroking into her, lifting her to unimagined heights.

But most of all, she wanted him to care about her wishes, to see her as a person worthy of his respect. And therefore she was going to refuse him, her husband and master. She was certain there was no one in the kingdom, her father and Mirielle included, who would stand with her on her decision to defy her husband. Once she said no to Dain, she would be alone as she had never been alone before.

There was nothing else she could do. She simply could not allow him to take her and use her for the sake of cold, unfeeling revenge against her father. What Dain's reaction was going to be she could not guess. She opened her mouth, preparing to tell him that she would not lie with him willingly, and that if he attempted to force her against her will, she would use her magical arts to prevent him.

He rose and took a step in her direction, and at first Emma thought he was going to grab at her. But he walked right past her, heading for the chamber door, and she realized that there was a great deal of noise coming from below, in the hall. She had heard it at the back of her mind, but in her concentration on Dain she had ignored it, until now, when it could no longer be ignored.

"My lord!" There were footsteps on the stairs, followed by a heavy banging on the door, and the excited sound of several male voices outside it. "My lord, make haste! To arms!"

"What in the name of the saints are you yelling about?" Dain exclaimed, pulling the door open so quickly that both Blake the page and a short, swarthy man-at-arms nearly fell into the room. "Sloan, you had better have a good reason for disturbing me."

"I have, my lord," said the man-at-arms. He gave Emma only the briefest of glances before turning his full attention to Dain. "A messenger arrived just a few moments ago. Trevanan has been attacked and looted."

"Has it?" Dain's mouth thinned, his eyes blazing. "We can both guess whose work that was."

"Aye, no doubt about it," Sloan agreed, nodding. "The messenger said three men and a woman were killed."

"My people," said Dain. "My responsibility. Where is Robert?"

"Here, my lord." A young, blond fellow pushed his way into the crowded chamber.

"Arm me." Dain snapped out the order to Robert, who was apparently his squire. Swiftly, he unbuckled his belt and threw off his tunic.

Ignored by the men, Emma gaped at the broad, suntanned chest revealed to her, and at arms with muscles like corded steel. How had she dared to imagine she could resist such strength? Dain's chest and his lower arms were lightly covered with hair that was sun bleached to the same pale shade

41

as the hair on his head. To her bedazzled eyes he
appeared as one of the great knights of legend—tall,
golden, incredibly handsome—and so immersed in
manly concerns that her presence in his chamber
was already forgotten. Perhaps he had forgotten
her very existence.

The squire Robert lifted the lid of Dain's clothes
chest and drew out first a plain linen undershirt and
then the padded gambeson and the head wrapping
knights wore beneath their chain mail.

"Let me help," Emma said. She caught up the
concealing woolen shawl that Robert had dropped
on the floor. Upon hearing the noise at the door,
Hawise had come into the room from her own
chamber, and now she brought Emma a pin to fasten the shawl she was draping over her shoulders.
Thus securely covered, Emma reached for the gambeson, to help Dain pull it over his head.

"My lady, I can do it," Robert said.

"Leave me, Emma," Dain commanded her. With
a smile for the squire, he motioned for the young
man to continue.

"I am perfectly capable of arming a knight,"
Emma protested.

"I am sure you are, but I prefer to have Robert
do it, and I do not want you here when you are
undressed. Go with your maidservant into the next
room, and stay there with her until after I have left."

"Where are you going?" Emma cried, not moving
from where she stood.

"To smoke out a band of brigands that dares lay
waste to my lands," Dain said. "This is the second
time in less than six months that they have looted
Trevanan. I thought I had destroyed them after the
first time they attacked. They will not have a third
opportunity."

"What will you do to them? And what can I do to aid you?" she asked.

"When I find them, I will burn them to ashes," he responded. "This is man's work. As for you, do not leave the castle until I return."

"Really, my lord," she began, "I can decide for myself—"

"You will obey me." Dain's voice was a cold knife slicing across her words. "It is common gossip in this area that I have taken a wife, so some of the same brigands may be lurking nearby in hope of seizing you and holding you for ransom while I am occupied at Trevanan. I do not intend to waste my time or risk the lives of my men in an effort to rescue a woman who is foolish enough to expose herself to abduction by leaving the protection of my castle walls. Do you understand me?"

"Yes, my lord." If she sounded meek, it was only because she did understand the danger against which he was warning her. "May I walk on the battlements?"

"If you have a liking for rain and wind, you may do as you please. I will probably be gone for several days," he said.

"I will see that Penruan is well guarded in your absence, my lord." She knew her duty as lady of the castle.

"You?" There was a world of derision in his tone. "In my absence you will defer to the orders of Sloan, the knight who is the captain of my men-at-arms. It is he who will guard the castle, not you."

"I have been well trained," she protested.

"No doubt you have. But as you, yourself, pointed out to me just a short time ago, I do not know you. Neither do I trust you."

"How dare you question my honesty?"

"It would be unwise of me not to distrust you," he said. "You are, after all, the child of my enemy. If you want my trust, you must earn it. You may begin to do so by obeying Sir Sloan while I am gone."

While they talked, Robert had finished arming him. Clad in chain mail from head to foot, Dain was a fearsome sight. He adjusted his sword belt, pulled his mail coif up over the cloth head wrapping, and with another smile and a word of thanks he accepted the gauntlets his squire held out to him. Dain's eyes had taken on the cold glint of the metal armor he wore, and his mouth was a hard, grim line. Emma could see no warmth in him at all.

"Until I return, my lady," he said, and made a slight bow in her direction.

Then he was gone, and his men with him. Hawise hurried to close the door after them, shutting out the draft that swirled along the stairs.

"My lady, I made sure to keep the door to my room closed tight while Lord Dain was with you," Hawise said, glancing at the bed, where the sheets remained undisturbed and the quilt showed only the imprint where Dain had sat. "Did he—? No, I see he did not, unless he has some very peculiar habits. But did he hurt you in any way? What is wrong with your arm?"

"This is my own doing," Emma answered. "I burned it on the brazier. Can you find the cowslip water among the medicines we brought with us?"

"You'll want a clean bandage, too." Hawise went to search among the boxes and baskets that were piled in the adjoining room.

Emma decided she could remain on her feet no longer. She staggered to the bed and sat on the edge, next to the spot where the impression of

Dain's thighs still showed. Lost in thought, she put out a hand to touch the indentation in the quilt.

"Here, my lady." Hawise returned and held out the uncorked bottle of cowslip water. Emma poured a little of the medicine onto the burned area and spread it around with her fingertips. When she was finished she let Hawise tie a strip of white linen around her arm. When Hawise was done she regarded Emma out of troubled eyes.

"I hope Lord Dain will not be cruel to you," Hawise said. "From what I have seen of him, I think he is not a kind man. Did he tell you that all of the men-at-arms and squires who came with us have been quartered in a separate barracks from his men, and that they are guarded wherever they go? One of our squires told me so when I was in the kitchen earlier."

"I am not surprised," Emma said with a sigh. "If Dain doesn't trust me, surely he won't trust them, either. For all he knows, our people may have orders to attack his men-at-arms and to open the castle gate to my father and a large force that is waiting to take over Penruan."

"Lord Gavin would never behave so treacherously!" Hawise exclaimed.

"Dain doesn't know that." Emma straightened her shoulders. "Before I am finished, he will know it. He will trust me, and my father, too, and he will understand just how ridiculous is the feud he reopened. In the future when he rides away to battle he will leave Penruan in my keeping, as it ought to be."

"How can you achieve such a change, when he holds all the power in your marriage?" Hawise asked. "A mere woman cannot gainsay her husband. Remember, Dain has the right to force himself on you if you dare to refuse him—unless you plan to use magic to prevent him?"

"He cannot know about my magic. Not yet, not until we know each other far better than we do now. You are correct, Hawise, when you say I have little power against him. By law I cannot withhold physical favors from my husband." As Emma spoke all of her conflicting thoughts and emotions came together in one determined purpose. "However, there is a way to change his mind and his heart."

"How?" Hawise asked.

"I intend to have the sweetest revenge possible, to pay Dain back for the way he has treated me in the last hour," Emma said, her eyes glowing. "I will drive him to his knees."

"Oh, my lady, do be careful," Hawise begged. "What can any woman hope to achieve against a man as hard as Lord Dain?"

"I shall teach him to trust me and to love me," Emma declared with all the assurance of youth and with an innocence only slightly tarnished by Dain's recent cool manipulation of her senses. "Furthermore, I will do it without using magic. I do believe it's the only way to assure a permanent peace between Penruan and Wroxley."

"*If* you can teach him." Hawise, who was three years older than Emma, and a bit more experienced with men, recorked the bottle of cowslip water and headed for the other room to put it away. "If Lord Dain owns a heart that is capable of love. From what I've seen of him, I sadly doubt it."

Chapter Three

In Dain's absence Emma made a point of walking on the battlements each afternoon. She saw the activity as asserting herself, even though Dain had granted his grudging permission. It wasn't a very pleasant form of exercise. The steady drizzle went on for days, making the stone walkways slippery. Emma could see little of the castle surroundings because of the rain and the fog that drifted in from the sea. When she leaned over the parapet she couldn't even see the rocks below the castle, although she could hear the waves crashing on them. Let Hawise mutter about the cold and damp, and the quaking ague that was sure to make both of them permanently ill; still Emma persisted in taking her daily walk. She repeatedly pointed out to her companion that, as both of them soon learned, walking was one of the few things she was allowed to do.

Though Emma vowed she was not going to defy the rules laid down for her by her husband, she did intend to stretch those rules as far as she could. She began by attempting to change the daily menu, only to discover the cook would not alter one single detail. She was polite to Emma but adamant.

"Before she left Penruan, Lady Richenda decided on all of the menus for each day of her absence," the cook explained. "We dare not vary any meal."

"What if someone brings in unexpected game or fish?" Emma asked. "Surely, you don't waste such largesse."

"Lady Richenda has made provision for that event," the cook said, exuding patience toward a newcomer who obviously did not understand the way Penruan was run. "Truly, my lady Emma, you need not concern yourself with the meals. Lady Richenda has everything perfectly organized."

Emma was wise enough not to insist to a servant whose loyalties lay elsewhere that *she* was now the lady of the castle and, therefore, the orders of the present baron's wife ought to take precedence over those of the baron's widowed mother. She decided to wait until Dain returned and speak to him about who was to be chatelaine of Penruan.

Bored by idleness and eager to use the skills she had spent years perfecting, Emma next moved onto housecleaning, to the laundry, to storage and maintenance of the household linens, to sewing, spinning, weaving. Everywhere she turned her efforts were balked by servants who very politely but very firmly informed her that her help was not needed or wanted. Lady Richenda had everything well in hand. Emma was expected to do nothing but rest from her difficult journey to Penruan while she awaited the return of Lord Dain.

She complained to Sir Sloan. He, adhering strictly to the orders given him by Dain, with great politeness pointed out to Emma what she already knew: that the domestic affairs of a castle were not within the provence of the captain of the guard. Lady Richenda had been undisputed mistress of the castle since the day she had arrived there as a bride more than thirty years earlier. If Emma wanted to change that arrangement, she would have to speak to Dain.

"I almost wish someone would be rude to me, so I could have an excuse to stand and fight," she said to Father Maynard. The early morning service was just completed and the castle folk who had attended were leaving the chapel to take up their daily work. Emma watched them go with envious eyes. "I shall run mad if I cannot discover something to occupy my mind. At Wroxley I was always busy, always needed, but here I feel useless. And unwanted," she added in a moment of self-pity. So disturbed that she could not remain still, she began to walk up and down, covering the space between chapel door and altar steps in a few rapid strides, then turning to retrace her path.

"You must understand that your position here is somewhat unusual," Father Maynard said.

"I do understand it; I just wish others would." She was instantly contrite for having snapped at him. "I am sorry, Father. You see in me an example of how idleness leads to ill-temper, and to feeling sorry for oneself. I cannot ride or even take a long walk, for I am forbidden to step outside the castle walls. And I am forbidden to *do* anything within these walls! It is unjust of Dain to treat me so."

"Perhaps, but it is also understandable. Dain wants to keep you safe and, until the outlaws are caught and punished, you are safest here, inside." Father Maynard watched her agitated pacing for a few moments more before he asked, "Have you visited the stillroom?"

"Of course not. I did ask about the room, only to be told it is kept locked, at Lady Richenda's orders. In the absence of Lady Richenda, the cook has the key, but she refuses to give it to me without a direct command from either Dain or his mother." Emma passed Father Maynard for the fifth time and would have continued striding restlessly between door and altar if he had not stopped her by putting a hand on her arm.

"My child, be still for a moment. Collect your thoughts, which are obviously scattered, and try to think reasonably.

"I was at Wroxley Castle for two weeks," Father Maynard said. "During that time I observed how you were given responsibilities beyond those of most unmarried girls."

"My father and my stepmother trusted me," Emma said, "and rightly so."

"As I recall, your special responsibility was in the stillroom, where you compounded medicines," Father Maynard said.

"That's true." Emma regarded him with interest. Of course he had been watching her while he was at Wroxley. Dain had most likely required a report from him on his return to Penruan. Father Maynard had been clever enough to conceal what he was doing, and Emma had not thought to hide her daily sessions with Mirielle, during which she practiced magical spells. More important than any spell casting were Mirielle's instructions in how to control her magical abilities. Thanks to Mirielle's gentle explanations over the years, Emma knew about her mother's evil activities in the past, activities that had almost destroyed Wroxley and its inhabitants, and she was determined to avoid Alda's fate of being consumed by a magic she could no longer contain. Emma wondered how much Father Maynard had learned, or how much he guessed, about her inborn magic.

"I am skilled at making medicines from herbs," she said to the priest, and braced herself for an interrogation.

To her relief Father Maynard asked no questions about her medicines. Perhaps, like the resident priest at Wroxley, he preferred not to know what she could do with herbs or with her spells, so he could with a clear conscience live side by side with an ancient tradition that in its own way brought as much comfort to people's bodies as Father Maynard's religion did to their souls.

"Even when Lady Richenda is here, the stillroom is seldom used," Father Maynard said, "which is too bad, especially during the late winter, when people often fall ill."

"They are sick because there isn't much fresh food left by late winter, except for cabbages and parsnips and a few other roots," Emma said, "though certain herbs can help the situation. Also, I am sure the men-at-arms develop serious coughs and running noses from standing long hours of sentry duty upon the walls in damp and windy weather."

"Perhaps during the coming winter your medicines will be of help to those poor men-at-arms," Father Maynard suggested.

"There are medicines I could make," Emma said, "but only if the fresh herbs are available to me now, in the summer season. Other herbs ought to be dried before winter comes, so I'll have them to use later. There is only a small herb garden here at Penruan, and the cook tells me that she uses most of what it supplies. If only I could go outside the castle, I could search for fresh herbs and even dig up a few plants to bring back and put into the garden. It's not too late in the year for transplanting."

"Now, there is a useful work to keep you busy," said Father Maynard.

"I am sure if I suggest it, I will be prevented by some unbreakable rule Lady Richenda has laid down about the uses of herbs, or about entrance to the stillroom," Emma exclaimed in exaspiration. "Everything I try to do is stopped before I can begin."

"I do think," said Father Maynard, "that you are a resourceful young woman." His smile held a wealth of unspoken meaning.

"What are you suggesting?" Emma asked. She was not sure she was reading him correctly. She did not, after all, know him very well, and if the actions she was suddenly contemplating should prove to be a mistake, the consequences could be devastating to her future with Dain. Emma sighed, wishing for just a moment that her life had taken a simpler path. But if there were no feud, if she had married an ordinary nobleman, she would not know Dain. And that was a painful thought.

"Why, my child, I suggest nothing," said Father Maynard, looking remarkably innocent for a man who had for years been listening to the confessions of men-at-arms, "though I do suppose that before you can begin your herbal work you will have to get into the stillroom and make an inventory."

"How am I to do that, except by stealing the key from the cook?" Emma demanded.

" 'Thou shalt not *steal*,' " said Father Maynard, straight-faced and serious. "The commandment is explicit."

"Ah." Emma broke into a grin as the certainty of his meaning dawned on her. "No, Father, I won't steal. I shall borrow, and later I shall return, the key."

"It's best if you say no more to me," Father Maynard warned.

"What a clever man you are. What a good and kind friend to me." Emma was tempted to kiss him on his stubbly cheek, but she feared he might take the gesture amiss, and so she restrained her bursting enthusiasm. All the way back to the lord's chamber she considered the problem of how to obtain the key to the stillroom.

She found Hawise just finishing with the new bed hangings. Bright blue wool with borders embroidered in red and green replaced the old, threadbare brown hangings, and the green quilt added an extra note of color.

The shutters were open to provide light for Hawise's work, and a gray, misty sky could be seen through the long twin windows. The chamber was a bit cool, but it smelled lovely from the dried lavender flowers and rosemary leaves that Emma kept in small bowls to freshen the air.

"How nice the bed looks," Emma said, smiling at Hawise.

"Now we have only the chair to assemble and the room will be remade to your liking." Hawise nodded toward a pile of boards that were cut into precise lengths, each length well sanded and oiled. "We will need a third person, but Sir Sloan claims that all of his men are too busy to assist us."

"We could ask Blake," Emma said, thoughtfully.

She was still mulling over the question of how to get her hands on the stillroom key, and an idea was forming in her mind.

"The page?" Hawise asked. "He's only a boy, not more than eleven or twelve, and slender for his age. Will he be strong enough for this job?"

"The carpenter at Wroxley showed me how the chair is to be put together," Emma said. "It only needs two pair of hands to hold the pieces in place while a third person drives the pegs into the slots to keep the pieces together. See if you can find Blake."

While Hawise was gone Emma laid the various pieces of wood out on the floor in order, so they were ready to be assembled. At the same time she assembled her thoughts, working out how to approach Blake, and how to accomplish her goal of making the stillroom her own place. She thought Blake's cooperation would be easy enough to obtain. Dain's consent was going to be more difficult. Still, she had to try. She simply could not spend many more days in enforced idleness.

When Blake came into the room with Hawise, Emma rose from her kneeling posture to face him with a friendly smile and a pleasant greeting.

"You really know how to do this?" Blake exclaimed in undisguised disbelief after she explained to him how they were going to assemble the chair. "A lady who understands carpentry?"

"Just do as I have asked and you will have proof of my claim," Emma told him.

"I knew you were going to be more fun than Lady Richenda!" Blake eagerly reached for the first piece of wood.

Under Emma's instruction, Hawise and Blake fitted the sections together and then held them in place while Emma drove in the pegs with the small mallet provided by the carpenter. It didn't take long to finish the chair. Blake claimed the right to be first to sit in it.

"If you ever want to move it or store it, you only have to knock the pegs out again," Blake noted. He ran his hands over the smooth arms, letting his fingertips rest on the nearest peg.

"Yes," Emma said, "which is why Hawise will now store the mallet in one of my boxes, in case we need it again. And in another box she will find the cushions for the chair seat and back." She handed the mallet to Hawise with a tilt of her head that told her companion to go into the adjoining chamber and stay there until she was summoned.

"What else can you do, Lady Emma?" Blake asked, gazing at her in near reverence for her accomplishments.

"I know how to make herbal medicines," she answered. "My father's wife taught me." It wasn't the entire truth, but it was close enough for her present purposes.

"Lady Richenda doesn't believe in medicines," Blake revealed. "She says all illnesses are the punishment of God. If a person falls sick, it's because he has committed a sin. That's why the men-at-arms are so often sick. Lady Richenda says they are all miserable sinners."

"The men-at-arms fall ill because they drink too much ale and wine, they stand long watches on the battlements in cold, damp weather, they live together in a crowded barracks, and they very seldom bother to bathe," Emma stated firmly.

"Lady Richenda wouldn't agree with you," Blake said.

"What about wounds?" Emma asked. "Does Lady

Richenda wash and sew up the injuries that men working with weapons so often sustain?"

"She says those are the Lord's doing, too," Blake said. "If the good Lord wants a wounded man to live, then he will live, regardless of how the wound is treated. If the Lord turns His face away, then the man's wound will suppurate and he'll die. But it's up to God, not to mere men or women."

"I cannot believe Dain feels the same way," Emma cried. "I'm sure he has seen enough men wounded in battle to know that some can be restored to health, while others, though they must die of their terrible injuries, can be made more comfortable with the proper nostrums."

"You're right about Dain," Blake said. "Sometimes he sends for a healer, an old woman named Agatha who lives in Trevanan village, to treat his men, but Lady Richenda says Agatha is a witch. Whenever Agatha comes here, Lady Richenda shuts herself in her room and won't come out until the healer has done her work and left. Then Lady Richenda runs to the chapel to pray, and she insists that Father Maynard say the Holy Mass at once. But Agatha is a kind person. Last winter she gave me horehound syrup to stop a cough that had made my chest ache for days."

"I would very much like to meet Agatha," Emma said.

"I'm sure you will meet her, if you stay at Penruan long enough," Blake told her. "I ought not to say this, but in the great hall and the kitchen people are laying wagers on how long you'll last after Lady Richenda comes home."

Emma decided to ignore that last piece of information in favor of pursuing her real reason for asking Hawise to bring Blake to the lord's chamber.

"I wonder if you would be willing to do a great favor for me," Emma began.

"It is a page's duty to perform favors for his lady," Blake responded solemnly. "Now that you have married Dain, you are my lady, at least until Lady Richenda returns. What's the favor? Are you planning something else that's fun?"

"What I want," Emma said, "is to obtain the key to the stillroom. I understand it is in the cook's keeping. Do you by any chance know where it is and how I might get it?"

"You want to steal a key?" Solemnity gave way to eagerness. Blake's face was alight with boyish mischief. "Oh, my lady, you are fun! You must have grown up with brothers, because you aren't like any girl I've ever known."

"I have three brothers, one older than me and two who are younger," Emma said. "I'll tell you about them sometime. Blake, I do not want to steal the stillroom key. I only want to borrow it, and that for just a short time. I will return it when I have finished in the room. Do you know where the key is?"

"Why do you want to go in the stillroom? I went there once, with Lady Richenda. That was a couple of years ago. It was dusty and there were cobwebs, and I only noticed a few herbs."

"That's what I was afraid of," Emma said. "But I want to discover for myself exactly what herbs there are, and what medicines."

"There probably aren't any medicines at all," Blake said. "There wouldn't be, would there? Not with Lady Richenda feeling the way she does. She'd think medicines work against the Will of God."

"I disagree," Emma said very firmly. "I think medicines are meant to work *with* the Will of God. I think the good Lord meant His people to be as healthy as possible, and happy, too, and I intend to do everything I can to see to it that the people of Penruan are both."

She had said too much. She could tell by the way Blake was gazing at her with wide, gleaming eyes and wonder in his young face.

"I'll get the key for you," Blake said.

"If you will just tell me where it is, I can borrow it for myself," Emma said. "I don't want you to get into trouble for my sake."

"No, no, I can do it. I know I can," Blake said. "You couldn't, but I know how to get it."

"How?"

"Don't ask me that. Just tell me when you want to do this."

"Right after the midday meal?"

"Yes, that's good. When you leave the table, go straight to the stillroom door. I'll meet you there. And Lady Emma . . . ?"

"Yes, Blake?"

"Promise you won't ask me any questions about what I plan to do."

"I promise."

Emma kept her promise, and she never did learn exactly how Blake was able to obtain the key. He was waiting for her at the stillroom door as they had planned. He refused to give her the key, unlocking the door himself and keeping the key in his own hand the entire time they were in the room.

They weren't there for very long. It was a good-sized room, with a shuttered window to let in light, though they left the shutter closed and used a candle to see by. There was a table in the middle of the room, and there were shelves from floor to ceiling on two of the walls. Bunches of cooking herbs and a few empty baskets hung from the ceiling beams. Three small jars grouped together on one of the shelves proved to contain old and musty dried herbs. There was no sign of any prepared medicine, nor were there any mixing utensils, bowls or pots, no source of heat, not even a mortar and pestle. As Blake had warned, the floor, table, and all of the shelves were dusty, and cobwebs were draped from the ceiling and in every corner. Clearly, the room was seldom opened and only rarely used.

Emma left the stillroom in silence, trying to think how to convince Dain to oppose his mother's wishes and allow her to make use of the room.

When Dain rode out to intercept the brigands who had wrought terror upon Trevanan, his thoughts were sharply divided between schemes for ambush and capture of the outlaws, and memories of the bride he was trying to convince himself he did not want. He had originally agreed to wed a child of seven, his secret plan being to find an excuse to repudiate her and thus break the peace between himself and Gavin before the girl was old enough to consummate the marriage. Instead, he was sent a bride who was a beautiful raven-haired young woman with mysterious eyes and an air of self-assurance equal to his own.

He had come so close—so dangerously close!—to consummating their marriage and thereby making it completely legal. He was grateful for the emergency that called him away from Penruan, knowing that if he had stayed, Emma would have spent her first night in his castle locked in her husband's arms. The lady was willing; he had seen longing in her incredible eyes, and had felt it in the way she clung to him, hungry for more of his caresses.

And he had been all too eager to bestow those caresses. It was because of his shocking desire for the daughter of his sworn enemy that he deliberately prolonged the search for the brigands, whose villainy extended far beyond what the messenger from Trevanan had reported. Two village men were dead, killed defending their homes and families, and three women abducted, carried off to the moorland camp of the outlaws among the rocky tors, there to be repeatedly ravished and beaten.

When they were found one woman was dead of her injuries, but the other two Dain at once returned to their grieving families. Whether the women would ever be fully received back into those families would probably depend on whether the coming months found them with child by their brutal captors.

Dain's mouth thinned at the possibility. He resolved to stay in even closer contact than usual with the village elders. If he learned from them that the women were scorned or mistreated in any way because of what had happened, he would remove them from Trevanan to Penruan and give them honest work there. He knew of several homes in the vicinity where orphans or unwanted children were joyfully received, and to those homes he would send the babes born of rape, if that was what their mothers wished.

As their liege lord, obligated to protect and defend those who lived under his rule, it was his duty to see to the futures of all of those innocent victims. He knew his mother would disapprove of kindness to such women, but on this matter Dain was not concerned about Lady Richenda's opinion. He felt completely sure that Emma, who insisted on proper treatment of her traveling companions, would care about the ravished and battered women, and she would commend him for what he planned to do. At the sudden realization of the direction in which his thoughts were leading he told himself with cold obstinacy that Emma's opinion on the matter meant even less to him than his mother's.

During the next few days he and his men sought out and killed every member of that particular outlaw band. Beset by frustration over his unacceptable desire for Emma, fueled by impotent rage against Gavin, who his king had forced him not to attack, Dain sought release from his conflicting emotions in violence against the brigands who threatened his people. He took grim satisfaction in the bloody work of retribution, offering no mercy to the criminals and fully living up to his reputation as a fierce, coldhearted warrior.

When it was over he ordered everything his men could find belonging to the outlaws heaped into one huge pile, with the outlaws' bodies tossed on top. At his command the pile was set alight, becoming a funeral pyre for those who dared to injure the people of the baron of Penruan. Let the other brigands who hid on the moors see the flames and take note of the fearsome vengeance they could expect if they chose to attack Penruan or Trevanan.

As soon as the fire was reduced to ashes Dain gathered together his able-bodied men, his wounded, and the one who had been killed on the very last day of fighting, and he rode home to Penruan sunk in a grief so deep he did not think he would ever recover.

* * *

61

At the cry from the sentries at the gatehouse, notifying everyone in the castle that Dain was returning with wounded, Emma hastened to the great hall to offer her help. She was relieved to see there were only four wounded men, and that Dain seemed to be unhurt. Then she saw and recognized the body of the squire being carried in on a litter and understood why Dain was so quiet and withdrawn, and why his attention was devoted to the mangled remains of what had once been a handsome young man.

"I am so sorry," she said, going to him with her hands outstretched. "On my first day at Penruan, when Robert came to the lord's chamber to arm you, it seemed to me that you were fond of him."

"So I was." Dain's face was hard, his mouth grim, as if he was holding back strong emotion.

Emma's heart ached for his grief. Placing both her hands on his arm, she offered the one comfort she could give to him.

"I can help Father Maynard to wash and prepare Robert for burial." When Dain turned his head to look at her out of bleak eyes, Emma explained. "I have performed that sad task several times in my life. I will do it again now, with proper reverence, if you will allow me."

"No," Dain said. "This is my work. I will do it."

"You?" Emma stared at him in surprise. "I know you loved him, but it's hardly a lord's duty to prepare the dead."

"Loved him?" Dain repeated. His burning eyes bored into hers. "Aye, I loved him. Robert was my son."

"What?" Emma's hand pressed hard against her bosom. "Oh, Dain, I didn't know. No one told me you were married before."

"I have never been married," Dain said, in a tone that implied he still wasn't. In a gentler voice he added, "Robert's mother was the first woman with whom I ever lay. I learned a useful lesson from her, that it only takes one time to create a child. I was fifteen and a squire.

"She was one of the kitchen maids at the castle where I was fostered," he continued, speaking as if he could not hold back the words that would explain an apparently unseemly grief. "She was a maiden when I first lay with her, and for a few months she doted on me, so I never questioned her claim that I was Robert's sire."

"Where is she now?" Emma asked, expecting him to say that his mistress lived in Trevanan, or perhaps in the castle itself.

"After Robert was born she married the blacksmith of the castle where she lived. She died in childbirth two years later. When Robert was old enough to become a squire I brought him here to Penruan to serve me, with the intention of eventually making him one of my household knights. I believe he would have made a fine and loyal knight."

Emma heard the slight crack in Dain's voice on those last words, and she knew beyond doubt that deep in his most secret heart Dain had cherished dreams for his illegitimate son.

"I am certain what you say is true," Emma said to him. "Judging by my brief knowledge of him, Robert was a devoted squire."

"Thank you for those words, my lady." Dain inclined his head to her, then turned on his heel and headed for the chapel.

"Dain, wait!" Emma cried. "There is something I must ask of you."

"I have already told you that you may not attend my son," he said in a low voice.

"I understand your reasoning, my lord, and I will not quarrel with you about it. There is another matter on which we must speak, and this moment seems to me remarkably appropriate."

"What is it?" Dain turned to face her again. He looked inexpressibly weary.

"My lord, I am possessed of excellent healing skills. From the glimpse I saw of Robert's wounds, no one could have saved him, but it may be that I can help others. It is your duty to protect and care for your people. As your wife, it is my duty to do the same." When he made no objection to what she was saying, she went on, "While you were gone I borrowed the key to the stillroom."

"Borrowed?" he repeated, eyebrows raised in clear disbelief. "Are you sure that's the correct word? The cook would never give it to you."

"She did not, so don't blame her," Emma said. "I did take the key, but I use the word *borrowed* because I kept it for less than an hour before I replaced it. It did not require very long for me to see that the stillroom is but poorly supplied with the herbs necessary to make medicines. Nor are the necessary plants growing in the kitchen garden, which is turned over primarily to vegetables and cooking herbs." She paused, trying to think how to explain what was needed without appearing to criticize his mother.

"What is it you want?" he asked.

"Your permission to leave the castle, to explore the countryside in search of useful herbs. Some I can gather and bring back here to dry in the stillroom. Others I can dig up and transplant into the kitchen garden. Once I have an adequate supply, I can begin to prepare various tinctures for open wounds, ointments for rashes or sore muscles, mixtures of dry herbs to use for brewing hot drinks that will clear stuffy noses and sore throats.

"Dain, if you give your permission, I may be of some real use to our people, and all of us will be healthier when winter comes. When you first came into the hall I heard you tell Sloan that you have eliminated the outlaws from the vicinity of Penruan, so I should be safe from the threat of abduction that you cited days ago as a reason to keep me here at home."

For a few long moments she thought he was going to refuse her offer, and she feared if he did, she would go mad, for she could not endure many more days of nothing to do.

"Our people?" he repeated softly. "Keep you at home? Do you truly see Penruan as your home?"

"Since we are married, anywhere that you live is my home," she responded, deliberately defying his earlier hint that he did not consider theirs a real marriage.

"An interesting idea," he said. "It's a pity I have no time to discuss it with you just now. Very well; you may tell the cook that I have given the stillroom key into your keeping. Do whatever you want with the stillroom, and with the kitchen garden."

"Thank you, my lord. I will need a horse for myself, and one for Hawise. There are baskets in the stillroom that we can attach to our saddles to carry the herbs we gather."

"You will also need a man-at-arms for protection," he said.

"A man-at-arms will only grow bored with my kind of slow, quiet work." At that point in the discussion Emma noticed Blake standing alone in the great hall, staring after the men who carried Robert's body to the chapel. Blake's face was white and he held his slender shoulders stiffly. He looked as though he was trying hard not to weep.

"My lord, would you give me Blake, instead?"

"Blake?" Dain's glance took in the boy, who chose that moment to sniffle loudly before bracing his shoulders again. "Blake is only a child." Dain's words could have been disdainful, but they were softened by the compassion on his face, which indicated his understanding that Blake, too, was suffering at the loss of Robert.

"He is a page who soon will be old enough to become a squire," Emma corrected her husband. "It is my duty as mistress of the castle to train him in manners and in how to attend upon a lady's wishes. I can do so while he is assisting me. I do think fresh air and sunshine will be helpful to his growth. From what I have observed of young boys, I also think Blake will enjoy the chance to tramp around in muddy streams or dig up plants."

"As you wish," Dain said. "Just be sure to tell Sloan or me when you plan to leave the castle, so we'll know where you are. If anyone questions what you are doing, send that person to me."

"Thank you," she said again.

"Is that all?" he asked.

"Yes, my lord."

"Very well." Dain raised his voice. "Blake, you are to obey Lady Emma's orders and attend to her wishes. As of this day, I make you her page."

He left her then, and Emma thought he went to the chapel with a somewhat lighter look to him, and a less dragging step. Perhaps her genuine interest in helping the folk who lived in Penruan was of some slight comfort to him. Possibly, her mention of the grubby activities in which young boys delighted had raised some happy memories for him. She hoped it was so. She could see that Blake looked a bit more cheerful after hearing Dain's order to attend her.

"If you can do what you've promised," said Sloan, pausing beside her, "if you can ease the winter aches and pains and stop the hacking coughs, then every person in this castle will be grateful to you." With a warmer glance than any he had bestowed upon her during the past week, Sloan followed Dain toward the chapel.

"Every person in the castle," Emma said softly, "with the exception of Lady Richenda, who from all I have heard will be dreadfully offended by what I plan to do."

Chapter Four

Dain did not join Emma in the lord's chamber that night. He was keeping vigil in the chapel, where Robert's body lay with lighted candles at the head and foot of the bier.

The funeral was the next morning, and Dain spent the second night after his return in the great hall tending to his wounded men. According to Blake, Dain also served the dawn watch on the battlements. The day after the funeral he and Emma bid farewell to Gavin's men-at-arms, who were returning to Wroxley. Once Gavin's men were gone Dain rode off to Trevanan to oversee the rebuilding of the houses ruined by the outlaw attack. He stayed there for several days.

Emma understood that he did not want to lie with her so soon after his son's death. She could not imagine how terrible it must be to lose a child, and she longed to comfort him, but for the present she was not going to object to anything he did. She would not do or say anything that might increase his distress. In the meantime, until he was ready to think about lying with her, she held his permission to begin to make herself a vital part of life at Penruan.

She started by ordering the stillroom cleaned, from its cobweb-hung ceiling to its dusty floor. At first the maids objected, but the cook and Sloan both bore witness that Dain had granted her the right to open and use the room.

By midday after Dain's departure for Trevanan the stillroom was scrubbed and all of the old, dusty herbs had been removed. It was time to begin replenishing the herbal supplies. Emma and Hawise spent the hours after the midday meal in the kitchen garden, cutting the few herbs grown by the cook.

"We have made a good start," Emma said as she hung the last bunch of mint from a ceiling beam. She jumped lightly down from the stool on which she had been standing. "Tomorrow we will begin searching the countryside for wild herbs."

The two women set out on horseback in early morning, taking Blake with them and heading for the high inland moors. The day was fair and warm, with only a few clouds dotting the deep blue sky. It was Emma's first real look at the Cornish countryside, and she was surprised to see how few trees there were. Most of the moorland was covered in low bushes, heather, and grasses. What trees did grow in that wild landscape were clustered near the streams and they were poor, stunted things, their branches permanently stretching toward the south, having been shaped that way by the constant wind that blew off the sea.

Most of this information was imparted by Blake, who possessed an apparently endless supply of knowledge about the area around Penruan. Emma supposed his knowledge was the result of boyhood explorations.

"We must take care to keep to the path," Blake said as they rode along. "Don't ever go wandering on the moor alone. You will have to live here for a long time before you learn just where the dangerous bogs are. Once, shortly after I came to Penruan, I was almost sucked into a bog."

"How did you get out?" Emma asked. She expected to hear a tale of boyish courage that involved Blake desperately grasping the branches of a nearby bush at the very last moment and slowly, with great effort, pulling himself out of the muck by his own strength. His actual response startled her.

"I am sure I would have drowned," Blake said, almost somber in his unusual seriousness, "but my life was saved by the beautiful lady who haunts the moor."

"You were saved by a ghost?" cried Hawise, her brown eyes going huge and round at Blake's words.

"No, not a ghost," Blake answered with a touch of impatience. "The lady is a benevolent spirit who warns travelers when they stray from the solid paths, and helps those who become mired in the bogs. Animals, too; I once saw her pull a lamb out of a bog while its dam stood by, bleating in fear for its baby."

"Then, you have seen this mysterious lady more than once?" Emma asked, her curiosity piqued by Blake's story. Mirielle had taught her that there were beings of air or water or fire, creatures not of the human realm. Like people, though, some of them were good and some were evil. Thus, she was ready to believe what Blake said and to agree with him that the lady who pulled him from the bog was most likely one of the good spirits. Emma had never met a non-human spirit. She wondered if she would meet such a creature while she searched for herbs. The possibility was unsettling, but exciting, too. Blake was obviously not afraid of the spirit he had seen. But Emma could tell that Hawise was frightened.

"I am not the only person who has seen her," Blake said. "Sloan has spoken to her, though he says she did not respond when he asked who she was and where she came from, and Dain has seen her from a distance. I once heard him talking to Sloan about the lady."

"And Sloan does not believe she is dangerous?" asked Hawise. She was looking much less frightened after hearing that grown men had encountered the wraith of the moors and come away alive, with their wits intact.

"Sloan said only that she was beautiful and very sad. I thought she was beautiful, too," Blake informed Hawise. Then, abruptly, he changed the subject. "Lady Emma, just ahead is the place where I thought we might begin to search for the plants you want. I remember seeing a few leaves there that looked to me like the kind of herbs old Agatha gathers, and once I met her there, collecting mosses. She told me she uses them to pack open wounds."

"You appear to spend a lot of time away from your duties at the castle," Hawise said in the same severe tone she sometimes used at Wroxley with Emma's younger brothers.

"As much time as I can without being punished

for it," Blake responded with an unrepentant grin. "I like the openness of the moor."

"It's too open," Hawise said, looking around at the vast, empty expanse of gorse and heather.

"In the winter it is unpleasant, when the damp wind sweeps in from the sea," Blake said. "But in the warm weather, when the castle begins to stink and feel overcrowded, the moor is a lovely place and the breeze can be refreshing."

Having reached a spot where a few stunted bushes grew, Blake halted his horse and dismounted. He assisted Emma and Hawise to the ground, then looped the reins around one of the bushes.

As soon as she stepped off the narrow path, Emma understood why Blake had stopped just there. Mosses grew around a dip in the ground where water collected when it rained. There were a few rocks nearby with lichens on them, three different kinds of ferns growing in the soggy turf, and in the shade of the rocks delicate fungi sprouted.

"No wonder Agatha comes here," Emma exclaimed, delighted by their find. "This little area contains more ingredients to cleanse and heal open wounds than I have ever seen in one place before. Look, there's adder's tongue fern. Hawise, bring one of the baskets." She moved toward the clump of fern, intending to begin gathering there.

"Don't stray too far from the path," Blake warned again. "There is bog land just on the other side of those rocks."

"It isn't much of a path," Hawise grumbled, detaching a basket from her saddle as she spoke. She squinted, looking into the distance. "In fact, I can hardly see the path. It wanders here and there, never in a straight line, and in some places it disappears altogether."

"The path marks out the solid ground," Blake said, unperturbed by the criticism. "If you are wise, you will stay on it."

They fell silent then, all three of them on their knees to collect plant materials as Emma instructed them.

"Don't take too much from any one place," Emma warned. "Leave enough root and leaf for the plants to grow back after we've gone. And leave enough for Agatha to gather when next she comes here."

Emma wished Agatha would come that day. She wanted very much to meet the healer of whom Blake spoke so fondly. But they labored alone, the only humans to be seen in all the wide landscape. There was so much to be gathered that it was a long time before Emma stood to stretch legs grown stiff from kneeling. She pressed a hand to her lower back and wriggled her shoulders. Then she turned slowly, looking toward the horizon.

The land sloped gradually upward, so that they were well above the height of Penruan's tallest tower. Emma was sure Sloan had posted a man-at-arms on the wall to watch over them during their expedition. If any ill befell them, Sloan would send a band of riders to their aid. It was an agreeable thought; it made her feel less alone in the vast, empty moor.

From where she stood Emma could see how Penruan was built at the edge of the cliffs, where the land broke off abruptly. Beyond the cliffs lay the sparkling sea. In other directions as she turned, all was moor, the sweep of gently undulating land dotted here and there by rocky outcroppings.

"That looks interesting," Emma said, shading her

eyes with one hand and pointing with the other. "And not very far away, either. Blake, I'm sure we have time to ride to that tall rock and search around its bottom for plants, and still be home before sunset."

"No, my lady," Blake said. "The light here on the moor is confusing your sight. That's Rough Tor you are looking at, and it is more than half a day's ride from Penruan. I know, because I've been there. I rode and rode for hours, and still the tor was as far away as it was when I first started. Some say it's magic, that the tors recede as you approach them, but Dain has told me it is only a trick of the light.

"Besides," Blake finished his argument with a solemn glance into the distance, "the tors are where the outlaws live, and there are other bands than the one Dain subjected to his justice. Dain would hold me responsible if I took you there and harm came to you. No plant is valuable enough to risk meeting a brigand while gathering it."

"No," Emma agreed, shivering a little at the thought of Robert, and of Dain's grief for his son. "We don't want to meet any outlaws. Where has the sun gone so suddenly? Just look at the fog rolling in from the sea!"

"In this country the weather changes fast," Blake said with a quick look at sea and sky. "My lady, we ought to return to Penruan."

Emma cast a final glance in the direction of Rough Tor, which had grown dark and ominous-looking in the altered light. Only one small outcropping from the main body of the tall rock shone golden brown in a single ray of sunshine that somehow managed to penetrate the thickening fog.

At the base of that sunlit portion of the tor Emma noticed a flash of white. She stared harder, willing her gaze to greater clarity, keeping silent so Hawise would not be frightened. There it was again; a quick motion of white against the background of glowing rock, as if a long, gauzy scarf was being unfurled to catch the last glimmers of light. Then the sunbeam was gone, swallowed up by the encroaching fog. The white object was gone, too, and a moment later Emma could not even see the tor.

The misty drizzle started before they reached the castle. Emma did not mind it. There was no wind to chill her, the moisture was soft and warm against her skin, and the torches flaring at Penruan's gate welcomed her home. Out on the moor, whoever—or whatever—had run along the base of Rough Tor in a swirl of white fabric was no doubt caught in the rain, too.

Emma did not speak of what she had seen. Once she was in the stillroom emptying the baskets of plants and lichens, cleaning and preparing them for drying, she began to wonder if that glimpse of flowing white was only an invention of her imagination. Neither Blake nor Hawise had noticed it. Perhaps, like the foreshortened perception of distance Blake had mentioned, the object was only a trick of the light.

All the same, she was unable to erase the memory of what she thought she had seen, and she tucked the image deep into her mind, holding it there in case she should ever see anything similar in the future. She looked for but did not see the mysterious white object when she and her companions returned to the moor the next day, nor did she see it on the day after that.

On the fourth day of Dain's absence Sloan informed Emma that he had chores for Blake to do, and Hawise was complaining of a sore knee, so they did not ride to the moor. Instead, Emma spent the morning working in the stillroom.

It did seem a shame to waste the fine weather by staying indoors, so after the midday meal she decided to discover what plants she could find along the cliffs. In answer to her persistent questioning, Sloan had told her about a steep but relatively safe path that led down the face of the cliff to the beach. According to Sloan, the path was regularly used by the lesser members of the kitchen staff, who were sent there to gather mussels and seaweed for the cook, and by a few men-at-arms who liked to fish.

On this sunny afternoon there was no one else on the cliff or on the path. Emma kilted her skirt up above her knees, tucking the extra fabric into her belt and pulling the belt tight to secure it. Picking up the basket that she was making a habit of carrying whenever she left the castle walls, she stepped onto the path. She was wearing her sturdiest pair of boots and she went down the path with sure-footed grace.

When she reached the beach she discovered the sand was soft and white, in stark contrast to the rather sinister black height of the towering cliffs. Above her on the left rose the walls of Penruan Castle, seemingly carved out of the cliff itself. Gazing up at it, Emma marveled at the imagination of the architect and the skill of the builders. From where she stood she could see the double windows of the lord's chamber and, directly below the castle, the jagged rocks on which the surf pounded without ceasing, the sound that filled her ears each night.

At the moment the sound of the waves was muted, for the tide was low and a wide strip of wet sand was exposed. Shells and long strands of seaweed lay scattered across the damp area. After being washed in fresh water and dried in the sun, seaweed could be stored for months. Later, it could be boiled and used in making jellies. Emma decided she would gather some of the green seaplant to give to the cook. But first, she wanted to explore.

The cliff curved inward from the headland where Penruan Castle stood, the curve forming the sandy cove where Emma was. To her right the high black rocks turned toward the sea again. Emma struck out for the point that jutted closest to the sea. It wasn't far away and she quickly reached it. When she peered around the point of rock she discovered another cove, deeper and much narrower than the one directly below Penruan. This second cove boasted a stream that ran from the bottom of the cliff and flowed across the beach and into the sea.

Looking northward, beyond yet another outthrust point of high cliff on the far side of the cove, Emma could see a long, gleaming white beach. A few small boats were drawn up on the beach and several more boats were in the water. Figures in the boats were doing something with a net.

"Fishermen," Emma said aloud, realizing that Trevanan village must lay over there, behind the longer beach.

Not being certain when the tide was going to turn, she decided against walking to Trevanan on the beach. She would go there another day, using the narrow road along the top of the cliff, for she was determined to meet the healer, Agatha. For the present, the little cove with the stream was remarkably interesting. She was sure the plant she saw growing near the base of the cliff was golden samphire, which was valuable for pickling and for preserving food. There was more of the same plant growing a bit higher on the cliff face.

Emma hurried forward and began to scramble up the rocks, plucking the samphire as she went. Soon she discovered other herbs. She scratched her hands, broke two fingernails, and scraped both of her elbows, but she hardly noticed. Like the place Blake had shown her on the moor, this particular cove was a treasure trove of useful plants. Before long her basket was almost full. She set it down on the sand so she could slip into a crevasse in the rock and better reach one last, well-grown specimen of samphire. She squeezed a little farther, stepping into deep shadow and the cold water of the stream, and suddenly she was in a cave.

Light filtered through the opening, and there was more daylight ahead of her shining from somewhere deeper in the cave. Evidently the stream in which she was standing had created the cave by the action of its water over many years, for the stream ran along one side of the cave before gushing out under the rock at the entrance. Emma stepped from the stream onto a floor of damp sand. All around her the smooth rock walls of the cave gleamed with moisture.

Beyond a bend of rock just ahead of her, Emma could see daylight reflecting in the water. She could not resist; she had to find out what lay in the next chamber. She moved quickly along the upward-sloping rock.

The inner chamber was much larger than the outer one, the roof much higher. It was well lit from a natural opening in the rock far over her head. Emma decided this part of the cave must be above the high-tide line, for the walls were dry and dry sand covered the floor.

There were footprints in the sand. A single line of prints led from the shallow streambed directly to the rock wall, and there they stopped. It was as if the person who made the footprints had arisen from the water to walk right into the rock.

The hair on the back of Emma's neck began to prickle.

Within a heartbeat she was in the outer chamber again, hurrying across it, squeezing past the rock at the entrance, tearing her gown in her haste to be away from the cave. She stumbled into daylight, into bright, clear sunshine, and she fell to her knees on the beach, gasping for breath.

When she was able to stand again she saw that the tide was noticeably higher. If she delayed in returning to the beach below Penruan Castle, she would very soon be trapped in the little cove, stranded there until the next low tide with whoever—whatever—had left those footprints in the cave.

Grabbing her basket, she raced for the strip of sand surrounding the outermost tip of rocks, sand that grew narrower with every wave that broke upon it. She was almost at the seaward point of the rocks when she heard a seagull screeching. Pausing in her flight, she looked up. The seagull wheeled far above her, screeching again as if to mock her irrational fear. For she was being irrational. No one was in the cave; perhaps no one had been there for years, or for centuries. She had sensed no living presence in those silent rock chambers.

She took a deep breath of fresh sea air, chuckling at herself for her foolishness, and glanced up at the gull again, watching as it winged its way over the cliff, heading inland.

And there on the cliff top, perched dangerously near the edge, was a figure clad in white. Ghostly white draperies blew out around it, streaming on the wind. Something gleamed blue and silver in the sunlight, as if the figure wore a talisman on its breast.

Emma could not tell if what she saw was male or female, but she experienced the oddest sensation that the creature was looking directly at her. As if to prove the accuracy of her instinct, the figure on the cliff lifted one slender arm in a gesture.

Emma did not stay to discover what the gesture meant. A wave rushed shoreward, swirling around her knees, filling her boots with icy seawater. Shocked back to her full senses and to her precarious situation by the sudden chill, she turned and ran from the hungry sea, splashing through the receding water, through the next incoming wave, and the next one, running for the cliff path and the safety of Penruan.

Emma reached the top of the cliff in a breathless state, with her gaze directed toward the place where she had seen the mysterious figure in white. There was no one on the cliffs. Not a single person. No one in all the wide vista that stretched upward toward the high spine of Cornwall until the moorland met a horizon broken only by the rocky projection of Rough Tor. With Penruan Castle at her back, Emma scanned the landscape until her ears detected a soft footstep on the grass behind her.

"Oh!" She spun around, and when she saw who it was she took so hasty a step backward that she nearly fell over the cliff. Some of the precious samphire tumbled out of her basket and bounced down the face of the rock. Before her loomed a tall, decidedly masculine figure in a blue tunic.

"Have care, my lady," Dain said, catching her arm. "Come away. You are too near the edge."

"You startled me. I didn't know you were home." His eyes were the same marvelous blue-green shade as the sunlit sea below them. The wind lifted a lock of his close-cropped hair, the sun on it turning it to silver. Emma clutched her basket tightly while she fought against the urge to lay her head on his broad chest. She wasn't sure whether the sudden weakness in her knees was the result of her mad rush through seawater and up the face of the cliff—or whether it was caused by the unexpected presence of her husband standing so close and looking so formidable.

"What is it?" Dain asked. Her face was remarkably pale, devoid of the soft bloom of color he recalled seeing in her cheeks, and her eyes were wide with alarm, the brown irises heavily flecked with purple. Something unfamiliar and painfully sweet twisted in Dain's chest as he searched the expression in Emma's long-lashed eyes. He seized on the first reason that came to mind for the fear he saw in those eyes. "If you are afraid of heights, my lady, then you ought not to try the cliff path again."

"It's not the height. I foolishly stayed on the beach too long and, as you can see, the tide is coming in fast. I got wet."

"The water only reaches to the lower section of the cliff path when there is a bad storm," he said, wanting to put her mind at ease. "Otherwise, there is always dry sand at the bottom of the path. You were in no danger."

"I will remember that in the future. I've been gathering plants."

"So I see." He spared only a quick glance for the wilted greenery in her basket. He couldn't imagine what she thought she was going to do with the sandy things, but if they kept her occupied in the stillroom, so she had no time to meddle in the running of Penruan, then let her drag in all the plants she wanted and let her stay in the stillroom all the time.

Dain had no intention of permitting himself to become a judge in a domestic struggle between his wife and his mother. He did not doubt for a moment that there would be war when Lady Richenda returned from visiting her sister. She had made her opinion of Dain's marriage, and of his submission to King Henry's will, very clear before her departure to the convent at Tawton where her sister was the abbess.

However placid and gentle Emma's disposition might prove to be—and from the way she had faced him down on several occasions, he doubted she would ever run from a quarrel—his mother was not going to accept the presence of another lady of rank at Penruan. Life was going to be easier for Emma, and for him, if she stayed away from his mother. Thus, his willingness to allow Emma free rein in the stillroom, where he hoped she would occupy most of her hours.

She bestowed a trembling smile on him, and again Dain was aware of a tightening in his chest—and of a harder, more urgent tightening in his lower body.

Perhaps he ought to take his wife to bed at once, and fill her belly with his seed before his mother came home. Surely even Lady Richenda's pride would bend enough to accept the woman who bore in her womb the next heir to Penruan.

No! He could not bed Emma. He did not want this cursed marriage that had been inflicted on him, and he was determined to leave open the possibility of having it annulled for lack of consummation.

With a smothered oath he turned away from Emma and started back toward Penruan.

"Dain, wait a moment," she called after him.

"Why?" He halted, not looking at her.

"Did you see anyone on the cliff before I appeared?" she asked.

"No," he responded sharply. Then, thinking it an odd question for her to ask and wondering if she had seen something that could pose a danger to Penruan, he added, "I arrived home just a short time ago. Sloan did not mention the sentries noticing anything out of the ordinary. It was he who told me you were on the beach."

And like a love-smitten page running after the girl who had enchanted his heart, Dain had left his men-at-arms and squires, ignoring Sloan's attempts to make a full report of all that had occurred while he was gone, and had run to the top of the cliff path to meet Emma. It was not like him to make such a foolish gesture.

"You rode directly here from Trevanan?" Emma asked.

"I did." He could not continue to speak to her when his back was turned, so he faced her again. He was glad to see she had moved away from the edge of the cliff. The late-afternoon sun shone full on her face, making her skin glow as if it was translucent. The wind lifted the sides of her simple white linen head scarf, allowing him to see the thick black braid of her hair.

His fingers itched to tear off the scarf, to pull out the hairpins and untwist the braid, letting the smooth length of her hair flow through his hands. He remembered with painful clarity how Emma's hair felt, how clean it smelled. He longed to take her face between his hands, to feel again the softness of her cheek against his callused fingers. He ached to press his mouth over her rose-petal lips. At the mere thought of touching Emma, of holding her in his arms, his body surged into eager readiness.

Sweet saints in heaven! What was wrong with him? After his first, youthful foray into lust, and his recognition of how easily untrammeled masculine passion could create a new life, he had never again found it difficult to restrain his bodily desires. He ought not to find it difficult now. She was, after all, his enemy's daughter. He was not—definitely not!—going to bed her.

"What is it you want to know, Emma?" he asked, rather more sharply than he intended.

"If you rode straight from Trevanan, you must have had a full view of the cliffs all along your way," she said.

"So I did. And all along the way I saw no one. That is what you asked, is it not?" He frowned at her because, after first looking nervously in the direction of Trevanan, she was now staring straight into his eyes, and it was all he could do to keep his hands at his sides.

"While I was on the beach, I thought I saw a figure dressed in white standing at the edge of the cliff," she said.

"Ah," said Dain, understanding. "You've seen the lady."

"Blake told me that you have seen her, too."

"Blake talks much too freely."

"Does she live in the cave just below?"

"So you've been exploring Merlin's cave, have you?" Of course she had; she was too intelligent not to be curious about her surroundings. Well, let her prowl along the beaches and poke into caves and bring home all the half-dead plants she wanted. He and Sloan and even young Blake could easily keep her under surveillance, to see that she came to no harm. And if she was caught out in a misdemeanor during her wanderings, he would have a perfect excuse to send her back to Wroxley, untouched, unbedded, still a virgin. . . .

"Are you speaking of the great wizard?" she asked in a hushed voice.

"The legend says Merlin lies enchanted in one of the caves below these cliffs," Dain told her, aware that the ending of Merlin's story presented a lesson that he, wed to a lady he dared not trust, ought to take to heart. He started walking toward Penruan and Emma went with him. From the expression on her beautiful face, she was entranced by the mention of King Arthur's friend and teacher.

"Even the greatest wizard of all was not immune to the blandishments of a lovely female," Dain continued. "His treacherous mistress, Nimue, lured him to a cave and, according to the tale, there she wove an enchantment that supposedly holds great Merlin entombed to this day. In fact, the local folk believe the ruins of Camelot are buried somewhere on the moor. It has even been claimed that a new castle being built farther east along the coast is laid out on the very site of Arthur's birthplace. I do not believe that last story."

"Do you believe the other tales?" Emma asked.

"I do not know whether the stories are true or not. Nor, I fear, does anyone else know for certain, and I doubt if anyone will ever prove where Arthur built his castle."

"What of the lady in white? You admit you've seen her."

"She appears and disappears," he said. "Sometimes she is not seen for months, or even years. She must be a creature of magic, to come and go so mysteriously. It's my opinion that it is always best to avoid magic. Too much of it is evil." He rubbed his forehead, aware of the faint, unpleasant ache that always accompanied sight or mention of the ghostly lady. After a moment the ache disappeared.

Emma looked as if she wanted to say something, but she shook her head and remained silent instead. For the rest of the walk back to the castle she was so quiet that Dain wondered if she feared the possibility of magic, or if it was just the vision of the lady in white that had frightened her.

They reached the deep moat that was cut through the solid rock of the headland. Originally, the moat had been a natural ravine created by the river. The chasm had been made wider and deeper by successive lords of Penruan until the castle was almost completely inaccessible to invasion. The moat was so deep that the drawbridge had a railing to prevent falls.

Dain watched as Emma paused to look over the railing at the jagged black rocks along the sides of the ravine. When she resumed walking her step was firm and steady. Plainly, she was not afraid of heights. She was going to make a brave, resourceful, and beautiful lady for his castle.

Dain was so startled by the direction of his thoughts that he halted in the middle of the drawbridge to stare at his wife's slender back. His gaze moved lower and he took considerable pleasure in the sight of her shaply calves beneath the skirt that was still kilted high. In that moment Dain was glad she could not read his mind, and gladder still to know his tunic reached to mid-thigh.

The bottom of Emma's skirt was so wet that she

dripped as she walked, and her boots left a trail of damp footprints in her wake. Wet or dry, she moved with graceful dignity, and it was delightful to watch her. She did not seem to notice that Dain was no longer at her side. Perhaps she had her own secret thoughts. That was a distinctly unpleasant idea, for Emma's secret thoughts might well be treacherous.

With a frown clouding his brow, Dain followed his wife into the shadows of the gatehouse.

Chapter Five

Later that evening Dain sat at the high table with Emma by his side. She wore fresh clothes: deep russet-brown wool for her gown, a simple gold mesh net over the thick, pinned-up braid of her hair, and a gold necklace set with amethysts, stones as darkly purple as the flecks of color in her brown eyes.

It was all Dain could do to keep his hands from her. Having decided that he definitely would not bed her, and having sternly lectured himself over his desire for her during the hour when he was supposedly listening with full attention to Sloan's report covering the days of his absence from Penruan, Dain had succeeded in convincing himself that he was immune to Emma's beauty, as well as to the more subtle allures offered by her low-pitched, musical voice and her intelligence.

After Sloan finished his report, Dain visited the

castle bathhouse to wash and to be shaved by the barber. Then he changed into a sober dark brown tunic that he felt emphasized his new determination to keep a cool but polite distance from Emma.

He had entered the great hall looking forward to the evening meal which, in celebration of his return, was to be embellished beyond the usual cold meats and cheese, bread, and ale that were its everyday ingredients. Cook had made a pigeon pie, and there was to be a salad composed in part of herbs gathered by Emma during her most recent excursion to the moor. The sweet was to be a custard served with the first plums of the season stewed with cinnamon and cloves.

Dain noted with pleasure the clean white cloth on the high table, the wooden trenchers, one for every two people, and his own silver drinking cup waiting for him at his place. He saw that the candles were already lit in the twin candelabra on the high table. All was as it should be, all prepared for the lord of Penruan.

And then Emma came down the curving stone staircase from the tower and into the circle of candlelight, a radiant vision of ripe autumn shades, of russet and gold and purple, and Dain experienced again that peculiar twisting in his chest, as if a dainty hand was locking itself firmly around his heart.

In his struggle against unwilling admiration of her lovely person, and against the tightness that would not release itself from his chest, he resorted to a coldness toward her that was almost rude.

"Where did you acquire such a necklace?" he demanded, frowning at the gold and amethyst splendor that caressed her throat. The neckline of her gown was demurely high and round, with no embroidery, the better to show off the fine workmanship of the necklace—and the smooth ivory column of her throat. Dain shook with the sudden desire to place his lips upon a tiny mole just below her left ear, a slight imperfection that only enhanced her beauty.

"It is a wedding gift from my father," she said. Her fingertips lightly stroked the largest purple stone, the one that hung just above the beginning of the soft swell of her breasts.

"A king's ransom of a gift," Dain responded. He did not say what both of them knew, that according to the law the necklace rightly belonged to him, just as Emma did, just as all of her belongings were now his, because she was his wife. *His wife* . . . to take to his bed, to possess in the most intimate of ways . . .

"It was a gift of love," she said. "My father loves me well."

Dain was shamed by the tender smile playing along her lips and by the warm look in her eyes when she spoke of Gavin. She did love her father; he could not question the honesty of her emotion. Nor did he doubt her claim that Gavin loved her. Yet she had left her loving family to come voluntarily to Penruan, to be wife to a man who was sworn never to love her, never to believe in her honesty, or in her father's.

Suddenly Dain's angry feud against the baron of Wroxley and his plan to reject Emma as part of his revenge against Gavin seemed but tawdry schemes. They felt like the workings of an unquiet mind that counted wounds received in open warfare and the loss of a small tract of land more important than the heart of a virtuous young woman. Never mind that the initial impulse to reopen the feud was not his own; he had been all too willing to heed the arguments that claimed revenge was his duty. He had accepted the responsibility and he could not lay it aside. The feud was his now.

And so Dain sat beside his wife at the high table, barely nibbling at the pigeon pie that he usually relished, scarcely tasting the spiced plum sauce over rich custard that was one of his favorite treats. He drank a little too much and warned himself to keep away from Emma.

"Will you return to Trevanan soon?" she asked him.

"Yes." Dain made a hasty decision. "I intend to return tomorrow morning. The men who are rebuilding the houses ruined by the brigands will work faster and better if I am there to oversee their efforts." They would work just as well for the overseer Dain had left at Trevanan, but if he did not return there, if he remained at Penruan, he would have to see Emma several times a day, speak with her, sit beside her at the high table during the midday and evening meals. Every night he'd have to fight anew the battle with himself to stay out of the big bed in the lord's chamber.

"May I ride to Trevanan with you?" Emma asked.

"There is no place for you to stay," he objected.

"I don't want to stay in Trevanan," Emma said. "I am sure the villagers are much too busy making the necessary repairs before the winter gales to have time to entertain me. Not to mention their urgent need to bring in and store the harvest, and to cure and salt down the fish they catch. The damage the outlaws did has only added to their late-summer labors. I don't want to disrupt their work. I only want to visit Agatha."

He gave her a cold stare while he tried to make

up his mind which part of her speech to object to first. How did she know about the strenuous efforts the villagers were making to harvest the fruits of both land and sea before the storms of autumn and winter arrived? He was aware that the weather was different in Lincolnshire than in Cornwall. Emma had grown up with harsh winters, yet she seemed to understand that at Penruan the winter days were ruled by rain and strong wind, rather than by ice and snow. Had she been questioning Sloan? Or cajoling that impressionable boy, Blake, into indiscreet talk? All of his people had been warned not to reveal to Emma any information that she could send to Gavin, that he might use against Penruan or its lord. Did she really care about the people of Penruan and Trevanan, or was her interest a ruse? And what business did she have with Agatha?

It was exceedingly difficult not to be able to trust one's own wife. It was even more difficult not to embrace her when she was so enchanting. Emma smiled at him and touched his arm, and Dain went rigid with the effort it took not to put his hands on her shoulders and draw her close for a kiss on her delectable lips.

"Dain, are you woolgathering?" Her breathy little laugh sent a shiver down his spine, followed immediately by a surge of heat. "Have you heard anything I've said?"

"I have heard you. I don't think you ought to intrude on Trevanan at this time."

"As I just told you, I have no intention of intruding. All I want is your company as far as the village. Once there, I will visit Agatha for an hour or two, and then I'll leave. If you'll let me take Blake along, he will be escort enough for my return to Penruan."

"Why do you want to meet Agatha?"

"Because, according to Blake, and to several of your men-at-arms, whom I have asked about the manner in which wounds are treated here, Agatha is the person you send for whenever a serious illness or an injury occurs that you or Sloan or the men by themselves cannot manage. Everyone I asked spoke of Agatha's skills, and also mentioned that she is very old and not likely to live for many more years. It was my idea that she could teach me what cures she uses, and provide information about local plants with curative powers, plants that I might pass by on my searches, because I am not familiar with them. I want to learn as much as I can from Agatha."

"I thought you came to me well taught," he said, sounding irritated. Which, in fact, he was, but not because she wanted to use old Agatha as a teacher. It irked Dain that he could find no fault in her. Emma was attempting to do exactly what the new lady of the castle ought to do. She was trying to use her skills as a healer for the benefit of the men and women of Penruan. It was his duty to give her every assistance.

"There is no person so well taught that she cannot learn more," Emma said. "If Agatha is as wise as I have been told, then there is much she can teach me."

She met his stern gaze with a look that Dain perceived as complete openness, and in that moment, charmed by her beauty and her sweet voice, he decided to disregard the other, more familiar voice in his mind that shrilly warned him not to trust her.

"You may go with me," he said, "and I will order one of my men-at-arms to accompany you back to Penruan after you have finished your business with Agatha. The lady of Penruan ought not to ride about the countryside without an armed escort."

"Thank you, Dain." She lowered her eyes, blushing, and her voice was soft when next she spoke. "Do you wish to join me in the lord's chamber tonight?"

"Is that to be my reward for agreeing to what you want?" he asked, speaking harshly to hide the warmth that flooded his body at the thought of lying down with her in his own bed and taking her into his arms. He was sure she noticed how hot his face was, and if she looked more closely at him, she would see the obvious evidence of his desire for her, evidence he was unable to conceal without making a fool of himself by tugging down his tunic or pulling the tablecloth across his lap.

"I only thought you might feel it was time," she said, still blushing. "You have kindly allowed me several weeks in which to recover from my long and difficult journey to Penruan, and I did understand that you preferred not to engage in marital relations immediately after the death of your son, and then there was the reconstruction of those houses at Trevanan to see to, but now you are home again."

"So I am," he said. And about to run away to Trevanan again in the morning, just to avoid her. That he, who had never fled from a battlefield or from any other fight, should depart from his own castle in unseemly haste in order not to sleep in the same bed with his wife seemed to him ludicrous. It was unmanly of him. Emma was his chattel, to possess or reject as he chose. He wanted her as he had never wanted any other woman.

If he took her, he might get her with child, might blend his blood with the blood of Baron Udo and of Gavin, the two men he had been taught for all his life to hate. To do so would be to betray his father and grandfather. The old voice to which he had listened for so many years echoed in his mind, telling him that it was far more manly of him to deny his yearning for Emma than to give in to it.

Yet there was another reason why he could not lie with her, a reason having nothing to do with his family's long-established hatreds. There was in Emma a gentle richness, a quality of her soul that called out to him with an almost irresistible strength. If he led her to the lord's chamber and stripped off her clothing and his, if he took her into his bed, he would also take her into his heart. He would not merely possess his wife, he would make love to her. And loving was weakness. So he had been taught.

"Not tonight, my lady," he said. "I have much to discuss with Sloan, and plans to make for gathering in our own harvest, here at Penruan."

"As you wish, my lord." She had gone a little pale, but her low voice was steady. He would not expect it to be otherwise. While she was in public Emma would not show disappointment at his rejection.

"Yes," he said, "it will be as I wish." With that, he pushed his chair away from the table and stood. Calling to Sloan to join him, he left the great hall.

"Our harvest?" Emma muttered. "I have not seen any fields under cultivation around Penruan."

She stood by the window in the lord's chamber, gazing out at a sky streaked with clouds of purple and pale pink, and at a sea that was far more calm than her own heart. The air wafting in through the window was soft and mellow, just lightly touched with the tang of salt.

"But there are fields, my lady," said Hawise, who was folding a basket of clean underclothes and laying the garments into a chest. "I have been making friends with the cook, and she has described how Penruan lands extend to a sheltered valley set well away from the sea winds, and there Lord Dain's villeins grow wheat and barley, and Cook says there's a fine apple orchard, and several kinds of plum trees, too, because they are Dain's favorite fruit. And, of course, a portion of all the crops grown in the fields around Trevanan come to the castle."

"How is it that you have been able to learn these facts, while no one will tell me anything about Dain's holdings, no matter how often I ask?" Emma exclaimed.

"Dain gave orders that you are to be given no information, not until after you have proven yourself trustworthy," Hawise told her. "I guess he thought Lord Gavin was planning to follow you to Cornwall with a large army, and that you would find a way to send information to him or, perhaps, to open the gates of Penruan to him."

"I know Dain doesn't trust me," Emma said with a sigh. "It explains much."

"Including why he hasn't insisted on consummating your marriage," Hawise said. "He is probably afraid to give you a child whom you might decide to take back to Wroxley and use against him."

"I have given him no cause to mistrust me."

"Well, it's the feud, isn't it? That, and Lady Richenda. From what I've heard since coming here, she preaches against Lord Gavin, and against your poor, dead grandfather, Lord Udo, as if she's calling for a crusade against the Saracens."

"When is Lady Richenda expected to return home?" Emma asked.

"From the way the cook talks, I'd say it will be

another week or two," Hawise answered. "Certainly not much longer. She has already been gone for a whole month, which Cook says is a long time for her; Lady Richenda likes to keep everyone and everything under her close control."

"Well, then," Emma said, "I shall have to teach Dain to trust me, and then to love me, in just one week."

Emma was dressing for the ride to Trevanan when the bedchamber door was flung open with such force that it swung around on its hinges and crashed against the wall.

In strode Dain. He was unarmored, but still, he presented an imposing sight. His dark blue tunic was snugged to his narrow waist by a wide leather belt from which hung his ever-present sword, and his long, muscular legs were thrust into brown leather boots. His brown cloak was tossed back over one shoulder, and the silver clasp that held it at his throat glinted wickedly, sending splinters of light onto his tight, angry face. He did not waste time in polite greetings.

"I have been told that you have altered my private room," he said, halting just inside the doorway. His mouth closed in a hard line as he looked around the chamber.

"One would scarcely know it is your room," Emma responded calmly, "since you have not entered it for weeks."

"Do you think to make me grow soft and weak with such luxury?" he demanded. He extended a hand, as if to feel the fabric of the new blue bed hangings, but pulled his hand back and rested it on his sword hilt instead.

"I do not believe anything will ever make you soft,

my lord." Emma decided her best course was to attempt to reason with him. "My only concern was to make you more comfortable in your own room, and thereby make myself more comfortable, too. I am not used to living each day as if I were on campaign with King Henry's troops."

"Are you complaining about the arrangments I have made for you?" Dain growled.

"No, my lord. I am only saying that in this one, private chamber your life, and mine, need not be so harsh. When I first saw it, the room was barely furnished." She moved closer, smiling at him. "Surely you know it is the custom for a bride to arrive at her new home with chests of linens, with silver plate, and with furniture, as well as her bride clothes, and to add these things to her husband's belongings so that, together, they may enjoy all of their possessions."

"I do know it." He was frowning at her. "You neglected to discuss with me the changes you wished to make before you made them."

"How could I?" she asked, keeping her voice sweet and a smile on her lips, so what she said would not sound like an accusation. "You have been absent from Penruan for much of the time since I arrived, and when you have been here, you've had far more important matters to think about than a new set of bed hangings, or a chair."

"Yes, a chair." He went to it, to run his fingers along the smooth arms of it. "Did you think we had no chairs at Penruan?" His voice was remarkably soft for Dain, as if he, too, was trying to avoid the impression that he was making an accusation.

"I was certain you owned as many chairs as you want," she said. "This one is my gift to you, especially made for you. I sewed the cushions myself, and stuffed them with my own hands." She did not tell him that Gavin owned the same kind of chair. She thought it best not to mention Gavin, not if she wanted Dain to accept the gift.

"Did you make the bed hangings, too?" he asked. "I notice the wool is the same as that on the cushions."

"Hawise helped me to sew the curtains. She is a fine needlewoman."

Dain moved to the bed and flipped the nearest curtain up to examine the underside. He tested the curtain lining with his fingertips, looked at the quilt and at the pillows covered in new linen. Then he looked into Emma's eyes. One corner of his mouth quirked upward, but almost immediately straightened again, as if he was fighting the urge to return her smile.

"Thank you," he said. "It was churlish of me to complain about what you've done, but I was surprised to hear of it."

Emma refrained from pointing out that if he had come to their bed, he could have seen for himself how she was altering the room, and not have had to hear of it from the servants.

"I hope you are pleased," was all she said.

"You will be well sheltered from drafts when damp winter comes," he said.

Emma bit her lip, determined not to annoy him by telling him that he, too, ought to be sheltered within the new bed hangings, with her. The thought of sleeping in Dain's arms made her cheeks burn. But it was clear that he held little interest for him.

"Are you ready to ride?" he said. "It's past time for us to leave for Trevanan." He was out of the room and halfway down the stairs to the great hall before she could answer him.

*   *   *

Trevanan was set in a protected fold of land where the cliffs broke off for half a mile or so. A river ran out to the sea along the north side of the village, just before the cliffs began again. Inland, the fields were tilled for barley and oats, for cabbage and root vegetables, but the chief food of the village and the source of its prosperity was fish.

As they rode along the cliffs and down into the valley, Dain explained to Emma how schools of pilchard were caught in great sweeps of netting that extended from boat to boat. The fish not needed for food for the village were salted and packed in barrels, then carted to the deeper water port of Camelford, from where the barrels were sent by ship to Spain or Normandy.

"I saw a few boats at sea yesterday," Emma said, "but there are none today."

"They were after some other fish," Dain said. "The pilchard don't arrive until later in the summer, which is a good thing, for we need every man here on land to work at rebuilding the houses."

The entire village consisted of no more than two dozen houses spread along a rutted, gravelly road that branched off the cliff road and ran straight to the beach.

"It's the path used by the heavy fish carts," Dain said when Emma commented on the deep ruts. "Agatha's house is the little building you can see across the meadow, just next to the river. She prefers to live apart from the village proper."

The men-at-arms and servants who had come with Dain to help with the rebuilding stopped at the two houses that were being restored from the ground up, while Dain and Emma rode on to Agatha's home. It was no more than a hut, sheltered within a stand of willow trees that were all badly stunted by the continuous wind from the sea.

As Emma and Dain approached, a tiny woman came around the side of the house. Agatha's face had been weathered by sun and wind, covered with fine lines, and her hair was thin and gray. But her silver-pale eyes were bright with intelligence and her voice and step were both firm.

"So, this is your new lady," Agatha said to Dain. She touched Emma's cheek with a wrinkled hand, and where her fingers trailed, Emma's skin grew warm.

"Teach her what you can," Dain said to Agatha. "Emma has some idea of being useful to Penruan. Lady Emma, I will send a man-at-arms to escort you home at day's end. I will be staying here at Trevanan for several days." With a hasty nod to the women, he remounted and rode away, heading for the work site.

"How that boy has changed since he was younger," Agatha said, looking after him.

"Have you known Dain all his life?" Emma asked.

"Aye. There was a time when Dain was often here at my cottage, despite the way his mother continually spews hatred against me into his ears, warning him to keep his distance. But Dain quietly defies his mother's wishes. He allows me to live here in the village because I am expert at healing the ills and injuries of his men, and because I keep the villagers healthy."

With a hand on Emma's arm, Agatha drew her around the little house and into the fenced herb garden at the back. The fence was woven of irregular branches, apparently picked up during Agatha's walks in search of herbs, the branches bound together with vines. Within the confines of the fence herbs grew in wild abandon. At one corner, where the fence had almost collapsed, it was held up by a great, spreading rosebush. A few late roses bloomed pink on the untidy canes, but most of the canes bore large, bright red hips.

"For jelly," Emma said. "I love the taste of rose hip jelly. Do you dry and powder the hips for a hot drink in winter, as we do in Lincolnshire? Oh, there is lavender next to the rose, and there's thyme, and rosemary and mint over there, in the shade."

"You do know the herbs," Agatha said, nodding her approval. "Come, sit with me and tell me how you plan to circumvent Lady Richenda's disapproval of any effort to minister to the earthly ailments of men and women."

"I was hoping you could tell me," Emma said. She took a seat on the bench Agatha indicated, a black stone slab laid on two rocks and placed beneath an aged apple tree. All three pieces of the bench were obviously cut from the nearby cliffs and were worn smooth by years of use. "Agatha, how long have you lived in Trevanan?"

"Since I was a little girl," Agatha said, settling herself next to Emma. "My granny was the healer before me. At least, she called herself my granny, so no one would act spitefully toward me while I was a child and unable to defend myself. But I'm not so sure that's what she was.

"Sometimes, when an unwanted babe is born, if a young mother is afraid of what her parents will do to her or to her lover, or if she's a servant at the castle and fears losing her place there, then she bears her child in secret and leaves it on the moor. I do think that's where Granny found me, for I never recall her speaking of a child of her own who could have been my mother. My sire could have been Dain's grandfather or one of his men-at-arms, or a fisherman from the village, or even one of the outlaws who will continue to live on the moor no matter how ferociously the lords of Penruan try to be rid of them.

"Who my parents were doesn't matter," Agatha said. "What's important is that Granny recognized me when she first saw me. She always told me she knew at once I would grow up to be the best healer in Cornwall. She knew me. Yes, she did. Just as I know you. I've been waiting for you to come, Emma. It's past time."

"You recognized me as a fellow healer, even before Dain told you?" Emma said.

"Aye, and more than a healer." Agatha's fingers rested on Emma's hand like the delicate brush of a dry autumn leaf across her skin. "You are like me in more ways than one. You aren't who people think you are. You aren't even who *you* think you are."

"What do you mean?" Emma asked. For just a moment she was afraid, and wished she could pull her hand away from Agatha's. But Agatha's soft old fingers lay lightly on hers, the touch strong as steel manacles. In that gentle, unbreakable touch Emma recognized one who owned an inborn magic far stronger than her own.

"Never mind," Agatha said. "All will be revealed when the time is right. That's the way it always is . . . when the time is right. That's what I tell the girl, too."

"What girl?" Emma asked, speaking softly because she understood that Agatha's mind was wandering into pathways where she, Emma, could not follow. She didn't want to disturb the old woman's thoughts until Agatha had said all she meant to say.

"Well, she's not a girl anymore," Agatha said. "Her time is coming, soon enough. And so will your time come. Now," Agatha said briskly, removing her hand from Emma's and thus freeing the younger woman from the spell that had held her, "come and I'll show you all of the herb garden and then my workroom inside, and afterward we can talk about what's troubling you and how to mend it."

An hour later Emma and Agatha were back in the herb garden, again sitting on the rock bench in the sunshine. Without quite knowing how it had come about, Emma had revealed to the older woman the circumstances of her marriage, including the fact that Dain had so far avoided the act of consummation.

"He doesn't trust me," Emma concluded her account. She sipped from a cup containing Agatha's herbal wine, which was marvelously cooling, and picked from a plate on the bench a food she had not encountered before. Agatha called it a pasty and claimed it was a commonplace treat in Cornwall. The baked half-round of crisp dough enfolded apples chopped with herbs and spices to make a savory filling.

"The villagers use meat or fish for the filling," Agatha said, "though I prefer vegetables or fruits. Either way, it's a convenient food to take along when traveling, or for the fishermen when they go out to sea for a long day of work. Now, Emma, about that cave you mentioned. Did you see anyone there?"

"No," Emma answered. "Just the footprints I told you about, that suddenly stopped at the rock wall. I know of no magic that will allow a mortal body to pass through solid rock." She paused, waiting to hear Agatha's reaction to her carefully worded statement.

"Well, you don't know all there is to learn about magic, do you?" said Agatha. "Did you tell anyone else what you saw?"

"I was going to tell Dain, but when I mentioned the cave he began to talk about Merlin and King Arthur, and about a lady in white who appears from time to time. He was so opposed to the very idea of magic that I said no more on the subject."

"That's his mother's doing. You haven't told Dain about your magical abilities yet, have you?"

"No. I feel I will have to gain his trust first. Then perhaps he will be able to understand that not all magic is evil." Emma paused to take another bite of the pasty she held and to wash it down with some wine. "I have seen the lady in white twice; once on the moor and again on the cliff."

"Have you?" said Agatha, as if mysterious appearances and disappearances were nothing very suprising to her. "There is no need to fear the lady."

"I gathered as much from the comments made by a few other people who also have seen her from time to time. Dain admits to seeing her, but only from a distance. From the way he spoke I assumed he'd rather not discuss her."

"This is a land of legends and magic," Agatha said. "No one ever learns the whole of it, not even after a lifetime of study and practice. There are still secrets to be revealed. But I shall know the greatest secret of all before long."

"What secret is that?" Emma asked.

"Why, don't you know?" Agatha smiled, her eyes silver bright and utterly without fear. "It's the secret of what lies on the other side. I expect to learn it in another year or two, perhaps sooner."

Emma stared at her for a moment before realizing that Agatha was speaking of her own death. Emma saw no reason to protest against a knowledge deeper and wider than her own.

"It will be a sad day for Trevanan," Emma said, "and for those at Penruan who are injured or ill."

"Not while you are here to take my place," Agatha said. "Years ago, I thought the girl would be the one, but she was banished. Wicked, wicked, to send her away like that!"

"What girl?" Emma asked for the second time since meeting Agatha.

"And so you were sent in her stead," Agatha continued, as if Emma had not spoken, "and we must make certain you remain at Penruan, for there are those who would force you outside, too, and lock the gate behind you, just as was done after *she* was thrust out to face the world alone."

Emma began to wonder if Agatha's aged mind was faltering.

"The first thing we must do is get Dain into your bed," Agatha went on. "I know the recipe for a potion. 'Tis the same magical draft that was given to Iseult and Tristan, that bound them together forever, through life and beyond, into death. I'll make it for you."

"No!" Emma cried, thoroughly alarmed by this idea. "I will use no magic to charm my husband. Dain will come to me in genuine desire, by his own will, or I will not accept him."

"What you want is rare, child. Dain knows little of love. His father, Baron Halard, grew into a bitter and unloving man, and as for Lady Richenda—well, she never was the kind to happily warm a

106

man's bed, not even in her youth, and she has always been as cold and unyielding a parent as ever Halard was. Perhaps, if the girl—"

"What girl? Agatha, what, or who, are you talking about?"

"I see Dain riding down the road, leading your horse and with a man-at-arms in attendance," Agatha said, rising from the bench. "It is time for you to return to Penruan."

"May I come again?" Emma asked, her mind whirling with unanswered questions. "Or will you come to Penruan?"

"I only go to Penruan when Dain summons me. Now, don't forget the basket I gave you. There are rooted herb plants packed in moss for you to set out in the kitchen garden, and a few ointments and tinctures already prepared and sealed in jars and vials, all tucked under those bunches of cut herbs for drying that I laid on top."

"There is so much I want to learn from you," Emma said, thinking of the lady in white, and the girl of whom Agatha had spoken, and the place she thought of as Merlin's cave; so many mysteries to be solved.

"You've learned more in this one day than you realize," Agatha said. "So did I learn more from you than I expected. We will meet again soon."

Emma rode away, back to Penruan Castle, thinking she must hasten her efforts to establish herself as the castle healer. Not only did she want to make her position secure before Lady Richenda returned, but she felt an urgent need to gather as much information from Agatha as she could. She did not doubt that Agatha foresaw her own death approaching. The thought saddened Emma, but she believed Agatha's declaration that she was meant to succeed the old healer. After Agatha was gone, if the folk of Trevanan knew they could look to the castle for aid in times of sickness or injury, not only would that be a good use of Emma's herbal medicines and magical skills, it would also strengthen Dain's position as lord.

There hadn't been time to speak to Dain about her plans before she left Trevanan, not with his man-at-arms and Agatha herself present. Emma resolved to discuss the issue with Dain as soon as he returned to Penruan.

She looked over her shoulder once and saw Dain still standing before Agatha's hut, talking to the old woman. And then Emma set her eyes upon Penruan Castle and rode on.

Dain vowed he would not gaze after Emma like some lovesick minstrel, so he kept his full attention on Agatha.

"It's an unusually warm day," she said, "and you look as if you've been working long and hard. Come into the garden, boy, and sit in the shade for a while and drink a cup or two of my herbal wine."

If anyone else had dared to call him "boy," Dain's sword would have been out of its scabbard in an instant. But Agatha was different from everyone else. When he was young she had welcomed him into her house and fed him treats and told him romantic tales of King Arthur and his knights. As a child Dain had always found Agatha's house and garden a sweet respite from his mother's harsh rule, until Lady Richenda discovered where he went when he left Penruan on his pony. Then Dain had stopped his visits in order to protect Agatha, but once he was lord of Penruan he made a point of asserting himself against his mother's protests whenever someone at the castle needed the healer's aid. And now he knew—no one knew better—that he was going to have to fight his mother again for the sake of the castle inhabitants, and for Emma's right to treat their illnesses. He did not look forward to the battle.

"Come," Agatha coaxed him again. One frail hand rested lightly on his arm, and Dain discovered it was remarkably difficult to resist her. "Sit here on the bench, while I get the jug of wine. There are a few pasties left, too. Have you eaten since morning? No, I thought not."

It was pleasant to relax in Agatha's garden, to sip her delicious wine and eat the sweet apple pasties he recalled from his youth. How agreeable it was to visit with a woman who expected nothing at all from him. Dain ate three of the pasties and drank a bit more wine than he intended before taking his leave of Agatha.

Later in the day she brought more wine to him where he was working, along with a basket of sweet cakes to supplement the fish and vegetable stew and ale the village women were providing to the laborers.

Dain planned to sleep with his men in Trevanan that night, like them rolled in his cloak on the floor of the house they had almost finished rebuilding. But sleep eluded him, for his thoughts were occupied by Emma. Her beauty and her eagerness to help his people combined to make him overlook his old hatred of her family. When Dain tried to remind himself of how much he despised Gavin of Wroxley, the image of that tall and formidable warrior was superceded by a more recent vision of Emma's warm eyes smiling at him. Every attempt he made to concentrate on his long-held, cold rage was interrupted by thoughts of Emma.

He could not get Emma out of his mind, could not forget the taste of her lips on his. His arms ached to hold her. Nor could he assuage his desire by thinking of other women. It was Emma, and only Emma, who was driving him mad with longing.

The sun was long set, the stars and a crescent moon were shining in a clear sky, and all of his men were fast asleep when Dain quietly saddled his horse and led it out of Trevanan to the spot where the rutted village road met the cliff road. There he mounted and set his face toward Penruan, and rode as fast as he dared through the dark.

Chapter Six

As he crept into his own castle, Dain couldn't help thinking of the legend of Uther Pendragon, who disguised himself with Merlin's help and crept into the castle where the lady Igraine lay sleeping. He sated upon her his uncontrollable desire and, in that sating, begat great Arthur. And now Dain walked quietly up the curving stone stairway, too familiar with every step of the way to require any light. He reached the top of the stairs and pushed open the door to the lord's chamber. As if it were enchanted, the heavy wooden door made no sound, nor did the hinges squeak.

Dain stood still in the doorway for a moment, aware that here, in his most private room, he was likely to stumble against the new chair and the tables and clothing chests his bride had brought to him. In his own chamber he was like a stranger who did not know where the furniture was placed. With a spurt of resentment he reminded himself it mattered not if he made noise; he had every right to be where he was.

The window shutters were wide open, allowing a faint light to enter the room. That was odd. Most folk closed and latched their shutters against the night air and against any demons who might be abroad during the dark hours. Somehow he was not at all surprised to know that Emma did not fear the night demons.

He tiptoed across the room to where a shadow darker than the other indistinct shapes told him Hawise's door stood open. When he pulled on the door it, like the outer chamber door, closed silently, as if by magic. Still, he discerned a slight stirring from the direction of the large bed. It was possible that Emma had heard him enter, that she was about to waken. Dain waited, motionless, until all was quiet again. Then he stripped off his clothing and headed for the bed.

Not wanting any interruption, Dain decided the best course was to kiss Emma quickly, before she could awaken and cry out in alarm at finding a man in bed with her and, thus, bring servants and men-at-arms running to her aid. The bed curtains were not closed, perhaps because the night was so warm, and his eyes were rapidly adjusting to the dim light. It was easy to make out the thick braid of Emma's dark hair and the pale oval of her face. He could tell she was sound asleep.

Dain knelt on the bed, bent over, and placed his lips on hers. Emma stirred and murmured something. Her mouth was soft and unresponsive, a sure sign that she remained deeply asleep. Dain lowered himself to the sheets beside her and gathered

Emma into his arms, sighing with the sheer pleasure of touching her.

"Who? Dain, is that you?" She pushed one hand against his chest, waking suddenly, and Dain kissed her again to stifle her outcry.

Her resistance ceased almost as it began. Her hand slid upward, to his shoulder and then to his face, where it rested, fingers stroking his cheek.

"You are supposed to be at Trevanan," she said in a lazy voice that told him she wasn't completely awake yet. "Why are you here? Is something wrong?"

"Yes," he said. "What's wrong is that I need you." He allowed one of his hands to cover her breast, and he took note of the sudden tension in her body.

"You did not need me before. Are you sure of your need now?" Her fingertips stopped their delightful motions against his cheek. Her voice was full of doubt. "Do you truly want me, Dain? Are you here of your own will, your own free desire?"

"I am here because I can no longer exist without making you mine," he whispered. He caught at the braid over her shoulder and began working at the silky hair, unwinding it with an urgency he could not understand. He only knew that he wanted to feel the long, smooth strands running through his fingers.

"I want you to learn to love me," she said. "I want a true marriage, children, affection that lasts beyond the first passion and into old age. Heaven help me, Dain, I want all of that with you."

Her voice broke and Dain, lying close against her as he was, could feel her gasp. She fell silent, as if she rued her impetuous words. He had no answer for her. He did not know how to love, so he responded to her plea in the only honest way available to him.

"I want you more than I have ever wanted any woman," he said. "I can think of no one but you. I ache. I burn. I rode here from Trevanan like a madman, just to lie with you. Give yourself to me, Emma. Don't send me away now, not when I am so close to you, not when I can hear your heart beating and feel your warmth."

"You would accept my refusal?" She sounded as if she did not quite believe what he was saying.

"I will never take you against your will," he said, "though I fear I will die if I cannot have you this night, and I will do everything in my power to persuade you to give me what I most desire."

"Oh, Dain." Her whisper was soft, as if her throat was choked with sudden tears. "Don't you know that I want you, too? I have wanted you since my first day at Penruan, when you came to me in this room and kissed me so passionately, and touched me until I feared my bones would melt from longing."

"I rudely mistreated you that day," he said. "I will not do so tonight."

"I do believe you." She caught her breath, and Dain was painfully aware of her breasts rising against his chest. Only the thin layer of her linen nightrobe lay between them. Dain longed to rip the garment from her lovely body. He told himself to be patient. However intense his own desire, however blinded by lust for her he was, still he must control himself. He did not want merely to ravish Emma. What he wanted was to unleash the passion he was sure resided deep within her, until she responded to him completely. Only then could he know fulfillment of the need that was threatening to tear him apart.

"I am not sure how to please you," she said. "I have never done this before, except for that one time with you."

"I'll show you what to do," he said. "I know you are a maiden, so I will treat you with care. I'll try not to hurt you."

"I trust you. Please say you trust me, too."

For the first time since he had entered the lord's chamber a faint chill settled around Dain's heart, slightly cooling his desire and thus enabling him to think about what he was doing. He did not, dared not, trust her completely. To trust Emma could invite disaster for himself and for all those who depended upon him. If he were a wise man, he would rise from the bed where they lay and leave the room, leave Penruan and ride back to Trevanan and stay there for as long as it took to rid himself of a need he ought not to be experiencing.

Then Emma shifted her position and her thigh brushed against his hardened flesh. The involuntary caress of her smooth skin sent a fire into his veins, and he knew he could not leave her. He would say anything, promise anything, if only she would give herself to him. He could not take; he had never done so with a woman, and he would not do so now.

"Please say you trust me," she whispered again.

"I do trust you to be all that a maiden ought to be," he said, magically finding the right words through the fevered urgings of both his body and his mind. "I trust you to care for my people with your herbal healing, and to be faithful to me."

"I trust you to care for me, to protect me and to be faithful to me," she whispered, as if she were speaking a solemn vow. "And I trust you to love me, in time."

It was not what Dain wanted to hear. He would have preferred words of hot desire. But he reminded himself that she was yet a maiden, unaccustomed to the ways of passion. She was his to teach. He was older and more experienced. Surely he could keep a portion of himself separate from her, so that he could continue to guard his life, his castle, and his people against Emma and any intrusion she might invite from Wroxley, while at the same time, he would be free to enjoy her favors as completely, and as often, as he desired. What a perfect, subtle form of revenge against Gavin it would be to keep Gavin's daughter so enthralled by passion that she would forget her loyalty to her father and cleave to her husband, instead.

He had barely finished the grim thought when Emma wrapped her arms around his shoulders and pulled him closer. For the first time it was she who kissed him, and Dain nearly took leave of his senses at the wonder of her embrace.

Her tongue touched his lips, and when he opened his mouth she entered as he had once done to her. Delicately she touched her tongue to his. The eager innocence of her action set him aflame. Dain's arms encircled her, crushing her to him as he began her first lesson. She learned so quickly that he was forced to tear his mouth from hers lest he lose all control and break his promise not to hurt her. He was hard put not to plunge into her immediately, in order to ease the desperate longing that was rapidly becoming a physical pain.

He drew a little away from her and began to pull at the hem of her nightrobe, easing the sheer garment up and over her head. She gave no sign of embarrassment, only raising her arms to let him finish removing it. With her covering gone, every bit of her body was available to him, to explore and caress, and Dain reveled in the smoothness of her skin, the soft, sweet-smelling length of her hair, the perfect modeling of her fingers and toes. Most of all, he delighted in her astonished yet eager responses when he touched her in places where he was certain she had never been touched before. Not once did she ask him to stop what he was doing. Instead, her startled gasps, her soft moans, and the fervent way in which she pressed herself against his searching hands all confirmed what he had suspected since the day of her arrival at Penruan. His virgin bride was more than willing to be a true wife to him.

Soon Emma grew bolder and began to return Dain's caresses. Her fingertips skimmed across his shoulders and upper arms, then downward along his spine to the cleft of his buttocks, and Dain shook with inner tremors from the sensations she aroused. She caressed his thighs and his calves, all the while murmuring admiring comments on his hard muscles and obvious strength, and Dain was forced to grit his teeth tightly together to keep himself from bursting apart.

When he kissed and suckled at her breasts, she did the same for him, and Dain was aware of an unfamiliar heat curling downward from his suddenly erect nipples to his tight and aching loins. When he stroked his hands over her smooth abdomen and rounded hips, and allowed his lips to follow the same path, Emma returned the caresses a few moments later. She gave so freely and openly of her affection that Dain was shamed by his calculating motives and by his dishonesty. Yet he was unable to stop the slow progression toward the goal that was the heated object of his overwhelming desire.

As his explorations grew more intimate, Emma became more eager. Her surprised gasps turned to soft whispers of encouragement, and when he finally touched the entrance to the most private area of her body he found her warm and moist, ready for him.

"Dain," she moaned, pressing herself against his searching fingers, "I need something, but I don't know what it is."

"I do know," he whispered. "I will be as gentle as I can."

She did not resist when he spread her thighs wider and let his hardness come against her. Bracing himself above her on rigid arms, he pushed deeper.

"Oh, yes," she sighed. "That's the place, that's what I wanted, only I didn't know it till now."

"It's what I want, too," he said, and moved deeper still.

He held no doubt at all about her virgin state, and he fully expected her to protest that he was causing her pain. He was prepared to deal with tears. Yet Emma accepted his entrance with every indication of joy. Dain moved slowly into her, and Emma's body stretched around him, opening to him as smoothly and easily as his own chamber door had opened. He felt a small obstruction give way and then he was entirely within her and her sheath closed tightly about him. Dain stayed perfectly still, not daring to breathe, feeling as though he was suspended somewhere between Earth and Heaven.

"Oh, Dain!" Her voice was soft, yet he could hear the wonder in it.

He looked down at her, at the sweet sacrifice to an old feud, and all thoughts of vengeance and warfare vanished. For Dain in that moment, there was only the incredible beauty of his body joined to Emma's, and his only wish was to give her pleasure.

He reached down to touch her where he knew she would be most sensitive, and when he felt her begin to shatter around him, he finally let his body move freely as desire urged him. Emma's cries of delight were music that softened his hardened heart, even as they strengthened his long, eager thrusts.

One portion of his exalted mind warned that he must be hurting her with his furiously passionate assault; another part noted that Emma was lifting herself to meet his every thrust, that her hands were clutching at his buttocks, her nails digging into him, urging him onward.

Then a piercing, hot sweetness shot through him, and Dain stopped thinking. He hung for an instant at the brink of an astonishing revelation, with Emma's body throbbing beneath him, and then he tumbled over the edge of ecstasy and soared there for a breathless eternity, aware of nothing but an incredible happiness and a sense of gratitude toward the woman who had bestowed such a miracle upon him.

He wakened toward dawn to find Emma cuddled in his arms. He vaguely remembered pulling her close again after their long and intense lovemaking was finished, when both of them were beyond words. Dain could not recall ever before being so moved by a woman. He had been touched by the open and honest way in which Emma had given herself to him. And he knew the memory of the instant of complete happiness that he had found in

119

her would remain with him for the rest of his life. When he was old and feeble he would remember that perfect moment, and for a little while he would be restored to youth and strength once more.

But the fire in his body was gone now. The early morning breeze blowing through the open windows was cool, and a sudden chill attacked Dain's mind and wrapped itself around his heart. He thought about the events of the previous day, of the unusual summer heat and his hard work beside his men-at-arms and the villagers. He heard again old Agatha's voice offering him cool, spiced wine; he saw her gnarled hand holding the jug and refilling his cup several times. Agatha had brought him more wine later in the day, and it was so refreshing, so cooling to his parched throat, that he had drunk far more than he ordinarily imbibed.

And then, unable to withstand the clamorous demands of his own body, he had ridden through the night to Penruan, to bed his maiden wife, to consummate the marriage he did not want made fully legal. Consumed by lust, he had spilled his seed into the daughter of his worst enemy.

Dark suspicion took root and blossomed, all in a moment's time. The fruit of his suspicion was so bitter that Dain nearly choked on it.

Emma stirred in his arms, murmuring softly, and her hand flexed and unflexed against his chest. She was a warm and fragrant weight against him, her soft body more alluring than any siren's. Dain felt his own body begin to rise into eager life in response to Emma's touch, and he cursed the longing that could so easily have led him to waken her with a kiss. It was a powerful urge that made him want to caress her into what he was sure would be ready compliance, so he could join himself to her again and find once more the brief, ecstatic happiness that had earlier transported him. He shuddered at the wave of desire that swept over him.

As quickly as he could without waking her, he slid Emma out of his embrace and left the bed. He drew the green quilt up around her shoulders to keep out the cool breeze that might waken her. Then, still unclothed, he went to stand at the window while he sorted out his thoughts.

The windows in the lord's chamber faced west— deliberately so, to prevent attackers on the landward side of the castle from shooting flaming arrows into the room. The arrangement meant Dain could not see the sunrise. But he could see the sky turning a soft shade of pink, and he could see the mist rising off the calm, blue sea. Far below him the waves crashed upon the rocks at the foot of the tower keep. He usually found their constant thunder a restful sound. Not so today. Dain's speculations were deeply troubling.

Being an honest man at heart, he began by admitting to himself that it was possible that the desire that had overpowered him and led to his mad ride to Penruan was the result of his own longing, what Emma had called his own will.

It was also possible that Agatha had mixed into the wine she gave him herbs intended to inflame his natural male readiness into uncontrollable lust. He had heard stories about such herbs, and if they actually existed, Agatha surely knew of them.

These musings left him with three questions. If Agatha's herbs were responsible for his midnight madness, why had she fed them to him? Having known Agatha for most of his life, Dain found it difficult to believe she would do harm to him. Agatha was one of the few people he trusted.

Did Emma know what Agatha had done? And if so, was Emma the instigator of the deed? It was easy enough to believe that Emma had wanted Dain to consummate their marriage in order to gain a tighter hold over him and perhaps to conceive a child by him.

When he reached this point in his thoughts, Dain turned from his unseeing contemplation of sky and ocean to stalk across the room to the bed where Emma still slept. She looked so small tucked beneath the heavy quilt, and so innocent with her cheek resting on one hand, that he could not bear to think of her as treacherous.

If she had not conspired with Agatha to drug him into consummating their marriage, then he must accept that she had given herself to him out of true affection and out of a longing for a happy marriage. It had seemed to him at the time that there was no withholding in her joyful reception of his embrace. But if he was drugged by herbs, how could he be sure his impressions were accurate?

Worse still, if he accepted that Emma was innocent of any intrigue, then he must lay aside long-cherished beliefs about the tainted descendants of Udo of Wroxley. If Emma was innocent, if her blood ran honest and true, then perhaps Gavin was equally honest, equally blameless in the old quarrel between Udo and Dain's grandfather.

It was close to heresy to oppose his lifelong training in hatred. Udo and all his spawn were wicked, treacherous creatures; so Dain had been taught since he was old enough to understand the meaning of wickedness. The shrill voice that echoed in his mind told him nothing had changed because he had lain with a woman.

As he stared down at Emma's sleeping form it

occurred to him that from sundown of the previous night until dawn of the new day rising outside his window, that demanding voice had been completely silent. Whether herbs had silenced it, or the demands of passion, in its absence he had experienced complete happiness.

He regarded Emma, whose innocent, awakening passion had led him to that brief happiness, and he knew he would give his soul to possess her again, and find with her the same intense and fragile joy.

But not if she was conspiring against him, not if she was part of a scheme inspired by Gavin of Wroxley. He had to learn the truth about Emma, and about her intentions toward him. He owed it to the folk who called him their liege lord to keep his wits about him and not give in to blind lust.

With a low, muttered oath he turned away from his bed and his beautiful, sleeping wife. As quietly as he could, he pulled on his clothes and buckled his sword belt at his waist. Then he tiptoed out of the room, down the stairs, and across the bailey to the stable. The sun was just rising above the high moorland when he set out for Trevanan.

Emma woke suddenly and sat up in bed, confused. She thought she had heard the door latch click, but there was no one in the room. Hawise's door was closed, though the serving woman had left it partly open before going to bed, in case Emma should need something during the night.

"Dain must have closed it before he came to bed," Emma murmured. She glanced around the room, searching for some sign of his presence. The events of the past night seemed to her a dream, until she looked at the pillow next to hers. It was one of the new pillows she had brought from Wroxley, plump with its fresh feather stuffing. There was an indentation in the pillow where Dain's head had rested, and in the center of the rounded impression lay a single cornflower, blue as a piece of summer sky against the white linen.

Emma picked up the flower and held it against her cheek, then pressed it to her lips. Here was evidence that Dain's appearance had been real. The flower, added to the tiny splotch of blood on the sheet and the smears along her thighs, and the wonderful, languorous ache in her limbs and far inside her body, all told her she had not been dreaming. Dain had come to her in the dark of night, had ridden to her from Trevanan. And while she had tried to teach him to love, he had introduced her to passion, to a desire that flared even now, in the bright light of morning. She longed to have him back in her arms. Her bruised lips ached for his renewed kisses.

The blue blossom she held as if it were a fabulous jewel was proof of Dain's thoughtful tenderness toward her. She did not pretend to herself that he loved her yet, but she held in her hand hope that one day he might learn to care for her. Surely he knew, for it was common knowledge even among men-at-arms, that cornflowers were used to make an infusion to treat digestive disorders, and that the juice from the stems could heal wounds. It must be why he had chosen to leave this particular flower for her, as a sign of his approval of her work with herbal medicines.

Emma could hear Hawise moving about in the next room. Still holding the precious gift, she got out of bed, wrapped a shawl around her shoulders, and went to stand at the window. While she watched the early sunlight glistening on the blue sea she tried to think of the best way to explain to Dain that she possessed inborn magical abilities. After willingly opening to him the most private secrets of her body, the next step was to tell him the innermost secrets of her mind, and to convince him that her gift was not an evil one. Then, after Dain understood and accepted what she was, they could truly be man and wife.

She did not think he would take the news easily, but she looked forward to the telling. From the first she had wanted complete honesty between them, and now, after the tender way Dain had made love to her, and with the flower he had left suggesting there was a hidden, gentle side to him, she was filled with bright anticipation and hope for their marriage. She would find the right words to explain her magic, and Dain would understand.

"Good morning, my lady. I thought I left this door open last night."

Emma heard Hawise come into the room, but she did not turn from the window. She heard Hawise step to the bed, to pull back the sheets so the linens could air for a while.

"My lady, there's blood on the sheet. You had your monthly flow just last week," Hawise cried. "Are you ill? Or injured?"

"Neither," Emma answered. Her cheeks were suddenly burning, so she kept her back to the room while she made her explanation. Somehow, it was easier to do when she looked at the flower. "Dain was here last night. It was he who closed your door."

There followed a silence that Emma sensed was filled with all the questions Hawise wanted to ask, yet would not.

"No doubt," Hawise finally said, "you have certain aching muscles that you will want to soak for a while in a warm bath. I will see to it."

When Emma was certain she was alone again she left the window and returned to the bed to stare at the tiny, reddish-brown spot that was proof of her lost maidenhood.

"I love you, Dain," she whispered. "Because of you, a wonderful, passionate magic has seized my heart. I only pray you will allow me to teach you to love as I do."

"Lord Dain left just at sunrise, my lady," said Todd, the man-at-arms who had been on sentry duty overnight.

He gave a huge yawn that made Emma want to yawn, too. Even in the shadows of the great hall she could see his eyes twinkling as he regarded her, and she saw his gaze rest upon the flower she wore pinned at the shoulder of her gown. Todd's nose, once broken and healed crookedly, gave his face a savage appearance, yet Emma knew him for a kind-hearted soul who loved his wife and infant son. He was the friendliest of the men-at-arms, an observation proven by his next words, which he delivered as if he wanted to offer reassurance.

"Dain arrived late at night and seemed to be in a great hurry. 'Tis not at all unusual for a newly married man to visit his wife. I wouldn't be at all surprised if he returns again tonight."

"Thank you for the information," Emma said, wishing her cheeks did not blush so easily. "Will you tell Sloan that Blake and I are going for a walk on the moor, to gather herbs?"

"I will, my lady. And thank ye again for the ointment you gave me when I burned my hand a few days ago. It's healing nicely, as ye can see." The guard held out his hand to show her. "We were blessed the day you came to Penruan, my lady."

Emma was grateful when Todd did not remark on her decision to walk rather than ride. In the aftermath of her passionate interlude with Dain there remained a few muscles not soothed by the hot bath Hawise had drawn for her. Emma did not think she could sit a horse without discomfort. How odd that she had not noticed any pain while Dain was with her, stroking deep inside her, luring her onward with him into a magical beauty beyond all the dreams of innocent maidenhood. Emma's cheeks flamed again at the memory. Her fingers lightly touched the blue flower.

Then she noticed Todd smiling at her, almost as if he knew what she was thinking. Emma excused herself and went to look for Blake.

Chapter Seven

Dain did not stop at the site where the rebuilding was almost completed. He waved to the workmen who called out their greetings as he rode past, shouted a promise to return shortly, and then rode on through the little village to Agatha's hut.

As he dismounted Agatha came to the door. With her was a stranger, a man whose dark, uncut hair and long beard showed graying streaks, who wore a plain brown cloak that displayed signs of hard wear, and whose brown tunic and boots were not in much better condition than his outer garment. The staff the stranger held in his left hand, his broad-brimmed felt hat, and the leather sack slung over his right shoulder told Dain the man was a pilgrim, perhaps one of the holy hermits frequently seen in Cornwall, who lived on the moor or, occasionally, resided in the cliffside caves.

"Thank you for your help," the stranger said to

Agatha. "The pain is much less now, so I can continue my journey to its end."

His voice was so clear and crisp and his accent so aristocratic that Dain looked more closely at him. There wasn't much to see; just dusty hair and beard, a deeply tanned upper face, and no sign of any weapon. The man held his right arm close to his body, and Dain saw that his right hand, which was partly hidden by his loose sleeve, was crippled, the fingers bent and the skin smooth and shiny, as if the hand had once been thrust into a fire and the seared flesh had never healed properly. As Dain often did on meeting such wanderers, he wondered what the stranger's story was.

After his quick but searching look at the man, Dain did not think he presented any danger to either Trevanan or Penruan. Listening to Agatha talk to him, Dain concluded that she had met the stranger during her wanderings in search of herbs. If she had brought him back to her house for treatment of some affliction, which Dain took to be the case upon hearing the man's words of thanks, then Agatha was not any more concerned about his presence in the village than Dain was.

"Your journey will not end where you expect," Agatha told the stranger. "Now, see that you do not forget my directions."

"I will remember. Thank you again," the stranger said.

With a slight nod to Dain, he walked away. He limped rather badly, and the set of his shoulders indicated a deep weariness. Dain watched him for only a moment before Agatha's greeting drove thoughts of the stranger out of his mind.

"Come into the garden and sit in the shade," Agatha said. "The day is hot again. I'll fetch a jug of cool wine for us to share."

"No, thank you. The wine you prepared for me yesterday was potion enough." Dain followed her along the side of the house and into the herb garden. There all of the rich and tantalizing fragrances of high summer greeted him; thyme, and the last of the roses, bee balm and hyssop, and mint springing thick and green in the shade. Agatha waved a hand in the direction of the bench, but Dain was too angry with her to sit. Planting his fists at his waist, he glared at his oldest friend.

"What did you put in that wine?" he demanded.

"Violets," Agatha said, not bothering to pretend she didn't understand his meaning, "and a drop of jasmine oil that was brought to me years ago from the East, a few honeysuckle flowers, and one or two other ingredients I prefer not to name."

"Why did you do it?" he asked. "You knew I intended not to consummate this marriage between enemies, so I could more easily have it annulled later."

"That plan was made when you expected to be sent a child bride," Agatha said. "Emma is not your enemy."

"Her father is."

"Are you sure of that?" Agatha asked.

"I have my mother's word on it," he said. "Agatha, you know I have promised my mother there will be no magic practiced at Penruan. The herbs you put into my wine broke that promise."

"I did not carry those herbs to Penruan," she responded, with no sign of repentance. "You took them there, in your own belly." Suddenly she grinned at him, and for a few moments her aged face resembled that of a mischievous child.

"Does Richenda really think she can keep all magic out, in a land where magic abounds?" Agatha shook her head as if in disgust at Lady Richenda's narrow way of thinking. "Dain, the herbs I put into your wine did you no harm. They only released you to do what you wanted to do long before you took the first sip."

"Did Emma order you to offer the wine to me? She was here, visiting you, just before you produced that jug of tainted drink."

"When was the last time anyone dared to order me?" Agatha asked with a laugh. "I swear to you, Emma did not know what I was doing. In fact, when I mentioned making a love potion for her to give to you, she forbade me. She wanted honest passion from you. However, I knew you to be so bound by the hatred of Emma's family that your mother has instilled in you over the years that you were incapable of taking the first step toward a true marriage unless you had my help."

"I am not my mother's puppet!"

"Never fear, I do know who you are," Agatha said. "Lad, your father died when you were much too young. There are things you have forgotten."

"My father died because of Udo," Dain said between gritted teeth.

"There has been no one to counteract the poisonous words Richenda has dripped into your ears day by day, year after year," Agatha said. "No one but me. I think it's why you visit me so often. I am the antidote to your mother. In your heart you know that, unlike Richenda, I have no other reason for what I say to you than my love for you."

"Do not speak ill of my mother." Dain's voice was gentler now. He sat on the bench and leaned his head back against the bark of the old apple tree.

"Why should I not?" Agatha asked, joining him on the bench. "Richenda does not hesitate to speak ill of me."

"I am weary of the conflict between you," Dain said. "I wish you would settle your differences."

"It will never happen, because Richenda has her beliefs and I have mine, and neither she nor I will ever change," Agatha said. "Has it never occurred to you that for a woman who professes a strong Christian faith, Richenda carries on an amazing number of feuds? There was the one with Lord Udo, which she has continued with Udo's son. There is the constant feud with me, which has lasted nearly thirty years. And you know as well as I that Richenda will return to Penruan as soon as she has quarreled yet again with her sister the abbess. I see food for thought there, lad. If I were you, I'd question the claims of a woman who quarrels with nearly everyone she knows. And then, there is the matter of the girl. Well, it's best not to speak to you of that. Not yet." Agatha lapsed into silence.

"Nothing you have said excuses your deed," Dain told her. "You should not have put those herbs into my wine. Now, thanks to you, Emma may be carrying my child."

"I do hope so," Agatha said. "I cannot think of a better way to end a senseless quarrel between nobles."

Dain considered the possibility that Emma was with child, that her slim figure might soon begin to grow round as his seed grew in her. The idea was so agreeable that he shied away from it as a nervous horse shies from an adder. He believed he knew better than to hope for anything good to come from the family of Lord Udo. To clear his mind of the beguiling image of Emma holding his child in her arms, he thought about Agatha's peculiar words.

"What was that you just said about my mother and a girl?" he asked, hoping to catch her off guard with the sudden question.

"What girl?" she said, not looking directly at him as she ordinarily did when they were talking together. "I'm just an old woman whose thoughts sometimes wander. Think nothing of it."

Agatha's thoughts never wandered, and they both knew it. She was hiding something from him. Dain was going to insist that she explain, but she took his hand in hers and smiled at him with all the warm kindness she had shown to him ever since he was a lonely child, and he did not have the heart to press his question further.

The cave was exactly where Agatha had promised it would be. With a murmured word of thanks on behalf of the elderly herbalist, the stranger set down his sack and removed his hat in preparation for squeezing past the rock at the entrance. He was a good-sized man and his booted feet made firm impressions in the damp sand of the outer chamber.

"Excellent," he said, looking around, appreciating the softer light inside the cave. "In here, I won't have to squint all the time."

The inner chamber was all he had hoped it would be. The stranger noted the dry rock walls rising high around him like a solid fortress, and the opening far above through which daylight entered and through which smoke from a fire could escape. He saw the impressions of small, bare feet that crisscrossed the sand as if someone had paced back and forth many times, always stopping in the same place at the face of the rock.

"Agatha's footprints, by the size of them," he said. "I wonder what she does in here, when the herbs she uses are all planted in her garden at Trevanan, or else growing wild out on the moors?"

With a shrug he dismissed the question and knelt to test the water in the underground stream. He dipped his left hand into the water and brought it to his mouth, finding it cool and fresh to the taste.

"Yes," he said, rising to his feet and looking around again. He had a habit of talking to himself whenever he was alone, which was most of the time. Talking out loud kept his voice from growing rusty, and the sound of a human voice helped to make his loneliness less difficult to bear. "Here I can be quiet, and perhaps at last I'll find the peace I seek. Here I can do no harm to those I love, and it's better for them if I never see them again. And if I die here, this is as good a tomb as any."

The stranger went outside to retrieve his hat and sack and carry them into his new abode. Then it was back to the beach once more to gather a few scarce pieces of driftwood for a fire. He made a third trip to the beach. This time he went barefoot and with the sleeves of his tunic rolled above his elbows. For the sake of easier movement he left his boots and his long cloak in the cave.

A search among the rocks at the edge of the sea yielded mussels, and seaweed to wrap them in while cooking them. The tide was coming in, and the stranger's sharp eyes detected a silvery shape within the foaming waves. Laying down the shellfish, he waded into the water and stood still. The next wave rolled in and the stranger bent suddenly, submerging his left arm up to the elbow. When he straightened he held a small, wriggling fish.

"I haven't done that since I was a boy," he said,

laughing in triumph. "Well, I'll not be greedy and ask for more. This will make a decent meal."

A short time later the stranger sat beside a driftwood fire laid on the dry floor of the cave, holding the cleaned fish over the flames on a spit fashioned out of a branch he had broken off a bush that was growing from the cliff face. The mussels in their seaweed wrapping were done before the fish, so he ate them first, sopping the juices from the shells with a loaf of round bread that Agatha had put into his sack. He also had a wooden cup in his sack, and this he used to dip water out of the stream.

"A finer wine than many I have tasted," he said, and filled the cup to drink again.

His meal finished, he took the fish bones and the skin outside and left them at the water's edge for the sea birds to pick over. His new living arrangements had taken considerable time, and by now the sun was setting. The stranger stood for a few minutes admiring the rose-and-gold-streaked clouds, waiting until the sky turned darker and the first stars appeared before he reentered the cave. There was just enough light still coming through the opening at the top of the chamber to show him the way. He spread his cloak on the sand of the inner chamber and added the last piece of driftwood to the fire.

"That's an indulgence," he said. "I didn't see much driftwood on the beach. Tomorrow, I'll ask Agatha where I can find wood or peat to use for fuel. Then I'll gather some wild plants to eat and hope another fish swims into my hands."

His stomach pleasantly full of bread and mussels and fish, his bare toes warmed by the fire, ne settled into the folds of his cloak. He was weary to his bones and to the depths of his mind and heart, but he was confident that he was safe at last, his long wandering ended. With a contented sigh the stranger gave himself up to sleep.

He woke once during the night. The fire had burned down to glowing red embers. Otherwise, the cave was dark and still. He was not afraid of the dark. There was nothing left for him to fear. When he glimpsed a wisp of white in the darkness he did not even lift his head. Surely it was only the last bit of smoke from his fire, drifting across the cave and disappearing into the rock wall.

"I don't understand it," Emma said. "Dain is at Trevanan, no one saw him enter the castle, he did not visit me last night, yet this morning I discovered a sprig of rosemary on his pillow."

"Well, it is his castle," Hawise said in her sensible way, "and Dain has lived in it for most of his life. He probably knows of some secret way to come and go. The cook tells me he used to sneak off when he was a boy, to get away from his mother's scoldings, and he would walk along the cliffs to Trevanan, or ride his pony there."

"I suppose he could have entered without being seen," Emma said, staring at the rosemary in her hand. Tiny pink flowers starred the green needles along the branch. Rosemary was a sign of love and fidelity. "But if Dain did come to our room last night, why didn't he wake me?" She met Hawise's eyes squarely, too perplexed to be embarrassed by her own question.

"I don't know, my lady," Hawise replied. She bent to pull up the quilt and smooth it over the bed. "Perhaps he couldn't stay long and only wanted to leave a token of his warm feelings."

"What, ride all the way from Trevanan just to lay

this on the pillow?" Emma frowned at the sprig of rosemary. "It doesn't make sense." She could think of no reason why Dain would not wake her to embrace her.

"You will have to ask Lord Dain what his reason was," Hawise said.

"So I shall. Perhaps I'll ride to Trevanan today, to see him."

"Sloan says the houses are almost finished." Hawise gave one of the pillows a hearty whack to fluff it up and then replaced it on the bed. "Dain may well come home before you can go to Trevanan."

Perhaps that was what the rosemary was for, to remind her not to forget him until he did return to Penruan. But he *had* returned, and he had not come into their bed. Still puzzled by the herbal offering, Emma laid the rosemary aside, carefully wrapping it in the same scrap of old linen in which she kept the blue cornflower that had been her first gift.

All thought of a ride to Trevanan was quashed in mid-morning, when Sloan sent Blake to tell Emma a messenger had just arrived from Lady Richenda, bearing the news that she would be at Penruan in time for the midday meal.

"Someone must hurry to Trevanan to inform Dain," Emma said to the page.

"Sloan has already sent one of the men-at-arms," Blake said.

"The cook will want to know." Emma's thoughts were whirling with the details of what must be done before her mother-in-law arrived. "Some special dish ought to be prepared to welcome her. Blake, can you tell me what sort of food Lady Richenda especially likes?"

"She doesn't like any food more than any other," Blake said. "Besides, she'd be very angry if the cook deviated from the menus she gave her before she left Penruan. Lady Richenda isn't going to be happy, anyway." Blake's youthful face was somber.

"Do you mean because I am here?" Emma asked. "But she knew I was to marry Dain. It's no secret that my coming here is the reason why Lady Richenda has been absent from Penruan for weeks."

"I do think Lady Richenda is expecting you to be a little girl," Blake said.

"And still she went away!" Emma exclaimed. "Leaving a little girl to the care of servants, with no woman to greet her or ease her fears about being in a new place. That was not kindly done. I am glad it was I who came to Penruan, instead of my younger sister."

Blake said nothing to this declaration, and Emma wished she had not spoken her thoughts aloud, for the boy looked most unhappy. He looked even more unhappy later, when Lady Richenda arrived and swept into the great hall like a disdainful queen. She fixed her sharp gaze upon Blake.

"Well?" Lady Richenda greeted the boy. "What mischief have you been doing during my absence, for which I will now be obliged to punish you?"

"No mischief at all, my lady." Blake went to one knee before her and bowed his head. "Welcome home, Lady Richenda. I am glad to see you in good health."

"You know nothing about the state of my health," Lady Richenda said. "As for mischief, I know you too well to believe you have been behaving yourself during these last few weeks."

"Indeed, my lady," said Emma, coming forward, "Blake has been very well behaved."

"Who are you?" Lady Richenda demanded, glaring at her.

"Allow me to join Blake in welcoming you to Penruan, my lady." Emma sank into a curtsy.

"I asked who you are," said Lady Richenda.

"I am Emma of Wroxley. I am Dain's wife."

"What?" Lady Richenda stared at her. "I expected a child of seven."

"Yes, I know, my lady, but my younger sister has been ill and so I came in her place." Emma was determined not to antagonize her mother-in-law, so she kept to herself her opinion of the way Lady Richenda had absented herself from Penruan during the period when Dain's bride was expected to arrive.

"A substitute bride, are you? No doubt your coming was the result of some vile trick perpetrated by Gavin of Wroxley," Lady Richenda said. She did not lower her voice, which, being both loud and shrill, carried easily to every corner of the great hall and beyond. When she ceased speaking a sudden stillness fell in the hall, as if everyone there was waiting to learn what would happen next.

Emma chose not to make the angry reply in defense of Gavin that immediately sprang to her lips. Instead, she took a moment to study her opponent.

Lady Richenda was tall and thin, her height emphasized by her severe dark robe and her plain white linen wimple. Her features were similar to Dain's, and she possessed eyes of the same startling blue-green shade. But where Dain's eyes could warm and smile on occasion, Lady Richenda gave the impression of holding no warmth at all. Her sharp-boned face was gaunt, as though the features were honed by long illness or by intense religious fervor, or both. For just an instant Emma felt a spurt of pity for her mother-in-law, until she saw the flash of malice in Lady Richenda's eyes and knew the woman was going to be an implaccable enemy to any hope of finding happiness with Dain.

"Your inability to speak and answer my accusation," declared Lady Richenda, "is the result of guilt."

"Not so, my lady," Emma said. "I have come here to be an instrument of peace between your son and my father."

"Peace!" Lady Richenda's shrill tone made clear her opinion of that idea.

"For my willing presence here, I deserve a respectful greeting equal to the one I gave to you," Emma said.

"You will get no such greeting from me," Lady Richenda told her. "I do not want you here."

"Mother." Dain strode into the hall, his spurs jingling softly in the tense silence. "Welcome home." As Blake had done before him, Dain went to one knee. He would have lifted his mother's hand to his lips, but she snatched it away.

"What have you done in my absence?" Lady Richenda's voice held an awful warning.

Dain rose to his feet, smiling as if he had not noticed the odd stillness in the hall, or the way every person there stood unmoving, watching the scene.

"I see you have met my wife," Dain said, still smiling. "I am sorry I wasn't here to present her to you, myself. I am sure Emma has made you welcome."

"I am not a guest, to be made welcome in my own home," Lady Richenda said with icy dignity. She looked from Dain to Emma and back again. "Have you bedded her?"

"That is not your concern," Dain responded.

"Indeed, it is! I will know the truth. How did she trick you into bed?"

"I do believe this is a matter we ought to discuss

calmly, in a more private place," Emma said.

"How dare you tell me where to speak!" Lady Richenda stood still as a statue, her face like stone. Only her burning eyes and her shrill voice betrayed any emotion.

"Emma is right," Dain said. "The great hall at midday, before servants and men-at-arms, is not the place to discuss such an intimate matter."

"Will you take her part?" cried Lady Richenda. "Choose your enemy's daughter over me? She has bewitched you!"

Emma gasped, wondering if Lady Richenda was able to discern her magical power. Then she realized it was merely a figure of speech, the worst thing that Lady Richenda could imagine. From the corner of her eye Emma saw Father Maynard enter the hall.

"The Commandments say, 'Honor thy father and thy mother,' " Lady Richenda intoned, speaking to Dain.

"And our Blessed Lord said that a man shall leave his father and mother and cleave unto his wife," Father Maynard said.

"Do not presume to contradict me in this," Lady Richenda snapped at him. "I will have obedience from my son."

"You will have honor and respect," said Dain, "but do not forget who is lord of this castle. Now, if you wish to continue this conversation, we will do so in my chamber."

Lady Richenda directed a cold look at him before she turned and headed for the tower stairs. Dain put out a hand to Emma, to usher her toward the steps. She held back.

"Father Maynard," Emma said, "will you come, too? That is, if you agree, Dain?"

"Yes, I do," Dain responded at once. "Come along, priest; we may need you as a peacemaker."

"What is this?" cried Lady Richenda as she took in the refurbished lord's chamber. "Who has dared to make these changes without my approval?"

"Emma has my permission for everything she has done in this room," Dain said. "I am far more comfortable now than I ever was in the past."

"You do not need new bed hangings, or cushions," Lady Richenda declared, almost spitting out the words. "You do not need comforts, my son. What you require is boldness and determination of purpose if you are to defeat your enemy. Let me remind you that your enemy is this creature's parent."

Emma bit her lip and remained silent, waiting to hear what Dain would say. She was pleased by the quick way in which he had defended the alterations she was continuing to make in his room.

"I have not forgotten anything you have taught me," Dain said to his mother. He gestured toward the cushioned chair, offering the seat to her. When she refused with a haughty shake of her head, Dain sat down. At once Emma went to stand behind the chair, as she had often seen Mirielle do with Gavin. Emma put one hand on Dain's shoulder and was encouraged when he did not shrug it off or tell her to remove it. Lady Richenda noticed, and her eyes narrowed.

"Why did you not send Emma back to her father as soon as you saw that she was a grown woman?" Lady Richenda demanded of her son.

"You know as well as I that the marriage was made at the will of King Henry. By the terms he imposed on Gavin and me, I could not refuse to accept my wife," Dain said mildly.

"Then defy the king!" cried Lady Richenda.

"I will not."

"What you mean," said Lady Richenda with great contempt, "is that you want to bed her again. Dain, where is your resolve? Where is the hatred for anyone of Udo's blood that I have tried so hard to instill in you?"

"My lady, I beg of you," Father Maynard protested, "cease this talk of hatred. Vengeance belongs to the Lord, not to mere mortals."

"I shall become the Lord's right hand, wreaking His vengeance for the wrongs done to my husband and his father. I shall do the Lord's work, if my son will not!"

Lady Richenda's fierce blue gaze met and clashed with Emma's, and Emma trembled inwardly, for she perceived in Lady Richenda a true fanatic. The woman hated her beyond reason, and Emma was sure if Lady Richenda ever learned about her magical power, she would use the information as a weapon against her, and against those whom she loved.

Therefore, Emma decided, she could not tell Dain the truth. If she did, he might reveal her magical ability to his mother, either inadvertently or deliberately. Emma's heart sank within her as she contemplated the lie of omission that she had intended to remedy at her first opportunity and now must maintain indefinitely. Lady Richenda had just driven a wedge of dishonesty between husband and wife, harming their marriage without ever knowing it.

"Lady Richenda," said Father Maynard in a stern voice, "you cannot know what the Lord's will is. It is possible that the Lord wants peace between Penruan and Wroxley."

"What *I* want," Lady Richenda told him, "is for you to say Holy Mass in thanksgiving for my safe return home before this enemy creature was able to cause any more harm to Penruan than she has already done. I have fasted since rising this morning; therefore, you will conduct the service before the midday meal. I will be in the chapel within half an hour, and I expect everyone who is in the great hall to attend. You may tell them so."

"My lady, I believe the midday meal is ready to be served," Father Maynard said.

"Then tell the servants to put the food on the tables before they go to the chapel," Lady Richenda ordered.

"The meal will be cold before the Mass is over," Emma protested. "That's unfair to the men-at-arms who have been on guard duty since dawn and who need warming food."

"Are you claiming their bodies are more important than their immortal souls?" asked Lady Richenda.

"I am saying that both are important," Emma said, and would have gone on to suggest that the food be kept hot in the kitchen, but Lady Richenda stopped her.

"You are wrong," Lady Richenda declared in the voice of one who is absolutely sure of herself. "Nothing is more important than a person's immortal soul, and if you think differently, then you are doomed to a most unpleasant surprise in the Hereafter. Dain, I expect to see you in the chapel." Lady Richenda stalked out of the room, pausing only long enough to indicate with a fierce look that Father Maynard should follow her.

"Dain, I am sorry," Emma said. "It was not my intention to quarrel with your mother."

"Then see to it that you do not quarrel with her in the future." He rose from the chair but did not look at her.

"I fear it will be a difficult task. She does not like me."

"Considering the bloodshed that lies between our families, can you blame her?"

"I thought she would accept the king's will." When he did not respond at once, Emma went to him and laid her hands on his rigid back. "Dain, please look at me."

He turned to meet her eyes, but there was no warmth in him. This was the same cold and distant man who had confronted her on her arrival at Penruan, and she knew it was his mother's harsh words that had changed him from the gentler soul she had just begun to know, the lover who had shown her unimagined delights.

"I want to thank you," she said, hoping to see in him some slight return of kindness.

"For what?" The words were abrupt, clipped off between his gritted teeth.

"For the gifts," she said, and let her hands stray upward along his arms, feeling the hard muscles that tensed beneath her stroking gestures. When she touched one finger to the corner of his mouth, he turned his head away.

"What gifts?" he asked.

"The flower, and the herb," she said, smiling at him.

Dain frowned at her as if he did not understand what she was talking about, but before he could respond, Hawise came into the room.

"I am sorry to interrupt you," Hawise said. "Lady Richenda insists that both of you must join her in the chapel at once."

"Yes, I know," Dain said.

When he started to pull away from her, Emma went up on tiptoe to kiss his cheek. He made no response, but stood still for a moment, then turned his back on her and went out the door.

Chapter Eight

"I have not seen that disreputable squire of yours," Lady Richenda remarked to Dain when Mass was over and the inhabitants of Penruan were finally assembled in the great hall for a very late midday meal. "Dare I hope you have finally had the good sense to take my advice and send Robert away?"

They were sitting at the high table, eating a meat pie that ought to have been steaming hot but instead was cold, and a rather unsavory cold vegetable stew. Over Emma's protests Lady Richenda refused to allow any of the food to be reheated, saying denial of comfort was good for the soul. The men-at-arms seemed to be making up for the lack of hot food by drinking more wine and ale than usual, and the great hall was becoming noisy. Emma could not help wondering if the noise was an attempt on the part of the men to blot out the constant, strident sounds of Lady Richenda's irritating voice.

Dain was sitting between his wife and his mother, and at Lady Richenda's unkind words Emma saw his hand clench around his wine goblet, while his mouth thinned in the way she was beginning to recognize as a sign of tightly reined anger. She marveled that his mother did not notice and stop her prying about Robert's absence.

"I trust we will not see him again," Lady Richenda said.

"No, you will not," Dain replied. "Robert was killed recently while fighting outlaws."

"Was he?" Lady Richenda put down the sliver of cheese she had been nibbling on. Bowing her head she made the sign of the cross, then clasped her hands and whispered a brief prayer. When she was finished she looked at Dain with no hint of warmth or sympathy in her gaze. "I always disapproved of your decision to take that creature of sin into your personal service. At least he died in a good cause. I suppose that thought will comfort you." She picked up her cheese again and resumed her meal.

"How can you be so hard-hearted?" Emma cried, unable to keep quiet any longer. "Robert was your grandchild."

"He was a bastard," said Lady Richenda, as if that coldly uttered statement explained her apparent indifference to a tragic loss.

"I only met Robert once before he rode off to fight and die," Emma said, "but he seemed to be a good lad, and devoted to his father. And Dain loved him."

"That's enough, Emma." Dain's voice was quiet, his hand on Emma's gentle. "I thank you for your kind words in my son's behalf, but please, say no more."

"Is that how you did it?" asked Lady Richenda, leaning forward to look at Emma across Dain.

"Did what?" Emma asked her.

"Did you lure my son into your bed by pretending to share his unseemly grief over a child born out of filthy sin? Did you take advantage of his sorrow and use it to soften his heart against his sworn enemy?"

"My lady," gasped Father Maynard, who was sitting on Lady Richenda's other side, "I do protest your unfounded accusations."

"So do I," Emma said. "Lady Richenda, I am not Dain's enemy, I am his wife."

"Not for long," said Lady Richenda.

"My lady!" Father Maynard exclaimed, openly horrified by the threat in her words.

"Be quiet, all of you!" Dain thundered. "If you cannot be still, then leave the table. I will have peace while I eat!"

There was silence in response to Dain's command, but there was no peace in Emma's heart. As if in protest against all the unpleasant emotions she was trying to conceal, her stomach rebelled. She could eat nothing more and waved away a bowl of egg custard flavored with almonds, offering only a weak smile of apology to the servant who carried the bowl.

As soon as Dain rose from the table, signaling the end of the meal, Emma excused herself and fled to the calm safety of the stillroom. There she heated water on the brazier and made an infusion, steeping mint leaves in the boiling water until their fragrance was released into the air. She dipped some of the infusion into a pottery cup, then sat on a stool by the worktable, holding the cup in both hands as she sipped at the mint-flavored liquid.

"Dain was beginning to trust me, and I know he desired me," she said, thinking aloud. "We might have created a good marriage, if only we had been granted more time together before his mother returned. But how can I convince him to give up this feud when Lady Richenda is so set against my family?"

She took another gulp of the hot mint brew, feeling it beginning to settle her stomach. Slowly, warmth and courage returned to her.

"There must be something I can do to bring peace to both our families; it's why I came here, after all. I will pay careful attention to everything that happens, I will keep my eyes open and listen well, and I *will* discover a way. I must!"

Her thoughts were interrupted by a sharp knock on the stillroom door. Before Emma could respond, the door was pushed open and Blake stumbled into the room. He was clutching at his right thigh with both hands.

"My lady," Blake gasped, "Sloan sent me. He thought you'd be here, and I prayed you would be. I've hurt my leg. Please help me."

"Oh, Blake!" Emma set down her cup and went to him. She did not need to hear his fragmented explanation of an accident while he was practicing with a battle-ax to see that the gash just above his right knee was a painful wound and could have been a dangerous one.

She made him sit on the stool she had just vacated while she removed his shoe and cut away his blood-soaked hose so she could better examine the wound.

"You are fortunate it wasn't deeper," she said. To distract Blake from the pain and fear she was certain he was feeling, she began to explain what she was about to do. "The wound won't require stitching, although later we will have to ask Hawise to sew another leg on your hose. But that's a small matter. No, don't touch the cut. Let it bleed a bit until I gather what I'll need. The mint water I brewed a while ago has cooled enough for me to use it to clean the wound, and I have a supply of sanicle that I brought with me from Wroxley. It's the best herb for treating open wounds. I'll soon have your leg treated and bandaged, and if you are careful not to get dirt into the cut until the skin closes, you should suffer no permanent damage. You will have a stiff leg for a time, but you can work out the stiffness with exercise. I'm sure either Dain or Sloan will be happy to tell you how to do that."

Blake was looking a little pale, so she gave him some wine mixed with water and a few drops of poppy syrup to hearten him and take away the worst of the pain, and then she set to work on his leg. She was just finishing with the bandage when Dain arrived.

"Sloan told me the boy was hurt. How are you, Blake?" Dain ruffled Blake's dark hair.

"He will be well enough in a day or two," Emma answered for him.

"Be more careful the next time you handle a sharp blade," Dain warned Blake. Then, to Emma, he said, "Thank you. When I heard what happened, I feared I might lose a second potential knight."

"No chance of that. The wound is a clean one. I don't believe it will fester," Emma responded, warmed by the light she perceived in Dain's eyes. "Blake ought to lie down and stay quiet for a while, though, so the bleeding doesn't begin again."

"And put on your second pair of hose," Dain advised, chuckling at the sight of Blake's bare leg and his none-too-clean foot.

"I will." Blake pulled on his shoe, then stood and

151

attempted a cautious step. "Ow! Oh! It doesn't hurt too much," he said, glancing at Dain.

"As I expected," Dain told him, "you will grow up to become a brave knight."

"Yes, my lord. It's what I hope to do." Blake limped toward the door.

Behind Blake's back Dain and Emma exchanged a smile of adult understanding that lasted only an instant, until Lady Richenda stalked into the still-room, with Father Maynard in attendance.

"How dare you use this room without my permission!" Lady Richenda exclaimed, coming to a halt just a few inches away from Emma.

"I have Dain's permission to use the room," Emma said, speaking as calmly as she could when confronted by Lady Richenda's cold outrage.

"Why?" Lady Richenda turned to her son. "Cooking herbs are stored in this room. Only the cook or I may enter it. Why have you entrusted the key to this outsider?"

"Because Emma asked it of me," Dain said with remarkable patience. "Because I believe she can do some good with her herbal remedies."

"Blake!" Lady Richenda had noticed the boy, who was standing partly hidden behind the door. One skinny hand reached out to grab Blake by the ear and drag him forth. As soon as Lady Richenda got a good look at him, she dropped her hand and stepped back as if in shock. "Why, you are half naked! As usual, you are a disgrace to your name and to my service. If you wish to remain my page, you will explain to me at once what is the meaning of your present state of undress."

"Blake was injured, as you can see by his bandage." Stepping forward, Emma put a protective arm around the boy. "In order to treat his wound, it was necessary to cut off one leg of his hose."

"And you allowed her to do this, knowing how I consider treatment of injuries and illnesses to be in opposition to the Will of the Lord?" Lady Richenda turned to Dain again. "Have you no faith at all? Those whom the Lord favors will recover from their afflictions without mortal intervention. I suppose you have invited that witch, Agatha, here in my absence, as well as admitting your enemy wife to my private room?"

"The room was virtually unused," Emma said, so appalled by Lady Richenda's cruel viewpoint that for the moment she could think of no other argument.

"The room belongs to me. Return the key to me at once. I do not want you or that godless, wicked Agatha to come in here ever again, to practice your vile herbal treatments. And as for this immoral page, he also belongs to me, and I intend to see him properly chastised for his nakedness!" Lady Richenda pointed a skeletal finger at Blake.

"He is not naked, only bare-legged," Emma said. She sent a look of appeal in Dain's direction, hoping he would speak up to protect Blake. To her relief, Dain did not fail her.

"In fact, Mother, I gave Blake to Emma, to attend her," Dain said.

"First my stillroom, then my page? Where is your loyalty, Dain?" Lady Richenda demanded.

"My loyalty lies where it has always lain," Dain told her, "with Penruan, and with the folk whose liege lord I am. The people of Trevanan have Agatha to care for their illnesses and injuries, but for too long those who live here in the castle have had no healer. Emma's knowledge of herbs is extensive, and so far she has served us well. She will continue to do so."

"You cannot trust her!" Lady Richenda cried. "She is one of Udo's spawn." She looked as if she wanted to say much more. Dain's furious face stopped her.

"I will not be caught in a quarrel between my mother and my wife," Dain said. "Emma will not exceed the permission I have given her. You, Mother, will not prevent her from carrying out the duties I have granted her leave to perform. I trust both of you understand me, and will obey my wishes."

"But . . . !" Lady Richenda exclaimed, plainly about to say much more.

"Thank you, my lord," Emma said, bowing her head to him.

"Ah, you are clever!" Lady Richenda cried, turning on her. "Meek and mild, and agreeable in bed, too, I'll wager. But you won't win. Dain is my son, and you are only an interloper, not to be trusted. You will not last long."

"If any harm comes to Emma," Dain said, "I will know where to look first. Father Maynard, you are witness to my mother's threatening words."

"Now you will use my priest against me?" Lady Richenda cried. "What have you left me?"

"Your noble dignity, if only you will assume it," Dain said. He headed for the door, pausing just as he reached it to look back at his mother. "Perhaps you need reminding that Father Maynard is not your personal priest. He has been assigned to the entire parish of Penruan and Trevanan, and thus he serves all of us."

"This is your doing," Lady Richenda hissed at Emma as soon as Dain was gone. "You have corrupted my son. But I will live to see vengeance done against you and all your wicked family. Come, Father Maynard." The very picture of righteous indignation, she walked out of the stillroom with her back stiff and her head high.

"I will endeavor to soften her heart," Father Maynard said, lingering for a moment. "I fear it will be a difficult task. As you have heard, she is firmly set in all of her prejudices."

"Father Maynard!" came the imperious voice from the corridor.

"Yes, my lady, I am coming." With a smile that encompassed both Emma and Blake, the priest took his leave.

"I've never seen Lady Richenda so angry," Blake said. "She must have had a dreadful fight with her sister."

"It's more likely that hearing Dain agree with me infuriated her," Emma said, too distressed by the quarrel to care if she spoke aloud an opinion better kept to herself. "I expected Lady Richenda to dislike me, but why does she express such a fanatic hatred of Agatha?"

"I suppose it's because Agatha is a healer," Blake answered.

"Yes, of course, but it's more than that. On the subject of Agatha, Lady Richenda is almost mad. But why?"

"I don't know, my lady. I think it has always been that way." Blake swayed a little, and Emma tightened the arm she still kept around his shoulders. She could tell by the slightly blank look in his eyes and the widening of his pupils that the poppy syrup was beginning to take full effect. He would sleep for a few hours, which was just what his body required for healing.

155

"Come on, Blake." She steered him toward the door. "I'll see you to your pallet and make sure your blanket is warm enough. Then I'll ask Todd to look in on you later."

"Thank you, my lady. You are kind, kinder than anyone has been to me since my mother died."

Dain joined Emma in the lord's chamber that night, but she could discern no warmth or tenderness in him. Icy, blue-green fire lurked in his eyes, and his mouth had a familiar hard look to it. He directed so fierce a stare at Hawise that the maidservant turned to Emma in concern.

"It's all right," Emma said in an undertone. "Go to your room and close the door. Don't worry about me; I'll call you if I need you."

"What are you whispering about?" Dain asked.

"I was only dismissing Hawise for the night." Emma approached him, smiling, both hands extended. "Dain, I want to thank you for shielding both Blake and me today. It was kind of you."

"It was no more than my duty."

"I am sorry, my lord, but you do seem to be caught between mother and wife, whether you wish it or not. Can you suggest any method I might employ to lessen Lady Richenda's intense dislike of me?"

"You could leave Penruan forever," Dain said, "or you could die. Those are the only two remedies I know of to placate her."

"Do you want me to leave?" It hurt her to ask the question, but Emma had to know what Dain would say. His remark about her dying sent a cold chill up her spine.

"What I want does not matter," Dain said. "You

are here because I agreed to accept the king's judgment."

"Did Lady Richenda also agree?"

"Not she. Not ever. She will hate your family until the end of her life."

"Do you hate me, Dain?"

"I wish to heaven I could. It would be so much easier if I hated you." There was pain in his face, and a smoldering desire that flared and glowed as he inspected her from head to foot. She was wearing only her shift and her hair was not entirely braided, since Hawise was not finished with it when Dain appeared. Dain had begun removing his clothes immediately upon entering the room.

"No," he said, pulling off his hose and standing naked before her. "I don't hate you, as you can see for yourself."

"What, then?" Emma asked. She refused to look at his erect male flesh. She persisted in gazing directly into his eyes, for she wanted more from him than lust.

"This." He caught her about the waist and pulled her hard against him. "And this." His mouth bruised hers.

"Dain." At first she struggled a little, but the truth was, she did not want to fight him. She opened her mouth, accepting his punishing kiss, weaving her fingers through his hair. She did not even protest when he picked her up, dropped her onto the bed, and lay on top of her.

She knew he was angry about the dispute between his mother and herself, and thus she did not expect tenderness from him, so she was surprised when, despite his anger, he took care not to hurt her. He handled her expertly, warming her flesh with his hands and his mouth until her body was ready to receive him. Then he took her swiftly, with a cold, hard passion that made Emma's heart ache and sent tears spilling across her cheeks.

She attained a brief release when Dain stroked deep within her one last time, but it was simply a matter of her body functioning in response to his skill. Her heart and her soul were not involved as they had been during their previous lovemaking, and when Dain withdrew from her to lie beside her with one arm thrown over his eyes she did not know what to say or do to bridge the chasm between them.

Dain lay still, keeping his arm over his eyes so he would not have to look at Emma and show her the shame that must be revealed in his gaze.

He was filled with shame, overflowing with disgust at himself and his actions. Emma deserved better from him than to be used as a device to relieve his rage. She had patiently endured his mother's hostility and sharp tongue. Except for her declaration that she was not her husband's enemy, Emma's words to Lady Richenda had all been for Robert's sake, and for Blake's protection. Dain refused to believe there was any evil in Emma's herbal cures. Sloan praised her competence and kindness, Blake was devoted to her, even Agatha approved of her.

As his rage slowly ebbed, long years of strict training intruded on his thoughts, making him angry all over again because of his weakness toward an enemy whom he ought to despise. Emma was the cause of the present dissension between himself and his mother. His immediate problems were entirely Emma's fault.

And yet, she was so openhearted and fair, so kind

and affectionate, so accepting of him and his uncertain temper. . . . Dain's inner conflict became so strong that he shivered before he could force himself to lie still.

"Dain?"

Emma's voice was soft and low-pitched. He could tell by the movements beside him that she was sitting up and probably looking at him, so he kept his eyes covered—and cursed himself for a coward for doing so.

"What is it?" He tried to sound cold and uninterested, when what he really longed to do was gaze into her wonderful eyes and beg her to forgive him for treating her as if her heart did not matter. He wanted to take her into his arms again and make love to her, and do it properly this time, so they could both rediscover the soaring joy they had known at their first joining. There had been no joy in the crude coupling just finished. There had only been a brief moment of relative calm at the end for him, and he suspected it was the same for her. He was afraid to ask her if that was true. Asking would reveal weakness, and he must remember always that Emma had the potential to be a danger to him and to his people. When he was with her, he must appear strong and certain of himself.

"May I ask a question?" she said, sounding distinctly unsure of herself.

"You may ask," he said, marveling at her bravery in the face of his frequent rejection. "Whether I choose to answer or not will depend upon what the question is." He braced himself for a subtle query about the strength of Penruan, or a request to have family members visit her, so they'd have an opportunity to spy on him.

"Why does your mother hate and fear Agatha?"

"What?" Startled out of suspicion and deliberate coldness, he took his arm from his eyes to stare at her.

Emma looked back at him, all soft eyes and tumbling night-black hair and skin like rich cream, and Dain wanted her with a need that nearly shattered him, because it suddenly occurred to him that it wasn't just her beautiful body he craved. He wanted Emma to love him; he wanted her heart. He didn't know how to ask for her love, or how he would deal with it if she gave him such a priceless treasure. Nor did he know how to love in return. His entire life was devoted to hatred, to the quest for vengeance. Or it had been, until Emma's arrival.

He could tell she expected him to respond to her question about his mother and Agatha, so he said the first thing that came to his mind, not pausing to consider the words he spoke until they hung in the air between himself and his wife like dark, glittering jewels that contained the essence of a truth he did not want to admit.

"My mother fears nothing except the wrath of God," Dain said.

"Not so." Emma's gaze was steady. "She is afraid of Agatha. I saw and heard the fear in Lady Richenda this afternoon, when she thought Agatha had come to the castle during her absence."

"You may be right," Dain said slowly, considering. "Fear may be a part of the reason why she hates Agatha so much. How odd that I never thought about her reasons until this hour."

"What was the original cause of their dispute?" Emma asked.

"I don't really know." Dain pushed himself up to sit against the pillows, so his eyes were level with Emma's. "I have always assumed they differed be-

Thrill to the most sensual, adventure-filled Romances on the market today...

FROM  LOVE SPELL BOOKS

As a home subscriber to the Love Spell Romance Book Club, you'll enjoy the best in today's BRAND-NEW Time Travel, Futuristic, Legendary Lovers, Perfect Heroes and other genre romance fiction. For five years, Love Spell has brought you the award-winning, high-quality authors you know and love to read. Each Love Spell romance will sweep you away to a world of high adventure...and intimate romance. Discover for yourself all the passion and excitement millions of readers thrill to each and every month.

Save $5.00 Each Time You Buy!

Every other month, the Love Spell Romance Book Club brings you four brand-new titles from Love Spell Books. EACH PACKAGE WILL SAVE YOU AT LEAST $5.00 FROM THE BOOK-STORE PRICE! And you'll never miss a new title with our convenient home delivery service.

Here's how we do it: Each package will carry a FREE 10-DAY EXAMINATION privilege. At the end of that time, if you decide to keep your books, simply pay the low invoice price of $17.96, no shipping or handling charges added. HOME DELIVERY IS ALWAYS FREE. With today's top romance novels selling for $5.99 and higher, our price SAVES YOU AT LEAST $5.00 with each shipment.

AND YOUR FIRST TWO-BOOK SHIP-MENT IS TOTALLY FREE!

IT'S A BARGAIN YOU CAN'T BEAT! A SUPER $11.48 Value!

Love Spell ✦ A Division of Dorchester Publishing Co., Inc.

GET YOUR 2 FREE BOOKS
NOW—AN $11.48 VALUE!

*Mail the Free Book
Certificate Today!*

TWO FREE BOOKS

Free Books Certificate

YES! I want to subscribe to the Love Spell Romance Book Club. Please send me my 2 FREE BOOKS. Then every other month I'll receive the four newest Love Spell selections to Preview FREE for 10 days. If I decide to keep them, I will pay the Special Member's Only discounted price of just $4.49 each, a total of $17.96. This is a SAVINGS of at least $5.00 off the bookstore price. There are no shipping, handling, or other charges. There is no minimum number of books I must buy and I may cancel the program at any time. In any case, the 2 FREE BOOKS are mine to keep—A BIG $11.48 Value!

Offer valid only in the U.S.A.

*Name*_____

*Address*_____

*City*_____

*State*_____ *Zip*_____

*Telephone*_____

*Signature*_____

If under 18, Parent or Guardian must sign. Terms, prices and conditions subject to change. Subscription subject to acceptance. Leisure Books reserves the right to reject any order or cancel any subscription.

A $11.48 VALUE

Get Two Books Totally
FREE —
An $11.48 Value!

▼ Tear Here and Mail Your FREE Book Card Today! ▼

PLEASE RUSH
MY TWO FREE
BOOKS TO ME
RIGHT AWAY!

Love Spell Romance Book Club
P.O. Box 6613
Edison, NJ 08818-6613

AFFIX
STAMP
HERE

cause Agatha avoids attending church, and my mother is deeply religious. Yet, Agatha and Father Maynard always meet on friendly terms. There is no hostility at all between them.

"Whatever began the quarrel," Dain continued, "it happened long ago, while I was still a small child. My only reliable memory of that time is of the day when my father died." Dain frowned, trying to recapture another memory that slipped away even as his mind grasped at it. He rubbed at his forehead, where a dull ache was beginning.

"How did Lord Halard die?" Emma asked.

"He lost an arm in his last battle with Udo," Dain said. "He never fully recovered from the wound, and he finally died a few years later, when I was just five years old." He lapsed into silence, trying to recall what else it was that tugged at his memory. The headache grew worse.

As if she understood that sympathy from her would be unacceptable, Emma said nothing more. She just laid a hand on Dain's bare shoulder.

"If you want to know what set my mother and Agatha against each other," he said, "ask Agatha. I am sure my mother will never tell you."

He could have taken her into his arms at that point and possessed her again. His body was more than willing, and he did not think she would refuse him. But if he took her while his mind was bemused by thoughts of his dead father and his eternally vengeful mother, there was a strong possibility that he would not find this time, either, the complete happiness he had discovered with Emma the first night they lay together.

"It was an illusion," he said, fighting his seductive memories of that night.

"What was?" Emma asked, looking puzzled at the change of subject.

"Be on your guard with Agatha," he warned, ignoring her question. "I know I should have been more careful with her."

"I am sure Agatha would never harm anyone, least of all you. She loves you and wants you to be happy."

"Is that why she gave me herb-tainted wine to drink?" he demanded angrily.

Emma's mouth dropped open, her eyes large and round, and Dain was so wickedly pleased with the effect his question had produced that he went on to reveal all of the story.

"Agatha knew full well I had no intention of ever consummating our marriage, and she knew why I would not. Still, she fed me herbs in my wine, herbs that sent me into a state of desire I could not control."

"I do not know of any herbs that can overcome a person's own will," Emma declared.

"You may not know of them, but Agatha most assuredly does. The herbs are the reason why I rode to Penruan so precipitously, in the dark of night, to lie with you."

"Why was your desire only toward me?" Emma asked. "Why not toward any convenient woman? Surely, there is at least one woman in Trevanan who would lie with you most willingly, and thank you afterward for the favor bestowed upon her. Why did you come to me?"

The question stopped his tongue. He could not tell Emma it was because, even before he drank the wine, his thoughts and his desire were already fixed on her, and her alone. He would not admit how much he had wanted her from the hour of their first meeting. But he could not hide the truth from himself.

Emma seemed to understand his inner struggle. She asked no more questions. She just put her head on his shoulder and her arm across his waist and lay quietly beside him. After a while, he knew she was asleep.

Dain could not sleep, not even after the pain in his head eased into a numb blankness that blocked out something important that he knew he ought to remember. He lay staring at the gray stone wall opposite the bed, not seeing it, seeing nothing but a series of conflicting images within his mind, until the candles guttered out and darkness enveloped him.

In the morning Dain was gone before Emma awoke. On his pillow lay a blue-green bead, large as the tip of Emma's little finger, and the exact shade of Dain's eyes.

Chapter Nine

"There are eight servants sick," Hawise said to Emma, "and twelve men-at-arms. The garderobes are all overcrowded this morning. I think it's because our food became tainted from sitting on the tables too long. Every dish was cold when we ate it."

"It is possible that spoiled food caused the illness," Emma said, "or it could be that Lady Richenda's retainers brought some illness home with them from Tawton Abbey. Are any of them sick?"

"Only two, my lady. Personally, I am glad I ate just a bit of bread and a chunk of cheese last night. It's a most unpleasant sickness," Hawise said.

"I will make an infusion of mint leaves and willow bark," Emma said. "Tell anyone who feels the need of medicine to come to me in the stillroom."

"They are sick of their own gluttony," Lady Richenda said in unconcealed disgust when she heard of all the digestive upsets. "The men-at-arms swill ale like pigs wallowing in their troughs, and they always overeat. What else can be expected but illness after such behavior? They don't deserve any remedy. Let them recover as best they can."

Emma thought a little compassion ought to be expected from the lord's mother, but she held her tongue. She was glad to see Dain had come to the great hall in apparent good health, if not in good spirits.

Blake was up and moving about the great hall, limping a little and basking in the voluble approval of the younger squires for the way he was dealing with his first real wound.

Blake gave full credit to Emma for his rapid recovery, and his adoration of her shone in his young face every time he looked at her.

"He ought to love me," Lady Richenda said to Dain as they gathered for the midday meal. "Me, and not that troublesome girl who is attempting to usurp my position."

"You cannot force Blake to love you," Dain said in a voice that suggested he was weary of arguing with his mother. "Love comes where and when it will."

"What do you know of love?" Lady Richenda exclaimed scornfully. "All you have experienced is the urge to rut like a beast in the field. And what did it get you, tell me that! Nothing but a bastard son, and why you should grieve for him, I will never understand."

"No, Mother, you don't understand," Dain said.

"Love, as opposed to lust, is holy, sacred, and far removed from the desires of the flesh," Lady Richenda told him. "So I have always taught you, and I wish you would remember it."

165

"I do require an heir," Dain said. "Surely you understand my reasoning. I have a grown-up, willing wife, and I need an heir."

"Consummating your marriage was not part of your original plan!" Lady Richenda screeched at him. "Oh, very well, then, go spend your lust on your enemy's daughter. Get her with child, if that is what you want. Afterward, you can devote yourself to more exalted objectives—preferably, the destruction of her family."

Emma was finding it difficult to keep her promise to herself not to quarrel with Lady Richenda again. She was forced to clamp her teeth together to prevent herself from speaking. She was heartened by the sympathetic glances she received from Sloan and Todd, and from a few other men-at-arms and some of the squires and servants. Hawise stood firmly behind her, waiting until Emma was seated at the high table before seeking her own place at one of the lower tables. And Blake came to her and took her hand, a gesture that earned him a scowl from Lady Richenda.

Once again Emma was unable to eat more than a bite or two of the midday meal. Feeling the need to get away from the castle, she told Dain she was planning to spend the afternoon searching for wild herbs and did not mention her intent to go alone. Blake's leg was still too sore for much walking, and Hawise had a full basket of mending to do. Emma slipped through the main gate with a wave for Todd, who was on sentry duty, and headed for the path that would take her down the cliff face to the beach.

The wind from the sea was brisk, blowing foam off the tops of the waves, sending the sand into little swirls around Emma's feet. She went to the water's edge and stood there with her face into the wind, letting it blow irritation and unhappiness out of her mind. Then she began to walk along the beach in the direction of Trevanan.

She quickly reached the outcropping of rocks that divided the cove below Penruan Castle from the next, smaller cove. The tide was just beginning to ebb, and as Emma came to the rocks the water washed seaward, leaving wet sand. She hurried around the rocks and into the little cove before the next wave rolled in. In one hand she held the basket she always carried when she ventured out to gather herbs, and she told herself she was in the cove only to pick a fresh supply of samphire.

"No, be honest, Emma," she scolded herself. "You are here because you want to explore the cave again, to discover if there are more footprints in the sand. There is nothing to fear. No ghost, no demon or spirit of air or water, could possibly be more fearsome than Lady Richenda's hatred or Dain's cold anger. Besides, everyone to whom I mention the lady in white claims she is a good spirit, so if I meet her perhaps she will impart some useful advice. Advice or no, it would be lovely to meet someone who would listen to me without despising who I am."

She headed for the rock behind which lay the cave entrance. As she had done the last time, she left her basket behind in order to get through the narrow opening. The first thing she noticed about the damp sand in the outer chamber of the cave was the footprints where there had been no prints on her previous visit. They were large prints, some made by bare feet and others made by someone wearing boots.

Cautiously, she moved toward the second cham-

ber. There she found the remnants of a fire. A
brown cloak and a leather sack lay at one side of
the chamber, and she could tell by the makeshift
spit that someone had been cooking.

The sand was so churned-up by the new footprints that the entire original row of small prints,
the signs that had frightened her on her earlier visit
to the cave, were completely obliterated.

Emma did not touch the cloak or the sack. They
were the property of the person who was living in
the cave. Feeling as if she was intruding into the
home of a stranger, she decided to leave, and had
just taken a step back toward the first chamber
when she heard a rather pleasant masculine voice.

"Agatha, I saw your basket outside. Have you
come to pay a visit?" The man who was speaking
appeared suddenly and stopped in surprise when
he saw Emma. "I beg your pardon. I thought you
were someone else."

"Do you know Agatha? Does she come here often?" Emma asked, hoping the stranger would say
yes and the puzzle about who had made that first
set of small footprints would thus be solved. She
required only a glance at the stranger's feet to know
he was responsible for making all the other footprints.

"Agatha told me about the cave and said I could
stay here. She hasn't come to see me since I moved
in. I was hoping she would come; she bakes wonderful bread. I assume she is your friend, too," the
stranger said.

He was staring hard at Emma, as if he could not
quite believe what he was seeing. It was a perfectly
natural reaction upon discovering an unexpected
person in the cave he was inhabiting. She thought
perhaps he was lonely, since he expressed an ea-

gerness to meet Agatha again. Then she remembered her manners and decided introductions were in order.

"I am Emma of Wroxley," she said, "the wife of Dain, the baron of Penruan."

"Are you?" Abruptly, the stranger turned to stare into the fast-rushing water of the underground stream.

Emma took the opportunity to look more closely at him, noting his untrimmed black hair and gray-streaked beard, and the way he held his withered right arm and hand close to his body, as if to protect the damaged limb. She thought she also detected a scar under the beard. His hair and clothes were clean, though the garments were well worn and patched.

She was not at all afraid of him. Far from being menacing, the strange man impressed her as carrying a great weight of sadness. Emma wished she could see more of his face.

"What shall I call you?" she asked.

"Call me?" He took a deep breath and squared his shoulders before he faced her again. "Call me Hermit. It's what I am. From now until the end of my life."

"If you are in trouble," she said, and made a motion indicating his hand, "or if you are in pain, I will be glad to help you. I have some skill with healing herbs."

"No." He swallowed hard, and it seemed to Emma that his eyes were suddenly very bright. "Thank you. It's kind of you to offer. Agatha gave me salve for my hand."

"She knows a great deal more about healing than I do." Emma began to feel awkward. "I apologize for venturing into your home without an invitation.

I didn't know anyone was living here." She began to edge toward the outer chamber.

"Do you come here often?" Hermit asked.

"I've only been to this cave once before, when I was gathering herbs that grow in the cliffs," she answered. "I promise I won't disturb you, and I won't come into your cave again."

"It's not my cave."

She paused, held by a sense of concern for him that she could not explain to herself, and by a feeling that he was of two minds about letting her go. Again, she received the impression that he was lonely, which was an odd quality in a hermit, a man who had deliberately chosen to live alone.

"Do you need food or clothing?" she asked.

"I am used to fending for myself," he said. "I want only to be left alone."

"Then, that is what I will do. If you should need help of any kind, just tell Agatha, and she'll get word to me."

"Good-bye, my lady," he said, in a way that made it clear he was dismissing her.

She left the cave and the little cove promptly, not pausing to gather any herbs. She took only a bit of seaweed from the beach below Penruan before she began to climb the narrow cliff path. When she reached the castle again, she found Todd still on guard, and she mentioned the stranger to him.

"So, you've seen the hermit, have you?" the man-at-arms said. "When I was in Trevanan yesterday, the local folk were talking about him. Some say he's a holy man. Others think he's a magician, because he first appeared in the village in company with Agatha."

"Which do you think he is?"

"I don't know," Todd responded, shaking his

head. "But I do know we ought not to tell Lady Richenda about him. She'll have him dragged out of his cave and brought before Dain for questioning. If the stranger is a holy man, that would be a grave sacrilege. If he's a magician, it could be a terrible, dangerous mistake."

"I agree with you. I will say nothing about the man while Lady Richenda is within hearing distance." Emma did not think the person who called himself Hermit was a magician. She had not sensed any magical power emanating from him. From what she had observed of him, she thought it was more likely that he was a holy man, driven to lonely wandering by some great sorrow. If he wanted to be left alone, she would respect his wishes.

She did not even mention Hermit to Dain, although she was sure he knew about the stranger. It was the sort of thing that one of Dain's men, or someone in Trevanan, would report to him as a matter of course, thinking Dain ought to be aware of any unknown people in the area. Apparently, Dain did not consider Hermit to be a danger and was not going to send him away from his cave.

For some reason that she was unable to explain to herself, Emma was pleased to know Hermit was going to be living nearby.

Hermit was almost asleep when he saw something in the darkness, a shape gliding along the wall of the cave. It was not the first time. On several occasions since his first night there he had sensed, or glimpsed, a movement at that particular spot.

He sat up slowly, so as not to startle whoever it was. The indistinct shape stopped moving.

"Who are you?" Hermit called softly. "Show yourself without fear. I won't hurt you."

There followed an interminable time during which Hermit sat where he was, still partially rolled in his cloak, and the form in the shadows stayed where it was, too.

"Come and sit by the fire where it's warmer," Hermit said when waiting became intolerable. "I have cheese and some fresh bread that a friend gave me late this afternoon. I'll share it with you, if you are hungry."

The silence continued, though Hermit could detect an alteration in the quality of the stillness, as if whatever was just beyond his sight was listening intently to each word he uttered.

"Do you know Agatha?" Hermit asked. "She gave me the bread and cheese, and medicine for my hand, too." He held up his ruined right hand.

There came a gasp from the shadows, followed by what sounded like a sob. Hermit continued to talk in hope of encouraging the unseen soul to come forward and reveal itself.

"Do you know the people at Penruan? I met the baron's wife today." Hermit fell silent, unable to say more on that subject. Again he waited for a response.

"Penruan." It was a whisper caught between a sob and a moan.

"Please join me. I'll put another piece of driftwood on the fire."

Slowly a shape separated itself from the shadows along the rock wall and came forward. At first Hermit thought it was a ghost, until the figure drew nearer, and he saw it was a short, slender female dressed in loose white robes. A silver amulet set with a large turquoise hung about her neck on a silver chain. Hermit recognized the stone; he had seen turquoise several times during his years of wandering.

The woman stood hesitantly, looking from Hermit to the fire and back to Hermit again, and he stayed where he was, making no movement at all, not wanting to frighten her away. Then she lowered herself gracefully to the sand and sat across the fire from him. As she did so, the white scarf covering her head slid off to reveal long waves of unbound auburn hair.

"I call myself Hermit," he said, and smiled in hope of putting her at ease. In the light from the fire he could see that she was truly neither ghost nor demon, but a pale woman some years past her youth, and her silver eyes held a sorrow far surpassing his own griefs. Out of respect for her sadness he addressed her gently. "Have you a name, my lady? Will you tell it to me?"

"You may not call me 'my lady,'" she said, still whispering. "No one may call me 'my lady' anymore. It is forbidden. I am Exile."

He did not question her statement. As he did not want anyone to pry into his past life, so he refused to pry into anyone else's.

"Well then, Exile, will you share food with me?" he asked. "It's in my sack, just over there."

Her eyes were still on his face, as if she was reading his soul, and he sat a little uncomfortably under her regard until she answered him.

"Agatha's bread? Agatha's cheese?" she whispered.

"Yes. Is she your friend, too?"

"My only friend. I will eat with you. Thank you for the kindness."

Her manners were dainty. She broke off small pieces of bread, and accepted with her fingertips the wedge of cheese he cut and offered to her. She nibbled at the food as if she were a great lady at a royal banquet. Hermit's curiosity was stirred by her obvious fine breeding, aroused to a point at which he decided to press her for just a little information.

"Have you been living in this cave since before I came here?" he asked. "I'm sure I've seen you several times, usually just as I am falling asleep."

"I live—in there." She seemed oddly hesitant, and the place she indicated with a brief gesture of one hand was the solid rock wall of the cave.

"I don't understand," Hermit said. "Is there a secret entrance?"

"It is hidden." Again she hesitated, her silvery eyes locked on his. "If Agatha sent you here, there can be little danger. She would not tell you about the cave unless she was sure you will not harm me."

"Indeed, I will not," Hermit said. "My dearest wish is never again to cause harm to any person."

Still her eyes held his. Eventually, she appeared to make up her mind, for she nodded and rose to her feet. She walked to the cave wall, to the solid rock into which Hermit, when half asleep, had seen her wispy, indistinct shape vanish several times.

"Watch," she said, and walked right into the wall. Before Hermit could scramble to his feet, she reappeared. Seeing his baffled face, she smiled.

"Magic," Hermit said, understanding at last. "You are a sorceress."

"So I have been told."

"Aren't you sure?" His nervous laugh rang out, echoing against the rocks.

"If I were truly a sorceress, all that I want would come to me," she said. "Instead, I am Exile. Alone. Bereft."

"I knew a sorceress once," Hermit said, almost to

himself. "She was wicked beyond all imagining. I don't think you are wicked."

"I have been called wicked." Her voice returned to its original sad whisper. "That is why I was banished."

"I find it hard to believe Agatha would befriend someone who is evil," Hermit said.

"Agatha has been my friend since I was a little girl. She showed me how to control my power and how to use the door that is not there. Several times, the door has saved my life, when searchers came here looking for me."

"Do you mean Agatha set up the magical door?" Hermit asked. Eagerly he searched the rock, but he was unable to detect any sign of the opening Exile had used. Still, it was there; he had just seen the proof.

"I do not think even Agatha's magic is strong enough for such a great achievement," Exile said. "No, the door has existed in this cave for centuries. When Agatha was very little, her granny taught her how to use it, as Granny was taught by *her* granny, and so on, back into the mists of time, for as long as people have lived in Cornwall."

"Did Agatha ever tell you who first erected the door?" Hermit asked, intrigued despite his personal prejudice against magic. He reminded himself that not all magic was wicked. He had known a few good and honest magicians in his time.

"There is a tale that long, long ago, the great magician, Merlin, came to this cave, lured here by the enchantress, Nimue. According to the story, Nimue misused Merlin's love for her to convince him to teach her his magic. Once she had learned all she wanted from him, she imprisoned him behind a door that is not there."

"Behind that door?" Hermit asked, again staring at the rock into which Exile had disappeared and from which she had reappeared.

"So the story says." Exile gave him another sad smile. "I have never seen Merlin. I have explored much of the cave that lies behind the door, but not all of it. Perhaps he is hidden in a secret room."

"The door is certainly well concealed," Hermit remarked. "No ordinary mortal could guess it exists." It was all he could do to keep himself from asking the questions that crowded into his mind. He longed to know where Exile had been born, how she had found Agatha, and exactly what kind of magic she practiced. Most of all, he wanted to know who she really was.

For just a moment he contemplated the possibility that Exile was in fact Nimue, then quickly discarded the thought. If she were the enchantress who had bound Merlin into perpetual imprisonment, he did not think she would tell him about it in the way Exile had, as if it were a sad event. Besides, for all her talk of magic and legends, her ability to walk through a rock wall, and her appearance of being something other than an ordinary woman, Hermit knew in his heart that Exile was as human as he was.

While he speculated about her possible origins and wondered what tragedy could have brought her to a cave where legends took on real life, Exile did something unexpected. She drew closer to him, lifted one delicate hand, and touched his temple.

It was as though he was drenched in flowers, in beautiful fragrances and lovely colors and the caress of countless soft petals against his skin. He saw Exile's face aglow with an inner light, and while her hand stayed where it was, just gently pressing against his head, all of his pain and grief disappeared, leaving him peaceful as he had not been for decades.

Then she took her hand away and he was Hermit again, standing in a seaside cave because he had no other place to go, as much an exile as she was. She blinked, and he saw tears in her eyes and knew that after touching him she understood all there was to learn about his past and his motives.

"Oh, what a pity," she said in a mournful whisper. "But you are right to keep silent. No one knows better than I that your secret must never be revealed. Revelation will bring danger and possibly death, which I am sure you do not intend."

"I thought this was a safe place," he said. "I hoped that here, I could avoid hurting others. Now I know better, and I am not certain what to do."

"Sometimes it is wiser to do nothing than to do the wrong thing," Exile said. "Sometimes, it is best to wait until the fates have completed weaving the threads."

"Earlier, I thought of leaving," he said. "But I am so weary. I have traveled so many years and for so great a distance, in hope of keeping my loved ones safe. And now this, when I least expected it, when I was unprepared." He dropped to his knees, bowing his head, unable to bear the pain or the guilt of what he had once done.

Exile knelt before him with tears running down her pale face. After a moment she touched him again, using both of her hands this time, one hand on either side of his head. Instead of the glorious profusion of flowers, what he sensed was a soft, welcoming mist, pale gray-blue and scented with lavender and rosemary.

"Sleep," Exile said, her gentle whisper blending

with the mist and the fragrance. "Trust to Time, and to Fate."

He wondered if this was how Great Merlin had been lured to his imprisonment, and for a single, confused moment Hermit imagined himself in a secret, inner chamber of the cave, his arms bound with golden ropes, his body suffused with an indescribable feeling of peace and contentment. Hermit wondered if he would ever wake up again, if he would ever be free of Exile's sweet spell.

Out of his past he recalled another spell that had been anything but sweet, a spell that had all but destroyed his soul, and he struggled against what was happening. But he did not struggle for long. The weariness of spirit that had brought him to the cave and kept him there for days prevented him from opposing Exile's magic. He could not fight her. He did not want to fight. His last conscious sensation was of her lips on his forehead.

Chapter Ten

"Dain, did you leave this for me?" Emma held out her hand to show him the delicate pink seashell resting in her palm. "I found it on your pillow when I woke this morning."

They were in the lord's chamber, and the day was still young. Emma was growing used to waking to find Dain gone. He often rose before the sun and went up onto the battlements with Sloan to hear the reports of the men who were coming off nighttime sentry duty. The times were perilous, and Dain kept Penruan in a state of readiness lest an enemy noble attack or the dispersed bands of outlaws reform into new groups and decide to destroy Trevanan more completely than on their previous foray. Though he never said so to her, Emma knew one of the hostile nobles he was guarding against was her own father. She knew the baron of Wroxley would never break the peace agreement, but Lady

Richenda continually poured her hatred and suspicion of Gavin into Dain's ears.

On this summer day Dain returned to the room they shared just as Emma was finishing her morning meal of fruit and bread. Upon seeing him she decided the time was right to ask about the mysterious gifts. Dain had not made love to her since the night when he had been so angry. He kept to his own side of the bed and rebuffed any attempt she made to become closer. Yet when others were present he treated her politely, and on several occasions he had defended her against his mother. And there were the objects that occasionally appeared on the pillow next to her. Every one of those gifts held a personal meaning for Emma, and suggested remarkable familiarity with her character.

"Why do you think I would give you a seashell?" Dain asked, frowning at it.

"Didn't you give it to me?"

"Of course not." He sounded surprisingly impatient. His next statement explained why. "My mother is ill."

"I am sorry to hear it." Emma closed her fingers around the seashell and tried not to let her disappointment show. If the gifts were not from Dain, then someone else was leaving them, and she would have to discover who. At the moment, there was a more important matter to consider. "What is wrong with Lady Richenda?"

"According to her maidservant, she has a severe pain in her belly and a cough that will not stop. She has apparently been suffering for several days while hiding her illness. The maidservant came to me to report that Mother could not rise from her bed this morning."

"Then she is very ill, especially if she missed early

morning Mass. Dain, I will gladly do what I can for her, but you know how she dislikes me. She may refuse to accept my remedies."

"I will go with you to her room," Dain said, "and insist that she answer your questions in my presence, so you can determine what is wrong with her."

"Very well. Just give me a moment." Emma opened her clothing chest and took out the linen in which she kept her mysterious gifts. She unrolled the linen and added the seashell to the other items.

"What is this?" Dain was watching her, and he bent forward to pluck the blue bead from the collection.

"That was my last gift before the seashell," Emma said.

"Intriguing." He held the bead up to the light so he could see it better. "I saw something like this before, when I was a boy, but I can't remember where."

"When I found it, I thought it was from you."

"No." Dain turned the bead over and over in his fingers, staring at it as if his sharp gaze could uncover its mystery. "When I look at this, I remember someone weeping, and I recall an ache in my heart, as if part of me was wrenched away. It's just a fragment of memory and I must have been very young, because I cannot connect what I remember with anything else." He handed the bead back to Emma and she put it away with the seashell and the cornflower and the sprig of rosemary, both of which were almost dry enough to crumble into pale dust.

"Could the weeping be a memory of your father's death?" she asked.

"Possibly. Whatever it was, I've forgotten it. Seeing the bead brought it back for a few moments."

Dain rubbed his forehead as if it hurt. "It cannot be important or I would still remember."

Lady Richenda's chamber was sparely furnished. Her bed was narrow, and Emma suspected it was hard, too. In keeping with the ascetic appearance of the room, there were no hangings to draw around the bed to shut out drafts. A plain wooden clothes chest sat beneath a tightly shuttered window. The only other objects in the room were a crucifix on one wall, bearing a particularly contorted, agonized figure, and a prie-dieu placed directly beneath the crucifix. No cushion softened the hardness of the kneeling bench that bore the hollowed-out evidence of Lady Richenda's years of frequent prayer.

A wrenching cough brought Emma's attention back to the emaciated figure on the bed. Lady Richenda glared at her with feverish eyes.

"I do not want her here," Lady Richenda said to Dain. "I gave Blanche orders to tell only you that I am not entirely well today." She transferred her angry gaze to the meek-looking maidservant who stood by the bed.

"Blanche obeyed your orders," Dain said. "It was I who told Emma, because I want her to help you."

"I will not ask an enemy for help!" Lady Richenda exclaimed.

"You don't have to. I have already asked her," Dain said.

"I do not believe in treating illnesses," Lady Richenda declared. "This affliction is visited upon me in retribution for a life that has not been completely holy." With a gasp she stopped, her body going stiff under the covers.

182

"My lady," Emma cried, "I can see you are in pain. Please, let me help you."

"I can bear it," Lady Richenda said. "Do not imagine you can soften my heart with offers of aid. I will not relent. I will have vengeance against your family before I die."

"While you are yet alive, you live under my rule," Dain told her sternly. "I command you to answer Emma's questions honestly, and to allow her to touch you as seems necessary to her."

"My lady, if you will tell me exactly where the pain is . . ." Emma began.

"No! You will not put your hands on me." Lady Richenda gave way to a fit of coughing that left her wheezing and clutching at her abdomen.

"Please, let me help. It grieves me to see you in such pain." Emma knelt by the bed and reached to press on Lady Richenda's abdomen. When Lady Richenda attempted to strike her, Dain caught his mother's wrists and held them. Emma shot him a grateful look and began to examine the sick woman.

"Well?" Dain asked when Emma was finished and Lady Richenda lay with her eyes closed, trembling in outrage and pain.

"She is suffering from severe spasms of the bowel," Emma said, "and an inflammation of the chest. The hard coughing makes the spasms worse."

"Can you treat it?" Dain asked.

"Yes, if only she will take the medicines I prepare for her," Emma answered.

"I will see to it that she does." Dain fixed her with a cold eye and added, "I will trust you in this because I must for my mother's sake. Do not disappoint me, Emma."

"*I* am disappointed to know you think you have to say such a thing to me," she responded with considerable heat. "I am bound as a healer to do all I can to alleviate suffering wherever I find it, and to cause no harm by my treatments."

"Then do for my mother whatever you think is right," he said in a kinder tone.

Emma sent Blanche to find some extra pillows, which she was instructed to use to prop her mistress into a higher position, so Lady Richenda could breathe more easily. While this was being done, Emma went to the stillroom. There wasn't much poppy syrup left from the supply Emma had brought to Penruan with her, but it was definitely the best medicine for Lady Richenda's severe abdominal pain, and to ease the cough that was making her pain worse.

Since the syrup also acted to befog the mind, Emma hoped it would help Lady Richenda forget, at least while she was under its influence, how much she despised her daughter-in-law. Thus, Emma's nursing tasks would be easier, and Dain would not be obliged to remain with his mother to be sure she followed Emma's instructions.

Two hours later Lady Richenda lay quietly in a half-sleeping state, suffering very little pain and coughing only occasionally. Emma sent the exhausted Blanche to her pallet to rest. The servant had been awake all night, tending to her mistress.

"Dain, I know you have duties," Emma said. "I will stay with Lady Richenda. Hawise will look in on us occasionally, and if I need your help, I'll send for you."

"Tell me the truth, Emma. Will she live?" Anxiety showed in every line of Dain's handsome face.

"I am confident that she will recover this time,"

Emma said. "However, Lady Richenda is not in good health. I noticed the first time I saw her how thin and drawn she is. There is an underlying ailment that I believe no physician can treat. I think she may live another few years, but not much more than that."

"I see." Dain's gaze was on his mother's quiet face, taking in every detail of her shadowed, sunken eyes, her hollow cheeks, and the thin gray hair that was usually hidden beneath her wimple. "Thank you for being honest with me."

"If you wish," Emma said, "I can talk to Agatha and describe Lady Richenda's symptoms and explain how I am treating her. It will be a good idea for me to see Agatha in any case. What poppy syrup I have will only last for another day or two. I noticed poppies growing in Agatha's garden, so she may have her own supply, or she may know of some combination of other herbs that will be almost as effective."

"My mother will not approve of Agatha knowing she's sick," Dain said. A faint smile quirked his mouth, then disappeared. "But we don't have to tell her you've spoken to Agatha, do we?"

"Of course not," she agreed.

"I'll send a man to Trevanan and ask Agatha to come here."

"Ask her to come tomorrow," Emma said. "I don't want to leave Lady Richenda today. By tomorrow she ought to be recovered enough that I can leave her in Blanche's care while I meet with Agatha."

Dain left her, and Emma settled down on the stool that Blanche had brought from the great hall. Lady Richenda slept for a while. When she woke she remained in the semilethargic state that often overtook patients treated with poppy syrup, and she made no protest when Emma raised her head to give her just a little more of the medicine. Even so, she soon made it plain that she was not going to allow Emma full control over her care.

"I don't want your help," Lady Richenda said a short time after swallowing the poppy syrup. "I don't need it. Go away."

"You are too ill to be left alone," Emma said, "and I have sent Blanche to take a nap. There is no one else available to sit with you just now. Try to sleep again. Rest will do you good."

"I can't sleep." Lady Richenda tried to moisten her lips. Emma responded to the motion by providing a few sips from a cup of water mixed with wine. "Why should you take care of me? You ought to hate me, as I hate you."

"I cannot," Emma said. "I don't know how to hate."

"Fool," Lady Richenda muttered. "Your mother didn't raise you well. I taught Dain to hate, never to love."

"And I fear I shall spend the rest of my life trying to undo your teaching," Emma said quietly. In a louder voice she added, "Other nobles have gone to war against each other, fought and been wounded or killed, and when the conflict was over the survivors returned to their ordinary lives without continuing their family hatreds. I do wonder why you are so set upon pursuing the feud with my family long after the men who began it are dead."

She knew Lady Richenda's mind was wandering under the influence of the poppy syrup, so she did not expect a sensible response to her remarks.

"You do not understand," Lady Richenda said.

"No, I do not." An idea struck Emma. She wasn't at all sure it was the right thing to do, to question

Lady Richenda in her present state, when she was probably talking more freely to her daughter-in-law than she ever would again. But Emma could not neglect a chance to glean information that might lead to a peaceful resolution of the feud that had persisted for far too long.

"Lady Richenda, perhaps I will be able to understand better if you will tell me your version of the quarrel," Emma said.

"Why would you care about my opinion?" Lady Richenda asked.

"Because I am trying to find a way to make peace between our families," Emma replied.

"There is peace only in heaven," Lady Richenda said. She lapsed into silence while Emma waited and tried to think of words that would encourage the older woman to reveal something of the past. It seemed that Lady Richenda was only pausing to gather her thoughts, for she slowly began to speak. Her words were a bit slurred from the effect of the medicine, yet they were clear enough for Emma to understand perfectly.

"Thirty years ago, in the time of King William Rufus," Lady Richenda said, "my father-in-law, whose name was Dain, laid claim to a piece of land in Shropshire. The same land was also claimed by Udo of Wroxley. Neither man would back down, nor was either willing to accept any other land in substitution. They were both incredibly stubborn."

"So that is how the feud originated?" Emma prompted when Lady Richenda fell silent once more.

"Dain and Udo took their rival claims to the king," Lady Richenda said, "to William Rufus, that wicked man. I heard whispers about him even as a young and sheltered girl, stories claiming he was no Christian king but a pagan. He levied forbidden taxes on church property and spent the money on jewels and silk clothing. He lured pretty boys to his bed and debauched them.

"Worst of all, William Rufus scorned the very idea of knightly honor. He laughed and mocked both men when Dain and Udo insisted on settling the dispute by hand-to-hand combat. But he allowed it, and he sat in his chair of state and watched them fight, watched while Udo slew the older Dain. Then he granted the disputed land to Udo, clasping Udo's hand over Dain's bloody body. I thank all the saints I was not present. My husband told me about it years later."

"Even today it is not unusual for disputes to be settled that way," Emma said. "The death of one of the combatants, and the king's decision, should have been the end of it."

"Before he met Udo that day, Dain made his son swear to continue the battle if he should fall."

"Over a piece of land so far away from Cornwall?" Emma shook her head in despair at the stubbornness of men.

"It was valuable land," Lady Richenda said. "After his father's untimely death, Halard continued to insist the land should be his."

"Halard, your husband?" Emma asked, fascinated by details she had never been told before and wanting to know all of the story.

"He wasn't my husband yet. At the time of the combat, Halard was married to a girl he claimed to love." Lady Richenda made an irritated noise. "What foolishness. Love is a weakness and Halard was never weak, not for a moment. He could not have loved her, for no sooner did his first wife die in childbirth and her baby with her, than Halard arranged with my father to marry me. Halard was a hard man, but an honest master, and I respected him. I learned all about the feud from him, and I agreed with his claim that his family had been cheated. Halard got me with child at once, so he would have an heir, and then he rode off to wrest the land that was rightfully his away from Lord Udo."

Emma did not think it appropriate to inquire whether Lady Richenda had cared for Halard. It was clear to her that softer emotions held little sway over her formidable mother-in-law. Emma could not imagine Lady Richenda in an amorous embrace. She had probably thought of consummation as a matter of doing her duty and had found no joy in her husband's attentions.

And what of Halard? Did he grieve for his first bride and compare her to Richenda? Emma could not help feeling a degree of sympathy for the unpleasant Richenda. Perhaps she had once been an eager, naive young girl, yearning for the affection of a stern husband who had none left to give her after the loss of his first, best-beloved wife, and of the child who should have been his heir.

"You gave your husband Dain for his heir," Emma said, speaking out of pity for a life lived without love. "Halard must have been proud of his son, and of you."

"Such a beautiful baby," Lady Richenda said. "That pale hair, those wonderful eyes. But *she* was always there, always present. He loved her. I could not bear it." She made a sound as if she was about to burst into tears.

"Lady Richenda, you have talked so much that you must be tired." Emma laid a hand over the other woman's thin fingers. Lady Richenda grabbed her hand, holding tight, hurting her. And she kept on talking.

"Halard rode north and attacked Udo while Udo was visiting the disputed holding. In the melee Halard lost his left arm. He came home alive, but the wound never completely healed, and when Dain was five years old, Halard died.

"Shortly before his death he made another attempt to have the ruling changed, but King William Rufus reconfirmed Udo in his possession of that cursed piece of land, and after King Henry came to the throne he also declared the land belonged to Udo. I swore to Halard that I would continue to fight Udo's family on behalf of our son's rights. I ruled Penruan while Dain was a child, and I taught him to hate the barons of Wroxley as his father and grandfather did, and as I still do."

Emma longed to say that the tale of the feud was the saddest, stupidest story she had heard in her lifetime. She wanted to say that no piece of land, however valuable, was worth three generations of bloodshed and hatred, especially not after one king had twice made a decision on the matter and his brother, ruling as king after him, had made a third decision, all of them in favor of the baron of Wroxley. It was madness to continue the fight. But she could see that Lady Richenda was worn out by so much talking, and so Emma held her own tongue.

When Lady Richenda became restless Emma gave her a few drops more of the poppy syrup, and when Blanche appeared in the room to say she could sleep no longer, Emma turned her patient over to the maidservant and went to the great hall to find something to eat. Having spent the day in a darkened room with the shutters closed, she was not aware of the passing of time. She was a little surprised to see that it was after sunset.

"There you are, my lady," said Sloan, rising from one of the tables. "I've a message for you from Agatha. She will meet you tomorrow afternoon on the beach below the castle."

"On the beach?" Emma repeated.

"I think she'd prefer to stay away from the castle because of Lady Richenda," Sloan said with a meaningful look.

Emma smiled her understanding and sent the captain of the men-at-arms back to his evening meal. She thought it was far more likely that Agatha was planning to visit with Hermit and that was why she would be on the beach, rather than out of any fear of Lady Richenda.

Emma was so tired that she went to bed as soon as she finished eating. But she could not sleep. After tossing restlessly for a while she got up and wrapped a shawl around her shoulders. She was kneeling on the seat in the window niche, watching the moonlit sea below, when Dain entered the room.

"I have been to see my mother," he said, standing so close behind Emma that she could feel the heat of his body. "Blanche said she swallowed a little broth and ate some bread. She is sleeping peacefully now."

"I'm glad. She was in dreadful pain when I first saw her this morning."

"I was wrong to mistrust you." Dain's arms came around her, pulling her back against his chest, with her head resting on his broad shoulder. "I should have known without question that you are too honest to do aught but good to someone who is under your care." His lips brushed across her temple, and a moment later his warm mouth found the spot where her throat and shoulder joined. His hands worked their way upward to cup and caress her breasts, his thumbs teasing both of her nipples at the same time.

Emma squirmed against him, feeling his overheated hardness probing at her. Warmth flared within her as he slid his hands down until he reached the place between her thighs.

"It has been too long," he said, echoing her thoughts.

He turned her to face him, and she imagined he meant to pick her up and carry her to the bed. Instead, he tore at his clothes, freeing himself, and then he sank onto the stone window seat.

"Here," he said, "with the moonlight on us."

He lifted her linen nightrobe, and with his hands on her hips he pulled her forward until she was straddling his legs.

"Dain, I am not sure what you want me to do."

"I'll show you. Put your hands on my shoulders and kiss me."

He began to touch her, his fingers working a wild magic on her senses, and when she tore her lips from his because she had to cry out or die of the passion she could not control, he began to suck on her breast through her robe, drawing the slightly rough, moistened linen into his mouth, pulling her flesh into his mouth, too. And all the time his hands were busy between her thighs.

"Dain!" She did not know whether she wanted to flee from him to get away from the erotic sensations that were overwhelming her or force herself closer to him. He solved the problem for her by catching her writhing hips in his big hands and lifting her a little, holding her steady as he slowly began to lower her onto his hardness, stretching and filling her, engulfing her in pleasure.

"There's an advantage to this," he whispered, his breath hot in her ear. "It's you who has to do the work."

"Not work," she cried. "Joy. Oh, Dain." She was full of him, they were one, and she shimmered into ecstasy there on the cold stone seat with the silver moonlight flooding over them. She heard his cry and knew that he had found the same ecstasy.

A long time later he stood, still holding her wrapped around him and finally carried her to the bed.

"You're shivering," he said, "and so am I. Even in summer that stone is cold. We'll not use it often when winter comes."

She held onto him, clinging for warmth and love, while he pulled the quilt around them.

"I'll warm you," he said, and began to rub her back, and her arms, and then her calves and thighs.

Then he was inside her again, hard and tender at first, then fierce and demanding, and the pleasure came upon her so suddenly that she screamed from the force of it and gave herself up completely to love.

She was not at all surprised to find him gone when morning came, or to discover on his pillow a green pebble, worn smooth by water, the sort of stone she often saw at the edge of the sea.

Since she knew it was not Dain who was making a habit of leaving the mysterious gifts, she wondered how anyone could enter her room without her hearing or sensing the person's presence. Except for the single blue bead, there was no material value to any of the gifts, but she was certain, without knowing how she could be so sure of it, that no harm was meant to her or to Dain, that the offerings were meant as gifts, and that they were given with love.

Chapter Eleven

Emma was just beginning her descent of the cliff path the next morning when she looked down and saw Agatha standing on the beach, engrossed in conversation with Hermit. The two of them did not look up as Emma crossed the sand to them and they seemed to be unaware of her approach. She heard their last few sentences clearly.

"A despicable deed that must be rectified," Agatha said with considerable passion.

"After so long, what can be done?" asked Hermit. "There is great danger if we try to set matters aright."

"The girl deserves better," Agatha responded. "The time for justice approaches. Truth cannot and will not be denied for much longer."

"Agatha," said Emma as she reached them, "shall I go away until you have finished your private talk?"

"There's no need." Seeming unconcerned at

having been overheard, Agatha handed a cloth-wrapped bundle to Emma. "Dain's messenger described Lady Richenda's symptoms, so I was able to choose the correct herbs for her. I've included a vial of poppy syrup, too. Be careful not to give her too much. I have known people to become so attached to the stuff that they want more and more of it."

"I don't think there's any danger of that happening with Lady Richenda," Emma said. "She resents everything I do for her, so I'm sure she will refuse all my medicines as soon as she begins to feel a little better. The syrup does make her loquacious, though. Yesterday she recounted her version of the feud with Lord Udo. What prideful foolishness it all is."

"Most feuds are born out of pride," Agatha said. "Take good care of that nasty old woman. If she should die while you are treating her, Dain will have an excuse to blame you and set you aside so he can resume the feud, thus providing Lady Richenda, in death, with the vengeance she so craves. She will not mind dying if death gives her the victory over you and the baron of Wroxley."

"She is a most determined lady," Emma agreed. Then, deciding there would be no better time to speak up, she added, "Dain told me about you putting herbs in his wine. That was not well done." She could not say more, not with Hermit standing there with them. She found herself blushing at the memory of what the passionate results of Agatha's herbs had been, and she could not look at Hermit.

"It was only a pinch," Agatha said, scoffing at Emma's irritation. "The boy needed a little encouragement to go where his heart directed."

"Dain is not a boy," Emma said very firmly. "Nor

is he under his mother's influence, whatever you may think. He often disputes with her and frequently takes my part against her."

"I am glad to hear it," Agatha said. "Perhaps time is moving more swiftly than I realized."

Agatha fell silent, her expression guarded, as if she was considering some deep secret, and Emma decided it was best to change the subject. She had already said too much about her private relationship with Dain.

"Good morning, Hermit." Emma turned to him, to find him regarding her with an eagerness that suggested he could not gaze at her long enough. In another man such a degree of intensity would have indicated a lascivious interest. She could not impute such a motive to Hermit. There was warmth and friendliness in his look, and sorrow mixed with some other emotion she could not define, but she saw in him no evil intent, no wish to harm her in any way. In fact, she felt comfortable with him, as if they were already friends of long standing.

"Good day to you, my lady." Hermit made a quick little bow and smiled at her.

Emma could not help smiling back at him, though she was able to overcome her sudden, absurd desire to hug him.

"I must be going," Agatha said. "I left some medicine brewing back at my cottage, and by now it will need stirring and a few more herbs added to the pot. Hermit, do not forget what I have said. See to the girl, and take great care. She must come to no harm."

"I understand," Hermit said.

"Thank you for the herbs," Emma said to Agatha.

"I gave them to you for your sake, rather than for Richenda, whom I would prefer never to help," Agatha responded. "What you choose to do with the herbs now that they are in your hands is entirely up to you." Leaving her companions, Agatha set off along the beach in the direction of Trevanan.

"She mentioned a girl," Emma said to Hermit when Agatha had trudged around the rocks at the side of the cove and was lost to sight. "Did she mean me? I cannot think so. I am not a girl any longer." Emma paused, eyebrows raised in a question, hoping he would reveal something.

"Not you," was all Hermit said.

"I have heard her speak before of a girl whose name she did not mention," Emma said.

"There are many girls in this area." Hermit's face became a careful blank.

"You are being evasive."

"Agatha is old enough to have many secrets. Some of them are not her own."

"And you are not at liberty to discuss this one?" Emma mused, nodding her understanding of Hermit's discretion. "I apologize for prying. It's just that there are so many questions I want to ask Agatha."

"About her magic?" Hermit met Emma's startled look with another of his warm smiles. "Or about your own?"

"You know?" Emma gasped. "Did she tell you?"

"Agatha would never betray your secret. She didn't have to tell me. I recognized you the first instant I saw you, when I looked into your eyes. I know *your* magic is meant for good."

There was some deeper meaning to what he said; Emma was sure of it. She saw a danger in his kindness and his ready acceptance of her ability. With a sense of urgency, she tried to explain without saying too much.

"Agatha knows, and my companion, Hawise, and now you," Emma said. "No one else must know. Please, Hermit, keep my secret. Lady Richenda is so much opposed to magic that she has forbidden Agatha to enter Penruan Castle."

"Agatha enters all the same," Hermit said. "When Dain summons her, she enters, and he allows her presence in defiance of his mother."

"That's true." Emma glanced toward the rocks around which Agatha had disappeared. "Could it be Agatha who . . . ? But why would she? Oh, how I wish I could talk to her for a longer time!"

"Perhaps I can help," Hermit said. "Ask me the questions you wanted to ask Agatha. What has her ability to enter Penruan despite Lady Richenda's ban to do with the confusion I see in you?"

"Are you a wizard?"

"No," he responded promptly, "and I thank heaven for my lack of magical ability. I know the power too well to want it for myself."

He flexed the fingers of his right hand, the movement drawing Emma's attention. To her eyes, the hand looked less twisted and more like a normal hand.

"Agatha has a salve to soften the burn scars," he said, as if he could read her thoughts, "and she has suggested I ought to try to use my hand more often and not favor it as I have done since it was injured. She says use will strengthen the bones and tendons. Emma, what troubles you? I will not repeat anything you confide in me."

She believed him. Something about Hermit's quiet manner, added to her perception of a deep sorrow hidden behind his gentleness, gave her the courage to reveal her troubles to him. She thought he would understand, so she said to him the things

199

she hadn't had the chance to discuss with Agatha.

"Agatha is eager to promote a firm marriage between Dain and me," Emma began. "I'm not sure if it's because she cares about him and wants him to be happy, which I am certain she does, or if her chief motive is dislike of Lady Richenda and disgust with the old feud between Dain's family and mine."

"It disturbs you that she put those herbs into Dain's wine so he would make love to you," Hermit said, looking out to sea and not at her, as if he were as embarrassed by the subject as she was. "You would have preferred Dain to come to you out of his own desire."

"Yes," Emma said, resolved to get through this first part of her explanation so he would better understand her questions when she came to them.

"Any honest woman would feel the same. Now, why wouldn't Agatha know as much, being a woman herself?" Hermit mused.

"Afterward," Emma spoke into an extended pause in the conversation, "I began to receive gifts."

"What gifts?" Hermit asked, slanting a puzzled look at her.

"From time to time, after Dain has left our bed, I find objects on his pillow. At first I thought they were from him, but he insists they are not. The gifts are nothing valuable, but always something with meaning for me. A flower, an herb, a blue bead, a seashell—"

"A bead?" he interrupted. "I have found a few beads in the cave. When I asked Agatha about them, she claimed they were left there by the Sea People who visited these shores thousands of years ago, looking for tin. According to Agatha, the foreigners traded the beads and small gold trinkets for the ore they considered to be far more valuable."

"Well, there you are, then," Emma exclaimed. "It must be Agatha, if she's familiar with the beads. The one left for me to find is almost the exact color of Dain's eyes. First the herbs in his wine, then the gifts. It does make sense, doesn't it?"

"You think Agatha is stealing into Penruan Castle to leave offerings on your pillow?" he asked, sounding as though he could not accept her conclusion.

"If I have judged Agatha correctly, she doesn't need to enter the castle," Emma said. "Her magic is strong enough to move those small objects into the lord's chamber without her having to venture anywhere near Penruan."

"My dear girl, you have it all wrong."

To Emma's amazement, Hermit burst into laughter. He sounded as if he hadn't laughed for a long, long time. It was as if the rusty, half-choked noises issuing from his throat surprised him as much as they did Emma.

"Is this some kind of game?" she demanded.

"No," he said, sobering. "No game at all. It's deadly serious. There's more here than you know. I'll tell you this much: you can trust Agatha, and me. But beware of Lady Richenda. That jealous, spiteful woman will do you any harm she can."

"Because of the feud?" Emma said.

"Out of jealousy," Hermit answered. "It's the reason for everything she does."

"Have you ever met Lady Richenda?"

"I have no desire to meet her," he said.

"Then how can you say such things about her, if you don't know her?" Emma cried.

"Are you defending her?"

"I am saying it's not fair to judge someone you don't know. Her life has been difficult."

"How innocent you are. I wish I could keep you

safe," he murmured. His left hand came up to caress her cheek. Then he rested his hand on her shoulder and looked into Emma's eyes until she broke away from his gentle touch. With an excuse about returning to the castle to check on Lady Richenda's condition she left him there, alone on the beach.

"I've been waiting for you." Hermit crouched by his smoky peat fire, feeding more turves into it. He did not have to look up to know when Exile entered the cave and came to join him.

"You are troubled," Exile said from across the fire.

"I met Emma again today," he said. "I do not know how much longer I can resist telling her the truth. Yet I must say nothing to her. She's not safe as it is, and the truth could put her into mortal danger—as it could do to you, too."

"Have you spoken to Agatha?"

"Her advice was the same as yours. I am to remain silent for the present, and to be patient. But it's not natural for a man to do nothing in the face of danger!"

"You are recovering," Exile said. "Your heart grows ever bolder. Even your hand is becoming more flexible. Soon you will be the man you once were."

"Oh, no," Hermit said. "I never want to be that man again. I'd rather die first. And if I must die, I'll do it in defense of that kindhearted enchantress who is forced to conceal her true self while she lives at Penruan!"

"Just because you have nursed me through this illness," Lady Richenda said to Emma, "don't think we will ever become friends. I still despise you."

"Then you ought to despise your son, too," Emma said, rising from the bedside stool. "Dain was eager for me to treat you."

"Only because he is under your baleful influence," Lady Richenda declared. "You lure him to bed each night and perform disgusting acts with him, but I warn you, arrogant young fool that you are, men do not long remain enchanted by a woman's body when there exists no other common interest. Dain will desert you soon enough. You will be left to sleep alone, with only your regrets for company."

A harsh response burned on Emma's tongue, until it occurred to her that Lady Richenda was speaking out of her own experience. Emma thought about Lady Richenda's herb-induced revelations of how she had been Lord Halard's second wife, and how Halard had left her to march north and fight Udo, returning to Penruan later with a terrible wound from which he never recovered. Lady Richenda had borne only one child and she had been a widow for more than a quarter of a century. Emma doubted there had ever been much love or tenderness in her mother-in-law's life. With that thought in mind, she stifled her angry words and turned to Blanche, who lingered in the shadows in case her mistress should require some duty of her.

"I do not think Lady Richenda needs my constant care any longer," Emma said to the maidservant. "You may give her the last of the medicine later this afternoon. By tomorrow she ought to be well enough to leave her bed."

"I, not you, will decide when I am ready to leave my bed," Lady Richenda snapped at her.

"Do as you please, my lady," Emma responded,

and walked out of the room before she forgot her good intentions and lost her temper.

It was a relief to be free of the dark bedchamber, with its oppressive atmosphere, but leaving Lady Richenda's room wasn't enough. Emma wanted to be away from the castle. The midday meal was over and there were only a few people in the great hall when she reached it. She did not see Dain anywhere. Emma paused just long enough to provide a report on Lady Richenda's improved condition to Father Maynard before she hurried across the bailey and over the drawbridge.

"I am going to look for herbs," she called to the sentry on duty at the gatehouse, and he smiled and waved her on her way.

When she went out alone she usually went to the beach. Not today. She did not want to chance meeting Hermit, or even Agatha. She had learned so much over the last few days, though she had been too busy to sort through all of the new information. If she was going to make sense of so many disturbing facts she needed to be alone without interruption for a time.

Emma set out for the moor, using the path she and Blake had taken several times. She was sure she could easily find the spot where the adder's tongue fern grew. Once there she planned to sit on one of the rocks in the sunshine until she had put her thoughts into order. Too late, she realized she had forgotten to take her basket from the stillroom, then decided she didn't care. Any herbs she picked in her present disturbed state would likely be useless.

Either she missed a turning in the path or she was so absorbed in her contemplations that she walked right past the place where she intended to stop. Before she knew it, she was high on the sloping ground, close to the top of the ridge. She wasn't overly concerned about getting lost, not as long as she could see Penruan below her, perched on the edge of the cliffs.

It was wonderful to be so free, to be surrounded only by blue sky and fresh air and the open moorland. Her spirits reviving, Emma looked toward Rough Tor. Blake always told her it was actually farther away than it appeared to be, yet today it was so close she thought she could almost touch it.

"This ridge I'm on is much higher than the rest of the land around here. Therefore," she reasoned, "it ought to be dry and safe to walk on. I'll walk a short distance, just to learn if Blake is right and Rough Tor does recede as I approach it."

She set off at a brisk pace. The wind was at her back, the sun was warm, and her concerns about Lady Richenda's hostility, the appearance of mysterious gifts, even the overriding worry about Dain's true feelings for her, all suddenly seemed unimportant. She was in a magical land and the tall rock formation beckoned.

No matter how far she walked, Rough Tor was never any closer. When Emma began to grow tired and turned once more to measure the distance between Penruan and the place where she was presently standing, she discovered she could no longer see the castle. Fog was creeping in from the ocean and even as Emma watched it edged closer, veiling the sun and threatening to conceal the few landmarks she was able to recall from previous expeditions.

She was going to have to turn back and hope she didn't stray from the path or wander into one of the bogs. She remembered all too well Blake's warnings about quicksand so deep it could swallow up small animals, sheep, or even humans.

The problem was, she had turned around several times while seeking spots she recognized, and now she wasn't sure in exactly which direction the castle lay. She could no longer see Rough Tor, either, so she couldn't take her bearings from it. At least she was still on the high path along the ridge. If she kept to it, sooner or later she would come upon a familiar landmark and would know how to proceed from there. She tried not to think about the brigands who infested the moors and who surely knew the area well enough to find their way through any fog.

Before she had gone more than a few yards the seeping fog reached her, enveloping her in damp, wooly gray so thick that she could not even see her own feet. She was forced to stop again while she reconsidered her situation. As the fog flowed about her the air became noticeably colder and damper, and the daylight began to vanish into a deep, gray gloom.

"I'm lost," Emma said to herself. "Completely, thoroughly lost, in an unfamiliar land. There is only one way I'm ever going to find Penruan again. I need to see through the fog to the correct path, and I must do it before either Dain or Sloan decide to send out searchers. I have no right to put anyone else into danger because of my thoughtlessness. What harm can magic do when there's no one here to see?"

Her decision made, she closed her eyes and stood quietly for a moment, concentrating, gathering the power, accepting the uprushing sense of joy as she unleashed her magic. It was such a relief after keeping that part of herself hidden away for months; it was rather like taking off a pair of too-tight shoes that constantly pinched and blistered her feet. Her heart soared at the release of all restrictions. She knew it was only for a short time, but still she reveled in her own ability.

She did not make the fog retreat, for banishing it would reveal the presence of a magician to anyone who was nearby, and Emma intended to keep her magical skills hidden. She let the fog remain, though she could see through it with vision so sensitive that she was able to recognize every pebble along the path. And the path itself was suddenly clear to her, heading gradually downhill, wandering a bit to avoid the boggy areas, yet leading steadily toward Penruan Castle. To Emma's intensely perceptive eyes the very stones of the castle at the end of the path shone with a welcoming glow. Penruan was home. She had known it before, but now she perceived it with magical clarity, understanding with her mind and soul, as well as with her most tender emotions, that Penruan was where she was meant to be.

She set out upon the path revealed to her, walking quickly, wanting to be close to the castle before any possible searchers found her, so she could pretend she hadn't wandered far and wouldn't have to make explanations she would prefer not to offer about how she had found her way back.

She came to a large rock that she hadn't noticed on her outward trek. She did not doubt the evidence of her sight; the rock definitely had not been there before. She stopped, drawing her magic about her for safety, though she felt no sense of danger. Then she caught a glimpse of something white floating, drifting on the fog, like a long scarf or a banner, and she relaxed a little in recognition.

"Who are you?" she called. "I know you are there.

I've seen you several times, on the moor and at the cliffs. If you are lost, perhaps I can help you find your way home."

"So you will, when the time is right," came a whispery murmur, the speaker hidden by the rock. "Agatha says you will."

"Are you a friend of Agatha's?" All the residual tension left Emma's body at mention of the familiar name. "I can show you the direction to her cottage."

"I thought you were lost," said the voice. "I came to help you. Now I find you require no help from me."

"Companionship on my walk would be pleasant," Emma said. "Please, show yourself."

From behind the rock stepped a figure draped in white, a scarf covering the head. A pale, slender hand reached out to Emma, who lifted her own hand, accepting the clasp and knowing in the instant of touching exactly what the stranger was. Though not who. There lay within Emma's knowing an empty place, a blank at the very heart of the ghostly creature. As soon as their hands separated, the odd sense of awareness that was not truly recognition ended abruptly. Still, Emma knew with absolute certainty that the strange woman was human.

"I am Emma," she said. "May I know your name?"

"Vivienne." The voice remained a whisper.

"A magical name," Emma said, recalling stories she had heard about King Arthur and Camelot.

"Magical," said Vivienne, "and cursed."

"Surely not, if you have Agatha for a friend."

"I have only two friends."

"Will you count me as a third? I don't have many

friends either. I'd consider myself fortunate to find a new one."

"Me?" Vivienne gazed at her in disbelief.

"Why not? You also possess inborn magic. I felt it just now, when you took my hand. We ought to be friends, don't you think? Our kind seldom find other folk with whom they can reveal themselves."

"Oh, yes." The scarf slipped from Vivienne's head, disclosing long auburn hair. Her features were delicate, her eyes pale silver. As the scarf slid off her shoulders, Emma saw the silver chain about her neck and the silver and turquoise pendant on her bosom.

"You mentioned Agatha," Emma said. "I assume she is your first friend. Who is the second? Another person with magical ability?"

"No." Vivienne's lips curved into a mysterious smile and her whisper softened into tenderness on the next word she spoke. "Hermit."

"The man who lives in the sea cave? I know him, too. At first I thought he was Merlin, till I realized he owns no magical ability."

"Hermit fears magic. Rightly so," said Vivienne. "As for Merlin, he's not in the outer cave. It requires magic more powerful than mine to find the great wizard. Perhaps no one ever will. Agatha thinks not."

"Vivienne, where do you live? How can we meet again?"

Before Vivienne could answer there was a swirling movement in the fog, an edying that warned Emma someone was approaching. She heard muffled hoofbeats and a familiar masculine voice.

"Emma! Emma, where are you?"

"Dain!" Vivienne's whisper suddenly conveyed an

urgent fear. "He must not see me. It is forbidden. Lady Richenda—"

"Lady Richenda is ill and in her bed," Emma said. "I do understand your concern. She is unalterably opposed to the use of magic, or even of medicine, though she hasn't refused my herbal help while she's ill. By the way, Vivienne, I haven't told Dain about my ability. I'm afraid he won't understand that someone who can work magic is not necessarily evil. Please, don't tell him."

"Tell him?" whispered Vivienne. "I dare not allow him to set eyes on me. How could I tell him anything at all? Ah, Dain, how I wish—" She broke off on a sob.

"Emma!" Dain's shout was louder, a sign he was drawing near. "If you can hear me, answer."

"I'm here," Emma called, "on the path, not far from you." In a lower voice she begged, "Vivienne, please stay."

But when Emma turned her companion was gone, vanished into the mist, along with the magical rock that had been her hiding place. And Dain appeared, riding out of the fog on his big stallion.

"What in the name of heaven do you think you are doing?" he yelled at her. "How could you be so foolish as to wander off without a companion on a day when a fog bank was hovering offshore and was clearly about to move inland?"

"There's no need for you to be angry," she said quite calmly. "I know exactly where I am and I am on my way home. I do hope you haven't sent any of your men out to search for me. They could easily become lost."

"It's you who might become lost," he said, reining in beside her. "You don't know this countryside."

"I have a wonderful sense of direction," she told

him, "as you can see for yourself. I am not lost." She said it with firm conviction, and with more than the obvious meaning. Using her magic had restored her self-confidence, which had been slowly ebbing away ever since her arrival at Penruan. The meeting with Vivienne had strengthened her even more. Emma felt capable of overcoming any obstacle.

When Dain reached down his hand she gave him a brilliant smile, accepting the offer, and lightly sprang upward to seat herself behind him on the horse's back. She wrapped her arms around her husband's waist and rested her cheek on his shoulder.

"Though I wasn't lost, I am very glad to see you," she murmured, rubbing her cheek against the blue wool of his tunic. "I have missed you, Dain."

He said nothing, though for a moment he did place his big hand over her interlocked fingers at his belt. Then they were trotting over the drawbridge and Dain took his hand away. He did not speak again until they were both in the great hall, with the stallion given over to a groom to stable and curry.

Awaiting them in the hall was Lady Richenda, fully dressed in her black robes and white linen wimple. Her face was pale except for a bright spot of red in each cheek, and her eyes, so like Dain's in color, were cold and hard as twin stones when they regarded Emma. Blanche hovered behind her mistress, looking thoroughly frightened.

"So," Lady Richenda said, skirts flaring as she stalked toward Emma, "you left the castle without permission. Were you meeting a lover on the moor?"

"I require no one's permission to leave Penruan,"

Emma said. "I told the sentry on duty where I was going. And I have no lover. How dare you suggest that I have?"

"I know you," Lady Richenda snarled, "spawn of a coward, of a cheat, of a thief."

"You husband's feud with my grandfather has nothing to do with my walk on the moor today," Emma told her. "My lady, you have been seriously ill. You ought not to be out of bed yet. I am surprised to see you standing, and amazed that you were able to negotiate the steps from your room to the hall."

"Are you suggesting that I am not in my right mind?" Lady Richenda screeched, fists clenched, face thrust forward as if to intimidate her adversary.

"I am suggesting that you are still weak," Emma said quietly. "If you continue to exert yourself beyond your strength, you may well have to be carried back to your bed, an indignity I am certain you would rather not endure."

"Dain!" Lady Richenda cried, turning to her son, "will you allow this slut to dismiss me from my own hall?"

"What I will not allow," Dain said, "is for anyone, even you, to insult my wife. Emma is a virtuous woman. And, incidentally, this is my hall, not yours. You'd do well to remember it."

"The wench has bewitched you!"

"I will not tolerate bickering between my wife and my mother!" Dain shouted. "Emma, go to your room!"

"Dain?" Emma put out protesting hands, a gesture intended to ward off his anger. "Don't treat me like a naughty child. I did not begin the quarrel."

"To your room, at once!" he roared at her. In a

quieter tone, he said, "I will speak with you later, in private. For now, do as I say."

The servants were staring, fascinated by the open dispute between the two ladies of the castle, and Emma was sure they'd soon be gossiping freely about what was happening, and very likely carrying the tale to Trevanan village. She saw the plea in Dain's eyes and, in the interest of curtailing the gossip as much as possible, she meekly assented to his command. She headed for the stairs.

"If Emma has no lover among the brigands on the moors," declared Lady Richenda, speaking loudly enough for everyone in the hall to hear, "then she does have a lover on the beach, a disreputable creature who lies with her in a cave beneath the cliffs."

Emma halted on the third step to look back at her accuser. For one dreadful instant she was sorely tempted to use her newly roused magic on Lady Richenda, to bind up her mother-in-law's vicious tongue and silence her. From the guilty expression on Blanche's face Emma guessed she had been carrying gossip to her mistress. Emma's visits to the beach to gather herbs were no secret, and just about everyone in the castle knew of Hermit's arrival. But of all the folk in Penruan Castle only Lady Richenda possessed a mind capable of turning simple facts and an innocent friendship into a sordid affair.

Out of jealousy, Hermit had said. *It's the reason for everything she does.*

Recalling Hermit's remarks, Emma used her knowledge to transmute angry magic into icy-cold scorn.

"If you are speaking of my friend, Hermit," she said to Lady Richenda, "he is a penniless old man, a homeless wanderer with a scarred face and a ruined limb. How could you possibly imagine I'd prefer him to Dain? My lady, I implore you, credit me with better judgment."

While Lady Richenda glared at her, struck speechless by her cool words and icy composure, Emma perceived a faint spark of amusement in Dain's gaze. It was quickly repressed, and he glanced pointedly at the upper level of the stairs. Emma nodded once in his direction and set her foot upon the next step.

In complete silence, keeping her head up and her backbone perfectly straight while servants, men-at-arms, squires, Blake, Lady Richenda—and Dain—all stared at her, she mounted the stairs to the lord's chamber.

Chapter Twelve

"You have been warned often enough about wandering alone on the moors," Dain said, confronting Emma in the lord's chamber an hour after the scene in the great hall. "You ought to know better than to be so foolish."

"You are completely in the right," Emma agreed. "I shouldn't have gone out alone."

"Why did you?" he demanded.

"Emma?" he prompted when she didn't answer immediately. "You do realize you put yourself into danger? You could have been captured by outlaws or fallen into one of the bogs. I might never have known what happened to you."

"I'm sorry."

"Sorry? Never do that again!"

He caught her wrists, forcing her hands against his chest, holding them there in an unbreakable grip. His blue-green eyes blazed into hers until

Emma feared she'd faint from the intensity of his gaze. Before she could determine whether he'd been truly concerned for her welfare or was just angry because she had disobeyed his orders, he raised her hands to his lips and kissed them. Never taking his eyes from hers, he released her wrists and took her face between his palms.

"Don't ever run away from me," he whispered harshly, just before his mouth covered hers.

There was anger in his kiss, yet Emma detected fear, too. He had been afraid for her sake. That meant he did care about her. Her response to the realization was instantaneous. Desire flared in her like dry tinder touched by a blazing torch. Dain was the torch and he was already ablaze, his hard body thrusting against hers when her arms encircled his waist and she moved closer.

"I cannot lose you," he muttered, tearing at her clothes. "I will not."

"I'm here. You haven't lost me." She yearned to promise he would never lose her, but her mind was on fire and Dain didn't give her the chance to say anything more, not with his renewed kisses effectively stopping her mouth. He separated his lips from hers only long enough to pull her gown over her head with a rough gesture and fling it aside. Then he picked her up and put her onto the bed.

"Your belt buckle is scratching me," she protested when he came down on top of her.

"Remove it," he commanded, his voice muffled because his face was pressed against her throat. "My hose, too. In the name of heaven, Emma, I must have you now, at once."

She quickly got rid of his belt, then lifted his tunic to fumble at his hose. It was difficult to keep her thoughts on what she was trying to do while Dain was sucking on one of her breasts through her linen shift and teasing at her other breast with his hand until she wanted to scream. She did succeed in pushing his hose down as far as his knees before she succumbed to the urge to hold him in her hands and drive him as mad as he was driving her.

"Ah!" he groaned, pushing himself against her caressing fingers. "Don't stop. Don't ever stop."

Emma heard a tearing sound and felt the fabric of her shift give way as Dain ripped it from throat to hem. He was still wearing his tunic and the wool rubbed against her sensitive skin. She didn't mind a bit, for his mouth was on hers, his tongue was plunging into her mouth, and she had both her hands around him, drawing him closer to the hot, aching place where she wanted him to be.

He raised his head in bemused surprise when she pulled him forward and opened her thighs to receive him.

"I want you," she said, lifting her hips to push her eager, yielding flesh against his hardness. "As I belong to you, so you belong to me."

He slid into her easily, two halves joining to make one whole, held together by the tightness of her stretched body. Dain was still staring at her as if he couldn't believe she had acted to bring about their joining before he could.

"Have you a complaint, my lord?" she asked in a throaty tone quite unlike her usual clear voice.

"No complaint at all, my lady. I shall endeavor to give you what you so plainly want," he responded with a knowing smile.

His sharp gaze became clouded then, as if he was looking inside himself instead of at her. Emma understood, for she was losing her ability to think as all of her own senses focused on Dain's huge masculinity deeply embedded inside her, stretching her, tormenting her with his overheated presence. When he began to move, she moved with him, wrapping her arms and legs around him, giving her mouth up to his searing kisses.

The fiery, soul-rending climax came upon both of them in the same moment. Emma felt Dain's heat pouring into her and screamed aloud with the joy of it, even as his shout rang in her ears.

"Never leave me," she heard him gasp in the next heartbeat. "I could not bear to live without you."

"I am curious," Dain said, much later.

He was sitting at the foot of the bed, at the very bottom of all the disarray of rumpled sheets and tumbled quilt and pillows left in the wake of their lovemaking, while he retied his hose. Emma was on her knees at the other side of the room, searching through her clothes chest for a shift.

"Curious about what?" she asked, rising with a new shift in her hands.

"According to the sentry, he last saw you on the ridge just as the fog was moving inland. That's some distance from the castle. How did you find your way back without becoming lost? I doubt if I could have done it through such a thick fog, and I've lived here all my life."

"Actually, I did become lost for a short time." She decided to take a chance and tell him part of the truth. Perhaps his response would provide a hint as to whether she dared reveal her deepest secret. They were in such tender accord and he had been so disturbed at the possibility of losing her that she couldn't believe he would hate or reject her when he learned about her magic. To give herself a moment in which to choose her next words, she pulled on her clean shift. Then she continued, watching closely for his reaction to what she said. "I wasn't entirely alone. While I was searching for the way home I met the lady in white who haunts the moors. I met Vivienne."

Dain went absolutely still. After a moment he frowned and rubbed his forehead as if it ached. Then he began to rub the back of his neck with the other hand.

"Are you in pain?" Emma asked.

"No." He stood, holding up one hand to prevent her from moving closer. "It's something I can't remember, something teasing at the back of my mind. The woman told you her name?"

"Yes. As I said, it's Vivienne."

Dain's lips moved, though he made no sound. As he tried, he began to look more and more distressed.

"I cannot say it," he told Emma. "I cannot make the word come out of my mouth."

"What word? Dain, are you ill?"

"The woman's name, damn it!" he shouted at her.

"Vivienne," she said again.

"V—V—" Horror filled his eyes. "What's wrong with me?"

"Sit down again," she suggested. "Perhaps you ought to lie down. Does your head ache?"

"I'm not sick, I tell you! There's a hole in my memory. Why can't I remember?"

"Has it something to do with warfare?" she asked, frantically seeking a way to help him. "Sometimes when men-at-arms see dreadful scenes, or when a young man is forced to kill for the first time, the hour that's too horrid to remember is blanked out as if it never happened. I recall two of my father's

219

men who suffered such memory loss. Could that be what's happened to you?"

"No," he answered, speaking more calmly. "It has nothing to do with fear."

"Horror and fear are not the same thing." To Emma's relief, Dain let her touch him, allowing her to catch the hand he was still rubbing across his forehead and move it away from his face. "Can you recall anything important that happened immediately before or just after the blank spot?"

"Not very well," he said. "I was a boy, no more than five or six years old. Something terrible—unbearable—" He broke off on a groan that sounded suspiciously like a repressed sob.

Emma's heart twisted upon hearing such a noise made by a man who kept his emotions well hidden. She could only guess at the anguish Dain was suffering and wanted desperately to relieve his pain.

"Five years old. Wouldn't that be about the time your father died?" she asked. "Surely the death of a beloved parent would be unbearable to a little boy. Perhaps that's it."

"I didn't love my father," he stated coldly. "I respected and feared him. We were never close. Anyway, I remember the day he died perfectly well. It was afterward—how long afterward? Dear God, *what happened?*"

Dain stared out the window, though Emma was sure he wasn't looking at the fog or listening to the crash of waves on the rocks far below. His eyes were as bleak and empty as the space inside his mind. At last he shook himself and looked at Emma again.

"We were discussing your foolhardy venture onto the moors," he said.

"Yes, and I was telling you of my meeting with Vivienne." Emma spoke the name deliberately, to discover what kind of response it would evoke this time. Dain merely shook his head, so she asked. "Have you ever met her?"

"I've only seen the lady from afar," he said.

"After the first time I saw her," Emma said, "I asked Sloan and Todd and some of the other men about her. No one seems to know who she is or where she lives. The men claim she's a ghost. Perhaps she told her name to me in hope I'd mention it to you."

"Why would she do that?" Dain asked.

"I don't know. She knows your name, and she recognized your voice when you called to me."

"Most people in this part of Cornwall know me by sight," he said, shrugging off the subject of the mysterious lady as if she were unimportant and ignoring the fact that Vivienne hadn't seen him at all. The fog had been too thick for them to see each other, except by using the means Emma had employed to see the path. Emma didn't believe Vivienne was unimportant, so she revealed what else she had learned about the lady in white.

"Dain, Vivienne is a magician. And she fears your mother with an abject terror."

"Now, *that* makes sense," he said, "though little else about the woman does. I'm sure you've heard my mother's opinion on magic. Agatha will have told you, when you discussed herbs and medicines with her. No doubt Agatha has warned the mysterious woman, whoever she is, to keep her distance from Penruan." He fell silent for a moment, thinking, though apparently his thoughts weren't on Vivienne, for he changed the subject.

"Emma," he said, casting a puzzled look at her, "is my mother the reason you fled the castle today? The sentry did say you left in haste. Now that I'm no longer concerned for your safety or upset over your carelessness, I can see it wasn't like you to behave so irresponsibly. Why did you leave?"

"It scarcely matters now, does it?" Emma responded, not wanting to criticize his mother to him. Nor, it seemed, could she tell him about her magic. Not just yet, not while he was afflicted with a memory lapse in addition to a mother who held a fanatical hatred of magic and medicine. Emma's truth was going to have to wait a little longer to be revealed.

"Answer me." Dain's strong hands clasped her shoulders. "Did my mother insult you before you left, as well as after you returned? I saw how she was in the great hall waiting for you, primed like a befouled pump with accusations of wrongdoing."

"One of the medicines I gave her when she was sick contained diluted poppy syrup. It loosened her tongue, so she rambled on about the feud and about her life. I imagine she regrets everything she said to me during those hours. I don't regret listening to her, for I understand her a little better now. She's a lonely soul who sees her power waning and her life drawing to its close, and here's a younger woman ready to step into her place. I might wish her disposition were sweeter, but I can sympathize with her feelings of helplessness and anger. Please don't scold her on my account."

"You are far too generous," Dain said. "Even when she was still young and strong, my mother was difficult to deal with."

"So can Agatha be difficult," Emma said with a smile. "I had words with her over the herbs she put into your wine. Then Hermit mentioned something that made me suspect Agatha as the source of the strange little gifts I keep finding on your pillow.

When I said so, Hermit laughed at me and told me I was all wrong in my suppostions, but he wouldn't answer my questions. So, after all of that, and after having listened to your mother's story with considerable patience, when she upbraided me earlier today and ordered me out of her bedchamber I wanted nothing so much as a quiet, uninterrupted hour to myself. That's why I left the castle, and I am truly sorry my absence alarmed you."

"You could have discussed your concerns with me," he said.

"You are a busy man and these are women's matters."

"Anything that happens in or around the castle is my concern," he said. "In the future, if you are worried or upset or frightened, don't run away. Speak to me, instead. I will have your promise on this, Emma." He sounded stern, yet the look in his eyes was warm.

"I promise. I will speak to you first and then, if the matter is too difficult and the demons are too persistent, perhaps we can run away together." She ended on a soft laugh, thinking of Lady Richenda's bitter tongue and unforgiving attitude. She sobered quickly upon hearing Dain's response.

"My life has taught me that the best way to fight demons is not to run away, but to stand and face them."

"In that case, we'll fight them together," she said.

"We will, if only I can remember what my demons are. I have to fill in that empty spot in my memory."

"I'll help you, Dain."

"I know you will." He bent and kissed her lightly. "I have duties awaiting me now, but we'll talk about this again later." With his gaze still on her face, he crossed to the door and flung it open.

Blanche nearly fell into the room.

"Were you looking for me?" Dain asked, eyebrows raised in surprise. "Or is it my lady you seek?"

"I—I—my lord—my m-mistress—L-Lady Richenda—" Blanche stuttered to an embarrassed halt.

"Yes, I know who my mother is," Dain said coldly.

"Well, Lady Richenda would like to speak to you as soon as possible. In her room, my lord."

"You may tell my mother I will wait upon her when I am free of my present duties," Dain said. He stood impassively in the doorway while Blanche curtsied and stammered an excuse and then fled down the steps.

"Her ear was pressed hard against the door," Emma said. "Which is why she was caught off balance when you opened it so suddenly."

"She is my mother's ears," Dain said, "and my mother's eyes. This has passed beyond a woman's concern. It's my problem; I will deal with it. Until I do, I suggest you avoid my mother."

"I think I will order a bath prepared," Emma responded with what she hoped was an enticing smile, "and I'll ask Hawise to bring me a tray of food and some wine. Would you care to join me?"

"Later in the evening, I will."

The warmth of his gaze delighted Emma. But she realized the next clash with Lady Richenda had only been postponed, for she couldn't believe her mother-in-law was going to be swayed in her opinions by Dain, however firmly he stated his objections to his mother's treatment of Emma, or to Blanche's eavesdropping. More than ever she longed to tell him about her inborn magic, so there would be no secrets left between them.

Dain did come to her later that night, as he had promised. He made love to her with a long, slow tenderness that bound her to him even more closely. In the morning, after he was gone, Emma discovered on his pillow a golden crescent no larger than her thumbnail.

She found Dain atop the castle wall, where he was supervising the masons who were making repairs to the merlons, where some of the mortar was crumbling. At first he seemed irritated by her presence among the busy workers, until he paused to regard her serious expression.

"Walk with me, Emma. What has happened?" he asked when they were well away from the masons and the sentries.

"I found this on your pillow." She opened her fist to show him the golden crescent. "You did require me to discuss my concerns with you."

"So I did." He took the crescent, holding it up between two fingers to look at it more closely. "It's good, solid gold, and finely made. See the raised border and the tiny hole in each point, as if it's meant to be sewn onto a piece of clothing, for decoration?"

"Or fastened to a larger piece of jewelry," Emma suggested.

"When did you find this?" Dain asked. "I only left you an hour ago, and you've taken time to dress completely and braid your hair, which means you rose soon after I departed the lord's chamber."

"I heard the door latch click when you went out,"

Emma said. "When I opened my eyes there it was, on your pillow."

"I didn't pull the door tightly shut. I didn't want to wake you. The latch did not click behind me. I took care that it didn't."

"Then the sound I heard was the person who left the gift closing the door."

"A stranger in the lord's chamber while you were asleep," he muttered. "I cannot allow it to happen again. We must discover who it is, and without arousing suspicion until I have the person responsible safely in my custody. You said yesterday that Agatha denies all knowledge of these incidents."

"She does. So does Hermit. In fact, he took the subject as a joke. As far as I know, he has never been inside the castle walls, so it can't be him. It surely isn't Lady Richenda who's leaving little gifts for me, nor Blanche, either. I can't believe Blake would creep into our room without permission. Certainly it's not Sloan or Todd, but I don't know the other castle inhabitants well enough to be sure of them. Can you think of anyone it might be?"

"No one at all," Dain said. "There are a couple of secret ways into Penruan, intended for use during warfare. Only I, my mother, and Sloan know of them, so I'm sorry to say I must conclude that someone who lives inside the castle is leaving the trinkets. But who? And why?

"I'm going to post an extra guard to watch the entrance to the lord's chamber and report to me who goes up and down the stairs. Todd is trustworthy, and I notice he's been coughing a lot lately. I'll provide a chance for him to stay indoors for a few days and keep warm and dry while still having a legitimate duty to perform. We'll soon have our gift-giver, and then we'll learn what is the purpose of this peculiar assortment of tokens. They certainly make no sense to me." Dain dropped the crescent back into Emma's hand.

"Thank you for your help, my lord." Emma wasn't sure the unseen visitor to her room would be caught as easily as Dain seemed to think. At one time she had suspected Agatha of transporting the gifts to Dain's pillow by magic. She believed Agatha's denial, but there was another person in the vicinity of Penruan who was capable of magic, and that person knew Dain well enough to recognize his voice in a thick fog.

"I thought today I'd search along the beach for seaweed, and try to locate more samphire in the rock crevices," she said. "I'm telling you so you'll know where to find me."

"Take someone with you," Dain ordered.

"Hawise doesn't like heights. She'd be terrified of the path down the cliffside," Emma said, "and Lady Richenda is keeping Blake busy, running errands for her. I know you said he's to be my page now, but I don't want to start a fresh quarrel with your mother. The beach is safe enough. The only people I've ever seen there are Agatha and Hermit, and neither of them will harm me. I won't need a guard." She wanted to go to the beach alone because she was hoping to find Agatha and question her privately about Vivienne. Surely Agatha would know whether Vivienne had a reason to send gifts to Dain's pillow by magic.

"You may be safer outside the castle than in it," Dain said, gently caressing the hand in which Emma held the crescent.

As it happened, Emma never left the castle that day. When she descended from the battlements to the bailey after talking with Dain, she found Hawise waiting for her.

"I'm worried about Todd," Hawise said. "His wife tells me he has been coughing up phlegm all night, though like most men, he refuses to admit he's ill. The wife wanted to know if you have a medicine that will help."

"At least that's good news," Emma said. "Not because Todd isn't well, but his wife's request means the folk here are beginning to trust me and the medicines I make. Do you know where Todd is right now?"

"He's in the wardroom, preparing to stand watch on the battlements," Hawise responded. "His wife is none too pleased about it, either, considering how cloudy the sky is, and how sharp the wind. She's afraid Todd will be drenched with rain and catch another chill."

"He won't be out of doors today," Emma said. With Hawise behind her, she set off briskly in the direction of the wardroom, which lay just inside the entrance of the tower keep. Weapons were kept there, and the men-at-arms coming off or going on duty on the castle walls used the wardroom while they donned or removed their chain mail. It was a noisy, thoroughly masculine place, smelling strongly of male sweat and of the oil and sand used to clean weapons and chain mail. The unexpected appearance of the lady of the castle brought a sudden halt to rough conversation. Several men-at-arms reached in haste for a shirt or a chain-mail tunic with which to cover unseemly nakedness.

"I ask your pardon for interrupting you," Emma said, making sure she kept her gaze well above the shoulder level of the embarrassed men. "I am looking for Todd."

228

"Here I am, my lady." Todd was holding his chain-mail shirt, which he was just about to pull over his padded gambeson. His face was flushed and his eyes were fever-bright.

"You may leave your chain mail behind. My lord Dain has a new assignment for you today," Emma said to him. "You are to come with me. If one of your comrades will speak to Dain, or with Sloan, they will have decided by now who is to take your place on the walls. Again, good sirs, I beg your pardon for intruding," she said to the men-at-arms. She flashed her sweetest smile at the men and stepped outside the wardroom to wait for Todd to join her.

"My lady," Hawise protested, "you shouldn't be giving orders to the men-at-arms, not while Dain and Sloan are both within the castle. It's not a woman's place to command men."

"Dain won't object. He has already decided to keep Todd indoors. He noticed that young man isn't well even before Todd's wife spoke to you," Emma explained.

"He's a considerate lord," Hawise said. "Sloan tells me Dain is aware of almost everything that happens in Penruan, and in Trevanan village, too."

"Sloan, hmm?" Emma was about to make a teasing comment on Hawise's increasingly frequent references to the knight who was captain of the men-at-arms when Todd appeared wearing a woolen tunic, with sword and knife at his belt. "Come with me to the stillroom, Todd. You, too, Hawise. I may need your assistance." Emma knew it wasn't necessary to tell Hawise to report to Todd's wife on his treatment. Hawise would be certain to provide whatever information was pertinent, and she'd carry additional medicine to Todd's quarters and explain how it was to be used. The anxious wife would see to it that her husband obeyed the instructions.

"What is it you want of me, my lady?" Todd stood just inside the stillroom door, looking warily around at the bunches of herbs hanging from the ceiling to dry, and at all the jars and pots of newly prepared medicines lined up on the shelves. Suddenly he gave way to a fit of coughing that bent his sturdy form double. Hearing the way he was gagging, Hawise snatched a small bowl from the table and thrust it into his hands.

"First," Emma said, pouring syrup from a jar into a large spoon, "we are going to ease your cough. Swallow this."

"What is it?" Todd stopped coughing long enough to take a backward step in the direction of the door.

"It's horehound syrup," Emma told him, offering the spoon. "I promise it won't harm you, and I'm sure it will help. Didn't your mother, or your grandmother, ever dose you with horehound?"

"Sometimes, when I was little." Todd regarded the spoon doubtfully.

"If you took it when you were a boy, surely you can do no less now that you are a grown-up man-at-arms," Emma said.

With undisguised reluctance Todd opened his mouth and accepted the medicine.

"It doesn't taste quite as awful as my grandmother's syrup used to do," he admitted.

"I disguise the taste with other herbs," Emma said, "and with a bit of honey. Todd, Lord Dain wants you to stand guard at the door to the lord's chamber. Someone has been sneaking in and out of the room. We want to learn who it is."

"A thief?" Todd asked. "Here in the castle? How can that be?"

"I don't think it is a thief. Nothing has been taken, but Dain and I are both concerned to know it's possible to get into and out of our chamber unseen."

"It shouldn't be possible," Todd said, frowning in thought. "There are always people in the great hall, and we have a good view of the staircase from there."

"And of the people going up and down the steps," Hawise added. "Who would notice one among so many?"

"Are you saying you think it's one of us?" Todd exclaimed in open disbelief.

"Neither Dain nor I can imagine who it could be." Emma spoke very firmly. "We want to disprove any suspicion that one of our own people could be at fault. That's why we decided you would be a good man for the job. You are honest and intelligent, and we know you'll be discreet until this mystery is solved."

"I will, my lady." Todd stood a little taller, looking pleased at the trust being reposed in him. "I'll say nothing to anyone, not even my wife."

"I knew we could depend on you. Now, you'll need to take the horehound syrup regularly to supress the cough. You don't want to begin choking just at a moment when you ought to be quiet."

"Quiet for what?" In a rustle of black robes, with Blake directly behind her, Lady Richenda entered the stillroom. "Are you devising some wicked scheme to use your noxious herbal medicines to disable my son so you can turn the castle over to Gavin of Wroxley?"

"I am obeying Dain's wishes," Emma said.

"What is the evil potion you've just fed to this

stupid boy?" Lady Richenda demanded, glaring at Todd as if he had done something wrong.

"It is only a syrup to stop frequent coughing," Emma explained. "My lady, I have Dain's permission for everything I am doing in this room."

"By gathering herbs and preparing tinctures and ointments from them, you are deliberately contravening the Will of the Lord," Lady Richenda declared in a loud voice.

Emma noticed the light of fanaticism in her mother-in-law's eyes and knew it was useless to try to argue with her. Even so, she wasn't going to back down. She had to stand up to Lady Richenda, for herself and her hopes for the future, for Dain's sake, and for the sake of all the folk whom she was certain she could help, if only she could prevent Lady Richenda from constantly interfering.

"It is cruel of you to allow the people who depend on you to suffer needlessly," she said.

"Suffering will cleanse their immortal souls," Lady Richenda proclaimed, sounding as if she spoke from a pulpit.

"I disagree," Emma said with great firmness. "When a person is ill or in pain, it's often difficult to think of anything but the body. Alleviating discomfort allows the afflicted soul to consider spiritual matters. At Wroxley I knew a man who sustained a dreadful wound to his side. It was clear he was going to die and he knew it, yet all he could think about was his intolerable pain. When he was given a calming herbal infusion mixed with a bit of poppy syrup the pain receded. He was able to make a full confession and receive absolution. He died at peace, clasping the priest's hand. Will you tell me that medicine did not help his immortal soul?"

"He was a weakling," Lady Richenda answered

in a voice filled with contempt. "If I do not prevent you, you will turn every man at Penruan into a similar weakling. Then you'll open the gates to Lord Gavin, which is what you've planned all along."

"That is untrue," Emma said, "as I suspect you are well aware. I have no such intentions."

"Lady Richenda," Blake spoke up, "I can't believe Lady Emma would work any harm to Penruan, or to the people here. She has been doing nothing but good since she arrived. She treated my gashed leg so it healed without festering, and the drink she gave me took away all the pain, so I slept well that night. I'm sure she was helping Todd just now, the same as she helped me."

"How dare you interrupt me?" Lady Richenda whirled on Blake, her right hand whipping out to slap him so hard he stumbled and would have fallen if Emma had not caught him.

"Enough!" Emma cried, her arms around the boy. "Dain gave Blake to me, to be my page. I make my claim to him here and now. You may no longer abuse him."

"What is this infernal racket about?" exclaimed Dain, striding into the stillroom, bringing with him a breath of cool, damp outside air that Emma found very welcome.

"Your cursed wife is determined to weaken every man-at-arms in the castle," Lady Richenda cried, "so she can turn the place over to Gavin of Wroxley."

"I treated Todd's cough," Emma explained, responding to Dain's questioning look in her direction, "and I protested when Blake defended me against Lady Richenda and she slapped him for it."

"I can see she slapped him hard." Dain's large hand caught the boy's chin, turning his face to better see the red mark on Blake's cheek. When he removed his hand from Blake, Dain touched Emma's arm, pressing it in a reassuring way. Then he turned and seized Lady Richenda's arm in what was clearly a much tighter grip.

"Mother," Dain said, "I will escort you to the great hall. You may remain there or retire to your own chamber if you wish. You are not to step within the confines of the stillroom again, unless you are expressly invited by Emma, or by me. Do I make my intention plain, my lady? Henceforth, you are to leave Emma alone to treat the castle inhabitants as she sees fit. I will tolerate no more interference from you."

"You are making a grave mistake," Lady Richenda declared. "This enemy wife of yours will lead you to ruin and debauchery. But you remain my son, and I know my duty to you and to the memory of your father. Whatever restrictions you impose on me, I will do everything in my power to prevent your destruction."

Chapter Thirteen

That day Lady Richenda did not appear in the great hall for the midday meal.

"She is closeted in her room with Blanche and Father Maynard," Hawise reported to Emma. "I pity the priest, for he's not a bad fellow, and I almost feel sorry for Blanche, though I cannot convince myself to like her. Blanche is too sneaky for my taste. Lady Richenda has refused a tray of food, so her companions will miss their largest meal of the day."

"Ask Cook to save something for them to eat later. They'll want more than bread and cheese by the time evening comes," Emma said.

The midday meal was a pleasant one, with the calm of the great hall undisturbed by any arguments. Just as the sweets were about to be served, Emma noticed a rather pale and tired-looking Father Maynard approaching his usual seat at the high table. Suddenly, the castle cook erupted around the end of the screened passage to race across the hall. She was moving so rapidly that Father Maynard halted his own progress to gape at her.

"My lady!" cried the cook, skidding to a halt before the high table. "There's a dreadful thing happening and I know you won't like it."

"What is it?" Emma asked.

"I needed a bit of fresh mint for one of the sweets. You did tell me to feel free to help myself from the garden whenever I needed fresh herbs."

"So I did," Emma said. "Pick as much as you require. There's no cause to worry about overusing the mint. Our plants have sent out so many runners, it would be impossible for you to destroy them."

"Not so," the cook cried, almost in tears. "Lady Richenda is uprooting all the plants, and the sweet I worked on all morning will be spoiled for lack of mint."

"What?" For just a moment Emma was so startled and so angry she couldn't move. She heard Dain's muttered oath and was aware of him leaping to his feet beside her. For his sake she made what she knew was a futile attempt to smooth over the cook's accusation. "Perhaps Lady Richenda wants herbs for her own use."

"Never," said Dain. "This is deliberate mischief."

"My lord," the cook said to Dain, confirming his suspicion, "she's tearing up every plant in the garden, not just the mint. All the new plants Lady Emma put in, and the seedlings, too—all the hard work that she and Blake and Hawise did has gone for naught. When Lady Richenda is finished the herb garden will be completely destroyed."

"By heaven, I'll make her replant the entire garden herself," Dain exclaimed. He stepped off the dais and headed in the direction of the screened passage. Emma followed on his heels, with the cook, Father Maynard, Blake, Hawise, and Sloan all close behind.

The herb garden, which was located near the kitchen door for easy access by the cook, and which also contained lettuce, carrots, and a few other vegetables, was in worse condition than Emma expected. Row upon row of plants lay on the ground, uprooted and trampled. Some of the plants had been chopped into pieces with a kitchen knife, which Lady Richenda was still brandishing while she stamped on a row of tiny seedlings. Her shoes and the hem of her black robe were muddy, there were smudges of dirt on her face and her white linen wimple, and her hands were scratched and stained green. Blanche stood off to one side, wringing her hands and weeping. From the cleanliness of the maidservant's clothing and hands, it was apparent that she hadn't been helping her mistress.

"Mother," Dain shouted at Lady Richenda, "what do you mean by this act of vandalism? You've done as much damage here as any barbarian."

"I mean to prevent that unwholesome creature you've been bedding from working her vile magic on you and your people," Lady Richenda exclaimed, facing him with an unholy fire in her eyes. "So, Emma will help you to exorcise your demons, will she? *She* is the demon!"

"I see," Dain said. Fists planted on his hips, he glared from his mother to Blanche. "Your maidservant reported a private conversation that she overheard while eavesdropping, and you misinterpreted a kindly meant remark, spoken half in jest, to mean something dire and evil."

"It's your wife who's evil," Lady Richenda cried. "Why can't you see what she's doing? She is trying to lure you into caring about her, so you'll give up the feud with Wroxley. Then, when you are weak, she'll strike. She will hand you, and Penruan, over to Lord Gavin."

"You are talking nonsense," Dain told her. "I am sad to have to say this to you, but since you cannot accept my wife, or even ignore her presence at Penruan, perhaps you ought to return to your beloved convent."

"Not just yet." Refusing to back down, Lady Richenda glared at Dain with unabated rage. "I have one last duty to my lord Halard. On his deathbed I gave him my solemn oath I'd see our son victorious in the feud against the lords of Wroxley. And so I will, by whatever means I can find."

"But not today," Dain said. He removed the knife from her fingers and took hold of her arm. "Your work is finished for this day. Come along, Blanche. I'll see you and your mistress to your chamber. Sloan, I want a guard posted outside my mother's door. Neither she nor Blanche is to leave that room without my permission."

"Aye, my lord," Sloan responded. "I'll see to it." After a disgusted look in Lady Richenda's direction, he turned his attention to the ruined garden, shaking his head at its sorry state.

Lady Richenda wasn't ready to depart from the garden. She wrenched her arm out of Dain's grasp and stood defiantly, looking from him to Emma, while she spoke with deliberate malice.

"Did you know, my son," said Lady Richenda, "that your wife's mother was a notable sorceress? And a notorious whore, too. In a packet of messages that arrived here this morning from court there was a letter to me from an old acquaintance of mine. In answer to a note I sent to her weeks ago she provided all the details of the wicked life and scandalous death of Lady Alda of Wroxley. I have no doubt that Alda's daughter is following in her mother's footsteps. It's a well-known fact that magical ability can be inherited."

"Sloan," said Dain, speaking through tight lips, "see that this damage is cleaned up. Call in house servants and men-at-arms if you must. Replant what can be replanted. Father Maynard, if you will kindly come with me, I believe my mother has need of you."

"Dain, we must talk," Emma said, stepping toward him.

"Not now, my lady." Dain's handsome face was every bit as cold and remote as it had been on the day of Emma's unwelcome arrival at Penruan. "I will deal with you later."

"Is my mother's accusation true?" Dain asked that evening. "Was your mother a sorceress?"

"I'm sorry you had to learn it in such an unkind way."

"Answer me." Dain remained on the opposite side of the lord's chamber from Emma, making no move to come closer, no attempt to touch her. "I will hear it from your own lips, and I warn you, my lady, you had better tell me the truth."

"Yes," Emma said, "my mother was born with magical ability. Unfortunately for her, no adult recognized her for what she was, so she grew up unschooled in the methods of controlling such power, until she met an evil man who encouraged her to join his wicked schemes. The two of them planned to take over Wroxley, and they almost succeeded."

"Was this during Baron Udo's time? Did Alda use her magic to help Udo get the disputed land away from my father?"

"So far as I am aware, my mother had no connection with the feud. From all reports she and my grandfather detested each other. She'd have been unlikely to help him in anything."

"I see. Go on. Tell me the rest."

To Emma's surprise, Dain appeared to be perfectly calm. It was more than she'd dared to hope for after he'd been with his mother since mid-afternoon. Still, she saw the steel in him and knew her only chance of maintaining some degree of affection between them lay in telling him all she knew of the old story.

"When Baron Udo learned what Alda was and tried to stop her, she killed him and his seneschal," Emma said. "She left a trail of folk who died by magic or by poison, until her accomplice killed her and then died himself, in a terrible confrontation with my father, who was newly returned from years in the Holy Land. I wasn't living at Wroxley in those days. My brother and I had been sent away for fostering. We were brought home just as my father arrived, too, and he quickly sent us off again, this time to a monastery, to keep us safe till Wroxley was free of evil magic."

"Exactly how did Baron Gavin succeed in freeing Wroxley?" Dain asked.

"With the help of a dear friend, a sage from Cathay who was a powerful wizard," Emma answered, "and of the Lady Mirielle, who later became my stepmother."

"Wroxley would seem to be a veritable den of magic," Dain remarked, his lip curling in distain.

"There is evil magic," Emma told him, "and then

there is magic that's properly controlled, so it can be used for beneficial purposes. Mirielle is a good, kindhearted, loving woman who would never harm anyone."

"So, your mother was a wicked sorceress and your stepmother is a good sorceress."

"Don't say it that way," Emma cried, stung by his sneering tone. "Don't mock Mirielle. She loved me when my mother did not; she taught me everything—"

"Yes?" Dain interrupted. "Everything she knows? Now we come to the crux of the matter, don't we? Are you a sorceress, too?"

"Yes," Emma said, unable in that instant to utter more than the single word. She saw Dain receive the admission like a blow to the heart. She could only pray the truth hadn't destroyed his newfound tenderness for her.

"How cleverly you have concealed your ability," he said, scorn dripping from each word he spoke.

"People with inborn magic learn early in life to conceal their ability for their own safety. Ask Agatha; she is more than just a healer."

"Does Gavin know of your ability? I cannot imagine he does not."

"He knows. And he knows I'll do no harm to any living being. I have spent my life trying not to be like my mother."

"Yet still Gavin sent you to me? To work your spells on me, perhaps? Is that why I've wanted you so often and so passionately?"

"No! I told you when I first came here that I was a substitute bride. I begged my father to send me in place of the younger sister he originally intended for you, who was too ill to travel. Dain, what's between you and me is entirely natural. The only magic I've used since coming to Penruan was to help me see my way through the fog, when I was lost."

"Dare I believe you if you swear as much to me?" He took a single step toward her, the first move he'd made in her direction since entering the lord's chamber.

"I would never hurt you or lie to you," she said. "I am pledged to you by a sacred vow. We are man and wife."

"So was your mother pledged to Gavin, yet apparently her oath meant nothing to her."

"I am not my mother. I am not evil, no more than you are the fierce and bloodthirsty baron you are reported to be."

She was gazing directly into his eyes as she spoke. He placed one fingertip under her chin and lifted her face a little higher still, and to her astonishment she detected a faint smile upon his lips.

"Never say so outside this room," he warned her. "It's my fierce reputation that keeps Penruan safe."

"I would die sooner than do anything to harm you or your people," she said.

"I'd like to believe you."

"I wish you would. Every word I've spoken is true. I've been afraid that when I finally told you, you'd disown me."

"Are you surprised that I haven't done so immediately? It's what my mother advised."

"And you refused her advice? Why?" She hoped he'd say it was because he loved her, not because he was bound to the marriage by the king's command, which was true enough. His explanation left her stunned. He began with what seemed to be an innocuous question.

"Have you ever wondered why my mother is so

opposed to herbal healing, and to the very idea of magic?" he asked.

"I assumed it's because she is so passionately, and rigidly, religious," Emma said.

"That's only part of the reason. In his youth my father took a beautiful first wife, a famous herbal healer, who was also rumored to be a sorceress. He loved Morigaine with his whole heart and soul, and when she died in childbirth my father was devastated. But he needed an heir, so he quickly married my mother and I was born a year later. No one at Penruan ever mentions Morigaine. I know her name only because Agatha told me the story and made me promise never to let my mother know I knew of it.

"I think my mother has always been jealous of the love my father felt for Morigaine, and that's why she has forbidden medicines or magic here at Penruan. I think she has tried to root out all memory of Morigaine. She has succeeded; it's as though the woman never existed."

"Lady Richenda hasn't forgotten her," Emma said. "When she was sick and her thoughts were wandering, she mentioned that first marriage to me, though she included few details."

"When Agatha told me the story she insisted that Morigaine was a good woman, a wise practitioner of her art," Dain said. "Now you tell me your stepmother is the same kind of benevolent sorceress, and you claim that you will use your magic only for good. Yet all my life I've listened to my mother speak of magic with fear and great hatred. What am I to believe?"

"Do you hate me for what you've learned about me?" Emma asked. From the way he was acting, she couldn't guess what his true feelings were. She didn't think he was terribly angry, but she couldn't be certain. For a reason as yet unclear to her, her own thoughts were fixed upon Morigaine.

"I don't know what I feel," Dain said, "or what I'm going to do about you. I need time to think."

"So do I," Emma mumured. "Dain, there is something about Morigaine's story—"

"I won't be sleeping here tonight," he interrupted. "My mother is right about one thing; it's dangerous for me to share a bed with you. I won't be using this room until I've decided whether to return you to Wroxley or hand you over to King Henry and his bishops."

"There is a third choice," she said, beginning to be frightened by the possibility of having to explain herself to clergymen who likely would not be as understanding as Father Maynard or the priest at Wroxley. "You could keep me."

He only shook his head at that suggestion. He gathered up a few items of clothing and then he left her alone, with Todd to guard the door.

The next morning Emma found a large blue bead on Dain's pillow.

"Todd, are you absolutely certain no one entered the lord's chamber last night?"

"My lady, I've told you twice; since Lord Dain left yesterday evening no one has come to this level of the keep."

Emma knew why Todd wasn't quite meeting her eyes. He was embarrassed because Dain hadn't spent the night with her. But someone had gotten into her room while she slept. She believed Todd's insistence that he hadn't fallen asleep. If he had been under a spell for part of the night he wouldn't remember it. He'd think he had been awake the entire time.

"If Lord Dain comes to see me, please tell him I've gone to the beach," she said.

"I'm sorry, my lady, but you may not leave the lord's chamber," Todd said.

"By whose order?"

"Lord Dain's, my lady."

"I see." So, Dain didn't trust her in spite of her reassurances. He probably didn't believe her claim that she'd do no harm to him or to his people. Perhaps his mother had talked to him again, and finally convinced him he'd married an evil wife. In that case, there was just one thing for her to do, one hope of salvaging her marriage and preventing the old feud from blazing up anew with Lady Richenda fueling it with charges of trickery and magic.

"Todd?"

"Yes, my lady?"

"Please look at me when I speak to you."

"I'm not sure I should. Is it true you're a witch?"

"No. I have some magic, but I only use it for good. Have I ever hurt you or anyone else that you know of? Did the syrup I gave you help your cough?"

"It did, but Lady Richenda says—"

Todd made the mistake of looking directly into her eyes, and Emma immediately took advantage of that fact. He would not know he'd been put into a trance during which Emma slipped past him and hurried down the steps. If Dain, or anyone else, came to the door of the lord's chamber and demanded to know where she was, Todd would insist with perfect honesty that he had seen no one going into or out of the room.

Several servants and a few men-at-arms were in the great hall, but Emma hurried past them with only a quick greeting, and they didn't try to stop her. It was still early, and everyone was busy with morning chores. She guessed that Dain hadn't told anyone except Todd that she wasn't to be out of her room.

She expected the men-at-arms who guarded the castle gate to be more alert than the men and women in the hall, so she placed three of them under spells similar to the one she had used on Todd. All of them would waken unharmed after just a few minutes, and none of them would recall her exit. Once she was over the drawbridge it wouldn't matter who saw her.

She ran to the path leading down the face of the cliffs to the beach and made her way to the sand below as quickly as she could without falling off the narrow trail.

The tide was in and seawater washed around the rocks dividing Penruan beach from the beach where Hermit's cave was. Emma pulled off her shoes and stockings and bundled them into her skirt, tying her belt tighter to secure the bundle. Holding her skirt up high, she began to wade through the water. She thought she heard a shout from behind her, but she was too busy trying to avoid being knocked off her feet by the surging waves to pay attention.

She almost didn't make it. A huge wave broke over her head, soaking her and threatening to pull her out to sea as it ebbed. She gasped and struggled shoreward.

"Dear girl, what are you trying to do?" Hermit caught her around the waist with his good left arm and dragged her out of the surf onto dry sand. "Emma, in the name of heaven, how could you be so reckless? What's in your skirt?"

"My shoes," she answered, sputtering from the saltwater she'd swallowed.

"They'll be as sodden as the rest of you." Hermit took the dripping shoes she pulled from her bedraggled skirt and, still with a supporting arm around her, led her toward the cave entrance. "Come along, child. There's a fire burning inside. I was searching for shellfish on the rocks and caught you, instead."

"You are using your right hand," she exclaimed.

"It's much improved." He held up her shoes so she could see how easily he carried them. "What are you doing out of the castle on a chill and misty day?"

"I need to see Agatha and thought she might be with you," Emma said. "If she's not here, I'll walk to Trevanan village along the beach."

"You'll go nowhere with the sea as wild as it is," Hermit told her. "There must be a dreadful storm beyond the horizon and we're feeling the edges of it. Squeeze through the opening now, and I'll see you warm and dry before I send you home."

"I can't go home until I've talked with Agatha." But she did as he ordered and slid through the narrow entrance and followed him to the inner chamber of the cave.

"Take off your clothes and wrap up in my cloak," Hermit said, picking up the garment from his pile of belongings and offering it to her.

"It will take hours for this woolen gown to dry at a peat fire," she objected.

"Perhaps you won't have to remove the dress after all," Hermit said. He shook his head at her as if she were a heedless child. "My dear, you ought to have complained about my suggestion that you undress."

"The thought didn't occur to me. I trust you. I know you'd never hurt me."

"Oh, Emma." Hermit's eyes were suddenly bright, as if they were filled with unshed tears. "Do you find me trustworthy? There's an honor I never dreamed of earning, and I thank you for it. All the same, I am going to provide you with a chaperone.

"Vivienne!" Hermit called, raising his voice. "Come out. Emma has come to visit and she needs your help again."

"Vivienne is here?" Emma turned in the direction Hermit was looking. At first she saw only the solid stone of the cave wall. Then Vivienne walked through the stone as if she was entering a room through an open doorway.

"How wonderful!" Emma exclaimed. "Vivienne, have you a special affinity for rocks? The one you hid behind up on the moor was created by magic, wasn't it?"

"Stones, and certain other objects," Vivienne said. "Why are you wet?"

"She tried to walk through the sea." Hermit responded to the question with exasirated impatience. "Vivienne, I beseech you, dry the foolish girl before she catches a bad chill."

"Of course." Vivienne moved her hands in a gesture that was familiar to Emma. In an instant Emma was dry and her hands and feet, which had been chilled by the cold sea, were warm again.

"I should have thought of doing that myself," Emma said ruefully.

"So you would have done, if Hermit hadn't been fluttering over you like a mother hen," Vivienne said. "Now that you are more comfortable, I shall scold you for risking your life on the moor the other day, and then again, just now, in the sea. You must

248

take better care of yourself. You are needed, Emma."

"Indeed, you are," said Hermit.

Emma was watching Vivienne, noting changes in the mysterious lady. Vivienne was wearing her usual flowing white garments, with the turquoise and silver pendant hanging upon her bosom and her auburn hair waving loose around her shoulders, yet to Emma's eyes she did not seem as distant and unearthly as in her previous appearances, and her voice, though low and soft, was no longer a whisper.

"You are drawing nearer," Emma said to her. "You are more substantial now."

"The time approaches," Vivienne responded.

"The time for what?"

"For an end to disguise," Vivienne said.

"For justice," Hermit interjected abruptly, his deep masculine voice severing the delicate linking thread that Emma and Vivienne were beginning to spin between them.

Emma felt a spurt of irritation when the thread broke; Vivienne only smiled.

"Tell me why you are here," Vivienne said to her.

"I came to the beach looking for Agatha, hoping she'd know where to find you," Emma said. There was a pocket sewn into the fabric belt that encircled her waist. Emma dug into the pocket and drew forth the blue bead she had tucked there for safekeeping. "This is the latest in a series of objects I have found on Dain's pillow. The guard outside my door insists no one entered the room all night, and I accept his word, for I think it's likely he was entranced. Did you leave this on the pillow?" She held out the blue bead for Vivienne to see.

"The gifts are meant for Dain," Vivienne said.

Before Emma could ask why Vivienne should be giving presents to Dain they heard voices in the outer chamber of the cave.

"That's Dain now," Emma said, clearing her thoughts and preparing herself to perform magic. "Agatha is with him."

Emma was poised to act, so the instant Vivienne made a movement to flee Emma caught her, holding her by magic, forcing her to remain where she was.

"Please don't," Vivienne cried, fighting magic with magic. "It means his death."

"Whose death?" Emma demanded. "What are you saying?"

"Dain may not look upon my face. It is forbidden. If you love him, and I'm certain you do, release me at once."

"Dain will die if he sees you?"

For the duration of a single heartbeat Emma's power faltered at the thought of Dain's death, and Vivienne broke away from her. In the next moment Vivienne rushed into the rock and vanished, just as Dain and Agatha arrived.

"Who was that?" Dain exclaimed, staring at the rock. "What did I just see?"

"It was Vivienne," Emma told him. "I wanted her to stay and meet you, but she claimed seeing her would mean your death."

"What are you doing here?" Dain glared at her, his face and eyes cold with fury. "Two days ago you promised never to run away from me again, yet you vanished from the castle. I can guess how you got past Todd. You used magic to circumvent my wishes and to break a promise I trusted. I will have an explanation from you."

"Aren't you afraid she'll use magic on you?" asked

Hermit. "Emma could turn you into a crab and eat you for supper if she wanted."

"I'll soon learn what you have to do with the mysteries that bedevil me," Dain said to him. "In the meantime, since I have suffered you to live on my land, I'll thank you to avoid making useless threats. There is no reason for me to fear Emma. She will not harm me."

"But I may, if you break her heart," Hermit said, very quietly.

"Who the devil are you, to threaten me?" Dain shouted at him.

"I have made no threat, my lord. I have merely offered a promise, which I will keep."

"Please, stop arguing," Emma cried, stepping between them. She held out her hand to show Dain the blue bead. "This is the latest gift, found on your pillow this morning, though Todd insists, and honestly so, that he saw no one enter or leave the lord's chamber. If you are looking for magic, my lord, here it is.

"I have not broken my promise to you, for I haven't run away. I came to the beach in search of a solution to this mystery, and believing either Agatha or Vivienne could provide the answers I want. Vivienne admits to being the one leaving the gifts. She says they were intended for you, and she was about to tell me why she would give you presents when she heard your voice and left." Emma wasn't sure Dain had heard all of her speech, for he was staring at the bead that lay on her palm as if he was transfixed by the sight of it.

"I had a bead like it once," Dain said, and began rubbing his forehead as he had done when Emma first mentioned Vivienne's name to him. "My mother took it away from me. It's part of what I can't remember." He fell silent, still gazing at the bead.

"Agatha," Emma said to the elderly healer, who had stood quietly at one side of the chamber since entering it, "what do you know about this?"

"Tell them," Hermit said. "It's time, Agatha. You know it is."

Agatha said nothing aloud; she merely made a gesture in Dain's direction, a gesture that Emma recognized as magical. Dain began to speak in an oddly slurred voice, as if he were half asleep.

"She gave it to me so I wouldn't forget her," Dain said. "Before she left Penruan she crept into my room and kissed me and put it into my hand. I can see her folding my little fingers around it and telling me she wouldn't forget me, either. 'I will love you always,' she said. Emma, help me! Am I mad?"

"No." Emma put the bead into Dain's hand and folded his large, adult fingers over it. Then she wrapped her arms around him and held him tight. "Not mad, Dain. Not you. But you have been held in a spell."

"What else do you remember?" Agatha asked him.

"My mother snatching the bead away from me, scolding me for having it, slapping my hand until my fingers were red and aching, telling me over and over that it was an evil object," Dain said, his voice growing steadily clearer as he spoke. "It wasn't evil, it was a gift. The last gift—ah! My head!" He pulled away from Emma's embrace, both hands at his head. The blue bead fell onto the sand and Hermit picked it up.

"It's his memory returning," Agatha said. "I have released the spell."

"Take his pain away now!" Emma shouted at her.

"Then I insist you tell us what you've done to him, and tell us who Vivienne is."

"Let magic undo what evil has wrought," Agatha proclaimed in a deep, sonorous voice. Drawing herself up to her full height, and then up again until she was at least a foot taller than the old healer, she reached out to touch Dain's forehead.

Dain's hands dropped to his sides. He took a deep breath and opened his eyes.

"Emma," he whispered, "the pain is gone. I knew you'd help me."

"Now Agatha is going to help you," Emma said. "Agatha is going to explain why she has held you under a spell for more than twenty years. I intend to see to it that you remember everything Agatha made you forget."

Chapter Fourteen

"A spell?" Dain said. "Agatha, why would you do such a thing? I've always considered you my friend."

"So I am," Agatha said. "The spell was an act of kindness, intended to protect you and to save Vivienne's life. Dain, there is a danger if I allow you to recover all of your lost memories. Are you willing to take the risk? I warn you, it won't be the danger you expect to find. Arms and armor will be of no use to you. The knowledge you gain will permanently alter your life."

"For years I have been pretending to myself that the emptiness inside me didn't exist," Dain said. "Most of the time it was easy enough to ignore, because no one ever spoke the strange woman's name. So far as I can tell, no one at Penruan, or in Trevanan village, even knows what the name is. Not until Emma learned it and spoke it aloud to me did the torment in my mind begin in earnest, and it has plagued me ever since. I must have answers! Agatha, if you are my friend as you claim, then break the spell and give me back my lost memories. Or teach Emma how to do it."

"It's you who hold the power to end the spell," Agatha said.

"I? There's no magic in me."

"We shall see." Agatha gestured, and the surface of the rock through which Vivienne had disappeared began to waver.

Dain blinked and shook his head, as if trying to clear his vision. Emma took his hand and stepped forward, drawing him with her to the rock. Though he was plainly puzzled, he didn't resist.

"Don't fight us, Vivienne," Hermit called. "Let us in. The time has come."

"Vivienne!" Agatha no longer spoke with the voice of an elderly woman. Her clear, commanding tones rang through the cave. "The time for fear has passed! Your exile is about to end."

A section of the rock wall suddenly vanished, revealing an arched opening. Still holding Dain's hand, Emma walked through the arch and into the room beyond. Above a smooth rock floor the walls and the high ceiling shimmered and sparkled with multicolored embedded crystals. From halfway up one wall a spring burst forth, its water falling with a soft, trickling sound into a depression at the base of the rock.

Vivienne's couch was covered in sea green silk. A clothing chest stood to one side. On a polished stone table lay a book bound in purple leather which, from the gold letters on its cover, Emma recognized as a treatise on magic. Beside the book a silver pitcher held a few moorland flowers. There was a chair pulled up to the table. A bowl and a cup sat upon a narrow rock shelf. Those were all the furnishings, yet the room gave the appearance of being a true home. The air was warm and fresh, faintly scented by the flowers, and daylight shone through a fissure high above.

Vivienne was nowhere to be seen.

"Come out at once!" Agatha ordered, and uttered a string of words that made Emma stare at her in disbelief.

"How can you know that ancient language?" Emma cried. "I read those words once and was warned never to speak them aloud. They are the property of—unless you are—?"

"Haven't you guessed by now?" Agatha said, grinning at her.

"What is it?" Dain asked. "What's wrong?" He broke off suddenly, and an incredulous expression spread over his face. Clenching Emma's hand, he stood perfectly still, gaping as the figure of a woman emerged from the crystal-studded rock wall. She stepped right through the falling water and into the room without a drop of moisture clinging to her.

"*He* made me return," Vivienne said.

"Of course he did," Agatha responded. "*He* knows what's best for you. As you see, the spell is almost completely broken. Dain looks upon you and lives."

"Dain." Vivienne moved toward him, her white robes floating about her as if touched by a breeze none of the others could feel. She lifted a slender hand to stroke his face, then stood immobilized, her hand inches from Dain's cheek, while tears streamed down her face. "Oh, my dear. I have waited so long."

"I should know you," Dain said, his brows drawn together in concentration. "I should remember."

"Greet your sister," Agatha said to him.

"I have no sister." Dain tore his gaze from Vivienne to look imploringly at Agatha, and then at Emma, seeking an explanation.

"Speak her name aloud and you will remember," Agatha instructed. "It's the last step in breaking the spell."

"*Viv-Vivienne.*" Dain obeyed Agatha's instruction, uttering the word with a gasp. Emma thought he would crush her hand, so tightly did he hold it. "Vivienne," he said again, sounding as if he could not quite believe the sound of his own voice.

"I feared you'd never remember me," Vivienne said.

"Nonsense," Agatha told her. "You always knew there would come a time for revelation. Now you are both free."

"Not yet," Dain said, in a way that told Emma he was far from satisfied with the working of Agatha's magic. "I am owed a fuller accounting than just, 'the spell is broken,' and I refuse to leave this cave until I receive it. Where are the memories I was promised? I do believe in my heart that Vivienne is my sister, but I know nothing else about her."

"Let us go to the outer chamber," Vivienne suggested, "where he will not follow us."

"He cannot pursue," Agatha said to her, "as you very well know. Not for centuries will he be released."

"Who is he?" asked Dain.

"The one who lives in there," Agatha answered, indicating something behind the glittering wall and the tiny waterfall.

"Those words you spoke in an unknowable tongue that I barely recognized," Emma exclaimed, realization flooding her mind.

"Speak not the name," Agatha hastily advised, hand raised in the beginning of a magical gesture that would prevent Emma from saying more than she should. "Names contain powerful magic, as we have just seen. Vivienne, is there anything you want to take from your old home?"

"Everything I have ever wanted is here with me now," Vivienne replied, her eyes on Dain as if she were making up for all the years when she could see him only from afar. She spared not a single backward glance for the inner chamber.

Emma walked beside Dain through the arch to the outer chamber. She did look back, in wonder and faint apprehension, toward the place hidden deep within the rock, where the greatest magician the world had ever known lay imprisoned until the time was right for him to be released. Then Agatha gestured, and the open arch vanished, and Emma knew it would remain closed for centuries to come.

"Now," said Agatha, moving toward Hermit's peat fire with the smooth stride of a young woman, "let us have a bit more light and warmth, and I will answer all your questions, save for the ones infringing upon the secrets of magic, which I am not permitted to answer." At a motion of her hand the fire blazed high, as if it were fueled by dry wood.

They all sat on the sand, with Dain between Vivienne and Emma, and Agatha facing them across the fire. Seen through the leaping flames, Agatha's face was alternately that of the elderly healer who was familiar to Emma and the visage of a younger woman of unearthly beauty. Dain did not appear to notice the continuing transformations; but then, he was seeking within his own mind for his lost memories. As for Vivienne and Hermit, they did not remark on the changes in Agatha, a fact that made

Emma suspect they had observed something similar in the recent past.

"Begin," Dain commanded Agatha, "by telling me what happened during the time I still cannot entirely remember."

"I will begin before then," Agatha said, "and Vivienne will add to the story as she thinks fit. Dain, you know already of your father's first marriage, to the lady Morigaine."

"Yes." Dain nodded. "You told me once that she died in childbirth."

"Bearing her second child to Halard," Vivienne said. "I was their first child. I was four years old when my mother died, and her just-born son with her."

"Until this hour, I did not know of your existence," Dain said to her.

"I made you forget," Agatha told him. "Listen, now, and hear the rest of the tale. You already know how Lord Halard wed Lady Richenda less than a year after Morigaine's death, and how you were born barely a year after that second marriage. You have been told often enough of your father's attempt to wrest a disputed patch of land away from Udo of Wroxley, and of the terrible wound Halard sustained during the battle."

"And died of the wound nearly five years later," Vivienne added, "when I was barely ten years old."

"I was five when my father died," Dain said to her. "That's old enough for a child to recall his own sister, yet I have no memory of you except for the moment when you gave me the blue bead."

"I am coming to the reason why your memory is lacking," Agatha told them. "Vivienne inherited her mother's magical ability. You know how Lady Richenda feels about magic."

259

"She is a bitterly jealous woman," Hermit put in, "and Halard dearly loved his daughter. But I doubt if he loved his second wife. He'd had his great love in Morigaine, you see, and lost her, and possibly blamed himself for the loss. Men sometimes do blame themselves when a wife dies in childbirth. Still, he needed an heir, so he married again as soon as he could arrange it, and it's likely he respected Richenda well enough."

Vivienne was weeping quietly. Dain reached over and laid his hand on top of hers.

"As soon as Halard was buried and the funeral guests had departed," Agatha continued the story, "Lady Richenda ordered Vivienne to leave Penruan."

"And go where?" Dain asked.

"She told me she cared not," Vivienne said, holding onto his hand with both of hers. "She said, 'Onto the moor, into the sea, wherever you like, but never come near Penruan again.' "

"You were only ten years old!" Dain exclaimed. "How could anyone be so cruel to a child?"

"Jealousy incites cruelty," said Hermit. "The two are close partners."

"I was at Penruan for the funeral," Agatha said, "for I liked and respected Lord Halard, and he had always accepted my close friendship with Morigaine. After the other guests left I stayed on, because I suspected Lady Richenda of preparing some devious scheme to cause harm to the stepdaughter she hated. I saw Vivienne run down the stairs from the lord's chamber to the great hall with Lady Richenda behind her, shooing her along as if the girl were of no more consequence than an errant chick that has wandered into a garden and started to peck up the seeds.

"Vivienne was crying so hard she ran right into me without seeing me. I hushed her and hid her behind my skirt, and waited for what I feared would come next. What I expected did happen. Lady Richenda spoke to a man named Wade, whom she had brought to Penruan from her father's house, who was bound to her service, and I guessed what murderous order she was giving him.

"It was then I struck my bargain with Lady Richenda. It was no secret how she detested me, though while Halard lived she could do nothing to rid herself of my occasional presence at the castle, any more than she dared rid herself of Halard's daughter while he lived. I offered to take Vivienne with me when I left and find a home for her far from Penruan, so Lady Richenda could avoid bearing the sin of murder on her conscience.

"Vivienne slipped away from me while we talked. That was when she went to Dain, to say her farewell and give him the blue bead. The next thing I knew, Vivienne was hurrying back down the steps and Dain was following her, crying to his sister to come back as if his heart was broken, for she was his dearest companion. I could see Lady Richenda wasn't going to accept my offer, not with Dain wailing and trying to reach Vivienne, and Lady Richenda's newly commissioned murderer holding the girl by one arm to keep her away from him. That dreadful woman was half mad with jealousy of the love those two young ones bore to each other, so I took advantage of her fury. I told her I'd remove Dain's memories of his sister so he'd cease to pine for her, and I'd place a spell on the entire castle, so no one else there would remember Vivienne either. Furthermore, I promised to teach Vivienne that Dain would die if ever they met face-to-face.

"Lady Richenda's own memory I refused to erase. She has remembered every single day for a quarter of a century what she did to Vivienne, and to Dain. It was the best punishment I could conjure on such short notice. At the time it seemed to me far more important to use my power to protect those two helpless children. Lady Richenda finally agreed, and I have kept my promises to her. Since that day she and I have not spoken. We have passed each other a few times when I was at the castle. She always looks the other way, as if not facing me keeps her pure of the taint of magic. But she knows her own guilt, and neither all her prayers nor the masses she orders said as soon as I have gone can cleanse her of the harm she's done to an innocent brother and sister."

"That must be why she hated to know I visited you," Dain said. "She always punished me when she found out."

"What your mother has never understood," Agatha said, "is the working of the human heart. Vivienne remembered you, Dain. I could not take her cherished memories away from her; doing so would have broken her heart and likely would have killed her. To convince her not to use her own magic to overcome my promise to Lady Richenda that she'd never see you, I was forced to swear to Vivienne that one day I'd bring the two of you together again and restore your memory. The moment I met Emma, I knew I had found my agent. There was no need to place any spell on her; all I had to do was make certain she saw Vivienne from time to time and let Emma's natural curiosity do its work."

"What of you, Hermit?" Dain asked. "What part have you played in Agatha's clever scheme? I am sure she used you as she has used Emma."

"No wicked part," Hermit said. "I came to this cave with a badly maimed arm and fully convinced my soul was in peril. I sought only a peaceful place in which to die. Agatha and Vivienne between them have treated my arm till it's almost completely restored. Vivienne's willingness to listen to the story of my long wanderings has helped to heal a heart that was originally in worse condition than my arm. No man could ask for two more faithful friends."

Vivienne made a strangled little sound and turned her face away from Hermit. He did not appear to notice, but Emma did, and understood Vivienne's distress as only another woman could. Emma began to wonder exactly what Hermit's story was.

"Can you honestly tell me you knew nothing about all of this?" Dain said to her, his sudden question jerking her out of contemplation of Hermit's association with Vivienne.

"Nothing," Emma said. "Looking back now, I can see there were hints offered to me, but at first I was so concerned with hiding my magical ability from you, and then later, with trying to find the right time to tell you the secret, and worrying whether you'd hate me when you learned of it, that I missed every lure Agatha cast in my direction."

"I don't hate you," Dain said, going directly to the heart of her fears. "How could I, when there's magic in my own family?"

"Not in your bloodline," Vivienne corrected him.

"Close enough." Dain smiled at his sister before returning to his wife. "Emma, I wish you had not kept your magic secret from me, though I do understand why you felt it was necessary, and perhaps you were right to fear I'd reject you if you revealed the truth to me at our first meeting. You and I will deal later with our differences on the subject. At the moment, there's a more urgent matter to settle. I intend to confront my mother. Will you come with me?"

"Of course I will." Emma was on her feet as soon as Dain stood up.

"Vivienne," Dain said, reaching down to help his sister stand, "I do have a last question for you to answer. Why did you leave those gifts for me?"

"I used to give you similar tokens when we were children, so I foolishly hoped they'd remind you of me," she said, "though Agatha warned that your memory of me was blocked so long as the spell endured. But I grew impatient and refused to wait any longer. Knowing Emma possesses magical skills, I trusted her to solve the mystery and reveal to you a truth you could not recall. Which she did, when she first spoke my name aloud to you. It's why I told her my name. The last gift, the large bead, is very similar to my parting gift to you so many years ago."

"Nothing can bring back the years we've lost," Dain said, "but restitution will be made. You will have justice, Vivienne. I'll see to it. Agatha, you will come with us." It wasn't a request.

"You needn't order me, Dain," Agatha said. "I've been waiting years for this day to arrive."

"Hermit, will you come, too?" Dain asked.

"I'd just as soon stay here," Hermit said. "I've no real taste for battles."

"Please?" Vivienne asked, and turned her soft gray eyes on him.

"On the other hand," Hermit said, standing to join her, "I'd like to see this through to the end, and I have never met the notorious Lady Richenda. Lead on, my lord Dain, and I will follow."

* * *

The tide was just beginning to ebb and the sea still washed over the rocks. Agatha and Vivienne simply walked through the water, emerging perfectly dry on Penruan beach. Emma was about to follow them when Dain scooped her into his arms and carried her around the rocks.

Emma didn't protest. She was content to wrap her arms about his broad shoulders and lay her cheek against his. For a few minutes she rejoiced in the warmth and strength of Dain's vigorous manhood, and dared to hope they could resolve all problems and banish all demons together, as they had promised each other just a few days earlier.

Behind them, Hermit splashed through the waves, grinning with the mischievous look of a little boy tramping his way through mud puddles, until he reached the dry sand. Then his scarred and bearded face assumed a grim expression.

"The look in your eyes," Emma said to him when Dain had set her on her own feet again, "tells me that you are ready to do battle for Vivienne's sake."

"Not for Vivienne only," Hermit responded. "I owe a debt to you, too."

"Come on, then," Dain ordered, speaking as if Hermit were one of his men-at-arms. "We'll use our wits first, and trust we won't have to resort to swords."

"I haven't handled a sword for years," Hermit told him, "but I still remember how, and I'll have no qualms about using one to defend our ladies."

"Good man." Dain clapped Hermit on the shoulder. "I don't expect to have to use cold steel against my mother, but when dealing with her, it's always best to be well prepared."

With Dain and Hermit in the lead they hastened

up the steep and narrow path to the top of the cliff and set out for Penruan Castle. The sentries on the battlements leaned over the edge to stare at the lord of the castle and at the shabbily dressed man in a flat-brimmed pilgrim's hat, who were escorting across the drawbridge the lady of the castle, the elderly healer whom most of them knew, and the mysterious lady in white who was commonly assumed to be a ghost.

So firm was Dain's control of his men that no one objected to the peculiar procession and no questions were asked, not even when they crossed the bailey, mounted the stairs, and entered the great hall. However, there were plenty of wondering looks. When Sloan saw them he set down his mug of ale rather abruptly on the trestle table. Todd sent a reproachful glance in Emma's direction. Hawise rushed to Emma's side, and Blake came with her.

"Where is Lady Richenda?" Dain asked of Sloan.

"In her chamber, my lord, where you ordered her confined," Sloan answered.

"You and Todd go to her and bring her to the hall, along with Blanche," Dain commanded. "What I have to say to my mother must be public knowledge. I will not have rumors making the rounds. This is a day for open truth."

Chapter Fifteen

Lady Richenda began her descent of the stairs with a confident air, as if she believed she had triumphed over her despised opponent. Blanche would have told her by now how Emma had escaped from the lord's chamber by magical means, and Emma could gather from the expressions passing over her stern face what her thoughts must be. With undisguised contempt Lady Richenda regarded Emma standing below in the hall with her hair pulling out of its braid and her shoes and the hem of her skirt soggy from sand and seawater. Obviously, the runaway wife had returned repentant to her husband's castle, to be chastised and placed in confinement again, with Lady Richenda in charge of her.

Watching her mother-in-law, Emma saw with the clarity of new knowledge the conclusions Lady Richenda was drawing, and she marveled at the way in which that pitiful soul could deceive herself as well as others.

Then Lady Richenda spied Agatha and halted her progress down the steps.

"How dare you bring that loathsome creature into my home?" Lady Richenda demanded of Dain. "And who are these other two disreputable beings? If they are friends of Agatha, or of Emma, I'll not allow them to stay. Remove them, Dain, and then I will speak with you, but not before."

She turned to remount the steps only to find Sloan and Todd standing squarely behind her, blocking her way. Blanche was stopped a few steps higher, from where she could do nothing to aid her mistress.

"Out of my way!" Lady Richenda ordered the two men.

Neither man moved.

"Come down, Lady Richenda," Dain said in a terrible voice. "I have something to say to you."

"I will not listen if you intend to speak to me in that tone," Lady Richenda responded.

"You will like my tone even less after I have finished with you," Dain said, his face and voice as chill as winter's frost. "Will you come into the hall on your own feet, or shall I order Sloan and Todd to carry you in?"

Lady Richenda lifted her chin a notch higher and walked with silent dignity down the last few steps. She acted as if she was completely oblivious to the servants and men-at-arms who were slipping into the hall by way of the main entry or the screened passage, drawn there by the hastily passed word of mouth that hinted of something important about to happen. Even Father Maynard appeared from the chapel, alerted by the murmurings of servants that he might be needed before long.

"What is this about?" Lady Richenda asked of her son.

"I have guests to present to you," Dain said. "First, Agatha the healer, to whom you have not spoken for many years, not since the day when you made a certain malicious bargain with her."

Lady Richenda did not respond to the provocative statement. She merely set her mouth in a stubborn, unattractive line and glared at Agatha. Only when she let her gaze move onto Hermit and then to Vivienne did she begin to lose her composure. She appeared startled by her first clear look at the strangers. Next she seemed puzzled and, finally, bewildered.

"Allow me to present our other guests," said Dain. "First Hermit, a kind and valiant friend."

"A man cannot be both valiant and kind," Lady Richenda snapped haughtily.

"Your son is," Hermit told her.

"I never taught him kindness," Lady Richenda said.

"Of that I am absolutely certain," Hermit responded, smiling a little when Lady Richenda disdained to place her hand into the one he politely extended.

"Here is our most important guest," Dain said, "though *guest* is not the correct word for her, since she rightfully belongs here." He drew the lady in white forward with an arm around her waist.

Vivienne moved gracefully, her robes floating about her in the invisible breeze that always seemed to surround her, and the air around her smelled of sunshine and the sea and of newly picked blossoms. A murmur arose from the onlookers, many of whom had seen the lady as she haunted the moor and the cliffs.

"This," said Dain to his mother, raising his voice so all could hear, "is Lady Vivienne, my sister, child of my father's first marriage, whom you banished from Penruan as soon as my father died."

Lady Richenda went as white as Vivienne's robes, her face absolutely bloodless. Emma expected her to swoon at the sudden appearance of the girl who she must have believed was long dead by now. Lady Richenda did not faint. Instead, she drew herself up and turned her cold, blue-green gaze on her son.

"This is a foul trick, perpetrated by that wicked healer, Agatha," Lady Richenda said. "No doubt she was assisted by your equally wicked wife. Dain, you have no sister."

"What I have," he said, taking a threatening step toward her, "is my memory of Vivienne during my earliest life, years too long forgotten and restored to me only today. How could you abandon the daughter of the baron of Penruan? You have always claimed to honor and respect Halard as your lord and master, yet you ordered the murder of his legitimate child, and it would have been done as you commanded were it not for Agatha, who took Vivienne away from here."

"My lady, is this terrible accusation true?" Father Maynard cried, hurrying to join the group facing Lady Richenda.

"It is true," Agatha declared.

"You have broken our agreement," Lady Richenda told her.

"An agreement made in haste and desperation," Agatha said, "to keep two innocent children out of harm's way. Tell me, Father Maynard, do you find any evil in what I did?"

"You used magic!" Lady Richenda cried, fists clenched in helpless fury.

"I saved Vivienne's life!" Agatha responded with equal passion.

"Lady Richenda," Father Maynard said, "it has long been clear to me that, while you rigidly observe the outward forms of faith, you lack the gentle and loving heart that ought to lie at the foundation of our religion. There are many ancient customs still alive in this land. I, myself, have felt their power on several occasions. So long as that power is used for good and not evil, as it is used in the healing arts, I do believe we ought to live peaceably, side by side with it. We have no right to take the comfort the old customs offer away from the souls we are tending."

"You are a poor example of a priest," Lady Richenda exclaimed.

"And you, my lady, are a remarkably poor example of a Christian," Father Mayard told her with an asperity most unusual for him. "Consider yourself fortunate if you are not formally charged with conspiring to murder a noblewoman. As your spiritual adviser, I suggest you make a full and prompt confession and accept whatever penance is laid upon you. If you would rather not confess to me, knowing my sentiments on this matter, then perhaps you will find a more accommodating priest at the convent where your sister resides."

"I thank you, Father Maynard," Dain said. "You have just suggested an excellent solution to a problem that has been sorely vexing me since I first learned of this lady's wicked scheming. I will not have a would-be murderer living in my home, even though she is my mother."

"Dain," Vivienne said, laying a hand on his arm,

271

"don't send Lady Richenda away. I know how painful it is to be forced to leave one's home. What she did was done out of love for you."

"A jealous, spiteful love," Dain said, "that led to an evil plan."

"I think she feared I would corrupt you with my magic."

"More likely, she feared I would love you better than I loved her. Do you honestly believe that, if I permit her to remain at Penruan, she will not try again to kill you?"

"I am older now, no longer a child, and in full control of my power," Vivienne said. "She cannot harm me."

"If Lady Richenda is left free and unpunished," Agatha spoke up, "she will do everything she can to cause trouble for you, Vivienne, and she'll try her worst to ruin Dain's marriage. She'll try to reopen the old feud, too."

"Ah, yes, the feud," Dain said. "That issue must still be resolved. Blanche, take as many servants as you require and pack up Lady Richenda's belongings—all of them! Todd, order horses saddled, and you'll need a cart or two for the baggage. Sloan will choose a dozen men-at-arms for you to lead as you escort Lady Richenda to Tawton Abbey, to pay a permanent visit to her sister, the abbess. She will be leaving Penruan before sunset. Father Maynard, will you be good enough to write a letter to the abbess, explaining Lady Richenda's sudden decision to devote the remainder of her years to prayer and penance? When it is finished, I will have you read it to me before I personally seal it, for Todd to deliver."

"You cannot do this to me," Lady Richenda said to Dain.

"Why not?" he asked, displaying no sign of warmth or affection, or even regret, toward her. "Would you prefer to spend the rest of your life in the castle dungeon? It's what you deserve, after the way you treated Vivienne, and me, too. And can you imagine that anyone here at Penruan or on the rest of my lands, having heard the tale of your perfidy, would be willing to serve you, ever again? You know how gossip travels. Everyone in Trevanan will be aware of your cruelty before this day is done."

"I did it all for you," Lady Richenda cried.

"You did it to maintain your own authority," Dain said. "With my father dead, you were full mistress of Penruan until I came of age. Even then, you continued to rule my household, and I treated you with respect because you are my mother, though often I disagreed with you.

"There is just one more thing you can do for me," Dain continued, "since you claim to have my welfare always at heart. Tell me everything you know about the feud between Halard and Udo."

"I have already told you, over and over, for years," Lady Richenda said. "Udo tricked and cheated Halard out of land that should have been his. Before Halard died of the wound Udo inflicted, I swore to him I'd see you victorious over Udo's heirs."

"Yet you did nothing to carry out your promise until this past year," Dain said. "Why did you nag at me to reopen the feud now? Why not sooner?"

"You'll get no more from me," she said. "I will tell you nothing, not so long as you harbor two sorceresses in my home."

"It is your home no longer. I bid you farewell." Dain turned his back on her and stalked away. He did not call her *mother*, or even *my lady*.

Emma saw the look of outrage that Lady Richenda cast at Dain's back, and the way her mother-in-law glared at Vivienne, and then at her, and she felt a dreadful premonition that Lady Richenda wasn't finished with them yet.

"I'll be going now," Agatha said as soon as the midday feast was over. "I have neglected my work of late. There are herbs to be gathered and medicines to be made before winter comes."

"I'll go with you," said Hermit, rising from his place at the high table, where they were all sitting.

"Surely you can stay longer." Vivienne's appeal was made to both of her friends, but Emma could see it was Hermit she wanted to keep nearby.

"You are welcome here," Dain said to Agatha.

"I know it," she responded with a smile, "and I'll return soon, I promise. There is much for me to discuss with Emma, and with Vivienne."

"Hermit, will you come again when Agatha does?" Vivienne asked, regarding him wistfully.

"Perhaps," Hermit responded rather abruptly. "Then again, I ought to be on my way. I can't live in that cave forever."

"Please don't go," Emma begged, having noticed the way tears were filling Vivienne's eyes. "Don't leave Penruan, or your friends."

"I won't leave until you—and Vivienne—are settled and happy," Hermit said. "You have my word on it."

With that rather vague promise both women were forced to be content, and Agatha and Hermit departed soon after.

"Dain," Emma said, "you and Vivienne will need time to learn to know each other again. Take her to the lord's chamber, where no one will disturb you and you may talk together without curious stares. I have plenty of chores to keep me occupied for a while, so I won't interrupt you."

"How good you are to me," Vivienne cried, and embraced Emma with a warmth that touched her deeply.

"Thank you for your thoughtfulness," Dain said with somewhat strained politeness.

Emma saw brother and sister off to their private conversation, and then attempted to immerse herself in the chatelaine's duties that now fell to her, with Lady Richenda departed. An hour or so later, while she was supervising the cleaning and preparation of the bedchamber Vivienne had once occupied as a girl, and where she declared she would prefer to sleep over any other room in the castle, Blake appeared, bringing with him a faint odor of the stables.

"I thought you should know," Blake said, "that shortly before Lady Richenda left, she sent a messenger riding off on an errand. I was in the bailey, helping to load up the carts, and I saw him saddle up and leave. When I asked where he was going he cuffed me so hard my ears rang and said the letter he carried was none of my business."

"Perhaps Lady Richenda was sending word to inform her sister she'd soon be arriving at the convent," Emma suggested, wishing she could permanently dismiss Lady Richenda from her thoughts. It wasn't likely. Dain's mother had ruled the domestic side of the castle with a stern hand, and Emma was once again encountering resistance to any alteration in long-established habits.

"I don't think so," Blake said in response to her comment. "I noticed how full Wade's saddlebags were, so as soon as I had a chance I checked his cot in the servants' quarters. All of his belongings are gone. I told Sloan, and he said good riddance. He doesn't like Wade. Not many people do. Wade isn't very friendly, and he often makes excuses not to do his share of work. But he was always ready to jump to do anything Lady Richenda asked of him."

"Did you say Wade?" Emma repeated the man's name, thinking how glad she was that Dain had taken Vivienne off to become reacquainted with her in private. Vivienne needed no reminding of Lady Richenda's manservant, who had been willing to murder a child at his mistress's command.

"You know him," Blake said. "He's the scrawny, gray-haired man who looks sour and seldom speaks. Maybe Sloan is right; maybe it is good riddance if he's gone. But I thought both Dain and Sloan ought to know, so when I couldn't find Dain, I came to you."

"It's probably just an ordinary letter Wade is bearing," Emma said, "and most likely, after it's delivered, he'll remain near the convent to attend Lady Richenda, since he is her servant, not Dain's. She's not taking the veil, you know, just living there, so she will have contact with the world outside the cloister, and no doubt she'll want someone to run errands for her."

But the matter tugged at Emma's thoughts, mingling with her belief that Lady Richenda wasn't going to relinquish her influence on her son's life. By day's end a nagging doubt was firmly lodged in Emma's mind, so when Dain came to the great hall for the evening meal she told him all that Blake had said and the conclusion she had drawn, that Lady Richenda wanted to keep her manservant nearby.

"You are the third person to carry the tale to me," Dain said. "First Blake, then Sloan, now you. There is another simple explanation for Wade's departure, which apparently hasn't occurred to any of you. My mother has two distant cousins and a few long-standing friends, all of whom she sees whenever we go to court. It is possible that she has sent Wade off to one of them with a letter requesting that he be given a place in another household. She knows I'd never keep Wade at Penruan after what I've learned about him, so it seems reasonable to me that she would try to find a new place for a man who has been faithful to her service."

"You are too accustomed to trusting her," Emma protested.

"I know it, and I will change my way of thinking. But there is little my mother can do except complain of me. I doubt if any relative or friend will raise an army in her behalf to bring her back to Penruan and force me to accept her presence here. Girls and women are sent off to convents all the time, and many of them are unwilling. To most men it's no great matter. I do thank you for your loyal concern, however." He paused, regarding her with a smile in his eyes that did not quite reach his lips.

"Will you join me later tonight?" she asked softly, taking courage from the look he bestowed on her.

"No." His warmth was gone, replaced by a cool consideration of her features. "Too much has happened in too short a time. I need to be alone, to think about what I've learned of your magical ability and how you concealed it from me for so long. I also need to think about Vivienne, and about my mother's duplicity."

"I do understand." She turned away so he wouldn't see how disappointed she was.

Dain did not join her the following night either, or the night after that. Seeking distraction from her longing for him, Emma plunged into her daily duties as chatelaine, and into seeing to the preparations for the coming winter. Harvest season was full upon them and there was grain to be stored, meat and fish to be dried or smoked, fruits to be preserved in honey.

Todd and his men returned to report that Lady Richenda had made no trouble about entering the convent. When asked, Todd declared that neither he nor his men had seen Wade.

"He has gone to live elsewhere, just as I assumed," Dain said to Emma. "He knows better than to stay nearby when I know so much about him."

The days and the lonely nights slowly slipped into weeks, and still Dain did not return to the bed in the lord's chamber. He was consistently polite to Emma, though always a little distant, and she often felt his speculative gaze, as if he could not quite decide what to do about her.

Vivienne was far more affectionate. The sisters-in-law were becoming close friends, drawn together by their mutual love of Dain, and by the relief each found in the opportunity to speak freely to a woman who would never betray the magical secrets they shared.

"Do you find it difficult to live confined in the castle after so many years of freedom?" Emma asked one day.

Vivienne had been well trained by Agatha in the healing arts, as well as in magic, and she and Emma were busy in the stillroom. Emma was shredding dried herb leaves into storage jars so they would be clean and easily available when needed, while Vivienne was compounding a salve for a kitchen worker who had burned her hand.

"I like it here with you and Dain," Vivienne said,

"though I do miss seeing Agatha every day." She fell silent, frowning at the bowl containing rendered goose grease and alkanet, which she was mixing together.

"What of Hermit?" Emma asked gently. "Do you miss seeing him? From what you've said, you lived in one room of the cave and he in the next, and you spent a good deal of time together."

"We did talk often." Vivienne gathered a few dried calendula petals in her fingertips and crumbled them over the salve. "Yes, I do miss Hermit." Her voice shook a little.

"Why don't you return to the cave and visit him?" Emma suggested. "Or he could come here. Dain has said he's always welcome."

"I don't think it's a good idea. Hermit has sad memories and conflicts in his past that only he can resolve. I am no help to him; I only complicate his thoughts. I believe he's eager to return to his traveling life."

"Did he say so? Hermit gave me the impression that he's very fond of you. He promised he'd not leave Penruan until you are settled and happy."

"I think he meant until Dain and I are close as brother and sister should be." Vivienne brushed away a tear and bent her head over the bowl of salve.

To Emma, that last remark indicated a conflict within Vivienne's heart, for the closer she and Dain became, the more likely Hermit was to forsake the cave and resume his wanderings. Emma didn't want to think about Hermit leaving, or about how empty the beach and the cave would be without him there. She had grown surprisingly fond of the bearded wanderer.

"You ought to talk to Agatha," Emma said. "She

knows Hermit well, so she may be able to offer some advice."

"Perhaps." Vivienne looked doubtful.

"I heard Dain telling Sloan that he is planning to ride to Trevanan tomorrow," Emma said, "to inspect the rebuilt houses. You could ride with him. I'm sure he wouldn't object. He enjoys your company, and I know he has been taking you along on short rides, to reaccustom you to horses."

"You and I were going to the moor tomorrow," Vivienne protested, still doubtful of the plan.

"I can take Blake and Hawise," Emma said. "They are used to helping me look for wild herbs."

When morning came Vivienne and Dain left early for Trevanan. An hour later Hawise made an excuse to stay at the castle.

"It's Sloan," Emma teased her. "You are spending more and more time with him. Don't think I haven't noticed."

"Do you mind? Blake is more agile than I when it comes to climbing on rocks or getting down on his knees to dig up plants. I usually end with my arms and hands itching. I'm glad to help you all I can in the stillroom, and you know I'm useful there, but I don't like the moor. It's so empty and windy."

"You are far more likely to fall into danger with Sloan than out on the moor with me," Emma said, still teasing. She wished there was a similar danger for her to fall into with Dain. "Very well, stay home if you like. Just be careful what herbal brews you feed to Sloan."

Shortly thereafter, with Blake at her side, Emma rode forth to the moor. The boy was as cheerful and talkative as ever, chattering on about his sword practice and Todd's promise to allow him to join in sentry duty during his next night on watch.

"Gather as much as you can," Emma said, interrupting the stream of youthful male plans. "We may not have many more opportunities to come here before winter arrives. You've told me how chill and blustery and wet the moor can be during the winter months."

There was no sign of unpleasant weather at the moment. The sky was cloudless, the sea sparkled in the distance, and a breeze blew gently, chasing away any hint of midafternoon heat. The moor was deserted, the only sign of humanity being a single horseman cantering along the road from Trevanan to Penruan. Emma watched him for a moment, thinking the mounted figure looked vaguely familiar. Then she shrugged and turned back to her work. The rider wasn't Dain, so he held little interest for her.

"It gets dark early in winter," Blake said, continuing their conversation. His voice was muffled as he bent low to dig up a plant. He pulled hard on it and the roots gave way, sending the boy rolling backward onto the damp ground with the plant on top of him. Laughing, he dusted himself off and placed the herb into his basket.

Within a short time all of the baskets were full, and they began to strap them to the horses's backs. They were so busy and Blake was talking so continuously that at first Emma didn't notice the soft sound of hooves on the spongy turf. Not until her horse whickered, acknowledging another equine presence, did Emma realize someone was approaching. She finished fastening the last leather strap that held her basket and turned, half expecting to see Dain. It was the horseman she had watched on the road just a short time earlier, and now she knew why she had found him a familiar figure.

"Wade!" Blake exclaimed. "What are you doing here? I thought you had left Penruan for good."

"Did you, now?" Wade leaned forward in the saddle to chat with Blake. "Whyever would you think such a thing, when I've lived at Penruan for more than thirty years?"

"All of your things were gone," Blake said, taking a step nearer to the wiry, gray-haired man, who smiled at him as if smiling hurt his usually sour face.

"Blake," Emma cautioned, noting the ice behind Wade's friendliness, and the sword and long knife at his belt, "come here to me."

"When I left, I was bound for a long ride," Wade explained to Blake, "and I didn't want anyone to steal my belongings while I was gone, so I took them with me. Here, lad, I've brought back a present for you." He reached out a closed fist, as if he was offering something he was afraid he'd drop if he wasn't careful.

"What is it?" Blake took another step toward where Wade sat on his horse. "It must be small if you can hold it in your hand that way. Is it a gold coin?"

"Come and see," Wade coaxed.

"Blake, no!" Emma cried. "Stay away from him!"

Her second warning was too late. Blake had moved a little closer to the promised gift, just close enough for Wade to seize the boy by his tunic and hoist him upward until Blake was flung facedown across the horse.

"Let him go this instant!" Emma commanded.

"Not a chance," Wade said. "Not until you do what I want."

"And what is that?" Emma asked, though she wasn't really interested in his response. She was gathering her magic, preparing to use her power to immobilize Wade and free Blake, when it occurred to her that she could learn more from Wade by pretending to be afraid of him and of what he might do to Blake. There was bound to be some dire reason why Wade had returned to Penruan after escaping Dain's justice, and Emma wanted to know what the reason was. Most likely, Lady Richenda was involved.

"Blake," Emma cried, managing to sound terrified, "are you hurt?"

"No," Blake responded, "but I'll be sick if I stay this way much longer."

"All the more reason for you to obey me without any further argument, my lady," Wade said with a nasty grin. "Start walking."

"Where should I walk?" Emma asked.

"To Rough Tor." Wade jerked his head in the direction of the high rock formation. He spoke his next words with a sneer. "Start moving now, my lady."

"It will be a long walk," Emma said. "Why don't I mount my horse and we can ride together?"

"Do you think I'm fool enough to allow you on a horse?" Wade demanded. "You walk; I ride."

"It will take until after dark to reach Rough Tor on foot," Emma said.

"Don't imagine I care if your dainty feet are blistered by the time we get there," Wade said. "You won't be spending the night on your feet, anyway."

"What do you mean?"

"You'll be spending the night sprawled on your back," Wade told her with a horrible, mirthless

283

grin, "unless they prefer to have you facedown. That's their concern, not mine."

"You're planning to give me to the bandits." She was so choked with rage and disgust that she could barely get the words out.

"They'll be glad to have you," Wade said, "considering all Dain has done to spoil their livelihood."

"Surely Lady Richenda never ordered you to do such a dreadful thing!"

"She told me to get rid of you by any means I chose," Wade said. "She left it to me. The witch Vivienne is next, after you're taken care of. Now there's a killing that should have been done years ago."

"No!" Blake yelled, kicking and struggling to push himself upright. "You can't kill women! It's dishonorable. I won't allow it!"

"If you want to live long enough to find out whether I'll do it or not, stay where you are," Wade told him, drawing his knife from his belt as he spoke. "Otherwise, I'll put my blade between your ribs."

"If you kill Blake, you've lost your hold on me," Emma said.

"If I kill him and the bandits have you, who's left to warn Dain or the witch?" Wade asked, calmly reasonable.

"What does Lady Richenda want?"

"You and the witch permanently gone, and her former place back." Wade answered so promptly that Emma knew he was speaking the truth as he had heard it from Lady Richenda's own lips.

"She's mad if she imagines Dain will ever let her return."

"Do you think he'll let *you* return after every brigand on the moor has had you?"

Emma had heard enough. Blake was retching as if he'd be sick at any moment, and she didn't want him frightened any longer. Nor did she think she'd get anything more out of Wade. She was sure he had told her all he knew of Lady Richenda's plan.

Emma summoned her magic and cast a spell on Wade, holding him in place where he was. He was so difficult to restrain that she began to wonder if he possessed some degree of magical ability. Surely if it was so, she'd have sensed it while he was living at Penruan. Nor did she think Lady Richenda would keep a magician for a servant, when she loathed the very idea of magic.

"Blake," Emma said, "get off the horse. You can do it. Wade cannot harm you. I won't allow it."

"I can feel the point of his knife in my side," Blake cried.

"He cannot use it. Trust me, Blake. I have immobilized him. Slide under Wade's arm and off the horse *now.*"

"I'll try." Blake moved with nerve-tearing slowness until, finally, he stood on the ground. He gazed up at Wade, who sat as if carved from stone, though the man's eyes blazed with impotent fury.

"You did it!" Blake cried, starting toward Emma. "You used magic to save me! Thank you."

"Don't touch me," Emma cautioned. "Wade is surprisingly strong and I want no distractions to my spell. Blake, I want you to mount your horse and ride back to Penruan."

"And leave you alone with this villain?" Blake cried. "I won't do it. I'll dishonor myself if I leave a woman alone and undefended."

"As you can see," Emma said, "I am perfectly capable of defending myself. I'm sure the sentries at Penruan have noticed how we've been accosted

285

here, and have ordered men-at-arms to ride to our aid. But just in case they haven't seen what's happening, I want you to alert Sloan and have him send men to escort Wade to the castle. I will hold him here until they come." She didn't add that she wanted Blake out of the way so Wade couldn't use him as a hostage for a second time. She couldn't be sure Wade wouldn't distract her long enough to kill Blake.

"Yes, I understand," Blake said, rushing to his horse. "You need me to summon help, to rescue you. I'll be as fast as I can."

"Be careful," Emma warned. "Mind the path and the bogs."

She couldn't watch Blake leave because she was having to use more and more magical energy to maintain her control over Wade. The hatred in the man's eyes was terrifying. She waited in tense silence, keeping her attention fixed on him.

Suddenly, from some distance behind her, she heard Blake shout. Fearing he'd been thrown from his horse in his haste to reach the castle, she allowed herself to be distracted for an instant.

It was long enough for Wade to take action. He wrenched himself free of the spell, leaving Emma gasping with pain that seared through her mind and her chest. Wade pulled a silver chain from beneath his tunic. From it dangled a rough, pitted black stone, half a finger in length. Emma recognized the remnant of a burned-out shooting star that had fallen to earth and broken into pieces, and she understood why keeping Wade within her spell had been so difficult.

"Here's a talisman that Lady Richenda gave me to use against your magic," Wade told her, letting the stone swing on its chain. "Iron that falls from the sky will destroy any spell."

"It didn't work very well against mine," Emma said. "Blake is free of you."

"No, he's not. I'll catch him before he can reach the castle and give the alarm. As for you, my lady, the bandits will take care of you."

With a last, cold glance and a shrug of his shoulders that left Emma totally perplexed, Wade kicked his horse's sides and headed for the cliff road.

Only then did Emma look around, searching for Blake. She quickly saw that he hadn't been thrown. He was riding as fast as he could, but not in the direction of the castle. Blake was galloping for the cliffs, where Hermit had just appeared at the top of the path, and where both of them, man and boy alike, were certain to encounter the murderous Wade.

"Oh, no! Blake! Hermit! Run to the castle!"

She wasn't sure they could hear her warning, and she feared she wasn't strong enough to capture Wade again by magic, when he was protected by his talisman. She could think of only one way to stop Wade. She'd have to chase him toward Penruan and trust Sloan to act quickly.

As she leapt onto her horse, Emma noticed a movement near Rough Tor. A moment later she was able to make out the shapes of a mounted band of men who were galloping toward her, and knew them for the outlaws to whom Wade had planned to consign her.

"That's why he left me so easily," she muttered. "He knew they were on the way. Well, they'll have to catch me first."

Then, to her despair, she recognized Dain and Vivienne riding along the road from Trevanan to

Penruan with just a few men-at-arms for escort. She didn't think Wade had noticed them yet. He was still following Blake.

With the brigands almost at her heels, Emma set out after Wade, heading for the spot on the cliffs where Dain and all the others were bound to meet and where, she knew, bloody violence was sure to occur.

Chapter Sixteen

As she raced toward the cliffs, Emma spared a hasty glance for Penruan Castle, off to her left. She was greatly relieved to see the main gate wide open and the glint of sunlight on armor and drawn swords as mounted men poured out of the entrance and across the drawbridge.

"Bless you, Sloan! Please, intercept the bandits before they catch up to me. Dain and his men and I will stop Wade and protect Vivienne."

Almost as if he could hear her murmured plea, Sloan led his men-at-arms directly toward the horsemen who were closing in on Emma. She needed only one look over her shoulder to know her pursuers were being neatly cut off, leaving her free to ride on unhindered.

She paid no heed to the sounds of battle rising behind her as the force from Penruan met the bandits. Her task was to stop Wade before he discovered his other intended victim, Vivienne, was on the road leading straight to him and drawing nearer with every moment that passed. Dain would fight to protect his sister, but Emma knew he wasn't wearing his chain-mail armor, and Wade was sure to be an unchivalrous opponent. Therefore Wade must be stopped at once.

Ahead of her, Emma saw Blake pulling up his horse beside Hermit, and saw the boy waving his arm toward the pursuing Wade, who had almost reached the cliff road.

"Faster! Faster!" Emma urged her horse, though the steed was already flying over the dangerous moorland with Emma bent low at its neck.

Wade must have heard her coming, for he pulled his horse around to face her just as Emma also reached the road. She tumbled down from her mount, intending to use magic on her opponent, no matter the cost to herself. She planted both feet firmly on the solid earth and began to gather her forces.

Before Emma could work her spell, Hermit was there, too, reaching up to grab Wade by one arm and yank him out of the saddle. Wade's reaction was rapid. He landed on his feet, sword in hand, and spun around to slash at Hermit, who leapt back just in time to avoid the killing stroke.

Emma sought deep inside herself, calling up reserves of magical strength, knowing Wade was going to use his talisman to oppose her magic. She had caught him by surprise once that day; he would not be surprised a second time. The pitted black stone swung back and forth on its silver chain, bumping against Wade's chest each time he moved.

Snaring him hurt. Pain ripped through Emma,

but she was determined to defend those she loved. She told herself she only had to hold Wade for a little while. The men-at-arms who were riding with Dain would arrive soon, and they would be strong enough to stop Wade by sheer force of arms before he could harm Blake or Hermit and, she hoped, before Dain became embroiled in the fight. And Vivienne would sense that Emma was relying on magic and be warned in time to protect herself by the same means. Emma exerted all her strength to bring Wade under her control.

She should have known Dain wouldn't send his men-at-arms ahead of him to see what was happening. He rode up leading his troops and took immediate command of the strange little skirmish that was going on in the middle of the cliff road. He wedged his horse between Emma and Wade, the combined interference of human and horseflesh making it even more difficult for Emma to hold Wade fast.

"In heaven's name, stand back," Dain ordered his wife. "I'll see to this villain. He's thoroughly outnumbered."

The sound of Dain's voice broke the last strands of Emma's magical connection with Wade. Freed from her control, Wade lifted his sword and slashed at Dain's horse. An instant before the blade made contact, Hermit seized Wade's sword arm.

"Halt!" Hermit ordered, and it wasn't clear until he spoke again just who it was he meant to stop. "Dain, this is my battle to fight. Blake tells me this villain has threatened both Emma and Vivienne."

"If he has threatened my wife and my sister," Dain responded, "then it is my fight."

"There's no need to fight," Emma cried. "Dain, let

291

your men-at-arms take Wade back to the castle and hold him prisoner there till you decide what to do with him."

"I'll never be a prisoner," Wade shouted, wrestling against Hermit, who was still holding onto his sword arm. "Nor will I be taken by magic, not while I have my talisman."

"You are right about that," Hermit told him. "No one will use magic against you. Dain, let me put an end to this man's villainy in my own way."

"He is my prisoner," Dain said.

"Not so," Hermit objected. "I captured him; I pulled him from his horse. He is mine. Please, Dain! I must do this."

"You are hardly fit for combat," Dain said, eyebrows raised in surprise at Hermit's vehemence. "Why are you so determined?"

"Once I was trained to use both sword and lance. In those long-ago days I knew the rules of chivalry, but I betrayed them, to my eternal shame," Hermit said. "Give me a sword and let me fight this battle as a man ought to fight. Let me earn the right to call myself an honest man again, before I die."

"Hermit, no!" Vivienne cried. "Your ruined arm—"

"Is growing strong again, thanks to you and Agatha," Hermit interrupted the protest. "I warn you, Vivienne, and you, too, Emma, I want no magic employed here. It must be a fair fight of man against man." Hermit released Wade and stepped back, awaiting Dain's decision.

"Well, Wade," said Dain, looking down from his high seat astride his horse, "will you accept Hermit's challenge?"

"Him? That weak, bearded pilgrim?" Wade responded, laughing at Hermit, who, in his wide-brimmed hat, tattered cloak, and worn boots, appeared to be anything but a fierce warrior. "What reward do I get when I kill him? For if it's a man-to-man challenge, then you cannot charge me with murder after it's over."

"Fair enough," Dain said. "I'll not imprison you if you win the fight. If you survive, you may leave Penruan lands a free man, provided you promise never to return. But if you lose the fight, you lose your life."

"Either way," Emma cried, knowing Dain would not change his mind now that it was made up, "you must hand over the talisman that Lady Richenda gave you."

"What, lose my security against magic?" Wade exclaimed. "I'll not do it."

"My mother gave him a talisman?" Dain asked, looking at Emma.

"To protect him against my magic, and Vivienne's, so he would be able to kill us," Emma explained. "He'd have killed Blake, too, because the boy got in his way. He used Blake as a hostage against me."

"You make me wish I had not offered him the chance to fight for his life," Dain responded, his mouth tight. "Unfortunately, I cannot renege on my word. For honor's sake I must allow the combat, so long as both men agree to it. I'll have that talisman now, Wade." He stretched out his hand.

"I'd rather put it in your lady's hand," Wade said, his mouth curling into a grim smile when Emma gasped.

"Give it to me," Dain ordered. "However the battle ends, be assured I will return it to its rightful owner."

"If I hand it over, can you prevent those two

witches from casting spells against me?" Wade asked.

"They will obey my orders," Dain said. "No magic will be used. You have my word on it. Give me the stone."

Instead of handing it up to Dain, Wade tossed the stone and chain at him. Dain caught it easily and tucked it into his tunic.

"Someone provide Hermit with a good sword," Dain commanded. "Everyone move well away from the cliff. The combat will take place here, on the road, where the ground is level and hard-packed."

He turned in his saddle to look back over the moor for a moment, to the place where Sloan was leading Penruan men to victory against the bandits.

"You'll get no help from your friends," Dain said to Wade.

"I have no friends," Wade responded, shrugging his shoulders to indicate that it mattered not to him whether the outlaws lived or died. "Let's get on with this."

While they spoke, one of the men in Dain's escort had offered his broadsword to Hermit. Blake, acting as squire, had taken Hermit's hat and was assisting him to remove his cloak. Hermit stood attired as Wade was, in tunic, breeches, and boots, though Hermit was a good deal shabbier than Wade. Hermit's tunic was roughly patched in several places, there was an unrepaired tear at one knee, and his long, untrimmed beard gave him a striking similarity to the outlaws who lived around Rough Tor.

Yet there was a quiet dignity to Hermit's stance, and a natural courtesy in the way he accepted the proferred sword from Dain's man-at-arms with words of thanks worthy of the grandest noble. He hefted the broadsword in both hands, testing its weight and balance, and his teeth flashed in a pleased smile that showed his approval of the weapon.

Then Hermit stepped to the exact middle of the road and silence fell over the group gathered there. From the distance, where the battle was winding down, came the faint sound of weapons clashing, and of a man's voice calling out an order.

Hermit looked directly into Emma's eyes and raised his borrowed broadsword straight up, saluting her. He turned a little to face Vivienne, who was still mounted, and offered the same salute to her.

"I am ready at your command, my lord Dain," Hermit said.

Dain considered Wade, who stood in a languid pose, running a finger along the edge of his sword to test the sharpness of the blade.

"Wade," Dain said, "give up your knife. Only swords are to be used here."

"What, don't you trust me?" asked Wade, with the unpleasant sneer that Emma was beginning to dislike intensely.

"No," Dain said quietly, "I do not trust you."

One of his men stepped forward and, with a look of disgust, Wade gave him the knife.

"Very well, then. Begin," Dain said.

The signal was barely out of his mouth when Wade lunged forward toward Hermit, obviously thinking he could end the fight without much effort.

Hermit parried the blow, the edge of his sword slicing open Wade's sleeve and leaving a bloody gash on his arm.

"I forgot to tell you," Hermit said, his eyes never leaving Wade's face, "lately, I've been practicing."

"Much good it'll do you," Wade responded.

The two men circled each other, slashing now and then, each man parrying, while the tension between them grew stronger and the men and women watching became completely quiet, until only the panting breath of the combatants, the clash of blade upon steel blade, and the crunch of their feet on the surface of the road broke the stillness. Wade cut Hermit's hand. Hermit opened another gash on Wade's forearm.

The afternoon wore on. Both men were drenched in sweat, and both were clearly tiring.

Suddenly Wade altered the pattern of circle and slash and parry. He began to press forward, slashing wildly, his teeth bared and his face assuming a mask of impotent fury as Hermit warded off the attack. Then, in a series of fierce and rapid blows, he drew blood from Hermit's left arm, sliced open his left shoulder, and tore a long wound in his left side.

"Now I'll have an end to this!" Wade shouted, and lifted his broadsword to bring it down on Hermit's neck, a blow that would surely sever Hermit's head from his shoulders.

With a wrenching groan that stabbed right to Emma's heart, Hermit raised his own sword and thrust aside the death that Wade intended for him. Then, before Wade could recover and come at him again, Hermit raised his own sword one more time, holding it in both bloodstained, sweaty hands, and struck Wade hard across his middle.

Wade stumbled backward, clutching at the wound with his left hand, trying to hold his ruined body together, though he must have sensed it was hopeless.

"You'll pay for this," Wade gasped, taking another backward step. "Lady Richenda will make you sorry."

"Catch him," Dain ordered his men, "before he goes over the edge."

"Don't—touch—me," Wade said, his words a moan of pain and fury. In his right hand he still held his broadsword, and he lifted it as if to ward off anyone who dared to approach him.

"Fool," he said to Dain, "to trust in magic."

"It's not magic that's done this," Dain said, "but hatred of magic."

Still keeping his broadsword extended, though no man made a move toward him, Wade stepped backward again, groaning at the effort it required to force his rapidly failing body to obey his will. Without another word he took the final step and went over the cliff. He did not cry out as he fell.

In the protracted silence that followed, Hermit drew himself up, standing straight and tall in his tattered clothing.

"I thank you, my lord Dain," Hermit said. "Today, at last, I am a true man again. My honor is redeemed. My loved ones are protected against evil." He looked at Vivienne, and then at Emma. Wonder and a wild joy filled his eyes and shone on his dirt-streaked, bearded face.

Emma started toward him, wanting to help, both her hands extended in concern over his dreadful wounds. Before she could reach him, Hermit collapsed onto the road and lay there, facedown and unmoving.

"No!" Vivienne shrieked, flinging herself from her horse to run to him.

Her cry broke the unnatural silence that had held them all in place, and suddenly the air rang with commands as Dain ordered one of his men to ride to the castle for a litter and a supply of bandages, commanded two other men to descend the cliff path to discover the remains of Wade and return them to the castle for burial, and ordered a fourth man to ride to the battle scene on the moor and bring back word of the results.

"I want to know how many men are wounded, how many dead, and how many captured," Dain instructed.

"Please," Emma begged, catching at his stirrup, "send one of the men to Trevanan to inform Agatha of what has happened and bring her to the castle. We are going to need her healing skills."

"Hermit's wounds are grave," Dain responded, dismounting as he spoke. "I have seen men die from lesser hurts."

"We can't let him die," Emma said on a sob.

At Vivienne's urgent call, she left Dain's side and went to help with Hermit. He was unconscious, his face bruised and cut where he'd hit the rough stone and gravel of the road. His wounds from Wade's sword were bleeding copiously. Blake was already at work, following Vivienne's instructions to bind up the gash on Hermit's arm using Vivienne's white scarf, and to pull it tight until the bleeding stopped. Emma tried to stanch the shoulder wound with her hands, while Vivienne struggled with the deep tear in Hermit's side. Though her face was white, Vivienne was amazingly calm, doing with admirable efficiency whatever must be done to stop the bleeding.

"He will require sewing," Emma said. "All three wounds need to be sewn closed."

"There will be other wounded men coming in from the moor who will also want help," Dain said, squatting beside Hermit's inert form. "He's still unconscious?"

"I'm glad he is," Vivienne said. "He won't feel the pain when we move him."

In fact, the men who came with a litter moved Hermit gently and carried him with great care to the castle and into one of the guest chambers in the tower keep. By that time Agatha appeared, having ridden pillion behind the man Dain sent to fetch her. She watched Emma and Vivienne for a few minutes before nodding her approval.

"He will do well enough under your care," Agatha said. "I'll see to the other wounded, the men from the battle, so you won't have to worry about them. Who can best assist me?"

"Hawise," Emma said at once, "and Blake, too. He's had a trying day, and helping someone else will be the best thing for him. Ask him to tell you how Wade misused him. He ought to talk about it, and I'm too busy here to listen just now."

"I'll see to the boy," Agatha promised, and left to start tending to the wounded men.

"Sloan is wounded, too," Dain said, hovering just inside the doorway. "That's where Hawise will be. What of you, Emma? Your day has been no less trying than Blake's."

"I haven't time to think of it just now," Emma responded, and firmly shut all thought of Wade and his wicked plans out of her mind.

By nightfall Wade and several of the bandits had been buried in an empty field at some distance from the castle, and the wounded, men-at-arms and outlaws alike, were bandaged and dosed with herbal medicines. Those who were strong enough to cause trouble were under close guard.

Hermit was beginning to move and thrash about

299

in his bed as he slowly regained consciousness. He was too weak to talk, but Emma could see that he did recognize her, and Vivienne. They each took one of his hands, and Hermit smiled and pressed their fingers. He obediently swallowed the spoonful of poppy syrup Emma offered to him, and a short time later he lapsed into a state of somnolence in which, Emma knew, there was no pain.

"Will he live?" Dain asked Emma as she came out of Hermit's room with a water pitcher for one of the maids to refill.

"If his wounds don't fester, I believe he will," Emma said.

"I'm glad to hear it," Dain said. "He's a brave man. Emma, I have a minor problem to discuss with you, if you can spare a moment."

"Of course." Emma handed the pitcher to a waiting maidservant before turning her full attention to Dain.

"I trouble you only because I promised Sloan I'd speak to you as soon as possible, and because I hope your answer will speed his recovery from his own wounds," Dain said. "Sloan wants to marry Hawise. Have you any objection?"

"None at all," Emma responded promptly, and discovered to her surprise that it was possible to smile at the end of the day's fear and pain. "I can't imagine Hawise will object to the idea."

"Nor I," said Dain, chuckling. "She has been with Sloan for so much of the afternoon that Agatha scolded her for neglecting the other wounded men. I do think Sloan will enjoy a speedy recovery."

"Let them be happy," Emma said, her gaze on the still figure she could see through the doorway, and on Vivienne bending over Hermit's form.

"Unlike Sloan, Hermit will have a long and slow

recovery," she said. "Dain, if you were to offer him a place here at Penruan when he's well again, I think he'd accept it now, and be glad of it. You saw today that he is no mean swordsman."

"A mere man-at-arms," Dain said, looking at his sister. "I wonder if it's wise to keep him here."

"Why don't we leave the decision to Hermit?" Emma suggested, her voice taking on a note of sharpness. "And to Vivienne, if Hermit offers her a decision to make."

Citing the need to remove the last of the bandits who were infesting Rough Tor before they could regroup and wreak vengeance on Trevanan village for the defeat of their comrades, Dain rode out at dawn the next day with a large troop of men. He was gone for almost a week. During that time two of the wounded bandits died and a third tried to escape and was recaptured. Todd, who was left in charge of the castle defenses during Dain's absence, ordered the man cast into the dungeon until Dain's return.

"If he's healthy enough to slip past his guard," Todd said to Emma when she inquired about the man's healing wounds, "then he's well enough to withstand being confined for a while."

Sloan, with marriage to Hawise promised in the near future, got out of his bed and limped into the great hall to announce his decision to return to duty.

"Only if you promise to rely on Todd," Emma warned him. "I will not allow you to disappoint Hawise by suffering a relapse."

"My lady, I will obey your every command," Sloan responded. "You've granted me my heart's desire."

"Actually, it's Hawise who will grant you that," Emma said. Noticing how Sloan winced when he tried to stand upright and square his aching shoulders, she winked at Todd behind his back and received an answering grin that told her the younger man would see to it that Sloan did not overexert himself.

Hermit's situation was not as cheerful as Sloan's, for one of his wounds began to fester. He developed a high fever and Emma, Vivienne, and Agatha, who remained at Penruan to help nurse the injured, all took turns sponging him with cool water and trying to force herbal medicines past his lips. Early one morning the fever finally broke, but he lay in a stupor for several days more.

"He'll live," Agatha assured Emma. "Rest and herbal brews and nourishment will restore him. You don't need me here any longer. I'm going back to Trevanan. As for you, my girl, see that you get some rest, too, or you'll be sick. Let Hawise spend a few hours with Hermit, while you and Vivienne sleep. It will do all of you a world of good. I'll return in a few days."

As soon as Hermit began to regain his strength Vivienne suggested that she shave his matted beard and cut his hair.

"Have you ever shaved a man before?" he asked.

"I haven't," Vivienne admitted, "but Emma could do it for you."

"I will, if you'll let me," Emma offered.

"No." It was as firm a refusal as his continuing weakness allowed. "Having seen the rest of me unclothed while I've been lying here helpless, now you want to see my bare face, too."

Vivienne giggled at the remark, but Emma detected something evasive behind the joking.

"We will do whatever you want, and not tease you for more," she told him.

"My old face is too scarred for gently raised young ladies to view," Hermit said. "Leave well enough alone."

"I was not gently raised," Vivienne reminded him.

"But you were," Hermit said, taking her hand. "You didn't learn to work fine embroidery, or to pin up your hair and wear silk gowns or play a lute, but Agatha taught you how to trust your kind and gentle heart.

"I will make a concession," Hermit said. "You may trim my hair and my beard, but I'll not be shaved."

"Speaking of fine embroidery," Emma said, "Hawise owns a pair of sharp embroidery scissors. I'll ask her for an hour's use of them." She left the room quickly, not wanting to stay there while Hermit and Vivienne gazed at each other with their hearts in their eyes and longing written clear to see on their faces.

As soon as Dain returned, Emma begged him to offer Hermit a place at Penruan. Though he again expressed his doubts about exposing Vivienne to the constant presence of a man about whose family and past he knew nothing, Dain made the offer, at a time when Vivienne was resting and Emma was with Hermit.

"It would never do," Hermit said at once. "I am grateful to you, Dain, for more reasons than I dare to reveal. You will never know how much these months I've spent on your land mean to me. But it's best if I resume my travels as soon as I am able."

"Will nothing change your mind?" Emma cried.

"My heart will always be at Penruan," Hermit said. "It's my mortal body that cannot stay here."

"Well, that's that," Dain said to Emma later. "Hermit obviously understands he wouldn't be well matched with Vivienne. Whatever the circumstances of his birth or his past, he is a man of honor."

"You needn't look so pleased," Emma retorted. "Vivienne will be heartbroken when he leaves."

"I left the choice to Hermit, just as you wanted," Dain said.

"So you did," Emma admitted on a sigh. Privately, she feared Vivienne's reaction when she learned Hermit was planning to depart—and she wondered what were the real reasons behind Hermit's decision to forsake the woman whom Emma was certain he loved.

Chapter Seventeen

"Hermit's belongings are still in the cave," Emma said to Dain the next morning. "I thought I'd go there and gather them up and bring them back to him."

"I'll go with you," Dain offered.

Emma was a bit surprised at the suggestion, but there was no excuse she could think of to keep the lord of Penruan away from a cave that was located on his own land, so she quickly assented. Perhaps, once they were removed from the castle, where the demands on his time and attention were constant, Dain would reveal his thoughts about their marriage. He hadn't returned to their bed since learning she could work magic and, though he treated her with scrupulous courtesy, Emma wasn't sure she could continue as his wife if he didn't soon tell her what was in his heart.

They walked out of the gatehouse at midmorning. The day was mild, though a haze hung over the sea, turning the sunlight to a milky-white glow. The sea was murky gray and oddly still.

"I am beginning to know the Cornish weather," Emma said as she followed Dain along the descent to the beach. "I recognize the signs of an approaching storm. We will have rain by midnight."

"You've been paying attention." Dain stepped off the path onto the sand and turned to offer Emma a hand.

"That," she responded, "is half the secret of working magic. Few people pay attention to what is happening around them."

She was slightly above Dain, still on the path and gazing downward into his upturned face, caught by the marvelous blue-green depths of his eyes. Her heart lurched within her and she wondered what she would do if he decided to send her away. She hoped she was strong enough to live without him, but she didn't want to. She wanted to live with him for the rest of their lives, to lie beside him every night and bear his children and help him to care for the people who depended on him. She belonged to him completely, yet for all her magical ability she could not read his mind or guess at the future he intended for them.

"Perhaps it's the mystery that tempts me so," she murmured.

"What mystery?" he asked.

"Men are such strange creatures," she said. Evading his outstretched hand, she jumped onto the sand and began walking toward the rocks at the far side of the beach.

"Do you think women are not strange?" he muttered, catching up to her on the damp sand at the edge of the water. "Emma, despite your claim, you

306

haven't been paying attention to the sea. The tide is in, so you'll get wet if you try to reach Hermit's cave."

"Think nothing of it," she said, and stepped into the water and began to walk around the rocks.

"Are you mad?" he exclaimed. "You could be swept away."

"Not while the sea is so calm. You see, my lord, I have been paying attention after all." She marched out of the water and up the beach without looking back to see if he was following her. She was inside the cave before he rejoined her.

"You are too damned independent!" he shouted at her, "thinking for yourself, making decisions on your own, choosing what is safe and what is not."

"Do you want a wife who cannot think?" she demanded, angry without really understanding why. "I know you wish you'd married a wife who cannot work magic, and who is not the daughter of Gavin of Wroxley, but you have me now and must make do with me, whether you want me or not."

"Must I?" he asked softly, a cool threat in his voice.

Frightened now, as well as angry, she spun away from him and made her way to the inner chamber, where Hermit's few belongings lay on the sand in a neat little pile topped by a folded blanket. The remains of his last fire occupied a shallow pit he had dug out of the sand. Next to his camp the underground stream that supplied his water rippled past on its race toward the sea.

Kneeling, Emma unfolded the blanket and began to transfer Hermit's possessions onto it. She tried to keep her attention on what she was doing and not think about Dain, who followed her to stand glaring at her as if she had committed some great sin. She did her best to pretend indifference to him, though she ached to know he cared about her.

"As for making do with you," Dain said suddenly, "at the moment, there is just one thing I want to do with you."

Emma paused with Hermit's leather knapsack in her hands. Dain knelt across the blanket from her. When he took the knapsack from her and set it aside she did not protest. A warm flush began deep within her and spread outward, melting any resistance she might have offered. Perhaps, just possibly, he did care. He wasn't the kind of lord who simply took for the sake of physical release.

"If I wait until we return to the castle," Dain said, "we will be interrupted. Someone will demand a moment of my time, or of yours, and it will be midnight before we are free of obligations. I do not want to wait, Emma. I cannot wait. I want you now."

"I don't think Hermit would mind if we use his blanket," she said, and shuddered with urgent need when he reached out to take her face between his hands.

"Proper wives cover their hair," he said. "I am glad you do not. Your hair is too beautiful to hide. Oh, Emma," he groaned, and without warning pulled her toward him. She fell against his chest.

"I shall never be a proper wife," she whispered, her face buried in his shoulder.

"I know it. Just for an hour, will you be an obedient wife?"

"I can try. What do you require of me, my lord?"

"Disrobe," he commanded. "Here, where no one will see or intrude upon us, remove your clothes while I watch."

"I will, and gladly," she said, "if you will, also."

"That's not obedience," he protested.

"No, it's not." She left his embrace with reluctance, to get to her feet and stand smiling at him in an attempt to disguise the improbable combination of rebellion and desire that was surging through her. She would—she *must!*—have him on her terms, as equals, and never would she use magic on him. She would meet him woman to man with a passion to match his own. Perhaps then he would understand how much she loved him. "It's a matter of cooperation."

He regarded her for a moment, as if making up his mind, then leapt to his feet.

"I have never in my life refused a challenge," he said.

He unbuckled his belt and laid it and his sword on the sand.

Emma untied her sash and cast it aside.

Dain kicked off his boots. Emma removed her shoes, unfastened the ribbon garters just below her knees, and with slow, deliberate movements, rolled down her stockings. The look in Dain's eyes as he watched her fingers sliding over calf and ankle sent exciting chills along her spine.

Dain pulled his tunic over his head. Emma lifted the damp hem of her skirt and very slowly, with Dain's overheated gaze still on her every motion, she removed her gown.

Dain grinned and began to unfasten his hose. Emma unbraided her hair and combed her fingers through it until it swung loose over her shoulders.

"Have a care, my lord," she advised, noting the hurried way he was fumbling with his undergarments. "It would be a great pity if you do yourself an injury at so vital a time."

He laughed at her remark, then tore off his last

remaining piece of clothing and stood naked and unashamed, letting her look her fill from his silver-gilt hair to his twinkling eyes, to his broad shoulders, narrow waist, and long, well-muscled legs and shapely feet. And then back again, upward to the flaunting, eager evidence of his desire for her.

"If cooperation is truly your intent, my lady," Dain said, "remove your shift. For, as you see, I have cooperated fully with you. I expect no less in return."

She lifted a trembling hand to push her wide-necked shift off her shoulders and let it fall. She stepped out of the circle of crumpled linen and went to him, to stand so close she could feel his warmth, yet not touching him.

"We are wanton," she whispered.

"I do hope so," he replied, and bent to kiss her shoulder.

Turning her head, she touched her tongue to the corner of his mouth. She felt his shiver of response deep in her bones.

Dain kissed her throat and her ears, her eyelids and her chin. She swayed toward him, wanting his arms around her, but he drew back a little, to look into her eyes.

"You are mine," he said.

"Only if you are mine, also."

"Will you never be obedient?" He sounded more perplexed than annoyed.

"I doubt it, my lord," she told him.

There remained an inch or two of space between them and Emma could no longer bear even that slight separation. She stepped forward, put her arms around his shoulders, and kissed him on the lips.

His strong arms almost crushed the breath out of

her. Dain lifted her off her feet and laid her on the blanket. He came down firmly on top of her, letting her feel his need, making clear his possession, telling her without words that she did, indeed, belong to him. He kissed her as if he would never get enough of her heated response, and he caressed every inch of her quivering skin.

"This cave is a magical place," he whispered so harshly that Emma knew he was making a desperate effort to restrain his ardor for just a little longer.

"But you don't fear magic," she said, and shifted her legs a bit to let him know she welcomed his increasing pressure against her liquid heat.

"You are the magic. I do not fear you, Emma."

She was unable to answer, for as he spoke Dain made them one, and Emma shook in the grip of an all-consuming pleasure. The wonder that lay between them seized her, holding her enthralled, opening her body completely to his driving masculine presence.

Only dimly, as from a great distance, did Emma hear her voice and Dain's crying out together at the final moment. She felt the warm rush of Dain's seed. The same magical knowledge that had once told her Dain was her true mate now informed her in a blaze of joy that in their joining they were creating a child. She was granted only an instant in which to accept that wondrous truth before the convulsions of her release came upon her and she lost awareness of time and place for a long, enchanted eternity of love.

"Now that the bandits are routed," Dain said, "and you and Vivienne are safe, I have one more important duty to perform."

They were lying together on Hermit's blanket,

still naked, and Dain's palm brushed lightly over Emma's breast, stirring a gentler fire than the demanding one they had recently extinguished. She turned to him with a smile that vanished when she heard his next words.

"I must go to Tawton Abbey and inform my mother that her plan to murder you and my sister has gone awry and, furthermore, the man she sent to perform the deeds is dead, himself."

"I do still wonder what message Wade carried for her," Emma said, "and to whom it went."

"Perhaps she will tell me." Dain sat up, reaching for his shirt. "We ought to return before Todd brings men-at-arms to the beach to search for us. He's remarkably efficient. What's this?"

Dain dug his fingers into the sand where his feet and Emma's had churned up the surface of the cave floor. He drew forth a golden crescent, twin to the one Vivienne had placed on his pillow weeks ago.

"Where do you suppose it was made?" he asked, holding it up for Emma to see.

"Agatha says there are bits and pieces of ancient jewelry to be found all along this coast," Emma said. "They were left here by folk who sailed to these shores centuries ago, looking for tin."

"Take it." Dain put the crescent into her hand and folded her fingers around it. "If you like, I'll have it fastened on a chain for you to wear, to remind you of the magical hours we've spent here."

Emma took the suggestion as a sign of hope, believing Dain would not have made it if he planned to rid himself of his non-submissive wife. Yet the bitter truth was that their wild and passionate lovemaking had not resolved the differences between them over what she was, and what he wanted his wife to be.

There was, also, the matter of the newly generated presence that she must keep secret from Dain until she knew with absolute certainty whether he loved her, or merely wanted her. If she told him what he had given her in the last, sweet instant of their joining, the knowledge would influence him in her favor. She wanted Dain to love her for herself, not for what she carried, still unformed, deep within. She had a few months before she must reveal her priceless secret, or he guessed it. She told herself to be patient, and to hope, and to trust in Dain.

"Why travel to Tawton?" she said as they walked along the beach toward the pathway up the cliff. The tide had gone out while they were in the cave, so there was no chance of either of them getting wet, but from the lowering clouds and the oily look of the sea the storm would not be long in coming, and then the waves would crash upon the rocks and the beach would be impassable. "Confronting Lady Richenda, knowing what she has done and listening to her vituperations will only upset you."

"She will never cease to plot against you and Vivienne until I face her down and formally disown her," Dain said.

"You need not see her, if you'd rather not. I know of an alternative, a way to put an end to her wicked scheming, but I won't do it without your permission."

"Permission to do what?" He faced her with a frown.

"To cast a spell on Lady Richenda, to make her sweet and docile."

"No mere human could achieve such an alteration in her nature," Dain scoffed. "Not even by magic."

"No one human could," Emma agreed. "However, Vivienne and I, together, can do it. If Agatha will agree to join us, the three of us can create a spell so powerful that no one will be strong enough to break it. Then we will all be permanently safe from Lady Richenda."

"It's cowardly of me to dread seeing her again," Dain said. "She is my mother and I owe her respect and affection, yet she is so wicked that even Father Maynard wants nothing more to do with her. He told me he's glad she is gone from Penruan."

"Once the spell is cast, if you want to visit her, she will be kind, and grateful for your presence, and never speak a word against Vivienne, or me. I propose to supress certain parts of her memory, so Lady Richenda can no longer recall the hatreds that have driven her for so long, or the wicked things she has done out of hatred."

"All that rage and jealousy, forgotten? There is an odd justice in such a sentence," Dain mused. "But what of her health?"

"The spell I intend to use will not affect her physical well-being. The illness with which she's already afflicted will continue its natural progress, for magic cannot alter its course. As I told you once before, Lady Richenda will live for some years yet. If you are concerned about my intentions toward her, if you cannot trust me on this matter, speak to Vivienne, or to Agatha. Either of them will confirm what I have just said. Lady Richenda will not be harmed, though from time to time she may be puzzled to realize there are details of her past that she cannot recall. I suspect those around her will find relief in the change and will comfort her with the explanation that her forgetfulness is the result of her increasing age," Emma ended dryly.

"I will consider your suggestion, and I will consult Vivienne and Agatha," Dain said. "Not because I lack trust in you, but because I find myself so eager to accept the simple solution you offer. I fear making a hasty choice that could be unfair to my mother. I, too, would find relief in the opportunity to visit her and hold a pleasant conversation with her, free of her usual rantings. But, however much she appears to change, I will never allow her to return to Penruan. Does my hardness shock you, Emma?"

"Not a bit. Like you, I grew up with a mother who was unpleasant, to say the least. I also understand your reluctance. We are taught from our earliest years to honor our parents. It's difficult to change."

"Yes." He took her hand and raised it to his lips. "But change we must, if we are not to be doomed by past mistakes."

They separated when they reached the castle gate, Dain excusing himself to climb the stair to the battlements and a conference with Todd. Emma strolled contentedly toward the keep, a smile curving her lips and hope warming her heart, while in the deepest recess of her woman's body the miracle that, thanks to her magic, she had been aware of from the very instant of its generation settled safely into its appointed place and began to grow.

The storm broke suddenly in late afternoon, bringing with it howling wind and heavy rain. The inhabitants of Penruan huddled indoors, with only a minimal guard sent to man the walls, for only madmen would choose to attack on such a night.

Dain never appeared in the lord's chamber,

though Emma doubted if the storm was keeping him away. She thought it more likely he was using the nighttime hours to consider the suggestion she had made about his mother. In the morning, the shadows under his eyes and the haggard lines of his face told her how torn he was between facing down Lady Richenda at Tawton Abbey to accuse her of conspiring to have murder done and ordering her into stricter confinement there, against handing her future well-being over to three sorceresses, every one of whom had compelling reasons for disliking the lady. Dain being Dain, he'd want to do what was right and just and fair, and the decision was a terrible one for any son to have to make.

In mid-morning the rain stopped and the skies began to clear. At the first beams of sunshine Agatha presented herself in the great hall.

"I've come to check on Hermit's condition," she said to Emma, "and on the other wounded men."

"I'm glad you're here," Emma responded. "I rather think Dain will want to speak with you in private." She then told her friend about the suggestion she had made, and Agatha nodded with satisfaction.

"It would provide an admirable solution. Otherwise, Lady Richenda will continue to attempt to destroy you, and Vivienne, too. I'll be happy to assure Dain that the greatest harm his mother will experience will be the quashing of her murderous impulses. Now, let me see Hermit."

As soon as the midday meal was over, Dain met with Agatha in the lord's chamber. A short time later he sent Hawise to ask Emma and Vivienne to join them.

"Agatha has banished the last traces of my reluctance," Dain said to Emma. "I spoke with Vivienne earlier and she has agreed to seek no other redress from my mother than the spell. You may work it whenever you wish. Is there anything you require of me beyond my approval?"

"You may stay," Vivienne said, "provided you promise not to interrupt once we have begun."

"You are going to do it now?" Dain sounded startled.

"Why wait?" asked Agatha. "All three of us are together, in private. Let us have an end to Lady Richenda's wickedness."

"A fine punishment," Dain said. "A woman who hates magic, to be held fast by magic and never know why she has changed her ways, or even that she has changed. Well, she prevented me from knowing my own sister, and from recalling several years of my life. Yes, let it be done immediately."

"Before we can begin," Emma said, "where is Wade's talisman? As I recall, Dain, you put it in your tunic after he threw it at you."

"I gave it to Father Maynard, to keep or to do with it whatever he wants," Dain answered.

"Good," Agatha said. "If it were in this room, it could act as an antidote against the working of the spell. But not if it's safe with a priest who will guard it carefully. Now, Dain, stand back and remain silent."

"I will," Dain promised, and put his shoulders against the door to keep it closed, in case anyone should interrupt. No one except the four of them knew what they were doing, so it was always possible for someone to seek him out with a problem or a request.

All of the women looked hard at him for a moment before setting about their magical business. Dain assumed they had noted and approved his serious mood, which well befitted a lord who was allowing just punishment to be administered. Secretly, he was filled with trepidation. It struck him as a peculiar time and place for magical incantations; not midnight, but during a clear afternoon; not on a foggy moor or deep in a chilly and hidden cave, but in the lord's chamber with the windows wide open to the warm air of an early autumn day and the golden sunlight streaming in to soften the gray stone walls.

Emma, Vivienne, and Agatha stood in a circle, their eyes closed, holding hands. They were silent for a time, and Dain was careful not to move or make a sound that might disturb their concentration. Agatha began the spell by speaking in a language Dain could not understand, though he believed it was the same tongue she had used to call Vivienne forth from her hiding place inside the cave. Next, Vivienne spoke, using a different language, this one totally alien to Dain.

Finally, it was Emma's turn. Dain could not understand a word she said, but he marveled at the rich, poetic sound of her voice, pitched to a deeper note than he was used to hearing from her. Emma's face was intent, and he knew she had moved deep inside herself, to a place where she and Vivienne and Agatha were joined in their trancelike state, a place where he could never venture.

Demanding, primitive, masculine need clamored inside him, urging him to seize his wife and shake her hard, to bring her back from her mystical trance to recognition of her duty to him and to their marriage. He reminded himself forcefully that what Emma was doing she was doing for his sake, and for his sister's safety, and he set aside his selfish male pride and tried to understand and appeciate

Emma's inborn calling. She could not help what she was, and she used her ability for good. Agatha had told him so, and he knew Agatha would not lie to him about something so important. Perhaps, Dain reasoned, he ought to have trusted Emma from the beginning, and not required someone else to confirm her honesty.

Suddenly, Emma was speaking in words Dain could understand, and he knew a prickling of very unmasculine tears behind his eyelids as he realized what she was saying.

"Bind Richenda of Penruan to peace and contentment, to forgetfulness of all hatreds, and to a quiet happiness in her holy retirement," Emma intoned. "For the rest of her life, let her do no more harm."

"No more harm," Vivienne echoed Emma's words, "for the rest of her life."

"Peace and contentment," Agatha chanted softly.

"Happiness and peace," Emma whispered.

It's more than my mother would have granted any of them, Dain thought, and swallowed hard to force down the lump in his throat.

The three women bowed their heads, and silence filled the lord's chamber for a while. Then Emma sighed and opened her eyes and looked at Dain. Looked at him, before anyone or anything else, as if he had been with her, in the back of her mind, through all the long conjuring. When she smiled at him, he ached to embrace her. He did not move, not being certain whether the spell was fully cast, or if there was still more to come.

"It is done," Agatha said. "The spell is made and cannot now be broken."

Dain did not know what to say or how to react. He had half expected smoke, or lightning and crashing thunder, or leaping tongues of flame. The quiet, almost gentle working of magic left him awed. He stared at his wife, his sister, and his elderly friend, and was hard put not to go to his knees before them.

Vivienne swayed a little, and Emma put a hand to her forehead.

"Are you—tired?" Dain asked, and then cursed himself for his stupidity.

"Always, after I work a spell," Emma said. "Agatha, I expect you to stay at the castle tonight. I should have said something before this. We will all sleep well, Dain, but in the morning we will be our usual selves. Have no fear for us."

"Agatha, come with me," Vivienne said. "You may sleep in my room." She put an arm around Agatha and they left the lord's chamber.

Emma went to the bed and sat down, moving slowly, as if she was exhausted. Dain stared at her, wanting to embrace her and not sure if he should.

"Is there anything you need?" he asked. "Food? Drink? Would you like wine?"

"Nothing, except to rest. Will you stay with me for a while?"

She began to remove her clothes. When she fumbled with the knot of her sash Dain set aside forbearance and went to assist her. He thought how different this undressing was from their passionate interlude in the cave. He saw Emma beneath the covers and drew up the quilt for her, tucking it in as if she were a sleepy child. Then he pulled the chair she had brought from Wroxley to the bedside and sat there, holding her hand till the sun set and the sky was dark and the stars began to shine.

Chapter Eighteen

Two days after the working of the spell on Lady Richenda, Sloan and Hawise were married. Dain proclaimed a day of celebration, and Emma supervised the preparation and serving of a hearty feast.

Sloan was so well respected that even the elders of Trevanan came to his wedding, bringing their wives with them. So far as Emma could tell, everyone in the castle rejoiced with the bride and groom. Even Hermit insisted on leaving his chamber for the occasion. Wearing borrowed clothing and leaning on Agatha's arm, he came to the hall to join the celebration and to watch while Vivienne acted as the bride's maiden attendant.

Hawise was dewy-eyed but composed in a new gown of fine blue wool that Emma had provided for her, with a wreath of moorland flowers made by Vivienne upon her unbound hair. Sloan looked appropriately nervous in a freshly washed tunic, with Todd and Blake as his groomsmen.

At the feast after the ceremony Dain bestowed upon the newlyweds a manor that lay within his holdings.

"A knight ought to have land on which to raise his children," Dain said. "You have earned this honor, Sir Sloan."

"But I'll still spend most of my time here at the castle," Hawise whispered to Emma, "for Sloan has important duties here, too, and he'll never shirk them just because he has taken a wife."

For their use while they were at the castle the couple was given one of the guest rooms. When evening came their friends escorted them to the chamber with much laughter and more than a few naughty jokes. Hawise blushed bright red to hear them. Sloan grinned sheepishly. Then Dain closed the bedroom door with lordly firmness and ordered everyone back to the great hall.

"Eat and drink all you want," he said, "but grant the lovers privacy."

Before Emma could retreat to the hall with the rest of the crowd Dain caught her hand to stop her from leaving.

"As for you, my lady," he murmured, his eyes shining, "I'd very much like to enact the bridal night we never enjoyed. I was rude to you when you came to Penruan, and the first time ever I took you to bed I was intoxicated by Agatha's herbal potion. I owe you a proper wedding night."

"Whatever you wish, my lord." She smiled into his eyes, touched and warmed by the tenderness she saw there.

He led her to the lord's chamber and barred the door. Then he made love to her, slowly and gently, yet with a burning need that told her far more surely than words could ever have that her magic presented no barrier to him. Dain knew her and knew what she could do, for he had observed her while she worked a spell, and still he wanted her. And he trusted her. He had said so.

As she shimmered into sweet ecstacy Emma dared to hope that in time—and, perhaps, not much time, either—Dain would begin to love her.

The wedding celebration continued well into the night but, while the newlyweds were allowed to linger in their chamber, everyone else was expected to be awake and at work at the usual early morning hour.

Dain had ordered a tray of bread and cheese and a pitcher of ale brought to the lord's chamber so he and Emma could break their fast. They were dressed and Dain was buckling on his sword in preparation for a ride to inspect one of his outlying farms, when Blake pounded on the door, yelling incoherently.

"What's wrong?" Emma pulled the door wide, exposing the white-faced, excited boy. "Blake, take a deep breath before you try to speak."

"My lord, my lady." Blake paused to gulp air. "I ran all the way from the gatehouse and up the tower steps."

"For what reason?" Dain asked.

In outward appearance he was calm, but Emma knew her husband well enough to see how carefully he attended to Blake's panting response.

"Todd sent me," Blake said. "I am to tell you there's a large, armed party coming this way, along the road from Trevanan. The fishermen were up before dawn and noticed the movement, so they sent a rider here to give warning before the army even reached Trevanan. Todd said to tell you that he can see their dust, and they are certainly headed to Penruan. He cannot make out their banners as yet and they have sent no herald to announce their arrival, so he is assuming they are enemies who mean to surprise us." He paused to take a breath.

"You will want your armor," Emma said to Dain. She knelt to open the wooden chest in which his chain mail was stored. "There's no need to call for assistance. Blake and I can act as your squires."

Dain was already unbuckling his belt and pulling up his tunic. Emma lifted the mail hose from the chest and handed them to him, while Blake pulled out the padded gambeson.

"Who can this armed party be?" Emma asked, noting the grim expression on Dain's face.

"I have no idea, but I will not go unprepared to meet them," he responded.

With Emma and Blake helping him, Dain was quickly armored and his sword refastened at his waist. With his mail coif loosely folded at his neck, his mail gauntlets tucked into his belt where they were easy to reach, and his helm under his arm, he raced down the stairs, Blake at his side and Emma at his back.

There were few men in the hall, and they were all servants too elderly to fight. Sloan appeared a moment later. Still adjusting his mail tunic, with Hawise carrying his belt and sword, he hurried to join Dain.

"Todd has alerted everyone," Sloan said. "The men are arming themselves. We are prepared to fight, if need be." He took his sword from Hawise and gave her a brief kiss.

When Dain and Sloan headed for the door, Emma and Hawise followed.

"Where do you think you are going?" Dain asked.

"With you," Emma said. "If fighting does begin, Hawise and I will return to the keep immediately and make ready to receive wounded men. If these prove to be guests, perhaps a party of King Henry's men who are riding on to St. Ives or Penzance, then we will want to know at once, because we'll have a fair amount of cooking to do if we are to feed everyone. We ate most of the bread and pies yesterday."

"They are more likely to be enemies than friends," Sloan said. "Prospective guests would send a messenger ahead to give their host time to prepare."

"I am going with you," Emma declared, looking deep into Dain's eyes. She expected an argument. Instead, he smiled and clasped her hand.

"You must promise to leave when I order you to leave," he said.

"Yes, my lord." From the look he gave her, she wasn't sure if he was going to rely on her meek assent. Dain was beginning to know her almost as well as she knew him.

The approaching force had nearly reached Penruan by the time Dain and his companions stepped out onto the walk atop the gatehouse, where Todd awaited them.

"It's not a very big army," Emma noted, peering through one of the crenels. The open intervals in the stone wall were meant to allow lookouts or archers a spot from which to watch an enemy and, for protection of the defenders, a crenel wasn't very wide. Even so, Dain put a hand on Emma's shoulder and pulled her back to a safer location, where she could still see some of what was happening below.

"They may have reinforcements coming later,"

Dain said, responding to her comment. "Who are they, Todd? Can you tell?"

"They haven't shown their banners yet," Todd answered.

"That bodes ill," Sloan grumbled. "Those men are too well mounted and well armed to be brigands come to avenge their fellows after you recently cleaned out their roost near Rough Tor. Dain, those are almost certainly some nobleman's troops."

The armed force reached the ravine over which the drawbridge usually lay. At Todd's command the gate had been closed and barred and the drawbridge had been raised, leaving no means of entering Penruan. The troops began to spread out in disciplined fashion to form a line three horsemen deep a few feet back from the edge of the ravine. Their leader, in full chain mail and astride a huge gray stallion, placed himself in position to be first across the drawbridge when—or if—it was lowered.

The horsemen immediately behind the leader drew apart, and now the squires at last unfurled their lord's banners, one on either side of a rider who came through the ranks to join the leader.

"A woman, by God!" Sloan exclaimed.

"If there is a lady among them, then we need not worry about a battle," Emma said. "Let me see better."

She pushed forward between Dain and Sloan to look through the crenel. Hawise did likewise at the next crenel, and both of them cried out at the same time.

"My lord Gavin!" yelled Hawise.

"Father!" Emma exclaimed.

"What?" Dain shouted at her. "Are you telling me

Gavin of Wroxley has brought an army against me?"

"It's his banner," Hawise cried. "See, blue and green diagonally divided, with a single gold scallop shell in the center. I'd know it anywhere."

"Damnation," Dain muttered. He leaned over Emma's shoulder so he could see what she was seeing. "That's Lady Mirielle with him. I recognize her now. We met once at court. She's brave to expose herself to my archers, and Gavin is a fool to put his wife into danger."

"My father is no fool," Emma said. "I am sure Mirielle knows you would never give an order to loose arrows upon a woman."

"Another sorceress at Penruan," Dain said, rubbing a hand over his face. "Well, Emma, can you tell me if they've come to besiege us? Or is Gavin likely to challenge me to mortal combat?"

"It's far more likely they're here to pay us a friendly visit," Hawise said stoutly.

"An uninvited and unwelcome visit," Sloan said.

"We must go down to meet them," Emma decided. "Todd, have the drawbridge lowered."

"No!" Dain thundered at Todd. Then, to Emma, "How dare you give an order to my man-at-arms when I am present? And what do you mean, *we?* This is war. You will remain here, behind the walls, where you are safe."

"I will not," Emma said, very distinctly. "The only way we can learn why my father and Mirielle are here is by talking with them. I am going to walk out of the gatehouse and across the drawbridge."

She headed for the stairs that led down to the bailey. Hawise went with her.

"Hawise!" Sloan shouted.

Emma turned back to see indecision on Hawise's

face as she wavered between her old loyalty to Emma and her new dedication to Sloan.

"Stay with your husband," Emma ordered, and went down the steps alone.

"I cannot decide," Dain said from close behind her a moment after she reached the bailey, "whether you are witless or I am. Todd will order the drawbridge lowered, and we will go out by the wicket gate. The main gate will remain closed for now. I'll decide later whether to open it."

"Thank you, Dain."

"I may have to kill him," Dain warned.

"Please, I beg you, talk to him first."

"For your sake, I will. I trust you, Emma. You, not Gavin. He has been my enemy for all my life."

The man-at-arms on duty at the gate unlocked and opened the wicket, a smaller door in the main gate, just wide enough to allow one person at a time to pass through. Dain went first, then Emma stepped out of the safety of Penruan's walls. She took Dain's hand, and they walked together across the drawbridge.

"Oh, my dear girl!" Mirielle had dismounted and, with tears running down her cheeks, she hurried forward to embrace Emma. "At least you are well enough to walk."

"Whatever do you mean?" Emma asked, hugging her stepmother with all the warmth she felt toward her dearest friend and teacher. But it was Gavin who answered her question.

"We have come to rescue you and take you home. We can protect you there."

Gavin tossed the reins of his horse to a squire so he could also dismount and embrace Emma. Even encased in chain mail, the circle of his arms was familiar and dear to her, and she returned his embrace as warmly as she had Mirielle's, hugging him until Dain interrupted their happy reunion.

"You intend to do what?" Dain exclaimed, one hand on his sword hilt. "If there is some danger to my wife, tell me what it is and I will protect her."

"You?" The look Gavin sent toward Dain would have made a lesser man tremble in terror. "You are the danger. I regret ever giving a daughter of Wroxley to you. We know what you have planned for our girl, and we won't allow it."

"I'll see you dead before I'll hand Emma over to you!" Dain yelled, and began to pull his sword from its scabbard.

"Stop!" Emma cried, daring to place her hands on top of Dain's, trying with all her strength to make him push the sword blade back into the sheath. "I won't allow you to fight. Dain, you promised we would talk with them. Mirielle, please, make Father stop threatening us."

"*Us?*" Mirielle repeated. She looked from Emma to Dain, a searching gaze that saw much. Then she faced her husband. "Gavin, I do believe you ought to be quiet, just for a few moments, and listen."

"Father," Emma said to the fuming Gavin, "why would I want to leave my husband, or Penruan?"

"Because Dain is planning to kill you," Gavin said, biting off each word. He had not removed his helm and his fine mouth, framed by silvery metal, closed in a line of fierce yet controlled anger. Like Dain, he kept his hand ready at his sword hilt.

"He most certainly is not going to kill me!" Emma cried. "How can you imagine an honorable man would commit such an outrage? Father, whence comes this unreasoning anger? You weren't this furious with Dain when the feud was reopened, or even when King Henry commanded you to send a daughter to marry the lord of Penruan. Why have you changed so drastically?"

"We have both changed our opinions," Mirielle said, "because we received a letter of warning from Dain's own mother, in which Lady Richenda informed us that Dain is planning to murder you and seize the disputed land. Emma, my dear, you are fortunate to have so devoted and honest a mother-in-law, who is willing to defy her own son for your sake. Of course, Gavin decided to set out from Wroxley the very next day after the letter arrived, and I could not let him come alone, not when you might need my skills to get you out of Dain's castle."

"Now we know where her messenger was sent," Dain said to Emma. "And to whom."

"Lady Richenda's accusation is completely and deliberately false," Emma told Gavin. "Dain would never hurt me. He has always been kind to me." It wasn't strictly true, but Emma wasn't going to mention Dain's coldness when she had first reached Penruan.

"If the accusation is false, as Emma says," Gavin asked with his gaze fixed on Dain like a hawk measuring its prey just before striking, "what reason would Lady Richenda have for sending such a damning message? She must have assumed I'd try to stop your plan. Didn't she understand how a claim of violence intended against Emma must inevitably lead to warfare between you and me?"

"I am certain she did know it," Dain said. "When my mother sent that letter she was depending on an armed reaction from you."

"Of course!" Emma exclaimed. "She wanted the feud to be reopened. After you sent her away the letter was her best chance of accomplishing her dearest wish."

"No doubt," Dain added, "she was convinced I'd win any battle fought on my own land against an opponent who is far from home and who has with him a smaller company of warriors than the large numbers I can quickly call up to join me."

"Let me understand this," Gavin said. "You are speaking of a mother who has schemed to send her only son into battle, to risk his life unnecessarily? Is she mad? Thanks to King Henry's command there was peace—uneasy and untrusting, but still, a peace—between us, until I received that frightening message."

"If you knew my mother, you'd understand," Dain said with bitter rage. "She has made perpetuation of that old feud between our baronies her life's work. She claims she swore to my father on his deathbed that she would see me the victor. Wretched, wretched woman!" Fists clenched, face distorted, he turned aside.

"Father," Emma said, in an effort to divert Gavin until Dain could recover from his emotional outburst, "tell me who delivered Lady Richenda's letter to you? Was it a sour-faced man with gray hair and a nasty smile?"

"An apt description," Gavin responded, his attention now on Emma, just as she wanted. "He said his name was Wade, and he declared that he had ridden at top speed with little rest, all the way from Penruan to Lincolnshire in a matter of days, rather than the weeks such a journey usually takes. I must say, he looked as if his story was true. But when I offered him fresh clothes, a bath, a bed, and food, and the chance to return to Penruan with my army for escort, as I intended to leave the next day, Wade refused. He insisted that it was his duty to report back to Lady Richenda as soon as possible, and an army would travel too slowly. I assume he reached home safely?"

"Oh, yes," Emma said, "and promptly thereafter he tried to kill me, and Dain's sister, and a boy who is my page."

"Then his life is forfeit to me," Gavin said.

"You are too late," Dain told him. "Wade's intended victims found a defender in a hermit who has been living near the castle in one of the cliff caves. Wade is dead, and the outlaws he called to his assistance are defeated in battle and either dead or imprisoned."

"You lead an exciting life here in Penruan," Gavin observed dryly.

"Lately, it has been too exciting by half," Dain responded.

"What of the brave hermit?" Mirielle asked. "We must thank him for helping Emma. May we visit his cave?"

"Hermit is staying at the castle," Emma said, "while he recovers from the wounds Wade inflicted on him. Dain's sister and I have been caring for him."

"It is a long and complicated story," Dain said to Gavin. "My lord, if you and Lady Mirielle are willing to enter Penruan Castle while leaving your army behind, I would be honored to entertain you, and I offer my personal guarantee for your safety. If you will forbid violence on the part of your men against mine, I'll order the main gate opened, so your people may freely pass in and out. I will also undertake to feed them. Thanks to Emma's hard work during this harvest season, our storerooms are full. We have more than enough food laid by to supply the castle for the entire winter and beyond. Feeding your troops will mean no serious drain on us."

"Which is to say, you are prepared to withstand a long siege if it becomes necessary," Gavin said. For the first time since meeting Dain the hard line of his mouth softened. Gavin reached up to remove his helm and hand it to a squire. He pushed back his mail coif, pulled off his gauntlets, and extended his bare hand to Dain.

"My lord, I do insist upon one condition to your generous offer," Gavin said. "I want to hear every detail of your long and complicated story."

"After you have heard the story," Emma suggested, "perhaps you and Dain can reach a peaceable final resolution to a dispute that seems to me more ridiculous the more I learn of it."

"I make no promises," Gavin said, "except a promise to listen."

"I accept that promise," Dain said, and he and Gavin shook hands.

A short time later the sentries on the walls of Penruan, who of late were growing accustomed to unusual occurrences, were treated to the sight of their lord strolling across the drawbridge in company with his lifelong enemy. The two men maintained a cautious distance from each other. Not so their wives, who walked arm-in-arm, talking and laughing. Scarcely were they all inside the bailey when Hawise, newly wed to the captain of Penruan's men-at-arms, threw herself into the embrace of the lady of Wroxley for a laughing, tearful reunion.

The onlookers also noted with astonishment the way Gavin of Wroxley clasped Hawise in his arms and told her that she was looking exceptionally pretty, and how, upon being introduced to Sloan, Gavin warmly shook his hand and informed him he was a very lucky man.

"If I hadn't seen it with my own eyes," Todd exclaimed in an original turn of phrase, "I wouldn't have believed it."

"Where is Lady Vivienne?" Dain asked the first maidservant he encountered in the great hall.

"She's in the herb garden with Hermit," the maid responded. "He wanted to see what Lady Emma has been doing there."

"Ask them to join us," Dain ordered.

Meanwhile, Emma was giving her own commands. The great hall was already swept and clean after the revelry of the previous day, and preparations for the midday meal were well in hand. Two unexpected guests at the high table presented no problem so far as food was concerned, and the guest rooms were always ready for visitors. But food and drink for Gavin's army would require considerable work from the kitchen staff. Emma gave specific orders, with Mirielle adding suggestions, for the army came well supplied to feed itself.

Both women were in the bailey, consulting with the knight who was in charge of overseeing food for Gavin's troops, when Vivienne and Hermit reached the great hall. Thus, they were not present to observe Gavin's reaction when he first met Hermit.

As soon as Emma came back into the hall, she saw the two men facing each other. She expected Gavin to be thanking Hermit most heartily for the way he had fought Wade to protect her and Vivienne. Instead, she detected an odd tension between them, and she saw a puzzled frown on Dain's brow. Vivienne stood close to her brother, keeping so still that her usually flowing white robes did not move at all.

"Mirielle, come and meet Dain's sister and Hermit," Emma said, taking Mirielle's arm to draw her

334

toward the little group standing in front of the high table.

Earlier, during their stroll across the drawbridge, Emma had told Mirielle about Vivienne's magical powers, so she was not surprised to see Mirielle smile and nod and make a certain gesture of recognition to Dain's sister. She was surprised when Vivienne did not respond. Vivienne's whole attention was fixed on Hermit and Gavin, as if she was entranced by the very sight of them. Or perhaps, Emma thought, Vivienne understood what was going on between the two men.

Suddenly, Mirielle made a muffled sound. She pulled her arm from Emma's light grasp and took a few swift steps to reach her husband's side. She was white-faced, her eyes wide with an emotion Emma could not define.

Emma gazed from Mirielle to Gavin to Hermit to Vivienne, and then looked to Dain, hoping he would supply an explanation for the taut posture, held breath, and rapidly rising anger she could sense in every pore of her body but could not understand.

"Brice," Mirielle said to Hermit in a strained voice, "Cousin Brice, what are you doing here?"

Chapter Nineteen

"Sir Brice is my cousin," Mirielle said to the three people who stared at her in astonishment. "He is also the former seneschal of Wroxley. I have not seen him for nearly ten years."

"After so long a time can you be certain of his identity?" Dain asked. "Perhaps it's merely a passing resemblance you see."

"I know my own cousin. From Gavin's manner when Emma and I entered the hall, it's clear that he has recognized Brice, too." Mirielle spoke as if Dain's question was an insult. To the silent, bearded man she said, "Tell them I am not mistaken."

"I am Brice," he admitted, as if confessing a crime, and closed his mouth on any further explanation.

"When you left Wroxley," Mirielle said rather sharply, "you claimed to be going on crusade. How did you find your way to Cornwall?"

"I did travel to the Holy Land," Hermit said, sounding as if the words were being torn out of him. "I remained there for years. When I returned to England last autumn, I was sick in body and spirit. Like a wounded animal yearning for its lair, I wanted only to find a quiet place far away from Wroxley. So I wandered south to the other end of England. It was a slow pilgrimage; I had to stop several times to regain enough strength to go on."

"Why couldn't you return to Wroxley?" Dain asked.

"I understand," Mirielle murmured before Dain could press more questions on Brice. "I do. But Brice, your withered arm is healed."

"My renewed health I owe to a remarkable local healer," Brice explained. "My newly optimistic spirit is Vivienne's doing."

"How was the arm injured?" Emma asked, seizing on what seemed to her the simplest question of the many engendered by what she was hearing. "Hermit, you never said how it happened, and I didn't want to pry into a past that was obviously painful to you."

"It happened during a terrible battle with a wicked magician," Mirielle answered for her cousin. "Brice was trying to protect me—and Gavin and the people of Wroxley, too."

"Just as you protected Vivienne and me from Wade," Emma said. "Dear Hermit, you are a hero as well as a crusader! Or should I call you Sir Brice?"

"Hermit will do," he responded in a voice roughened by emotion.

"What I would like," said Gavin, "is to hear how Brice fought to protect Emma from this Wade person. Dain, you have promised Mirielle and me a full accounting of Lady Richenda's activities, and of why she sent that man, Wade, to Wroxley with a letter meant to convince us that you wanted Emma dead. I gather those are all parts of the same complicated story. When may we hear it?"

"It is a remarkable story," Hermit told him, "and one that does great credit to Emma."

"There is another story you ought to hear," Vivienne spoke up. "It is the tale of how my brother and I were reunited, thanks to Emma, and how the missing pieces of Dain's memory, taken from him by magic, were restored by magic."

"Certainly I will want to hear that," Mirielle said, smiling at her.

"Let us sit," Dain suggested. "Emma, Vivienne, and I will tell you all of it while we eat."

With a somewhat forced politeness intended to conceal his emotional turmoil, Dain led his guests to the high table. He still did not fully trust Gavin, which was why he took note of how cleverly Gavin had turned the subject away from Hermit's past to a good deed performed in the present, and of how readily Mirielle and Hermit followed Gavin's lead. Dain silently vowed to learn the entire truth about Hermit—or Sir Brice, as he ought now to be called. If there was something unsavory about the man, he'd see to it that the erstwhile hermit left Penruan before he could cause irreparable damage to Vivienne's heart.

Dain's fiercely held desire to save his sister from any future unhappiness made him look closely at Brice. Beneath Brice's freshly trimmed beard Dain could detect a resemblance to Mirielle, who sat between Dain and her cousin, thus affording an easy comparison of the two. Brice's face was years older, scarred, and definitely masculine, yet the basic bone structure was similar, as was the thick, straight black hair. Brice's hair was threaded with silver, while Mirielle's was still entirely dark and gleaming with health. Mirielle wore her hair wound around her head in a thick braid, and she left it uncovered with the same blithe disregard of fashionable dictates for a married woman that Emma frequently displayed. On this day, Emma's own staight, black locks were also worn in a single braid fastened with ribbon at its end and allowed to hang down her back without any covering at all.

It was natural for Brice and Mirielle to have hair of the same color and texture. They were blood relations. But why would Emma, who was the daughter of Gavin and his first wife and, therefore, no blood relative to the other two, have hair so remarkably similar to theirs? Or a chin and cheekbones so like Mirielle's?

Dain watched his guests with eyes suddenly grown sharp and ever more suspicious. Gavin and Mirielle were listening with rapt attention to Emma's account of her dealings with Lady Richenda. Brice was gazing at Emma with despair in his eyes. Dain looked toward Vivienne and received a frightened glance that told him that his sister knew, or guessed, the answer to the dreadful presentiment that threatened to drive him from the table to grab his sword and challenge the man who, he was beginning to believe, had tricked him in the most outrageous manner.

Dain began to consider the possibility that his mother had been right about Gavin, after all.

"I understand the situation better now," Gavin said to Dain as soon as Emma finished her story. "It was Lady Richenda, not you, who instigated the revival of the feud."

"She insisted, it's true," Dain said. He told himself to control his rising anger so he could learn Gavin's real intentions in sending Emma to him—and his real reason for coming to Penruan.

Dain did not forget for a single moment that Gavin's men-at-arms were moving freely in and out of Penruan Castle—at *his* invitation! Before Dain or any of his men dared sleep that night he needed to know if treachery was afoot. He spoke slowly, as if he was thinking through all the ramifications of the old feud, though actually he was trying to decide how best to defend Penruan against an invader who was already within the walls. "I was agreeable to my mother's insistence, in part because I was raised to believe my father and grandfather were cheated by Udo of Wroxley, and that Udo caused my father's death."

"Here sits a man who may be able to tell us how the feud began," Mirielle said, and added a statement that startled Dain out of his reverie on defense. "Brice was at Wroxley during most of the time when Gavin was absent in the Holy Land."

"You were away from Wroxley?" Dain asked Gavin in surprise.

"For more than a decade," Gavin said. "I thought it best to leave. My wife and I were constantly at odds, and our bitter quarrels upset everyone around us. Only later did I learn Alda was a wicked sorceress. In my absence she poisoned my father, and the seneschal before Brice."

"Yet you married another sorceress," Dain said, then scarcely attended to Gavin's response. Gavin had been away from Wroxley for years, leaving his estranged wife behind. During those years Brice had been the seneschal and, no doubt, in frequent contact with the lady of the castle. Emma bore a remarkable resemblance to Brice. It would take a stupid man, indeed, not to see the implication.

"I don't know much about the feud," Brice said. "It was over and done before I was at Wroxley. The battle in which Lord Halard lost his arm had already been fought, and the king had confirmed Lord Udo in his possession of the land that both men coveted. To me it was just an old story told on winter evenings by the men-at-arms who could remember those exciting days. I expect most of them are dead by now; they were middle-aged at the time. The only one alive who knows the details of the feud is Lady Richenda. It's my opinion that she will keep to the story she has always told, the version that casts Lord Halard in a favorable light."

Dain noticed how Emma sat listening to all of this without a sign of guilt on her lovely features. Did she know? he wondered. Or was she an innocent victim of Gavin's plot to end the feud in his own favor?

But the feud was already ended in Gavin's favor, by the king's command. Gavin held that patch of long-disputed land. So, what purpose could possibly lay behind the deception he had foisted on Dain?

It required all of Dain's considerable self-control to force himself to sit at the high table and play the agreeable host while he dissembled his mounting suspicions. As soon as he decently could, he made an excuse to leave his guests, saying he must speak to Sloan.

"Warn the men-at-arms to be on the alert for treachery," Dain ordered.

"Hawise insists that Gavin is an honest lord," Sloan objected. "She knows some of the men who have come with Gavin, and is friends with their wives. Hawise is a fine judge of character. I cannot believe she would befriend a villain."

"Nor do I want to believe Emma is involved in treachery," Dain countered his friend's protests. "Yet we both know that even clever women can be misled. See to my command, Sloan."

"Aye," Sloan agreed with undisguised reluctance. "It's always best to be prepared, and it will do the men no harm to stand ready for a night. But we need to know more, Dain. We can't assume the worst based on guesses alone, nor can we act on supposition against a powerful lord who is a guest in your home."

"My thoughts exactly," Dain said. "I intend to confront Gavin in private, and I will have the truth out of him. If what I suspect is fact, guest or no, he won't leave Penruan alive, and I'll gladly answer to the king for my actions, knowing Henry will absolve me of guilt when I explain. Meanwhile, see that the men are ready for a fight."

Not until some hours later, with the castle inhabitants in their beds or, in the case of Sloan's men-at-arms, standing guard in tense readiness, did Dain approach the chamber where Gavin and Mirielle were to spend the night. To his surprise he found the door ajar. To his even greater surprise, he recognized the low-pitched voice of Sir Brice coming from within. Dain paused, eavesdropping without shame in hope of discovering whether his castle was threatened or not.

"I have told no one here at Penruan," Brice declared. "Nor will I. The secret is safe with me. Surely, you know I'd never wish harm to Emma."

"Your very presence may harm her," Gavin said. "You ought to have left on the same day you learned who she is, and found another place to hide."

"I know it." Brice's rough tone softened into reflective tenderness. "The cave where I was living is a magical place, so when I first beheld Emma there it was perfectly reasonable for me to think for an instant or two that she was an image of Mirielle as I remember her during her youth. They are so much alike. Surely you've noticed the resemblance? By the time I understood that she was real, not a ghost figure but Emma grown up and beautiful, I knew I could not leave her. She was lonely in her new life, and a bit frightened, and I foolishly dreamed of becoming her friend. She seemed to need a friend."

"You call it foolishness," Gavin said harshly. "I call it madness. Have you no sense at all?"

"Why was Emma afraid?" Mirielle asked.

"No one wanted her here," Brice answered. "Dain was indifferent to her and Lady Richenda was her implaccable enemy. Yet Emma has made a place for herself. She has earned the respect and affection of every person in Penruan, and of many in Trevanan village. Dain values her now, all the more so since Emma helped to restore his sister to him, along with his missing memories of Vivienne. I do believe Dain and Emma can be happy together."

"Only if you go away," Gavin said.

"So I will. It will break my heart to leave my girl for a second time, especially after knowing her as a lovely young woman, but for her sake I'll do it. Gavin, I do swear to you, Dain will never hear from me that Emma is my daughter. But I demand a promise from you in return. Let them live in peace. Dain is an honorable man; he'll keep to the terms of your agreement. Don't you be the one to reopen hostilities between Wroxley and Penruan."

"We only came to Penruan out of fear for Emma,"

Mirielle said. "Brice, if you are as convinced as I am that she is in no danger, and that Dain will keep her safe and honor her as a husband should, then there is no reason for us to go to war against him. Is there, Gavin?"

"No," Gavin said. "You have my word; I'll not attack Penruan. We will stay for a day or two, then take a friendly leave of our host. I suggest that you leave with us, Brice. You can say you want to visit longer with Mirielle. Once we are away from Penruan, you may go wherever you like, so long as you do not return here. And Dain need never know that I am not Emma's father."

But Dain already knew. He had heard every word, and was now fully aware that a misbegotten girl had been foisted on him in place of the legitimate daughter of the baron of Wroxley whom he had been ordered by the king to marry. Knowledge of the deception was far more disturbing than his earlier concern about the possibility of armed treachery within Penruan's walls.

The lies and the humiliation of being tricked were more than his noble honor could bear. Or his temper.

He did not trust himself to enter the chamber without inflicting violence upon the occupants—and that would only precipitate the armed conflict he'd prefer to avoid for the sake of the women and children who were dependent upon him. However, there was one person on whom he could vent his rage, and he'd force her to reveal her part in the ruse. He raced up the stairs to the lord's chamber.

"Dain?" Emma was combing her hair before braiding it for the night. Hearing the door slam behind him, she turned with comb in hand and a question in her eyes. Dain saw no fear in her. Not yet. "Whatever is wrong?"

"Did you know?" he demanded, advancing on her with barely controlled fury. "Have you known all along, and kept the secret for Gavin's sake? Or was your intention to make a fool of me, to gain one final advantage after King Henry settled the feud?"

"I don't know what you're talking about," she said, sounding calm, though the hand that set down her comb trembled slightly. "There's no reason for you to accuse me of wrongdoing. Explain yourself. What is it I'm supposed to know, and to be keeping from you?"

"Are you claiming you don't know that Brice— your precious Hermit—is your natural father?"

"What?" She stared at him as if she feared he'd gone mad. And in a way, he had. If he were in full possession of his wits, he never would have told her so bluntly. Nor was he going to stop. Outraged pride drove him on.

"I perceived the truth just by observing you and Lady Mirielle and Sir Brice together," Dain informed her with cold anger. "Do you expect me to believe you never noticed the family resemblance?"

"How could I notice any such thing?" Emma cried. "Like most children, I saw little of the grown-ups, except for my nurses and a few maidservants. When I was six years old I was sent away for fostering. Years later, I returned for just a week or two, before my brother and I were sent to a monastery for safety. While we were gone my mother died and Sir Brice left Wroxley.

"Oh, Dain!" she exclaimed, as if the awful meaning of his accusation had just struck her. "Are you saying that Brice and my mother were lovers?"

"I have heard your parentage confirmed from

Brice's own lips," Dain said. "He was talking with Gavin and Mirielle and I overheard them."

"Dear heaven." Emma's hands covered her face, hiding her expression. "How could they lie to me about something so important?"

"I gather it was to protect you from knowledge of your mother's adultery," Dain explained in a gentler voice, his fury abating slightly when he realized the depth of Emma's shock and pain. She had not known; he was suddenly certain she was not part of the conspiracy to deceive him. The relief that flooded through him left him as weak and stunned as Emma appeared to be. Dain could not, at that moment, afford to examine why he was so relieved.

Emma took her hands away from her face so she could look directly at Dain. She stood with fists clenched at her sides and her chin lifted in a gesture of courage that tore at Dain's angry heart and made him ache to embrace her. But he couldn't, not till he had learned everything she knew, or could guess out of her knowledge of Gavin and Mirielle, about the deception practiced on him. No, he corrected himself, the deception practiced on both of them.

"The man I knew as Hermit was old and scarred, with a beard and a withered arm," Emma said, as if trying to organize her fragmented thoughts. "I can barely recall the Sir Brice who was once seneschal of Wroxley Castle, except for a vague impression that he was handsome. Until this hour I never connected Hermit and Sir Brice. Why should I? I hadn't thought of Brice for years before Mirielle called Hermit by that name. I always took Hermit to be who he said he was.

"I do comprehend your problem, though," Emma went on. "I am not the wife you were promised. After what you have learned, you have every right to reject me. But my father—I mean, Gavin—never meant to defraud you. He fully intended to send Alys, his oldest daughter with Mirielle, to marry you. It was I who insisted Alys was too fragile to make the long journey and that I should come in her place. If there is fault in our marriage, it's entirely mine, not Gavin's. Let the blame rest with me and do not, I implore you, reopen that idiotic feud now that it's settled. Be content with punishing me."

"I never took you for a martyr," Dain said.

"An illegitimate martyr, my lord," she responded with a wry laugh, while tears ran down her cheeks. "The responsiblity for this debacle is mine."

"No, it is not." Unable to watch her misery any longer, Dain grabbed her shoulders so tightly that she winced. "The responsibility rightly lies with the adults who never told a little girl the truth."

"I'm sure they did it to protect me, just as you assumed. My mother was even more dreadful than yours. All the same, I had a right to know my real father."

"And a right to be angry after learning of their deception," Dain said, wishing she would display some temper, instead of meekly accepting a truth he found unacceptable.

"I'm not angry," she said. "Just stunned. I do admit to feeling betrayed, as much for your sake as for my own." She paused, swallowed hard, and then asked, "What shall we do now?"

"There is only one thing to do," said a soft voice from the doorway. Vivienne moved into the room, her white robes flowing and drifting about her slim figure, her eyes filled with pity and understanding. "Dain, you must forgive the lie. Emma, you must accept the truth."

"Impossible!" Dain uttered the single word through gritted teeth.

"Will you permit a well-meant fabrication to tear your marriage apart?" Vivienne asked.

"Well meant?" Dain repeated with a sneer. "Am I wrong to think you knew about this *fabrication?* Did Hermit tell you?"

"He didn't need to tell me," Vivienne answered with perfect calm. "I guessed by observation and confirmed the guess by magic. Brice loves his daughter. That's why he gave her to Mirielle to raise. He would sacrifice anything for Emma."

"Including you?" Dain asked.

"Brice long ago repented of his sins, and expiated them by going on Crusade, as many other men do. He is trying to live a better life now."

"How touching."

"Will you hold a grudge for decades, the way your mother used to do?" Vivienne asked. "What of your life, Dain? Suppose Gavin had refused Emma's plea to send her to Penruan and had kept strictly to King Henry's commands. Suppose little Alys had been sent to you, instead. If Alys had survived the journey, which from all I've heard of her would be a doubtful proposition at best, what would have happened? I can tell you without resorting to magic. Dear brother, you'd have found yourself burdened with a sick child for a bride. Lady Richenda would still rule Penruan with an iron hand and a cold heart, and you would still be ignorant of my very existence and lacking years of your memory. Would you prefer that life, or the life you now enjoy with Emma?" When Dain did not respond at once Vivienne said, "If you would rather answer that question in the silence of your own heart, then do so.

Just be certain you answer honestly. Don't let injured pride interfere."

Dain looked from his sister's imploring face to his wife. Emma's shoulders were rigid, her hands tightly clasped at her bosom. Her marvelous purple-flecked eyes were wide, her gaze fixed on his face. He wondered what she read there.

Did Emma love him as much as he loved her?

Dain nearly choked on the unexpected thought. Uncomfortably aware of the presence in his room of two women who were capable of working magic, he tried to close the unwelcome idea of love out of his mind, attempting to convince himself that the idea was in some way their doing. He did not want, or need, any further complications in his life.

Then Emma dredged up out of her undoubtedly roiling emotions a small, tremulous smile, and Dain knew with complete and blinding certainty that he did love her, with all his heart and all his being, and the emotion was not conjured by magic. He loved Emma because of who, and what, she was, and it mattered not one whit who had fathered her. Emma was honest to her core, and the magic she practiced was as good and pure as her heart. He longed to tell her so and grieved to realize that he must postpone his declaration. For Emma's sake, he had to confront Gavin and Brice and settle their differences before he could be free to reveal his unexpected discovery of love.

"Both of you," he said to his wife and his sister, "come with me."

Not allowing them a chance to argue, he caught each woman by an elbow and swept them together out of the lord's chamber and down the stairs to the next level of the tower keep.

Chapter Twenty

Dain led Emma and Vivienne to the chamber occupied by Gavin and Mirielle. There he pounded on
the latched door so hard that several curious faces
appeared from other doorways and from around
corners, and Blake hastened from the stairs to
Dain's side to see what was wrong.

"Has Sir Brice left this room?" Dain demanded
of the boy.

"Aye, my lord. I saw him going to his own chamber a short time ago," Blake answered.

"Bring him here," Dain commanded. "At once!"

Blake scurried off to do his bidding, just as the
door opened. Dain pushed his way inside, with the
two women following at his imperious nod.

It was apparent they had interrupted a romantic
moment. Gavin was naked to the waist and Mirielle
was hastily pulling on a robe. Neither of them objected to the intrusion. Perhaps, Dain thought,

Emma's accusing gaze and Vivienne's solemn expression warned his guests that the three of them were there for a serious purpose.

Dain stalked across the chamber to confront Gavin face-to-face and speak before Gavin could demand to know what was happening.

"You have broken the terms of the agreement King Henry imposed upon us, to which we both agreed and set our seals," Dain said, daring to poke a finger at the broad, bare chest of the baron of Wroxley. "I have every right to challenge you to mortal combat."

A slight stir at the door told Dain that Brice had arrived.

"Blake," Dain ordered, momentarily taking his gaze from Gavin's astonished face, "close the door and guard it from the outside. On peril of your life, allow no one else to enter here, and never repeat a word of anything you may overhear."

"You have my word of honor on it." Blake closed the door, and Vivienne, who was avoiding Brice's questioning glance, moved to latch it securely.

"Now let us be blunt," Dain said, returning his full attention to Gavin. "I have by chance learned who Emma's real father is. Emma claims that her coming to Penruan was at her own insistence and is, therefore, no fault of yours. I would hear your side of it, Gavin, and then yours, my lady Mirielle. If you tell me the entire truth, it's just possible that we can prevent bloodshed."

Dain did not look at Brice as he made this speech, but kept his shoulder resolutely turned toward the miscreant knight. He would deal with Brice later, depending on what Gavin and Mirielle had to say. However, Dain was acutely aware of Emma stepping forward to stand beside him. Emma did not touch him; she did not need to. Her close presence was support enough.

"Since the first day I met Emma, when she was barely ten years old," Gavin said, "I have thought of her as my true daughter. I love her as a daughter."

"I had the raising of her," Mirielle said. "I taught Emma to use her inborn magic for the benefit of others, so she could avoid the untutored excesses of her mother, and would never fall prey to evil, as Alda did. As for Brice, I believe Alda seduced him for her own wicked purpose, and used magic to do it. Brice was not entirely to blame for what happened. He has paid dearly for his mistakes."

"Mirielle, I will not allow you to make excuses for behavior that was beyond excuse," Brice said. "I should have resisted Alda and did not. I nearly died for my weakness of character. The only good result of my adulterous affair was Emma, whom I believed to be Gavin's daughter until Gavin and Mirielle told me the truth of Emma's birth. I regret everything about that dreadful time, except for Emma's existence."

"And so, having learned she was your daughter, you then consigned her to Gavin's care and left Wroxley?" Dain asked in a voice filled with scorn at the very idea of a father abandoning his child.

"It was the best thing I could do for her," Brice said. "I bore terrible sins on my conscience, sins that required a long penance before I could be absolved of them. I was not fit to raise an innocent girl."

"You should have told me," Emma said to the pair who faced her and Dain. "If not before, then when I begged to come to Penruan in Alys's place. Mirielle, you should have told me!"

"We wanted to protect you," Gavin said.

"When you have children of your own," Mirielle told her gently, "you will understand how far parents will go to ensure their child's safety and happiness. And you are the child of our hearts, Emma." She reached for Emma, who sidestepped her embrace to move behind Dain, as if seeking shelter behind a dependable rock.

"You cheated Dain!" Emma cried. "You betrayed both of us! You owed us the truth!"

"I cannot deny it," Gavin said. "Dain, you have the right to demand satisfaction for the lie that permitted Emma to wed you as my daughter."

"Yes," Dain said, regarding him coldly. "Be certain of it. I intend to have full satisfaction."

"If you want to have your marriage annulled and to reopen the feud and contest that piece of land again . . ." Gavin began.

"I am sick of that cursed feud!" Dain shouted at him. "Nor do I intend to give up my wife." His arm was around Emma, drawing her closer, holding her where she belonged.

"Then what do you want?" Gavin asked, voicing the question Vivienne had asked earlier, in a different way.

"As for the feud," Dain said in a quieter tone, "if my mother could lie to me for years, as I know she did about Vivienne's existence, then it is possible she also lied to me about the origins of the feud. For all I know, my father on his deathbed swore her *not* to bind me to that old conflict. We have only my mother's version of Halard's final hours, and her word cannot be trusted. Perhaps we will never know the full truth."

"Does it matter now, after so many years?" Brice asked. When Dain turned a fierce glare on him, he said, "You are a reasonable man. So is Gavin. I can prove that claim with one simple statement: Neither of you has killed me for what I've done. Why don't you forge a new agreement, making the infamous piece of land that caused the feud the inheritance of the first child born to Dain and Emma, whether the child be a boy or a girl? I cannot imagine King Henry will object, not when his primary interest is peace among his nobles."

There followed a few moments of surprised silence at so sensible and reasonable a suggestion, until Gavin spoke.

"I can accept that," Gavin said to Dain. "I'll gladly bestow the land on your firstborn, if only you and Emma will allow Mirielle and me to act as grandparents toward your children. Whatever the two of you may think of Mirielle and me at this moment, we love Emma as our own, and we will love any child she bears."

Dain looked at Emma, seeing her tear-filled eyes and quivering lips, and he knew he could not allow her heart to be broken by a dispute that no longer meant anything at all. Whatever the right or wrong of the old feud, or of Gavin's decision to send Emma to Penruan, Dain wasn't going to quarrel anymore.

"Agreed," he said, and held out his hand to clasp Gavin's, thereby signifying his acceptance of the compact they were making. But he could not let it go at that. He wanted Gavin to understand exactly what he meant. "Though I will need time to accept all I've learned tonight, I will not break faith with you, nor will I abjure the oath I made to King Henry. The feud is truly over. As for the circumstances of Emma's birth, no one but we in this room need ever know what has passed here."

"I thank you," Gavin said formally, "for the generous spirit you've shown to us, as well as to Emma."

"I will have Father Maynard draw up the document, so it can be signed and witnessed before you leave," Dain said.

"There is a provision I would add to the agreement," Vivienne announced, stepping forward. "Brice must remain at Penruan, so he and Emma can learn to know each other. It would be cruel to deprive Emma of her natural father as soon as she has discovered him."

"Will the provision be for Emma's sake," Dain asked with a frown, "or for yours?"

"For both of us," Vivienne answered. "Please, Dain."

"Emma," Dain said, "this decision is yours to make. Do you want Brice to stay or to go?"

"So many lies," Emma whispered, looking around the room. "Except for Dain, every person here has lied to me, either directly or by failing to reveal a vital fact that I had a right to know. And each of you has excused the falsehoods, claiming they were committed out of love."

"Never doubt it," Brice said, his eyes moist. "Emma, I loved you even before I knew I had fathered you. After I learned you were mine, I longed to stay with you, or to take you away with me. But you were so young, so innocent, and in those days I was a lost and broken man, guilty of adultery and worse. How could I drag you from your home and force you to join me on my long journey of penance? I did what I believed was best for you. When I see the fine woman you have become, I cannot think my choice was wrong. But if you cannot forgive me, I will understand. I'll go away and never contact you again."

"So have I lied," Emma said, "by not telling Dain about my magical skills."

"You had good reason for keeping that from him," Brice exclaimed. "Even more so after you knew Lady Richenda. Emma, your lie was a minor infraction. Mine was far more serious, and it has haunted me every day for more than a decade. No night has passed since I left Wroxley when I have not gone to my knees to pray for your welfare."

Emma regarded Brice for a long while in silence. From her oddly bland expression Dain could not tell what she was thinking, or what decision she would make.

"Vivienne thinks you are worthy of love, and I have learned to value her wisdom," she said at last. "I think we ought to know each other better, don't you, Sir Brice? I cannot promise to love you as a daughter, but we have been friends, and you did save my life at the risk of your own. You may remain at Penruan."

"Oh, thank you, Emma!" Vivienne cried.

"I accept Emma's wishes, Brice," Dain told him. "You may stay, but know that I will be watching you, and I will protect my sister, as I will protect my wife."

"I would expect no less of you," Brice responded, and offered his hand. After a long, tense moment, Dain took it.

"I don't entirely trust Brice," Dain said to Emma later, in the privacy of the lord's chamber, "but I won't attempt to influence Vivienne against him. I love her enough to let her find her own path to happiness."

"Wise man," Emma murmured. "I am still shaken by tonight's revelations, and I scarcely know who I dare trust. Except that I do trust you, always and forever. Dain, are you sure you want to keep me, now that you know whose daughter I am?"

"Are you saying you will let me find my own path to happiness?" he asked, an odd gleam lighting his blue-green eyes.

"I suppose I am." Emma discovered that she was holding her breath as she awaited his answer.

"Well, then," he said, looking serious, "let me consider the matter. In your favor, you have improved the lives of all who live in Penruan Castle. Thanks to your knowledge of herbs, everyone is healthier than before you came here, and the food is infinitely more tasty. You've brought me joy, tenderness, freedom from old hatreds, and my beloved sister. I believe, given a bit of time, all of us can learn to live with our newly acquired knowledge."

"I am not the wife you deserve," she whispered, scarcely daring to believe what she was hearing.

"I thank God you are not!" he exclaimed. "After the way I treated you when you arrived, I don't deserve you at all. Emma, tell me honestly: Is there a chance that you could forgive me and love me? For I love you with my whole heart."

To Emma's amazement, Dain went to his knees before her, where she had once sworn to see him and where, now, she did not want him to be. Dain belonged at her side, as her true mate and partner in life.

"Oh, Dain, don't you know?" she cried, tugging at his shoulders to urge him to his feet again. "I've loved you since the first moment I saw you."

"Even though I was a brute to you?" Dain, the fierce and ruthless warrior, actually looked frightened, until Emma seized his trembling hands from his sides and pulled them around her waist so she could nestle close to his heart.

"You ought to hate me for the rough way I mauled you that day," he said in a shaky voice.

"How could I hate my one and only love?" she asked. Seeing the smile overspreading his face, she lifted her own face in hope and expectation of his kiss.

He did not disappoint her.

"There is one last secret I must reveal to you," Emma said later, when they lay entwined on the bed in the sweet aftermath of loving. "I am carrying your child."

"A son!" Dain rose on his elbows to look down at her in the candlelight.

"No," Emma said, one hand on her abdomen. "This child will be a daughter, and she will possess the same inborn magic that I have. Never fear for her; Vivienne and I, together, will teach her well."

"How can you be so sure it will be a girl?" Dain asked.

"Because she was conceived in Merlin's cave," Emma said.

"Ahhh," Dain murmured, smiling in remembrance. "That incredible afternoon."

"The next baby will be made here, in your bed, as is right and proper for your son and heir," Emma told him. "I promise."

"I see." Dain's eyes began to sparkle like ocean waves in summer sunlight. "You are telling me, my lady, that you are going to have need of me for the next few years. I must admit, I find that an encouraging thought."

"I will have need of you, my lord," Emma said, "for the rest of my life."

When she lifted her arms and wrapped them around Dain's shoulders and pulled him down to her for a closer embrace, he forgot all about feuds and guests he'd rather not have in his castle, and gave himself up completely to the magical delights of love.

Epilogue

Agatha stepped through the rock and entered the innermost chamber below the cliffs. Here the ceiling glowed with jewels far surpassing the crystals of Vivienne's abandoned little room. Emeralds and sapphires, amethysts and rubies all caught the light from the fire blazing on a hearth carved out of solid rock. The walls of the chamber were covered with shelves, all of which were crammed full of books and scrolls, and with long tapes made of plant fibers upon which the ink was created from tropical fruits. Slabs of stone carved in languages long dead leaned against the shelves.

"There you are at last." A handsome, dark-haired man sitting at a table with an ancient book open before him looked up at the familiar footstep. "Is it all settled?"

"Very nicely settled. It is finally safe for Agatha to die of old age. Soon a new and younger healer will arrive at Trevanan. I haven't decided what to call myself the next time. I'll think of something. At least wickedness is banished for a while, a feud is resolved, and two couples are set upon happy paths. For the moment I am content."

Agatha stretched, shedding her elderly guise. Her stooped figure grew tall and slender, and her unkempt gray hair changed to lustrous pale gold that fell in a straight sheaf to below her knees. Agatha's dark wool gown began to shimmer with pearly luminescence while her once heavy shawl floated sheer and ivory pale about her delicate shoulders.

"Wickedness is always banished only for a while," the man said, rising to face her. "If you were to release me, Nimue, I could go with you to the outer world. You and I, together, would exert a greater effect upon evil."

"I could release you," she said, and ran a finger lightly along his lips, "but I won't. You are too clever for me, Merlin. After all these centuries, I know you well. The instant I freed you, you'd bind me to perpetual imprisonment, thus reversing our present positions. I am not foolish enough to imagine you love me as I love you. If you were free, I'd never see you again. Whereas I visit you occasionally, to report what's happening in the world and to lighten your loneliness."

"You are too kind," Merlin said with a wry smile.

"You know full well I will release you eventually," Nimue said. "I must; it's a requirement of the enchantment that holds you here."

"How many centuries more?" he asked.

"A few. Nine—ten—eleven, perhaps. No more than eleven, surely. The world will need you by then."

"The world will have me sooner, once I've found

the formula to break the spell you've bound me with," he said, glancing at the shelves where all the knowledge of the ages was contained.

"Never think you'll learn the secret there, in books or scrolls, on tapes or on stone tablets," Nimue said, laughing. "Shall I tell you what it is?"

"Will you tell me true?"

"Have I ever lied to you, Merlin?"

"Just once," he said. "It was enough. Your single lie brought me here."

"You must love me as I love you," Nimue said. "That is the secret. Unfortunately, love is the one enchantment to which you have always been immune. Those mortal souls who live above us on the surface love so easily. Love makes their short lives bearable." She sighed, smiling wistfully at him.

"I am willing to learn," Merlin said.

"I know you are, and I am always glad to teach you," Nimue responded, laughing softly. She slid her arms around his neck and let her fingers weave into his thick hair. "It has taken only a thousand years for you to begin to think seriously about me. Perhaps, in another thousand years, you will know why I keep you here."

"Sweet enchantress," Merlin whispered, embracing her, "I am yours to instruct."

"I knew you would be," Nimue said, and kissed him.

A LOVE BEYOND TIME

FLORA SPEER

Accidentally thrust back to the eighth century, Mike Bailey falls from the sky and lands near Charlemagne's camp. Knocked senseless by the crash, he can't remember his name, but no shock can make his body forget how to respond when he awakes to the sight of an enchanting angel on earth. Headstrong and innocent, Danise chooses to risk spending her life cloistered in a nunnery rather than marry for any reason besides love. Unexpectedly mesmerized by the stranger she discovers unconscious in the forest, Danise is quickly roused by an all-consuming passion—and a desire that will conquer time itself.

___52326-4 $5.50 US/$6.50 CAN

Dorchester Publishing Co., Inc.
P.O. Box 6640
Wayne, PA 19087-8640

Please add $1.75 for shipping and handling for the first book and $.50 for each book thereafter. NY, NYC, and PA residents, please add appropriate sales tax. No cash, stamps, or C.O.D.s. All orders shipped within 6 weeks via postal service book rate. Canadian orders require $2.00 extra postage and must be paid in U.S. dollars through a U.S. banking facility.

Name_____
Address_____
City_____State_____Zip_____
I have enclosed $_____ in payment for the checked book(s).
Payment <u>must</u> accompany all orders. ❑ Please send a free catalog.
CHECK OUT OUR WEBSITE! www.dorchesterpub.com

Love Once & Forever

Flora Speer

Laura has traveled here, to this time before the moon has come to circle the earth, to embrace Kentir beneath the violet-and-ochre brilliance of the Northern Lights. In his gray-blue gaze, she sees the longing he cannot hide. His lips seek hers and find them. In his kiss she tastes the warmth of amber wine and the urgency of manly desire. She drinks deeply, forgetting that for them there can be no past, no future; for he is of a time that is ending, while she belongs to one that has yet to begin. Closing her eyes to the soft shadows of the lantern lights, she gives herself to him, determined to live out her destiny in this one precious night.

___52291-8 $5.99 US/$6.99 CAN

Dorchester Publishing Co., Inc.
P.O. Box 6640
Wayne, PA 19087-8640

Please add $1.75 for shipping and handling for the first book and $.50 for each book thereafter. NY, NYC, and PA residents, please add appropriate sales tax. No cash, stamps, or C.O.D.s. All orders shipped within 6 weeks via postal service book rate. Canadian orders require $2.00 extra postage and must be paid in U.S. dollars through a U.S. banking facility.

Name_____
Address_____
City_____State_____Zip_____
I have enclosed $_____ in payment for the checked book(s).
Payment <u>must</u> accompany all orders. ❏ Please send a free catalog.
CHECK OUT OUR WEBSITE! www.dorchesterpub.com

Love Just in Time

FLORA SPEER

After discovering her husband's infidelity, Clarissa Cummings thinks she will never trust another man. Then a freak accident sends her into another century—and the most handsome stranger imaginable saves her from drowning in the canal. But he is all wet if he thinks he has a lock on Clarissa's heart. After scandal forces Jack Martin to flee to the wilds of America, the dashing young Englishman has to give up the pleasures of a rake and earn his keep with a plow and a hoe. Yet to his surprise, he learns to enjoy the simple life of a farmer, and he yearns to take Clarissa as his bride. But after Jack has sown the seeds of desire, secrets from his past threaten to destroy his harvest of love.

___52289-6 $5.50 US/$6.50 CAN

Dorchester Publishing Co., Inc.
P.O. Box 6640
Wayne, PA 19087-8640

Please add $1.75 for shipping and handling for the first book and $.50 for each book thereafter. NY, NYC, and PA residents, please add appropriate sales tax. No cash, stamps, or C.O.D.s. All orders shipped within 6 weeks via postal service book rate. Canadian orders require $2.00 extra postage and must be paid in U.S. dollars through a U.S. banking facility.

Name_____
Address_____
City_____ State_____ Zip_____
I have enclosed $_____ in payment for the checked book(s).
Payment <u>must</u> accompany all orders. ❑ Please send a free catalog.

Destiny's Lovers

FLORA SPEER

She is utterly forbidden, a maiden whose golden purity must remain untouched. Shunned by the villagers because she is different, Janina lives with loneliness until she has the vision—a vision of the man who will come to change everything. His life spared so that he can improve the blood lines of the village, the stranger is expected to mate with any woman who wants him. But Reid desires only one—the virginal beauty who heralds his mysterious appearance among them. Irresistibly drawn to one another, Reid and Janina break every taboo as they lie tangled together by the sacred pool.

___52281-0 $5.50 US/$6.50 CAN